Not Everything is what it seems...

Prince wasn't charming.

Not as far as I was concerned.

He stood in the middle of the castle drawbridge, his wheat-blond hair a mass of tangles, his jowls sagging, and his vacuous black eyes fixed unblinkingly on me. As I returned his stare, a thick strand of drool spilled over his lower lip and stretched down to pool between his front paws. A threatening growl rumbled up from his barrel-shaped chest, and he tipped his snout to display his sharp teeth.

No, Prince wasn't charming at all.

—From "Suede This Time"

...In a world filled with witches, robots, biplanes, and—of course—cats.

This and That

and Tales about Cats

The Collected Short Stories of Jean Rabe

by Jean Rabe

Walkabout Publishing • 2008

Walkabout Publishing
S.D.Studios
P.O.Box 151
Kansasville, WI 53139
www.walkaboutpublishing.com

Cover design by Jean Rabe and Stephen D. Sullivan.
Cover photo copyright © 2008 Adivin and IStockPhoto.com.

ISBN: 978-0-9802086-7-2

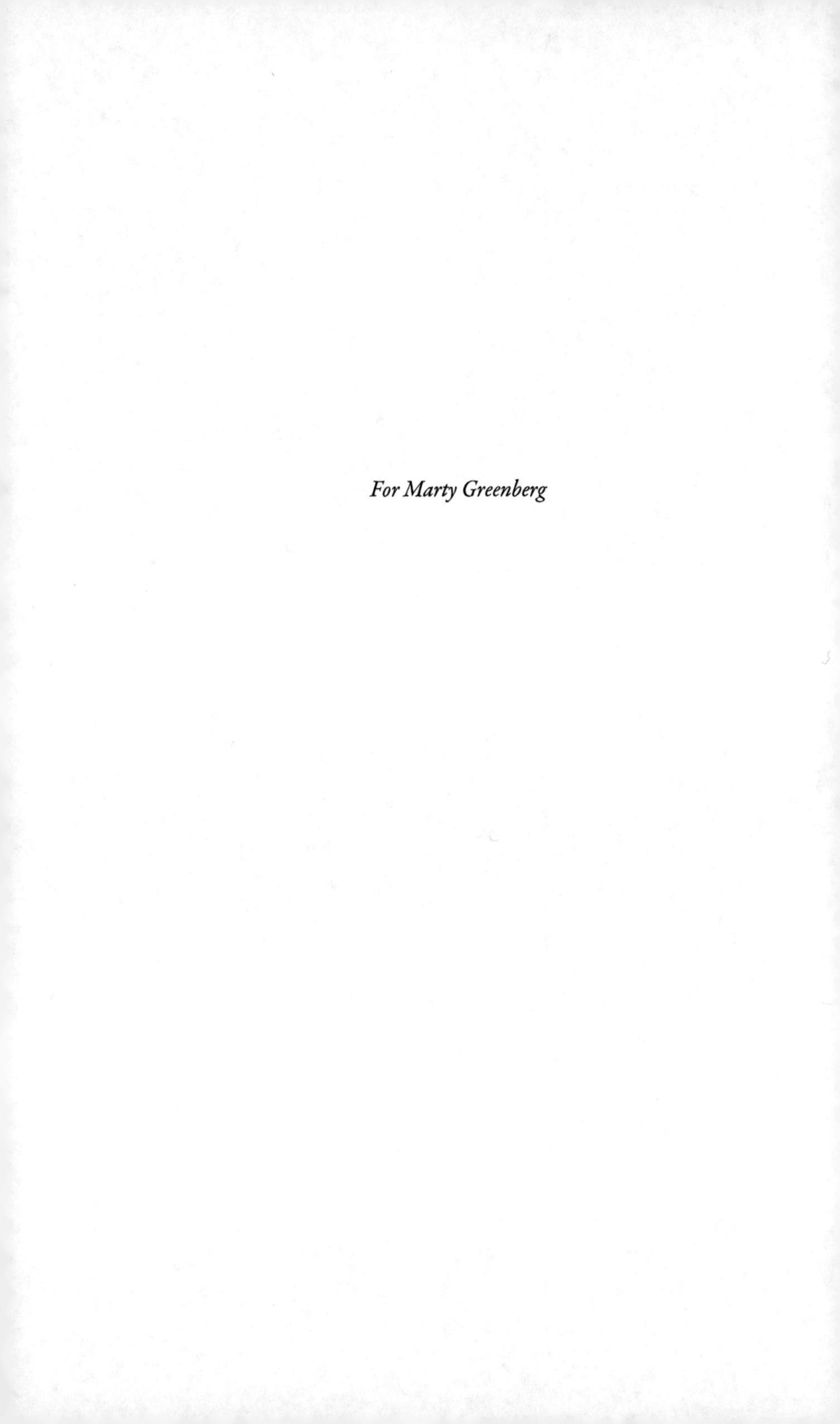

For Marty Greenberg

CONTENTS

Ramblings about This and That

I used to hate to write short stories. I could do as many as four rewrites on one, while only needing to do a light rewrite on a novel. Short fiction just didn't come easy for me, and so I avoided tackling anything under 50,000 words when at all possible.

Until that proverbial light bulb came on.

I think I was trying to cram too much story into a story—rather than looking at a short story as a slice of someone's life—an hour instead of a whole day, a day instead of a month, or a year instead of a lifetime.

So when I finally figured out what I was doing wrong, I came to love short stories. I've written more than forty of them, many for Dragonlance anthologies, which can't be reprinted in a collection like this. Most of the tales in *This and That* are from anthologies published by DAW Books, which were packaged by Tekno Books in Green Bay, Wisconsin. Thanks to the editors of those anthologies—John Helfers, Denise Little, Kerrie Hughes, Janet Deaver-Pack, Ed Gorman, and Brian Thomsen—for inviting me to participate. Thanks to the folks at Popcorn Press for first giving me the opportunity to assemble a chunk of my tales into one collection. And thanks to Walkabout Publishing for putting out the new edition of the book.

Short stories have given me the chance explore the caves of Hannibal, MO; traipse across a haunted Civil War battleground; prowl through an abandoned space station; skitter about in the Field Museum after hours; look at the Salem Witch trials through different eyes; and listen to sweet, moldy jazz in Nawlins.

They have also given me the chance to write about cats.

Marty Greenberg called me one morning years ago and asked me if I knew about cats, was familiar with them, and understood them. He was packaging a book for Barnes & Noble called *100 Crafty Little Cat Crimes.*

I own two dogs, and they are wrapped around my feet as I write this. I've never owned a cat or been owned by one. My husband is terribly, terribly allergic to them, and so one will never be afforded the chance to curl up on a couch in our home.

But I told Marty that of course I understood cats.

Then I proceeded to go out to breakfast with a friend who was owned by a few, and I picked her brain about how they moved, sounded, and in general acted. The result was "Nothing Newsworthy," which I've put at the end of this collection.

I've written several cat tales since, three of which appear in *This and That.* And I've a few more cat tales swirling around in my head.

I hope you enjoy *This and That and Tales about Cats.* I certainly enjoyed putting it together.

Best,

Jean Rabe

Misery and Woe

A beautiful, buxom woman at a science fiction convention in Chicago inspired this story. She sauntered up to an elevator, where her friends were waiting, and she happily embraced them all. One asked her how the "twins" were doing, and it took me a moment to realize he was talking about her...assets. She'd named them Mischief and Mayhem. In this story, I've renamed them Misery and Woe. This tale first appeared in the DAW Books anthology Maiden, Matron and Crone, *published in 2005.*

Willum tried his best to look around the kitchen, glancing first at a pot dangling over the fire and simmering with something sweet, next at a cluttered shelf midway up a smooth earthen wall.

The shelf was brimful with stones and feathers. There were also a few unlit tapers on it, along with some odd-looking objects he didn't take time to register. He knew that the shelf served as the witch's altar to some goddess she'd mentioned on his first visit, and whose name he'd subsequently forgotten. Besides, there was nothing interesting enough up there to hold his attention.

Then he tried to study his fingernails, a scar on his thumb, the whorls in the kitchen tabletop he flattened his palms against—all of it just to be polite. He was seated at the table, one he gave the witch last week as payment for a month's worth of mixtures of sage, ginger, and nettles to cure a cold, a sore throat, and other assorted ailments he didn't have. The village's carpenter, he moments ago promised her two matching chairs as payment for his next several sessions and for whatever additional herbs he could coax from her today.

"Elspeth," he said, his gaze finally leaving the table and meeting her ice blue eyes. He put on a doleful, pained expression. "I'm still feeling a bit untoward. My stomach gives me fits and keeps me up at night. Do you have something to quiet it and set me aright? So I can get some proper sleep?"

Before she could answer, his gaze dropped to her considerable bosom.

Elspeth Linn of Skarnhold Shire was more than well-endowed.

And try as Willum might to look at her unblemished face or her beautiful hair or to glance about her immaculate kitchen, he couldn't long keep his eyes away from her cleavage.

She sat opposite Willum at the narrow table, the surface of which gleamed in the sunlight that came through the window. Studying him, she tried to determine if he truly had a malady and thereby decide what mixtures and poultices might best treat him.

"Is there a sharp pain, Willum?" Elspeth's voice showed her concern. "This pain in your stomach? Or is it a dull ache?"

He didn't answer, just continued to stare, his eyes widening.

"Does the pain spread up toward your neck? How long does a bout linger? Is it every night? Or just after evenings that end with big meals? After certain foods?"

It seemed he hadn't heard her.

"Willum?"

Perturbed by her visitor's fixation with her chest, she sucked in so deep an irate breath that she threatened the seams of her bodice. As a result, Willum's eyes grew wider still and a thin line of drool spilled over his lower lip.

"Or is it nothing at all that bothers you Willum Smithson? Nothing but what rumbles 'round in your empty head each time you visit? Like always, you look as healthy as the village ox."

Again no answer.

"Willum." She repeated his name louder, then louder still. "Willum!"

"Huh?" He didn't lift his eyes. "So do you have something to ease my stomach, Elspeth?"

He didn't see her lips stretch into a threadlike line and her icy eyes narrow tetchily.

She rose and retreated to a cupboard at the back of the kitchen, one he had made for her, rummaging around amid the jars and pouches, measuring something into her hand and putting it in a small clay cup.

"Charcoal powder," she pronounced. "Just in case you really are feeling untoward. If you're not ill, neither will this bother you." She put some dried parsley into a small cloth packet and returned with both to the table. "The parsley should help settle you."

He looked up, his eyes not quite able to reach her face. "Charcoal?" He forced the word out through a mouth that had somehow gone dry. "I should eat charcoal?"

"Put it in something," she instructed. "Pudding, tea, soup. It will chase the toxins right out of your system and thereby ease your stomach problems so you can get proper sleep at night." And in the process likely get the scours, she added to herself.

She thrust the cup and packet at him and he shook his head to clear his senses.

"Thank you, Elspeth. Thank you mightily." He reluctantly got up and turned to leave. "If I have any other troubles, I can come to see you again? Next week?"

The witch opened her door each week on the middle day for the villagers to visit and seek her counsel and remedies. She made no exceptions to this rule and did her best to avoid them all other days, keeping to her garden and herself.

She halfheartedly nodded. "Of course, Willum. Next week on the middle day. And you'll bring those chairs?"

"Aye, Elspeth."

She was quick to close the door behind him.

Elspeth sighed. She had hoped this village would be different than the last one, and the one before that. She had hoped that the folks here would come to her for honest ailments and problems. Not just to...to...look.

"By the goddess!"

Oh, some did come to her when they were truthfully feeling ill, and for this she was grateful and quick to help. But most of the men who visited—and it was mostly men who did come to her door—were only interested in ogling her. She knew Willum only came to stare, and she knew she should turn him out. But he was a good carpenter, and she needed the chairs and another cabinet. And there was always the possibility he was ailing, and therefore her oath demanded she aid him.

A slight possibility. Very slight.

"By the goddess!" Elspeth hissed.

She wasn't a young woman anymore. It had been worse when she was, all the attention she got then from men of all ages, even boys. She turned the head of any man in her young years—when she was in the waxing time in the first aspect of the threefold goddess's energies. And she turned down one offer of marriage—or companionship—after another and another and another.

But she wasn't an old woman yet either. Not yet. She was a good stretch of time from that, she told herself. Matronly, she decided, on the lean edge of her middle years, only a few strands of gray weaving their way into her auburn mass of curls. No real wrinkles yet, just a sprinkling of faint lines around the edges of her eyes and at the corners of her mouth. And no one seemed to notice those imperfections, or had spied the one brown spot on the back of her left hand. Folks were always looking at her other...features.

"Maybe when I am an old woman and I sag. Maybe when I'm flat, then they'll pay more attention to what I say and brew and will look elsewhere about me. And maybe in the meantime I should look elsewhere for another home." She'd been in this village called Skarnhold Shire only a year. The place had caught her eye because it was nestled comfortably at the mouth of a low valley, the farmland spreading rich and away from it, a thick stream close and musical. All of it lovely. "Or maybe this time I'll stay for a long while and the ogling be damned. Stay until I'm old and flat. Be buried where I plant my herbs."

It was the nicest home she'd made for herself so far, occupying a cottage that had been abandoned when the old man who owned it died, buying it from the village in exchange for helping with their crops last spring. Last fall's harvest was impressive, and they begged her stay to help again this year. It was a good feeling to be wanted.

Elspeth took in her kitchen. It was tidy and simple, with the table Willum had fashioned and two old chairs that matched an old table since turned into kindling. There were three large cupboards, one filled with dishes and pots, the others with herbs, roots, and various things she'd gathered for brews and infusions. And there was a high counter on which was neatly arranged her athame, or spirit blade, the knife she used to prepare not only her magical and medicinal concoctions but her meals as well. There was a grinder for powdering roots, and a strainer for teas. And there was a soapstone mortar and pestle that she hoped to replace with a marble one when a traveling merchant who sold such things came through. Marble would serve better for crushing and bruising herbs. Her possessions were few enough that they could be carried on the back of a donkey or in a small cart—in the event she could no longer stomach the ogling.

But she was adding to her possessions each month. The carpenter, blacksmith, cobbler, and chandler were among the villagers trading her goods for spiritual sessions and medicines.

A light woolen blanket, festooned with an embroidered leafy design and used as payment from the village weaver, hung in a doorway that led to a small bedroom—where there was a heavier woolen blanket from the weaver and soft pillows from a man who kept fowl. Propped up against either side of the doorframe were twin brooms she'd fashioned herself. A lovely village and a lovely home. Lovely people—for the most part. Even Willum was tolerable, she decided.

"Wouldn't hurt to sweep again, I suppose." Elspeth started toward the brooms, but was stopped by a firm knock on her door.

"Elder Kendal." She greeted him with a smile.

He tipped his hat and nodded, stepping past her on bowed legs, clumsily striding to the table and sitting down.

"What can I do for you this afternoon, Elder? Does your wife know you're here? You know she disapproves of..."

He thrummed his fingers and made a show of settling in more comfortably.

"I've only come to you a handful of times since you moved into the village," he began. "'Cause of my wife's wishes. And 'cause the other elders think I'm being a fool consulting a kitchen witch. Not that they haven't consulted you themselves. Renald comes here often enough."

"I prefer hearth witch," Elspeth said as she took her place across from him. "Or hedge witch if you must."

"Kitchen witch," he repeated, taking a quick look around her kitchen before resting his eyes on her bosom. At least Elder Kendal occasionally raised his gaze to meet hers.

She crossed her arms in front of her, which only served to deepen the crease between her breasts and cause Elder Kendal to sharply suck in a breath. "All right, yes, I am considered a kitchen witch, as you say. The kitchen is, perhaps, the most basic approach to the craft."

Elder Kendal raised an eyebrow, perhaps out of interest in her talk.

Elspeth continued, happy for a chance to discuss her profession. "Food supports the circle of life, you see. A meal brings families together and nurtures them. Festivals are filled with food. Praying in advance of a meal is honoring the goddess. And in turn a rich harvest is seen as a gift from the goddess. In preparing food and spices, I work in rituals and direct positive energy. Community, health, food, these are things I devote my magic to."

"So, witch, can you tell me the future?" Elder Kendal met her gaze, then returned to his staring. "I'm getting up in the years, and I was wondering the other day just how long I might have left. Only curious, you understand."

She shook her head, a mix of disappointment and amusement flashing across her face. "You call me a kitchen witch, Elder Kendal, and then you ask me to look into your future? How can you possibly think that..."

"A witch is a witch, ain't it? 'Sides, I ain't got no ailments today, kitchen witch. Wife ain't sick neither." He looked into her eyes again, but only briefly. "Corn and beans are in, and no weeds are showing yet. So I ain't got no other reason to come see you 'cept to ask about my future, how much of it I have left. An' I know well enough that you'll be more than busy when the sun starts going down. The fellas done with their work and coming by here for herbs and the like and a look at you before going home. So I figured I'd best ask about my future now before you get busy."

Elspeth noticed his breathing was in time with hers, and that his head bobbed slightly with the rise and fall of her chest. "Elder Kendal..."

"I give you beans come harvest, you know that from last year. Corn if you want it."

The air hissed between her teeth as she edged away from the table and went to her altar-shelf. She selected two tapers and some incense, a small dish, and a polished piece of granite.

"A hearth witch isn't the sort of witch who stirs cauldrons and casts spells, Elder Kendal. I use my brooms for sweeping, not riding through the night sky." She returned to the table and arranged the incense on the dish in a star-shaped pattern, set the granite in front of her and lit the two tapers. "I focus on the kitchen and home. I do not perform banishments or cast shielding spells. I have been known to brew love potions, as that relates to family. But I cannot divine your future."

He pointed a callused finger at the candles. "What do you use those for?"

"Candle magic and color magic combined," Elspeth replied. She scowled to note he hadn't looked her in the eyes for a few minutes. "The white candle symbolizes purity and healing."

"Said I ain't sick."

"And the blue is water, peace, and tranquility."

"So what do I need with peace and tranquility? I got me enough of those things."

"Elder Kendal, I thought that since you are here, and since no one else has yet come to my door, I might try to sooth you. Chase your worries away, so to speak."

"Ain't got any worries," he said. "Got my corn and beans planted, I say. Left my nagging wife to her cleaning. Just was wondering about the future."

"I can't help you there."

"Some witch you are." He shook his head, his eyes only leaving her bosom for a moment, and that to give her a stern look. "A witch is a witch, or should be. Well, I suppose I'll come back next week and see if you can tell me the future then." He sat there for several moments, still staring, not saying anything else.

"Next week then," she said finally, sucking in another perturbed breath and again menacing her seams.

"Next week." He was slow to rise and slower to the door. A tip of the hat and a nod. "You think about my future in the meantime. All right?"

Elspeth didn't quite get the door closed behind him before there was another rapping. This time insistent and soft. She stepped back to admit her next visitor.

"Anna Cla..."

"You...you...witch!" The retort came from a comely young woman in a well-worn skirt and peasant blouse. She and her clothes were clean and smelled of lilacs, and there was a hint of rouge on her cheeks. A spot of flour on her arm and a trace of cinnamon indicated she'd been baking. Her dark eyes danced angrily. "Witch!"

Elspeth opened her mouth to say, Yes, I am a witch, and you well know that. But thought better of it. She simply regarded the young woman, breathing quickly in her ire, balled fists set against her narrow hips.

"Witch. Witch. Witch."

"Anna..." Elspeth slid to the side and opened the door all the way. She gestured to her table. "Would you like to come in and talk about what is troubling you?"

The red spread from Anna's cheeks to the rest of her face. "You're what's troubling me, witch. Troubling me and Dela and Huberta and even Isamu. Poor Dela, I know her Willum was here a little while ago. I saw him coming out your door."

"I don't understand what you're upset about. Anna..."

"Upset? Yes, I'm upset. You're what's troubling us—me and Huberta and Isamu, Dela especially. Look at that table Willum made you! You're troubling us fiercely. Have been for some months now. You and the twins."

"Twins?"

Anna thrust a finger at Elspeth's bosom. "The twins."

Elspeth looked down. Rising above the edge of her bodice, she had to admit her large breasts resembled the bald heads of infants suckling.

"The twins," Anna repeated, pointing with her finger again at each one. "Misery and Woe I call 'em. The twins. Misery and Woe." She made a huffing sound and tossed her head, her dark eyes wide and wild. "Our men visit you almost every week, getting potions and whatnots, claiming to feel sick, claiming we're sick and needing your herbs. But what they're really doing is just getting a look." Another huff, this one so loud it sounded like dry leaves shushing across the ground. "When you go to the market, they stare at you. When you tend your garden, they just happen to stroll by. It's not that the rest of us don't have what you have, witch. We just don't have near as much of it."

Elspeth stared slack-jawed at Anna's tirade. "I'm no threat to you."

"Threat? Misery and Woe there certainly are threatening our happy homes." She slammed her fists against her hips. Spittle flew from her mouth. "I've stayed quiet until now, just talking with Dela and Huberta and Isamu, cursing you. I've kept my tongue all these months. But last night my man was chattering in his sleep. I heard him say your name quite plainly."

"I'm sorry, Anna. I mean no..."

"I thought you kitchen witches were supposed to help families, not tear them apart. I thought..."

It was Elspeth's turn to be angry. "I've caused no trouble here. I've nurtured the fields with my spells. I've healed the sick. I've..."

"Drawn the attention of our men, who bring you the bread we bake and who make furniture for you, who repair your roof...who come by to get a good close look at Misery and Woe." Anna made another huffing sound. She balled her fists so tight her knuckles turned white. "You and the twins aren't welcome here. Not welcome by me or Dela or Isamu or Huberta. Not welcome by other women either, I'm certain. You threaten our homes. You and the twins threaten this entire village, you...you...witch! And you haven't heard the last from me."

With that, Anna spun and nearly bumped into the chandler, who was striding up the walk, bundle of candles in hand.

"No," Anna said, as she stomped off. "You and the twins haven't heard the last."

For an instant, Elspeth considered packing up and leaving this very day. But only for an instant. To give in when she'd done nothing wrong would not be honoring her craft. This village was lovely. Her home was lovely. The candles Ordney was thrusting at her were lovely and scented with vanilla. She liked it here.

Witches were persecuted elsewhere, Elspeth knew. It seemed to be part of their lot in life. People were suspicious and fearful of them, wary of the magic, and hounding them because they were not of the same cloth as a commoner. Persecution was rife. But she suspected few were victimized because of being so well endowed.

"And what can I do for you today, Ordney?" Elspeth accepted the candles and gestured to her table. "Oh!" Her breath caught when she noticed the still-burning tapers. The white was burning properly, little of the wax had melted, and the candle was straight. But the blue had burned down far more than it should have in the scant time, and it was bent and twisted like a gnarled tree branch.

"Looks like you needed these new candles," Ordney said. "Never seen one of 'em burn quite like that. Odd."

"Indeed," Elspeth hushed.

* * *

That night she studied the remains of the twisted, blue candle. It was an omen of some sort, she decided. Water, peace, tranquility—that's what blue stood for. And candle magic? In general to Elspeth it represented the power of fire. A candle could burn away bad influences and could release positive energy. The chandler used beeswax, the finest kind.

"A bad omen to be certain," she pronounced. "Perhaps Anna's tirade shattered the tranquility and so ruined the candle."

Elspeth selected the broom to the right of the doorframe. It wasn't used for sweeping dust and catching spiderwebs. The other broom served that purpose. This broom was blessed during its making, and she used it to sweep out the negative energy that collected in her kitchen. And there was always some trace of negative energy on the middle day of the week when the villagers came to call. The residue of their problems—when they actually had problems—gathered under her table and settled in. She swept them out.

Tonight she swept the floor again and again, getting into every corner and into every crack. Then she swept one more time, her arms heavy and tired from the task.

"Perhaps it was Anna," she mused, as she climbed into bed and pulled up the cover. Her head relaxed into a thick goose-down pillow. "Perhaps she brought so much dreadful energy to my home that she indeed ruined the candle and disturbed my peace."

In the morning, Elspeth lit another blue candle and watched it burn. Next to it she lit a green one, for luck, and again a white one for healing and harmony and protection. Within moments the blue candle twisted.

"By the goddess!"

She added a yellow taper that symbolized clairvoyance. And as the blue continued to burn uneven, she stared at the yellow's flame. Perhaps she could look into the future as Elder Kendal intimated. Other witches could, and in her earliest days in the craft she'd studied under a matron who had such ability and tried to teach Elspeth the same. But at the time Elspeth was interested in other things and was determined to specialize in hearth magic.

The flame grew brighter as she placed her thumbs against the base of the taper.

"Does something threaten the peace and tranquility of this village? A force other than jealous Anna Clayborn?" She edged closer to the candle until her face became warm. A trickle of sweat rolled down her cheek. But she saw only the fire and felt only the increasing warmth.

The blue candle she lit the following day also warped. And another yellow taper provided no clue that she could discern.

* * *

Twice more before spring ended Anna came on the middle day to complain about the twins and to spout her wrath. Perhaps in response Elspeth worked in her gardens in the early morning, wearing filmy skirts and blouses with skimpy bodices, bent over in her weeding so she was facing Anna's house. On more than one morning Elspeth caught the young woman staring angrily at her. Elspeth offered a friendly wave.

In the spring afternoons, save on the middle days when she accepted villagers into her kitchen, she strolled through the market in her finest clothes, hair tied up with ribbons to show of her neck. Sometimes she saw Anna and Isamu there, glaring at her. The men never glared. Stared, yes, and with either smiles on their careworn faces or mouths hanging open in appreciation. She talked to none of them, save the few vendors she dealt with.

There'd been little rain throughout the spring, and so early evenings found Elspeth and her handcart at the creek, filling ceramic bowls and jugs so she could water her herbs. Some of the farmers also gathered water, and most of these did so at the same time of day as Elspeth. Ogling her as they toiled. But the majority of the village farmers had fields too large to be helped by a few jugs of water.

Elspeth's herbs were growing, though not as vibrantly as the previous year.

* * *

Summer had come and the days were hot, almost fiery so.

When was the last time it had rained? she wondered. The herbs weren't getting enough water. The water she drew up from the stream wasn't sufficient. The farmers' crops were doing no better, and the men were coming to her on the middle days seeking remedies while still seeking to stare at her cleavage.

Water, Elspeth thought.

The blue candle represented water. The tapers had twisted months ago trying to tell her something, to show her a future with no rain and a dying stream. Elspeth's eyes flew wide. When she was at the stream last night she noticed how it had been shrinking away from its banks. It was no longer the thick creek that made music. It was struggling. Like the crops were struggling.

"Blind," she cursed at herself. "The candle was trying to tell me something months ago. Warn me. Elder Kendal asking about the future...the goddess was speaking through him, trying to warn me of the dry weather to come."

She paced in the kitchen, her long skirt sweeping the floor. "I could have advised the farmers to plant differently, to draw water from the stream and hold it in barrels for the drought. To conserve their food, to pray to the goddess for rain. I could have done things differently. I guess I should have..."

There was a knocking on her door. It wasn't the middle day, but Elspeth answered it nonetheless.

"Anna."

"He talked about you in his sleep again last night." The young woman thrust her finger at Elspeth's bosom. "You and the twins aren't welcome here, I say. Misery and Woe and..."

Elspeth brushed by her and hurried down the walk, heading straight toward Elder Kendal's. "There's still time to conserve," she said. "If we all work together we can save the crops and get through this. We can..."

"How dare you ignore me!" Anna sputtered. She caught up to Elspeth and shook her finger wildly. "How rude!"

Elspeth sped up, leaving the younger woman puffing behind her and taunting the "twins."

"There's time, I know it," Elspeth told herself. "We'll take from the stream now, before it completely goes. Fill every container we have. Take mud from the bank and set it around the melon mounds and around the carrots. We can meet this challenge."

She vaguely registered the men staring at her as she went, eyes fixed on what they usually were fixed on, smiles on the faces of some, mouths hanging open on others. Her breath came ragged, and she was jeopardizing the lace on her bodice. She gleamed with a thin layer of sweat by the time she reached Kendal's.

He'd been smoothing at a rail on his porch and had seen her coming, strode forward on his bowed legs to keep her in the yard—where his wife wasn't. He beamed at her.

"Elder Kendal..."

"Kitchen witch! So good to see you. And what a surprise. It's not a middle day. I don't think you've ever..."

"I need to talk to you, Elder."

He looked into her eyes for a moment before dropping his gaze. His breathing matched hers, and his head gently bobbed up and down in time with her heaving breasts.

"Elder, you asked me to look into the future."

"That was months ago." There was a trace of drool at the corner of his mouth. "Thought you said you weren't a diviner. Thought you said a witch wasn't a witch."

She tried to calm herself and slow her breathing. Elder Kendal's head bobbed slower in response.

"I am a..."

"Kitchen witch. Yeah, I know. Glad you came for a visit. Want to sit on the porch?"

She shook her head. "This weather."

"Hot ain't it? Burning my beans. I ain't faulting you for it. You can't make it rain."

"No," she admitted. "But about the future."

He raised an eyebrow, perhaps a reaction to her comment.

"It seems I can tell enough of the future to know that this drought is going to continue for some time. The stream is going to dry up. It's just a matter of days perhaps. We need to take water from it, while it's still running. We need to..." Her words trailed off. "Elder Kendal, are you listening to me?"

He nodded, eyes still fixed, drool more noticeable.

"You need to speak with the rest of the elders, and all the farmers in the village. Hold a meeting. I'll be happy to talk and explain what we must do."

Another nod.

"So you'll set up this meeting?"

Elder Kendal stroked his chin. "Don't see where's we need one. Sometimes this happens, kitchen witch, this lack of rain. It's the valley, you know. The mountains stop the wind and rain on either side. Sometimes. We'll get past it. We always do. Nothing for you to worry about. Hey, maybe you need to light one of those blue candles for yourself, get you some peace and tranquility."

Elspeth drew in a deep breath, preparing to repeat her request.

Elder Kendal's eyes swelled.

"Jon! Jon Kendal you come inside this very minute!" This came from Elder Kendal's wife, who was standing in the frame of the front door, nearly filling the space. Her eyes were daggers aimed at Elspeth. "Jon! You get away from that witch. It's not a middle day, and you've chores to tend to. D'ya hear me? You get away from that witch and the..."

Twins, Elspeth knew she was going to say. *Misery and Woe.* So Anna's wagging tongue had made its way around the entire village.

Elder Kendal took a last look at Elspeth, before shrugging and turning toward his wife. His shoulders stooped as he shuffled toward the cottage.

"Think about a village meeting. Please," Elspeth said. Her voice was thick with urgency, but she doubted it registered on Elder Kendal.

Then he was swallowed by the shadows in the cottage, and his wife firmly closed the door behind him.

* * *

Elspeth visited the other village elders, and Willum and the chandler. At each stop she explained that the drought would continue—perhaps throughout Lammas, or Lughnassadh, the witch festival of the First Fruits, the First of the Three Harvests.

"There might not be a harvest," she told Willum, who couldn't seem to raise his head high enough to look her in the eyes. "This drought could wipe everything out and seriously cripple this village." This lovely village in this lovely valley.

Willum mumbled that he'd be sure to tell his farmer friends. And would she like another shelf in her kitchen...in exchange for some herbs to help his achy joints?

The chandler and weaver paid her insufficient heed, though both were elated by her visit. The fowl tender offered her a goose-down quilt come the fall, as trade for some oils for his hands and a potion or two. It seemed he "didn't quite catch" what she was trying to say about this unforgiving summer.

At last she stopped by Anna Clayborn's cottage. She hoped to find both Anna and her husband at home. But there was only irate finger-pointing Anna.

"So the witch and her twins have come to pay me a visit. You've been stepping up on the stoops of everyone else, why should I be left out, eh? Well, I'll not invite you in. Misery and Woe have no place in my home, I say!"

Elspeth squared her shoulders, inadvertently better displaying her chest and causing something worse than anger to scud across Anna's face. "I need your help, Anna Clayborn." Before Anna could offer a retort, Elspeth continued. "This summer is fierce and will get no better. The stream is dying and there is no rain. This village needs its crops, and they are withering in the fields. I need your help. People listen to you. The goddess knows that you have every woman in town referring to my..."

"Twins," Anna hissed.

"Yes, my..."

"Misery and Woe."

"They listen to you, Anna, the people of this village. They hang on your wagging tongue, it seems. We need to gather water. We need to take the mud on the banks. We need..."

"You need to leave my property, witch. Misery and Woe have no place here."

* * *

The summer grew hotter and the grass around the village cottages became dry and brittle. Elspeth's herb garden was barely surviving, and yet it was faring better than the crops in the fields. The witch had gathered water, as she'd begged the townsfolk to do...and as she repeatedly told each man to do who came to visit her on the middle day.

It was past the time of the first harvest. Lammas had passed and there were no crops to cull. There were only stumpy dry cornstalks and withered bean shoots. The villagers were living by slaughtering the sheep and cows. All the geese were gone, their meat dried and spiced to serve in the coming desperate months.

Elspeth feared there might not be enough meat to take them through the winter. She would manage all right, as she started putting things aside when she realized the drought would continue. But the others were only now starting to plan ahead. And it could well be too late.

"Misery and Woe you've brought upon us," Anna told her again one day. "The men cared only about watching you, mouths all agape. They didn't pay enough attention to the weather and the fields. It's 'cause of you we're suffering so!"

That night, the thatched roof of Elspeth's cottage caught fire.

In her heart, the witch knew it was Anna's doing, the young woman's desire so strong to drive her out of the village. But there'd been no wisdom in the gesture, only anger. And like the flame of Elspeth's red candle, the one that by its color symbolized fire and energy, the blaze grew.

Everything so dry, the fire spread down the walls and leapt to the quilts and blankets the weaver and fowl keeper had given her. Elspeth managed to grab her mortar and pestle, a change of clothes and a few jars of herbs. These and a lone blue taper she threw in her handcart and started away from the village.

This lovely village, she thought. This lovely valley.

The fire spread from her cottage, an angry red beast racing across the brittle grass to the next cottage and the next. The flames danced up barns and across fences. And from a distance Elspeth watched. There was no water to put it out, and a breeze had picked up to aid the conflagration.

"Misery and Woe you brought upon yourselves," she said, as she finally glanced away and looked to the south. There would be another village where she could make her home. And then another and another after that.

She'd settle for good, she decided, "when I am old and flat." She breathed deep, threatening the threads in her tight blouse. The air was hot and filled with the smells of Skarnhold Shire. "When I am flat, then they will listen."

Trading Fours with the Moldy Figs

My friend John Helfers was editing an anthology called Little Red Riding Hood in the Big Bad City, *and he asked if I might have a "fairy tale" to offer. I immediately thought about the Big Bad Wolf, who I believed was a much more interesting character than "Red." I considered setting the story in Milwaukee or Chicago, either of which are closer to my Kenosha, WI, home, and both of which I'm reasonably familiar with. But neither city seemed appropriate. I needed a place where Big Bad could really howl. So I settled on New Orleans, which I'd visited a long time ago during my high school band's summer tour. This story was originally published by DAW Books in* Little Red Riding Hood in the Big Bad City, *2004.*

Music bombarded Bigbad—rock, pop, new age, rap, heavy metal, country, and jazz. Mostly it was jazz, with its muted trumpets and thrumming basses. And some of that was blues, some of it Dixieland, a hint of fusion and ragtime thrown in for good measure. It came at him from every open door and window, pulsed through the brick sidewalk to vibrate in three-quarters time against the pads of his aching feet.

Bigbad loved music, and he'd expected plenty of it here. This was New Orleans, after all, and the beginning of Mardi Gras. He just hadn't thought there would be quite so much music. It was all so painful to his sensitive ears.

Nor had he counted on the so-garish-it-made-your-eyes-hurt-rainbow-clad crowd, all highlighted by the glaring streetlights and flashing neon signs that held the night at bay. He'd anticipated tourists, just not the shoulder-to-shoulder-to-shoulder laughing, shrieking, singing, pressing, smothering, swarming mass surging like an inexorable wave down the Bourbon Street sidewalk and sweeping him along in its wake.

Women leaned over black iron railings and waved at him, some wearing little more than strands of plastic beads and several layers of makeup. Vendors hawked their wares on every corner—urging him to buy T-shirts, lemonades, flowers and more—but their pitches were lost in the pandemonium.

Costumed folk with overlarge masks jiggled and danced and drank beer and bumped annoyingly against him. Fortunetellers waved to him from shadowy archways. An occasional policeman threaded his way through the press—and these Bigbad worked to avoid.

So many, many people. Too many.

So much noise and color and odor. Too much!

So hard to think!

Bigbad set his feet against the wave and tried to ask directions to a jazz club from an old woman selling roses. Fortunately she seemed to understand what he wanted, jabbering back and nodding, pointing. Bigbad couldn't separate her words from the rest of the ruckus, but he followed her finger, seeing a flickering sign halfway down the nearest side street. He would have missed it! He grinned wide, and the rose-woman stepped back, frightened by all his sharp-looking teeth.

"It's just a costume," he said, though too softly for her to hear.

Indeed, he seemed to be attracting surprisingly little notice despite all his fur. Perhaps because Bigbad walked on his hind legs, the throng took him for one more costumed reveler instead of the wolf he really was. That had been his hope, after all.

He struggled through the crowd and narrowly dodged a horse-drawn carriage to reach the narrow side street, where the lighting was poor and where there were thankfully fewer people. He leaned against a wall and took a deep breath, told himself to relax—the building he was looking for was only a dozen yards away. The taste of the salty ocean air filled his mouth.

"Compose yourself," he said.

Put on a dignified front. Make a good first impression.

He closed his eyes and shut out all the riotous colors of the people and the buildings and the neon. Away from the bulk of the horde, Bigbad could smell more than sweat and the warring fragrances of cheap cologne. He picked up the delightful scent of fried clams and something spicy he couldn't put a name to. His stomach rumbled; it had been nearly two days since he'd stopped for something to eat. Or had it been three? Little time to eat when you're on the run.

Only a dozen yards away, the building.

He'd go there, take care of business, then get something to eat. Find a place to stay. Lose himself in New Orleans. Be safe. Really, really relax.

He allowed himself a brief pleasure, rubbing his shoulders against the wall. The bricks still held some warmth from the afternoon, and the roughness felt good. After a few moments he opened his eyes and looked down the street again and up at the flickering sign the flower woman had indicated.

"Les Lupes," it read. Wolves.

Music came from that building too, a slow and familiar ragsy piece.

"Rock-a-bye your baby with a Dixie melody," a craggy voice sang.

Bigbad wouldn't call it a "good" voice, but it was engaging like Louis Armstrong's had been. It had a touch of a French accent, and it settled in his ears just fine.

"When you croon, croon a little tune from the heart of Dixie!"

Al Jolson, Bigbad thought. Jolson recorded that tune back in...oh...1918 if his musical memory served. He had it on wax at his old place, two copies. Had a lot of albums there—33s, 78s—all left behind when he fled. Maybe in time he could replace the collection. Certainly he could buy some of the old stuff in this city. This city, where he could be safe.

"Just hang that cradle, Mammy mine, On the Mason-Dixon line, And swing it from Virginia to Tennessee with all the pull that's in ya."

"Rock-a-bye your baby with a Dixie melody."

Bigbad let the rest of the tune wrap around him and tug him into the establishment. The room was fairly small and crowded, only two vacant seats that he could see. "Intimate," a Yellow-Pages ad for the place might read. The lights were low, mostly stubby candles in glass jars burning merrily, and a spotlight on the band. It was a four-piece group, all wolves—a saxophonist, piano player, drummer, and someone handling the clarinet and flute...and currently playing the latter. A weathered placard near the stage proclaimed the group the Moldy Figs. Once upon a time there were five of them, but Bigbad had learned that something unfortunate had happened to the bass player a month or so back. Fortunate for himself. He was here to fill that vacancy.

He shuffled toward the empty seat nearest the stage; the couple occupying the table didn't seem to mind the intrusion and paid him the slightest attention, only a brief nod of greeting, their eyes riveted on the musicians, their fingers drumming in time on the edge of their plates.

His stomach growled again.

The couple finished their wine and left, and Bigbad hefted a leg across one of the chairs to discourage others from joining him. A waiter appeared and cleared the dishes.

"Shrimp Creole," Bigbad told him. "And a beer. Make it a Heineken, and make sure it's very cold." He had enough money in the pouch at his side to cover it, and hopefully the deposit and first-month on a shabby apartment, a little left over for a day or two of groceries. He'd upgrade his digs after his pay from the band—and from other sources he would develop—started rolling in. He eased back and continued to listen. The Moldy Figs were better than he expected, and they performed three more tunes, ending with something Bigbad hadn't heard in ages.

Siver-gray told the audience the band was taking a break and would be back in fifteen minutes for its final set. Even speaking, his voice had a hoarseness to it, a whisper cocooned around its French edges. He bowed his head to acknowledge the applause, then he and the pianist, a smallish black wolf with a patch of white fur on his throat, threaded their way through the tables and toward Bigbad. The other two wolves disappeared into the kitchen.

"Bigbad Wolf," Bigbad said as an introduction, offering his right paw in a handshake and taking his leg off the seat.

Silver-gray and the black slid into the empty chairs.

"Didn't 'spect you 'til the end o' the week," Silver-gray said. "Name's Gautier. This's Jamie-Lou. Says you can stay with him 'til you find a place o' your own." The black nodded. "Jamie-Lou's on keyboards and plays trombone from time to time. He's known from 'The Wolf and the Man.' Skip and Buzz in the kitchen, drums and woodwinds,...they's from 'The Wolf and the Seven Little Kids' and 'Gossip Wolf and the Fox' respectively."

"Grimm tales, all of them," Bigbad observed.

"Jacob and Wilhelm Grimm," Gautier said to make it more formal.

"The Grimm brothers got our stories mostly right," the black said. "What's your tale Bigbad?"

Bigbad didn't answer right away. So Gautier did the talking for him. "Bigbad here's from Kentucky. Ain't that right? He's got a hankerin' for *le porceau.* Me, I favor *coq au vin* followed up with *crème brulèe.*"

"*Porceau,*" the black snickered. "Piglet. You's the wolf from 'The Three Little Pigs.' And speaking of dinner, I'm gonna get me a bite if you don't mind." He shook Bigbad's paw and headed toward the kitchen.

"Didn't 'spect you 'til the end o' the week," Gautier repeated. "Your letter said you'd be comin' on Saturday most likely."

"Change of plans," Bigbad said.

"Not that I mind. We really need a new bass player, and the demo tape you sent showed you sure can play. It's the bass what really holds the sound together, I think. Good for us you were lookin' for a change o' scenery. None o' the wolf bass musicians in town were lookin' for work. Already had gigs. Got us a bevy o' wolf clarinetists, though, out o' work. Regular Pee Wee Spiteleras and Pete-gushing-Fountains."

There were dozens of questions Bigbad wanted to ask Gautier. Pay, hours, were there gigs on the side—things he certainly would have covered in the last phone conversation had he not been in a rush. Did the police frequent this place? Was the band in any trouble with the law?

"Good for me you put that ad on Wolf-dot-Net," Bigbad said. "I was getting tired of playing bluegrass in backwoods bars to good-ol'-boys soused on moonshine. No way a wolf could land a solid job with a city band in Lexington or Louisville. Not even in Paducah. City people in Kentucky wouldn't accept it. But wolves seem to be accepted here. Is it because of Mardi Gras?"

Gautier shook his head. "Can't rightly say what it is that lets us walk freely. We play every week to a full house. And there's another all-wolf band, plays rag only, on the north side. Two on the south are into country." He spat the last word out like it was a piece of spoiled meat. "Must be about fifty or so o' us in the musicians' guild here. We have no trouble walkin' in the open in broad daylight. Oh, we all get occasional looks from the tourists, but nothing to ruffle our fur. Maybe folks expect a strangeness here. Somethin' different. We're accepted, is all that matters. 'Spect that's why you're interested in the job."

Bigbad drew his lips into a thin line. "Yeah. I guess I need to find a good fit." A place to hide in the open and play music.

"Lots o' wolves here," Gautier continued. "And lots o' music. You'll like it, an' you'll fit well."

Bigbad knew that most people, including the police, thought all wolves looked the same. It might be impossible to pick him out from the pack in New Orleans.

Did any policemen frequent this place? And how expensive were apartments? When would he get his first check? Would there be an advance? Did the Moldy Figs have a recording deal in the works? He'd have to change his name if something was going to appear in print. Did the Figs write any of their own pieces? Did they have any "ins" with the local black market? And if so could they arrange some introductions so he could establish a second income? There were so many questions he wanted to ask Gautier.

"How long you been in New Orleans?" Bigbad asked instead. Ease into it, he thought. Be all friendly at first. Don't seem desperate or panicked or greedy.

"Long? Nah, not long. Only 'bout a hundred years," came the raspy reply. "I came to N'awlins..." Gautier pronounced it *Naaaaawlins* like a native, the word drawn out nice and deep like a contra-alto clarinet holding a note. "...just before the Great War."

"Is that when Red dumped you?" Bigbad immediately regretted that question. Friendly! he cursed at himself. You need to keep this gig for a while!

Gautier's eyes narrowed. "Me an' Red...Bernadette...split long, long before that. Jus' after we started living together on the outskirts o' Paris." He laid his head back against the chair railing and let out a deep breath. "Bernadette broke with me right after that Charles Perrault fellow penned my tale."

"Little Red Cap. Little Red Riding Hood," Bigbad supplied.

A nod. "Yeah, that be the one. She broke with me because o' a typographical error."

Bigbad raised a hairy eyebrow.

"A typo, can you believe it? When I was dictatin' my story to Perrault, I told him I was walking with Red in the woods one day an' told her I wanted to meet her grandmother. Bernadette an' her grandmother were real close, you see. I figured if I was going to marry Bernadette, I should get to know her family."

Bigbad's expression urged Gautier to continue.

"Well, Perrault was getting on in years, and his hearin' must have been failin' him. He didn't write that I wanted to 'meet' her grandmother. He wrote that I wanted to 'eat' her grandmother. And when Bernadette's grandmother turned up missin'...and then Perrault printed my tale with that typo...that would be in 1697...well, Bernadette figured I'd offed the old lady an' really did eat her. An' she got so angry that she split on me. Found out several years later that grandma had run off with some German woodworker named Gepeto. I tried to get back with Bernadette then, when all the truth came out an' Perrault admitted his mistake, but she'd found someone else an' had moved to Switzerland. Last I heard she was workin' as a waitress to help pay the mortgage 'cause her husband couldn't keep a full-time job. Pity. Me an' Red were good together."

"That is a pity," Bigbad agreed.

"So I traveled a bit, heartbroken natu'lly. Finally came to the States an' eventually settled here. I like Naaaaawlins. Fits me. It'll fit you, too. My favorite color is this city."

"Color? I don't..." Bigbad started.

"Color, my man. There's a color to this city, an' it's the blues." Gautier laughed. "Naaaaawlins is a blues town. It's the Wolverine Blues, Dippermouth Blues, Jackass Blues, Wildman Blues, Farewell Blues, Basin Street Blues, Tin Roof Blues, Beale Street Blues, Dallas Blues, The Jazz-me Blues, Sidewalk Blues, Sobbin Blues, St. Louis Blues, Tishomingo Blues, and the Weary Blues. That latter being one o' the best that Mort Greene an' his friends wrote before the Great War. Oh, but I love the blues."

"Beats bluegrass," Bigbad said.

"You can start with us tomorrow night. Seven o'clock. Get here a few minutes early so you can get accustomed to the bass. You said you weren't bringin' your own, right?"

Bigbad looked sad, thinking of his polished six-string bass fiddle in the house he abandoned. "No, I didn't bring my bass. Had to leave a lot of things behind."

Bigbad got directions to the black's apartment and left halfway through the Moldy Figs' final set. Gautier was singing scat on 'Stompin' at the Savoy.' Bigbad asked one of the bartenders on the way out if policemen frequented this club and was relieved to hear they were noticeably absent. Coming here, to this musical city, had been the right thing to do.

Bigbad got up early the next morning, intent on exploring his new home before starting work. He'd concentrate on the narrow streets and secluded courtyards of the French Quarter today, branch out in the days after that and test Gautier's claim that wolves were accepted in broad daylight. Indeed, he drew only a few looks as he made the rounds, taking in the folks dancing in the middle of the street and singing off-key. Gautier had slipped him an advance of two hundred-and-fifty, so he figured to spend some of that during his explorations.

A soulful, seductive city, Bigbad decided, a sensuous spot of civilization surrounded by swamp. He watched an elderly couple sway beneath a massive oak tree. He noted that five-star hotels on Bourbon Street were not far from strip joints. That men in suits and ties partied alongside shabbily dressed college students. Sensory pleasures abounded everywhere on this piece of crescent-shaped land that had been carved by the Mississippi River. A passionate, friendly city, dressed-up in mansions and flowers and restored historic buildings, dressed down in quaint jazz spots. An insouciant city, though a respected, dignified one with southern good manners and playfulness, and fun around every corner.

Crescent City, Isle d'Orleans, The City that Care Forgot, The Big Easy, wrapped up with the motto "Let the good times roll"— *Laissez les bon temps roulez.*

Bigbad hoped he could find an apartment he could afford in the French Quarter, or *Vieux Carréé,* as some of the natives called it. Old Square. A brochure told him the Quarter was established in 1718 by the French, intended as a military outpost and a commerce port. That it became a place filled with so much food and music...and life, amazed him.

Food...he was hungry again. Bananas Foster, Shrimp Remoulade, Oysters Rockefeller, and more were invented in this city. Cajun and creole dishes, French, Italian, African, and other cuisines begged to be sampled. He could smell a variety of dishes cooking as he walked, could hear music still coming from every open window and door. But he was learning to send the sounds to the back of his mind, so he could truly enjoy this place.

On Decatur Street he stopped at the *Caféé du Monde* for breakfast and had *caféé au lait* and *beignets,* small puffs of fried dough covered with powdered sugar that ended up dusting the hairs on his chest and stomach. Lunch was at *La Marquise Patisserie de Roi* on Chartres Street. For an early dinner he feasted on *Pompano en Papillote* at Antoine's, then he went for a drink back on Decatur at the Marie Laveau Voodoo Bar. He made mental notes to try the Clover Grill on Bourbon Street and the Pelican Club Restaurant and Bar on Exchange Alley later in the week.

In between meals he visited a fortuneteller in Jackson Square for a tarot reading, and made an appointment for next Thursday with a *tasseomancer,* tea-leaf reader at the Bottom of the Cup Tea Room on Royal Street. On Rue Conti he stood outside the Musee Conti Wax Museum, and decided he'd take a look some other day. It was said to depict in wax figures of legend and the supernatural.

Bigbad paused outside of a cafe to hear an old black man play a trumpet. It was improv and sounded more spiritual than straight jazz. At another stop, he listened to a trio play tunes made popular by King Oliver's Creole Jazz Band in the early 20s, and some of the Hot Five and Hot Seven pieces Louis Armstrong had recorded a few years later.

By luck, he caught a "jazz funeral" on the edge of the Quarter, then heard some unscripted ensemble work. Bigbad would have pursued more music, but an antique street clock showed it was past six and time to head toward Les Loupes.

"My favorite color is this city," he said to himself, as he ambled along. "Lord, why hadn't I thought to come here before?" Like Gautier, he figured he might never want to leave.

"This city is incredible," Bigbad told Gautier. The two wolves were in an alley behind Les Loupes, it was the only place Gautier said they were allowed to smoke...the establishment's ordinances and such. "All the music. The food. It's...amazing."

"So you fit," Gautier said.

"Like an expensive leather glove," Bigbad returned.

"we'll play some traditional stuff tonight and some improvisation. Make things easy on you."

"The Big Easy," Bigbad said, still caught up in the city.

"Get you some sheet music you can go over tomorrow. An' you can get us a list o' pieces you already now."

"I want to see the bass," Bigbad said. His claws were itching to play.

* * *

The candles were burning merrily and the spot was on the band. The silver-gray wolf stepped forward.

"Ev'nin' ladies and gents. We are the Moldy Figs, an' we aim to please you tonight."

Bigbad scanned the crowd. People were seated at every table, and a few he recognized from the previous night. The Moldy Figs evidently had a following.

"We's moldy for certain," Gautier continued. "Oh-so-very moldy. Moldy Figs is a borrowed term, one the beboppers a couple decades past came up with. It be a derisive term for folks who favor the old style o' jazz, particularly the moldy traditional stuff. Moldy means you're not up to date." He let out a low snarl that stretched to the corners of the room. "Come get moldy with us."

The audience applauded, and Gautier began to sing, the first several words of "Do You Know What it Means to Miss New Orleans" drowned out by the clapping. There was a rightness in the rhythm that made Gautier a real "monster," a master jazz musician who, when he wasn't singing, could lay down a perfect a line with the sax between the bass and the main melody.

Next came the "Basin Street Blues," and "It Don't Mean a Thing," both thick with improv. The Figs traded fours among them: The drummer started, playing a four-measure section, then turning it over to the wolf on clarinet, then to Bigbad. Gautier and Bigbad traded back and fourth in a chase for two choruses before everyone joined in for the finish.

Bigbad thought the night was as close to heaven as he'd ever get, especially when he was handed large sections of an 1883 piece, "My Ragtime Baby," and then "Crazy Blues" from the 1920s. They were fairly obscure pieces, he thought, and wondered if the Moldy Figs were testing his repertoire. Between sets he either went into the kitchen for a nibble or out in the alley to talk with the rest of the Figs.

"So what's your tale?" the drummer asked.

"Told you," the black wolf growled. "He's from the Three Little Pigs."

"So what's your tale?" the drummer repeated. "The Grimms got us mostly right, but not completely. What got messed up with your story? Any tragedies stemming from typos?"

Bigbad didn't tell them the first night, or the first three weeks for that matter. He had to know them better, know for certain he was going to stay, that this "fit" was truly perfect. He didn't need the sheet music Gautier provided, he knew the tunes well enough. Bigbad could play by ear when he wanted, a trait many wolf musicians possessed.

The days passed with trips to a smattering of creole and cajun restaurants, where Bigbad sampled seafood dishes he'd seen mentioned in *Food and Wine.* There was time for the wax museum, a trolley ride, and a tour of the City of the Dead, the famous cemetery where the voodoo queen Marie LeVeau was buried. After the band was finished some evenings, he spent a few early mornings looking for Marie's ghost in the ten-hundred block of St. Anne Street, where sightings had been recorded. In the afternoons he sampled various imported and local beers, made time to walk by the grand homes in the Garden District, and toured the D-Day Museum on Magazine Street, though he balked at the seven-dollar admission price. He met a young wolf one Sunday night on Decatur—the Figs never played on Sundays. She gave him a *gris gris,* a voodoo goodluck charm, and they passed a few hours at what she called a *'fais do-do,* a cajun dance party.

"This city is amazing," he told Gautier, while the pair sat on crates in the alley behind Les Loupes. "I'm going on a riverboat ride this weekend."

Gautier smiled. "Told you wolves're accepted here, Bigbad. You should've come here years ago."

"So true."

The Figs didn't repeat a single tune during a three-week stretch. There were enough moldy songs to keep everything seeming new. Bigbad became a fan-favorite because of his flashing grin and snazzy presence, and he watched the nights melt quickly by playing "All of Me," "Blue Skies," "Can't Help Lovin' Dat Man," and "Gee Baby, Ain't I Good to You." His world became "Have You Met Miss Jones?" "How Deep Is the Ocean," "Mood Indigo," and "Moonglow." He lived for "My Romance," "Solitude," "When I Take My Sugar to Tea," and "You Took Advantage of Me."

"So what's your tale?" the drummer asked again one night.

"It's not the 'Three Little Pigs,'" Bigbad admitted. "Well, not pigs in the 'les porceaus' sense. More in the *la gendarme* sense." He'd learned a few French phrases and was proud to show them off. "Police...pigs."

The drummer scratched at his face. "What about all the huffing and puffing you were said to do?"

"The only huffing and puffing I did was when I took trumpet lessons about eighty years ago. Didn't have the lips for it. Don't know where that huffing and puffing and blowing your house down thing came from. Maybe a typo or misprint, as Gautier is fond of saying. Oh, don't get me wrong, in my younger years I treasured roast pork, especially in fried rice dishes. But I bought it in restaurants and at the grocery store. No way would I skin and cook pigs myself."

Gautier joined them and pulled up a crate. "So if not three little pigs..."

"It was three *gendarmes*...police...in Henderson, Kentucky, just a stone's toss south of Indiana." Bigbad put on a sad face, thinking of his record collection and his prized bass fiddle he'd left behind. "Me and my friends weren't making enough playing the backwoods spots. So we did some other gigs on the side...running booze into some dry counties...peddling a little of Kentucky's number one cash crop."

"Pot? You mean you sold marijuana?" The black wolf sounded incredulous, a rare *naif.*

"Only in the summers and sometimes into the fall," Bigbad continued. "We grew it in some of those abandoned barns, ones where the roof had fallen in so the sun could get to the plants. Most of the cops looked the other way. Heck, some of the sheriff's deputies were in on it, particularly the liquor-running."

"So what about the three policemen?" The black couldn't hold his curiosity.

Bigbad laughed. "They were rookies."

"*Les porceaus,*" Gautier supplied. "Piglets."

"They were so new to the force the tags were still hanging on their uniforms." He chuckled. "Anyway, it was a small force, Henderson being a little place to the west of Owensboro and sort of north of Paducah. They kept dogging me, these three newbies, trying to catch me in the act and make a name for themselves. Well, I caught them."

The black wolf sat on the edge of his crate, eagerly waiting for the rest. A strand of saliva spilled over his lip and stretched to the alley floor.

"They were working on a report late one night, were the only ones in the tiny station house from what I could gather. I got them—and all the goods they had on me—in that proverbial one fell swoop. I guess I really did huff and puff and blow their house down. You see, I'd managed to get my paws on some plastique, and it leveled the place. Yep, I blew their house down but good." He leaned back against the wall and put on a self-satisfied expression.

"Wow," was all the black could muster.

"Wow indeed," Gautier said.

The drummer scratched at his face, and the clarinetist sputtered.

"But if you got rid of the cops," the black started, "why'd you come here? Why didn't you keep your business going as usual?"

Bigbad's expression clouded. "I got rid of one problem only to find myself in a worse one. Seems there was a witness to the bombing, a night dispatcher heading toward the place. Next thing I know, my mug's plastered on the front pages of the Henderson Gleaner and the nearby Evansville Courier. The Feds were called right away. Them backwoods cops didn't take kindly to me offing three of their own, even if the three were piglets."

"So you fled." This from Gautier.

"Yeah. And it was a good thing I'd seen your ad on Wolf-dot-net the day before I'd lit the fuse. I sent out the demo tapes I had made on a lark several months ago, then cleared out of my place before the Feds came into town."

The black shook his paws. "But aren't you worried..."

"That they'll find me?" Bigbad let out a deep breath. "Not in this city. I fit in here, and there are lots of wolves."

"We all look alike to most people," Gautier said.

"Got that right," Bigbad said.

That night finished with "You're My Everything," followed by two encore numbers—"Any Ice Today, Lady?" and "Did You Ever See a Dream Walking?" Bigbad was "in the pocket" for all three, playing flawlessly on his bass in the center of the beat.

The next night was not so smooth.

There were policemen in the audience, for the first time in recent memory of the establishment. A dozen officers sat at tables in the front row, and nabbed Bigbad right away before he could entirely realize what was happening.

"Why?" Bigbad hollered, as the *gendarmes* ushered him out the door.

"Shouldn't've told us you're tale," the black wolf snarled. "We's a group that keeps our noses clean. Don't want our music tainted."

* * *

It was nearly a month before the Moldy Figs found a new bass player, one who was even better than Bigbad. It was the first woman the group had accepted, a large brown bear who never missed a note when trading fours on "Who Will Take My Place When I Am Gone."

"What's your tale?" the black asked her in the alley during a break after the second set.

"My baby bear grew up and went to college," she said. "Papa, he ran off to the far north with a polar bear he'd met while surfing some site on the Internet. The den seemed kinda big after that. And I was feeling pretty blue."

"My favorite color is this city," Gautier sighed. "It's the 'Rooster Blues.'"

"The James Street Alley Blues," she traded back. "It's the 'Deep River Blues,' 'Dying With the Blues,' 'Minor Blues,' 'Shake Man Blues,' 'Squabbling Blues,' 'Hard Luck Blues,' and "Fore Day Blues.' It's the 'Bitin' Fleas Blues,' 'Evil Man Blues,' the 'Twelfth Street Blues' and 'Mama's Got the Blues.'"

"You gonna fit here just fine," Gautier said.

Hell Matter

Once upon a time I lived in Quincy, IL, which wasn't far from Hannibal, MO, the boyhood home of Mark Twain. I'd spent more than a few of my days off wandering around all the tourist attractions, including through the caves. I snapped up lots of books, attended summer plays about Tom Sawyer that were held in an outdoor amphitheater near the river, and in general became a Mark Twain devotee. When I was asked to write a cat mystery years later, I immediately thought about setting it in Hannibal. Mark Twain loved cats. "Hell Matter" was originally published in Kittens, Cats & Crime, *Five Star, 2003.*

It was barely evening, the sun just set, and the smell of the wet earth was strong. The rain—it had rained all afternoon—was nearing an end, I thought, as the sky was merely spitting now and then in an irregular rhythm that I found most annoying.

I hated rain.

I hated it especially when in this, the height of Missouri's summer, it did nothing to cool things. Somehow despite the time of day, it only served to make everything steamy and more uncomfortable, and thoroughly, thoroughly sodden. Had I not sequestered myself just beyond the opening of this cave I would have been thoroughly wet too, and hot and miserable—rather than dry and only slightly miserable, and terribly, terribly bored.

As I watched the slowing drops, I heard the cicadas start their song. And from somewhere off I heard a steady and repeated slosh and crunch, the heavy sound of men's boots tromping through puddles and across stretches of gravel. An unremitting "shush" told me they were dragging something. Perhaps they would come past this cave and I would have something to watch other than mud and rocks. And if they talked, I would have something to listen to other than this odious drizzle and the simple drone of insects.

I waited, and after several moments the sloshing and shushing grew louder, and the rain began to drum harder—making me realize it had only teased me moments ago into thinking it might stop. The wind picked up suddenly, sending some of the rain inside. There was a flash, lightning. The rumble of thunder followed. I retreated farther into the dry darkness, listening to a patter that was coming angrily now, listening to the sloshing, to the men, who had finally started talking and who were slogging uninvited into my favorite cave. I hoped they were only coming inside to escape the storm, and that they would leave when the rain no longer toyed with me and truly stopped. I did not care to share this place.

"Hate this rain," one said.

I was amused at this, that a man would have something in common with me.

"The weather's nothing to be bothered up about. It's good that it's raining," the other said. I could tell that there were only two of them. "It'll cover our tracks. Folks're staying in their houses tonight. No one saw us leave town. No one way out here to see us."

Except me. I could see fairly well in the growing darkness.

What they'd been dragging was a boy, their hands under his armpits. They dropped him when they came even with me, the shorter man letting out a deep breath, thankful to be free of his burden. The boy didn't move, and I wondered if he was dead. I didn't much care for boys, as I'd met more than a few mean ones in my years—pelting me with rocks, tying things to my tail, chasing me, trying to set my fur on fire. I didn't much care for boys at all. But I didn't want this boy to be dead. I didn't want him rotting inside my favorite cave and fouling the air.

The taller man pulled a small lantern from a pack. He fumbled to light it, as I crept 'round a rock to keep out of sight. From the shadows I continued to watch them, glad that my boredom was banished and still worried that the boy was dead and would soon begin to stink.

I have a keen memory, and so I recognized the men from my trips into town. They were disparate, and it seemed odd that they would keep company. I'd seen the taller one along the river, where the steamboats and barges tie up. He dressed finer on the bank, all ruffles around his neck and wrists, gold rings flashing on each hand, hair smoothed back and dark as oil, and head topped with a cap with a shiny black brim. An important man. But the rings didn't flash much in the lantern's soft light, and he was dressed in the color of night, clothes in good repair, though not so fancy as his river attire.

The shorter one? His clothes were dark, too, but old and spotted. Not an upmarket soul. He had the craggy, drooping face of a bulldog, and he walked with his right foot turned slightly out. I remembered seeing him most often in the shadows of the town's buildings, sometimes in the backs and in the alleys, where people carelessly threw out food. That's what I went into town for, the discarded food. I was getting older and slower, and only old, slow mice were finding their way into my belly. I'd come to—sadly—appreciate the people's garbage.

The boy? I might have seen him, too, but I would not have recalled it—I did my best to avoid boys. In truth I hated them only a little less than the rain.

"We should tie the boy up," the tall one announced. "Don't want him running off on us."

Not dead, I sighed gratefully. There would be no horrible odor in my favorite cave.

"Tie Sammy up? He ain't going anywhere, Hobe. You walloped him good. He's unconscious."

The tall man nudged the boy with his boot. "Mebee he's unconscious. Mebee he's not. Could be playing possum. We can't take any chances he'll slip away." He fumbled in his pack and pulled out a length of rope. The two men propped the boy up against the opposite wall of the cave and tied his hands behind his back, then tied his ankles together. He was a lean boy, with a hawkish nose and unruly hair. His clothes were worn and thin, holes at the knees and elbows, and he was caked with mud from being drug here.

"Not sure I like this, Hobe, killing a boy. I ain't got no hankering to..."

"Can't take any chances, I told you. 'Sides, who's really going to miss him?"

"I hear tell he works for Joseph Ament. So Ament'll miss him."

"Ament can find another cub," the one called Hobe said. "I'm not willing to take the chance. I'll not go to jail 'cause some boy heard us jawing."

"Should've drowned him in the river, then," the shorter man said. "Wouldn't've had to come way out here in this weather. Sammy's always down by the river, folks'd think he slipped."

A shake of the tall man's head. "My crew's on my boat. An' there're a few hands working on the river—in spite of this weather. Someone might've seen us. Nobody'd see us around here."

The shorter man shrugged, drawing his shoulders up practically to his ears. "Guess you're right, Hobe. No one comes out to these caves, 'cept some kids, maybe a trapper once in a while."

"That's right."

"And I guess we're not really killing Sammy, eh, Hobe?" He let out a raspy chuckle. "We ain't doing the actual deed. The cave'll do that, eh?"

Hobe didn't reply. He was in his pack again, this time retrieving something I had no name for. I noticed the boy was stirring behind them and mumbling something.

"Sammysammysammy," the shorter man said, the words hissing together like a teakettle left too long on the stove. "Shouldn't've been out in this weather, Sammy." He started tsking, and he added a finger wag for emphasis. "Shouldn't've been creeping around behind the Hawkins' house. Shouldn't've overheard us."

"Didn't hear nothin'," the boy managed. He poked out his bottom lip. "Didn't hear..."

The tall man roughly backhanded the boy, pitching him onto his side. The boy groaned.

"Sammysammysammy," the other man hissed. "I bet you heard me an' Hobe just fine. I bet you heard real good."

"I didn't hear nothin', I said. But even if I did, I wouldn't tell," the boy offered. "Ain't nobody would believe me anyway."

" 'Cause you're just a kid? Or 'cause you're always telling wild stories? I might go along with you, Sammysammysammy. But Hobe, here? Captain Hobart? He's not the type to take a gamble. Can't afford to." The shorter man bent over and righted the boy. "Hobe says you've got to die."

The two men worked quickly then, double-checking the boy's ropes.

"I didn't hear nothin'. And if I did, I wouldn't tell," the boy repeated. "Honest."

Hobe let out a clipped laugh. "If you're Ament's cub, you'd tell him about me—and mebee, just mebee he'd believe you. Can't have my ship jeopardized 'cause of you. Can't risk losing all I've worked for. Can't go to jail. You understand, boy."

"I could leave town," the boy continued, the desperation thick in his voice. "Go south to St. Louis or east to Springfield. My folks wouldn't miss me. My pa died last year."

"How old are you, boy?" Hobe leaned close.

"Thirteen."

"You won't be seeing fourteen."

Hobe started backing toward the cave's entrance, and taking the object I couldn't name. He stuffed a cord in the center of the thing and motioned to his fellow.

"Someone's gonna find you out!" the boy hollered to them. "What you're doin' is wrong. Someone else'll overhear you. You can't steal from people like you're doin'. It ain't right." His defiance grew with his hopelessness. "And if I get out of here, Captain Hobart, I aim to see that you and Jim rot in jail forever. You're pirates!"

"Pirates? Told you the boy overheard us," Hobe said.

"Didn't think he knew my name," the short man said, as he returned to the boy and stuffed a rag in his mouth to quiet him. Then he snatched up the lantern. "All shit and no sugar, Sammysammysammy. You're just too dangerous to let live. Light the fuse, Hobe. The way it's thundering, ain't no one going to hear the dynamite."

Then the men were outside, and suddenly the object I couldn't name was sputtering and sitting in the cave's mouth, the cord attached to it burning merrily. I hesitated, looking between the boy and the way out. A part of me was urging me to follow the men, not to stay here. A part of me somehow knew "here" wasn't safe. But I was curious about the boy. Aren't all of my kind so vexed with a natural inquisitiveness? And so I hesitated and crept closer to the boy. I heard the thunder boom outside, and felt a trembling beneath my paws, heard a hurtful, rumbling clap of thunder coming from the cave mouth—louder than anything—and it set the stone floor to shaking. In an instant my favorite cave was quaking, sending bits of rock and dust down on me like rain. The dust was so thick I found breathing difficult. The rumbling continued, and I was tossed about, the cave trembling like a frightened beast, its walls cracking, the ground continuing to pitch. For the first time ever I felt a true, profound fear, and as my heart hammered loud in my ears. I fully expected to die.

The utter darkness was sudden and absolute. The entrance to the cave was gone, and the rocks that filled the once-opening kept the twilight and lantern light from slipping inside. Kept all hint of light at bay. I sensed my stomach was rising into my throat. The dust continued to come down, and I struggled to take a breath.

I was surprised I didn't die. And as moments passed, the trembling subsided. The only rumbling now came from the thunder I knew was booming outside. The boy was still alive, as I could hear his ragged breath. I couldn't see him, though, couldn't see anything.

I'd found myself in this terrible blackness once before, when I'd ventured so far into this cave the light didn't reach me. I retraced my steps on that occasion. On this occasion, I didn't know what to do.

"Mmmmph." This was coming from the boy.

I didn't like boys. But...

I padded close to him, relying on my hearing and sense of smell. He continued to make the "mmmphing" noise. He smelled of sweat and fear and the wet earth that clung to his threadbare clothes. I could tell that he was struggling against his ropes, and he jostled me in his gyrations as I slid past.

"Mmmph?" He'd felt me, and he stiffened and stopped wriggling. If it was possible, his breathing became more rushed and ragged.

I didn't like boys at all, but I moved around behind him, my whiskers brushing first against his fingers, then the rope. I started gnawing, and finally his breathing slowed. When I'd cut through enough of it, he managed to work his hands out. In the blackness he fumbled for the gag in his mouth, then set to untying his ankles.

"Who're you? What're you?" he asked.

Of course, I couldn't answer in a way that he could hear.

Then his fingers were groping through the blackness, finding me and grabbing, fluttering for me when I slipped away.

"A cat," he pronounced. He kept his voice low. "You're a cat."

I felt the air stir, his fingers still futilely searching for me. He gave up, and I heard his feet scrabble over the rocks as he stood.

"Thank ya cat," he continued. "Thank ya mightily."

Faintly, I heard his arm brush against the cave wall.

"My head hurts somethin' fierce," he said. "That ol' Captain Hobart hit me hard."

His feet started shuffling away from me. He grunted, finding the collapsed entrance and trying to move aside the rocks.

"Ain't gonna be able to get out the way I came in, cat. Not that I want to run into them thieves again anyway. They'd surely kill me this time. Shoot me or..."

His feet were shuffling again. Now I could tell he was going deeper into the cave.

"Don't think I been in this cave before," he continued to prattle. "Unless I came in another way."

I'm not sure what I expected of the boy, but it wasn't this—going farther into the utter black. I wanted him to move all the rocks that had fallen down in the entrance. I chewed him loose, and in payment I wanted him to dig us out of the cave.

He continued to move away from the entrance. That he couldn't see didn't seem to worry him overmuch.

"You here, cat?"

I relied on my hearing to follow him, keeping what I guessed was a safe distance. One could never trust boys...even ones who owed you.

"I gotta find me a way out, ya know. I can't let ol' Captain Hobart and Junkman Jim get away with it."

I wondered just what it was the two men were getting away with. And though I doubt the boy was able to sense my thoughts, he supplied the information.

"Them two is bad," he continued. "And they's right, I overheard 'em. I was on my way to Laura's house. She was gonna help me with some schoolwork. They was in the alley behind her house, talkin' so fast they sounded like bees. Seems ol' Captain Hobart keeps real close watch on his steamboat passengers. Finds out who's got money and jewelry. And he finds out which gamblers won big stakes."

He paused in his words and steps. I heard him bump against stone. "Careful, cat. Find the wall and press close against it. There's a drop off, and I don't want to find out how deep it goes."

I took his advice, though I was certain I would have felt the edge of any rocky ledge and could have stopped myself from tumbling. We traveled very slowly now, until he was certain the footing was safer. I heard a rustling overhead.

"Bats," he said.

He spoke the obvious.

"They ain't gonna bother us none if'n we don't spook 'em." His course was taking us still deeper, and we were twisting down one unseen path after another. There were other sounds intruding, a plopping of drops on water.

"Maybe I have been in this cave before."

Finally I sensed that we were moving up. The going was more difficult, as the boy was constantly bumping into stalagmites and rocky outcroppings.

"Junkman Jim... When ol' Captain Hobart docks his steamer, I think he goes straightaway to Jim. Tells Jim about the passengers, which ones to follow, which boarding house they're staying at. He tells Jim which ones to rob, and they split the take. They's been doin' it for some time, cat. I'm Ament's cub, all right, and so I read every paper he prints. There's always somethin' there about a robbery. Every week, it seems. Wealthy folks that came down the river and are only stoppin' in Hannibal for a day or two. No one stayin' here long has been robbed. Bet this has been goin' on for better than a year. They's pirates, Hobart and Jim."

The boy continued to chatter as he stumbled, lost. "I gotta get me out of here, cat. I gotta tell Ament, gotta get to the judge so Hobart and Jim can be stopped. Ain't right what they're doin'." He stopped suddenly. "And more than stealin', cat, they's guilty of tryin' to kill me. My heads still achin'. They's gonna be in jail a long time."

We started down again.

I don't know how long we meandered disoriented. Hours upon hours, I was certain. It was long enough that the pads on my feet were sore and bleeding and my legs ached like they'd been set on fire. My throat was dry and my tongue felt thick. I was so very, very thirsty. And hungry. I'd intended to go to town after the rain quit, to search through the people's garbage.

"You there, cat?" The boy had paused again, and by the rustling of his clothes, I could tell he was sitting. "I gotta stop for a piece, catch my breath." His fingers were questing through the darkness, and in an uncharacteristic move, I let him touch my fur. "Yep, cat, you're still there." He settled back against a wall, and I lay nearby. Every few minutes his fingers fluttered along my back. "I like cats," he said.

Perhaps this one boy was all right.

He dozed for a time. I could not sleep. The darkness and my thirst were too disconcerting. Eventually I nudged him, and he clumsily got up.

"Guess you want to get goin', huh, cat? Me, too. Gotta stop ol' Captain Hobart and Jim. They's gonna give the river and steamboats a bad name. I aim to be a steamboat captain someday, cat. An honest one."

I had to nudge him twice more in the hours that followed, on the latter occasion prodding him to his right, where I felt the air moving. My senses were far superior to his, and I knew that if I did not take the lead now, we would either die of starvation in this black place or fall down some hole and break our necks.

The air smelled fresh, and this sped my sore paws. In it I could pick out traces of damp earth and wildflowers. And when I listened closely, and shut out the sounds of the boy's shuffling feet and quick breath, I could hear the cry of some bird and the tinkling of a nearby creek. And I could hear the cicadas singing their blessed, monotonous tune.

I nudged him a final time, and by now I think he heard the sounds of outside, too. He became clumsy in his excitement, slipping on skree and falling to his knees more times than I bothered to count. I fell back so he would not tumble on me, and I only took the lead again at the very end, when a grayness intruded into the black and the insects' song grew louder.

"Hurry, cat," the boy urged, though he didn't have to. I had moved several yards ahead, and my legs were working with a speed they hadn't shown in quite a while. "I've found us a way out of here, cat!"

You found us?

It was only minutes later that we stumbled out of the cave. The air was warmer out here, but for once I didn't complain about the sweltering summer. There were stars overhead, evidence we'd passed at least an entire day in the cave. I was exhausted, and I stretched out on the ground. In a moment I would worry about the creek and getting a drink. In a long moment.

"We have to hurry, cat." The boy was looking down at me, hands on his knees, and sucking in great gulps of this August air. "We have to get into town and tell Ament about ol' Captain Hobart and Junkman Jim. We gotta get the judge."

I raised my brow. We? We didn't have to do anything. We were out of the damnable hole in the ground. We were safe. The creek was near. With some effort I rose and trotted to it and started drinking. The boy was talking again, but I let his words drift to the back of my mind and I concentrated on the sound and sweet taste of the water.

"We gotta go," he said.

You can go where you please, I thought.

Then he scooped me up and nestled me under an arm. I was squirming in protest, but my motions were so feeble, so completely tired was I. I knew the boy was heading into town—Hannibal, he called the place. And so I finally stopped squirming. I was hungry, and Hannibal would feed me. It was night, and so I would be able to pick through people's garbage undisturbed. And then I would find somewhere to sleep.

"It's only a mile," he continued. "Not far. Me and Laura used to come out here once in a while. Don't think it was to that cave, though. Ain't never goin' back to that cave."

I agreed with him. I could find a better place to stay out of the rain, and somewhere not so far from town. The past several times my legs had been arguing with me over the journey between town and my once-favorite cave.

Somehow the boy managed to pick up his pace, and as we came down a hill I could see the town's sparse lights. It was late, as most of the homes were dark, but there were streetlights burning. Perhaps this Ament the boy was intent on seeing had left choice scraps outside his backdoor.

It didn't take us long, and we were darting down one street, then down a dark alley. Soon he was bounding up front porch steps and pounding on a door. The boy was impatient, and he began rocking back and forth on his heels, fidgeting with his free hand, then he was pounding again. A light was lit inside, and I could hear slow footfalls and a thin voice.

"Give me a minute." Then the door swung open and a stoop-shouldered man, barechested and in creased pants, loomed over us. "Sam?"

"Mr. Ament," the boy began.

"It's late."

"I know, Mr. Ament, but..."

"Samuel, you weren't at work today. I needed you. I have a mind to fire you and get me another cub. One that won't..."

"Mr. Ament, Captain Hobart and Junkman Jim just tried to kill me...and all because I overheard 'em talkin' behind the Hawkins place." The words flew furiously from the boy's lips. He left nothing out, though the part about our escape from the cave was not nearly as harrowing as he made it seem. The boy was quite the storyteller. When he was finished, Ament shook his head.

"Sam, I usually don't mind your tall tales, but this one is a bit too stretched. If you made it up to justify why you didn't work today..."

"I'm tellin' you the truth Mr. Ament. I didn't whitewash nothin' and..."

"Hobart is one of the most successful riverboat captains on the Mississippi. He wouldn't set folks up to be robbed."

"But there have been robberies," the boy persisted. "We've printed stories about 'em in the paper!"

Ament yawned and shook his head again. "Tell you what, Sam. I'll not fire you. Not just yet. And first thing Saturday morning..."

"That's two days away."

"First thing Saturday, I'll start looking into Captain Hobart. Poke around, ask some questions. Investigate like any good journalist would. There might be something in what you say, but..."

"But Captain Hobart will be gone then, especially if he knows we're askin' questions. Off down the river settin' more people up to be robbed in another town by someone like Junkman Jim. We can't wait."

Boys are so impatient, I realized. But this one had reason. I found myself wishing Ament would take him more seriously.

"Sam, I will investigate this first before we print anything. And maybe we'll have a story by next Thursday or the one after. And maybe we won't." Then Ament shut the door.

The boy raised his fist to the wood again, but I nipped him in the side.

"Cat, I can't wait. If ol' Captain Hobart sees me in town, he'll come after me again—and this time he'll kill me for certain. And I can't hide while Ament 'investigates' this. If ol' Captain Hobart catches wind of someone checkin' up on him, he'll kill me and then he'll be gone, never stoppin' in Hannibal again. I have to do somethin'."

I admired the boy's fervor. He had a purpose other than bothering cats. There was something almost noble about him. The way his arm was crooked beneath me left his fingers just beneath my chin. I moved my head and nipped at his thumb, not so hard as to draw blood, though. And I rubbed my jaw against his fingers.

Be a smart boy, I thought. Look to yourself for the answer.

The light from the stars and the light from the lamp inside the Ament place was enough. The boy could see his hands. They were dirty, from being dragged in the mud and from running along the walls in the cave. But there was more than dirt, there was a black settled in the whorls of his fingers. Ink from being Ament's cub.

"I set type," he told me.

Smart boy.

Then we were off again, down another alley and then turning on a street that paralleled the river. "What we're doin' ain't legal, breakin' into a place like this—even though I work here. But our crime ain't near so bad as what Hobart and Jim are guilty of. Our's is a good crime...if there's such a thing." He moved around to the back of a building and worked at the doorknob before it gave up and turned. "Lock doesn't hold none too good," he explained.

Inside, he finally set me down, and I watched as he lit a few lanterns. We were in a shop filled with cabinets and paper, big containers of ink, rollers, and a great contraption of metal larger than a bear. The boy continued to babble on, and I realized that in all my years boys had never talked to me, only at me as they were throwing things.

"I don't normally wet it down until Saturday, cat," he said, gesturing at the great contraption. "Turn it Sunday. See, we're a weekly, and the paper comes out on Thursday. That means one came out this mornin'. No wonder Ament was mad. I wasn't around to deliver it at dawn. 'Cept, I can't wait until next Thursday or the one after to tell my story. We're gonna print us up a special edition, cat. Tonight! And ol' Captain Hobart'll have the front page all to hisself. Gotta get the date right. August thirteenth, eighteen forty-eight."

I watched the boy work. "Only one page, cat, and I'll use the large type to take up space. Hope I can spell everythin' right." His fingers were plucking pieces of metal from racks—letters, he explained. Nearly all of these he arranged in rows, but he threw some bits away. "These're no good," he said. "Bent, worn, can't get a good print from 'em." He tossed them in a box. "Gotta throw the bad pieces away, into the hell matter." He paused. "I think ol' Captain Hobart and Junkman Jim belong in the hell matter, too." He smiled wide. "Jail is a hell matter box for bad people."

Despite being up so many hours, and frequently complaining about his sore head, he toiled without stop. Me? I slept off and on and wondered in between if the boy might think to feed me. I had, indeed, rescued him from the cave. I saved his life. And I had, by nipping his thumb, urged him to tell his tale to all of Hannibal now, rather than next Thursday. The boy owed me a meal.

It was dawn when the boy was finished pressing his one-sheet newspapers. He read the headline to me:

Respected Riverboat Captain Daniel Hobart

Mastermind Behind Scheme to Rob Passengers

Hannibal's Junkman Jim in Kahoots

"Not the best turn of phrase, cat," the boy told me. "But then I ain't had me a chance to write the news before. Good for a first effort, don't you think?"

I meowed my approval.

Later I clung to the buildings, watching him as he scurried from business to business to house to house, delivering his special edition and knocking on doors to wake up those still sleeping inside. He was careful to stay away from the river, not wanting to cross paths with Captain Hobart. And when he spotted Junkman Jim—fortunately Jim was looking the other way—the boy disappeared down an alley.

He did feed me well when he was finished, and he carried me up to a room above a drugstore, where both of us lay down on a small bed and slept the rest of the day away.

* * *

It was a week later, a fine Thursday morning, that Sam and I sat on the bank of the river, watching a steamer pass by. Captain Hobart and Junkman Jim were safely tucked away in a hell matter box—Hannibal's jail, and word was they were to be shipped down to St. Louis to begin a long sentence. More would be joining them, as Hobart had others like Junkman Jim working for him in several river towns in Missouri and Iowa.

Sam had delivered all the regular editions of the Hannibal Courier—that contained more detailed stories about Hobart and his gang—and was declared finished for the day. Ament hadn't fired him, rather he'd given the boy a modest raise and the title of assistant editor. Sam seemed pleased at this.

I was pleased, too.

For the first time in my long years, I had a home. Above a drugstore in the heart of Hannibal, a place at the foot of Sam's bed. For the rest of my days I was fed well and given saucers of milk, and I went to work with Sam on all the mornings my legs felt like carrying me.

I never cared much for boys.

Except for this one.

Two quotes that inspired this tale:

Samuel Clemens (Mark Twain) said this in an address at the Typothetae dinner, given at Delmonico's, January 18, 1886, Commemorating the birthday of Benjamin Franklin.

> *"The chairman's historical reminiscences of Gutenberg have caused me to fall into reminiscences, for I myself am something of an antiquity. All things change in the procession of years, and it may be that I am among strangers. It may be that the printer of today is not the printer of thirty-five years ago. I was no stranger to him. I knew him well. I built his fire for him in the winter mornings; I brought his water from the village pump; I swept out his office; I picked up his type from under his stand; and, if he were there to see, I put the good type in his case and the broken ones among the "hell matter"; and if he wasn't there to see, I dumped it all with the "pi" on the imposing-stone—for that was the furtive fashion of the cub, and I was a cub. I wetted down the paper Saturdays, I turned it Sundays—for this was a country weekly; I rolled, I washed the rollers, I washed the forms, I folded the papers, I carried them around at dawn Thursday mornings."*

And:

> *"Of all God's creatures there is only one that cannot be made the slave of the leash. That one is the cat. If man could be crossed with the cat it would improve man, but it would deteriorate the cat."*
>
> *—Mark Twain Notebook, 1894*

Shifting Gears

I wrote this story for no particular reason other than that I had the notion for it rumbling around. I was running a Star Wars role-playing game campaign at the time—the old game with all the six-sided dice, and I think the droids inspired me. Looking back on it now, I should have put a cat in Amalk's shop. Things might have turned out differently. "Shifting Gears" originally appeared in the magazine Fantastic Stories of the Imagination, *DNA Publications, 2001.*

"Lovely planet they sent us to, El-Tee. Pos'tively rustic. Might go so far as to call it a Class-A ball-o-dirt."

The Marine lieutenant scowled at his second-in-command, a gawky Texan who looked sixteen because of his boyish face, but the records proved him almost twice that. "A little dirt never hurt anyone, Marsh. 'Sides, we won't be here long. We cut through that gap an' surprise the Dakfars on the other side. There aren't many of them, according to Intel's spies. This'll be easy."

"Easy," Marsh sarcastically repeated, wrapping the word around his tongue and using his practiced Western drawl. "Easy. Easy."

"We free the miners," the lieutenant continued, "then it's leave time for all of us back on Earth."

"Nothing's ever easy out here." Marsh squatted and studied something on the ground, a bootprint that didn't match his unit's footgear. His dark eyes followed the tracks. "Lone man," he whispered. "Maybe a pirate scout. Maybe a miner passing through. Can't tell how long ago." His gloved hand traced the print, then he rose and reached for the pulse-carbine slung over his narrow back. "Wish we never tried to settle in this part of space. Wish we hadn't plopped miners here. Straight in the path of the Dakfars. I hate this dust." He drew his lips into a thin line and eyed the rest of the Marine force—one hundred and twenty recruits shipped out from basic training. Dreamy-eyed freedom fighters bent on making the central quadrant into Earth territories, Marsh thought.

Marsh let out a long sigh, which sounded like dry leaves shushing across the ground. He had resigned himself to the mission, was actually looking forward to it in a way, a fight to shake his boredom. "Couple dozen Dakfars. Slimy, greedy pirates. Too bad there aren't more, eh El-Tee? If I gotta shoot somebody, it might as well be Dakfars." He worked a kink out of his neck and met his commander's gaze. "Let me take point."

The lieutenant nodded, and Marsh scuttled silently ahead. The rest of the Marines trailed several dozen meters behind. As the stars winked into view, the men quietly made their way toward a gap in Torrant IV's iron-rich hills.

Marsh sneezed. "I really hate all this dust," he cursed, as he ran a spindly finger across the carbine's trigger. "Almost as much as I hate Dakfars." He reached the far end of the gap and glanced across an uneven arid field. "I could take them all out by myself without a bother. Add a medal to my collection. To the heart-o-the-sun with pris'ners. And then leave time in Dallas with..." His breath caught in his throat and his legs locked in place as he spotted something at the edge of his vision. The dust swirled around him as his comrades caught up.

*   *   *

"It's all this dust!" the thickset spacer groaned. He nudged the robot forward and slammed the shop door shut behind him. "Dust 'n sand. Every time I stay on Janu for more'n a few days, the stuff gets in my bot's joints. Makes it act up or shut down or not hear right to translate."

The shop consisted of one large room, which when it was built would have been called spacious. Now it seemed small and crowded. The walls were lined with robots. Like soldiers, a few dozen vaguely human in appearance stood in a row, their silver, gold, brass, blue, and bronze metal plating gleaming in the light that filtered in through a grime-streaked window.

Nearby were several squat constructs resembling barrels and columns, some with spiderlike appendages, others with tubes, wires, and paddles sticking out of them. Robots with four and six legs, some with multiple heads, were arranged on the floor. Handheld robots in the shape of spheres and blocks hung from the ceiling, all blinking and whirring like dancehall decorations.

There were also mining robots with shovels attached, companion robots built to mimic Earth dogs and cats, domestic units with vacuum cleaners in their chests and hoses for arms, and entertainment robots that played all manner of music and could catch the signals of any planet-based vid station—while serving cocktails and appetizers. Behind the counter were shelves upon shelves filled with metal legs, arms, wheels, treads, spools of wire, circuits, chips, and hundreds of small tools. And behind that was a metal-beaded curtain through which shuffled the proprietor.

The spacer cleared his throat and scratched at the stubble on his chin. "Can you do somethin' 'bout this bot, Mister...?"

"Amalk," the old man replied. He had never been a tall man, but age had stooped his shoulders, making him look small next to his burly customer. His skin was wrinkled and the shade of an eggshell, and his hair was smoke-gray and wispy like spiderwebs. The old man's eyes were his one dark feature. They were intense and alive, and they carefully regarded the spacer's sand-pitted robot, a silvery model with the vague form of a human. It looked in better shape than its ragged owner.

"You shouldn't leave him outside on Janu," Amalk suggested. "Janu's dust wouldn't be a problem for him if you kept him on your ship while you're wandering."

"Can't keep it on my ship. I need it nearby 'n case I come across some foreigner I wanna talk to. For business. It translates for me."

Amalk appreciatively ran his doughy fingers over the robot's arm. "An interpreter robot," he said. There was a hint of admiration in his thin voice.

"Yeah," the spacer returned. "A bot with lots o' languages floatin' around inside its metal head. It helps me with business."

"And you conduct your business out on the street? In the open where the dust always blows?"

The spacer ran his thick hand over the top of his head, smoothing his straggly hair. "Sometimes. 'N sometimes in the bar. Well, a lot o' the times in the bar. But the 'tender...well, he won't let me take it inside. 'Only Humans,' the sign says. The 'tender don't like aliens or artificial-intelligent types. Says they make him uneasy. So I keep my bot just outside the front door. Just outside's the next best thing."

The old robot engineer glided closer and ran his age-spotted hands over the silver's worn face. It was a kind gesture that was lost on the spacer. "You're in need of a good cleaning, my new friend," Amalk said softly. "Hammer out a few of these dents and give you a shiny finish. Ah, you'll gleam like distant Sol."

"Huh?"

Amalk straightened. "I said fixing him shouldn't be too much of a problem. It looks like his light-receptors are damaged."

The spacer raised an eyebrow and his lips parted in an unspoken question.

"Light-receptors," Amalk explained. "Your robot's eyes, the minute electronic devices that snag the light rays—natural and manufactured—and convert them into signals that are processed by the secondary computer at the base of his head. The computer essentially translates those signals into images so he can see. It all operates on the same principle as human eyes, probably a little better. He'll never need ocular implants as he gets older. In any event, the fittings are cracked. Dust got inside and choked the workings."

"Hate all this dust," the spacer grumbled.

Amalk's eyes narrowed and he returned his attention to the robot. "Hmm. Not just the fittings. You have some other problems, too, don't you fellow?"

"What's that noise?" the spacer cut in. "That squawky stuff?"

"It's your interpreter. He's talking to me."

"I can't understand it. The fuzz. Like insects buzzing. Is somethin' wrong with its...vocabulator?" The spacer puffed out his chest, pleased that he'd spewed out what he considered a highly technical term.

Amalk cocked his head. "Do you mean its speech-vocalizer?"

"Yeah." He deflated a bit. "Vocalizer. That's what I meant. Is it broken, too? Is that why I hear fuzz?"

"It's not fuzz," the old engineer muttered, sadly shaking his head. "It's language."

"Not one I understand."

"Few do."

But Amalk was one of those few. What sounded like insects buzzing around the cramped shop's interior was a specialized program language created more than a century ago on Earth and refined as man spread out into the galaxy and built an increasing number of robots to help his exploration efforts. Robots often used the program language to communicate among themselves and to computers. It was largely unintelligible to humans. Amalk buzzed back fluently—questions upon questions tumbling from his lips. And the robot quickly provided answers.

"So you travel a lot, I imagine, being a pilot," Amalk said, finally returning his attention to the man.

"Yeah. Got my own ship. I haul stuff for people."

"Get to see much of the Eight Quadrants?"

"Yeah. I get around."

"Ever travel in Dakfar territory?" Amalk popped the chestplate off the robot and peered inside.

"Yeah. Sometimes. Not that it's any of your business, though."

"I'd bet that's dangerous. The Dakfars keep stretching their lines toward Earth settlements. Dakfar gun-shuttles flitting around, maybe even an entire pirate fleet. But then you look like you're not afraid of much."

"I'm not afraid of anythin'." The spacer puffed out his chest again, straining the fastenings on his faded shirt. "Besides, it's not all that dangerous for me. And the Dakfars're not that much different from us. Their skin's just a little thicker, eyes a little bigger, an extra finger or two. They talk funny, but my bot translates it. Anyway, I got some contacts with the Dakfars, do some odd jobs for them now and again. Stay friendly with them and you're better off. Healthier and wealthier. Know what I mean?"

"Indeed I do." Amalk's fingers prodded the robot's wires and circuits. "Hmmm. What have we here?"

The pilot tried to look over Amalk's shoulder.

"Not good," Amalk tsked. "Not good at all. See this?"

"What? Dust got inside there, too?"

"Some. But that's not the problem. The loco-mechanism. It's wearing out. It will need to be replaced right away. Your robot probably won't be able to take more than another hundred steps or so under his own power before the mechanism burns out and locks his leg joints."

"Good thing I brought it to you to fix then." The pilot looked delighted with himself. "Back at the docking bay, they said you was the best. Also said that you was a bit off your feed...if you know what I mean. Said you think more of robots than people. Don't matter to me none about your preferences. Me, I'm just passin' through, an' I need you to fix it."

"Him."

"Huh?"

"Fix him. Fix your robot interpreter."

"Yeah. Is a loco-mechanism expensive? An' what is it? I know ships 'n all. Been flyin' my hauler for years. Robotics, well, that's somethin' I never took to studyin'."

"A loco-mechanism is a series of wires and interconnected boards that gives your robot—and most other humanoid robots—signals for moving their arms and legs. In short, it provides them the ability to walk, to move, to copy a human's way of getting around."

"So can you replace this mechanism? Without it costin' me much?"

"Yes. Though not at the moment. I don't have any spares in the shop. At least not for a model like this. I can order one. But it will take some time."

The spacer slammed his fist on the counter. "So whadda I do?" I gotta be leavin' in a day, no more'n two. Got someplace I gotta go. Somethin' to haul. I need it to translate for me."

"Him."

"Yeah. I need him to translate for me."

"You could buy another one." Amalk eased away from the spacer's robot and gestured at his shop's walls.

"I kinda like that bronze one with three legs," the pilot said after looking everything over. "Haven't had a bot with three legs before. Does it translate good?"

"He."

"Well, does he?"

Amalk nodded. "A good interpreter with all the Earth dialects and with several dozen languages spoken in the central quadrants."

"Dakfar?"

"Yes. He can speak Dakfar. Trade in this robot, which I'll repair when I get the loco-mechanism shipment, and throw in seven hundred."

"Six."

"Six-fifty."

"Deal." The pilot fumbled in his pocket for a counter. The three-legged bronze interpreter cast a last glance at Amalk, looking almost sad. Uttering a string of rushed sentences in a program language, he followed his new owner down the street.

"Is the man gone?" This from an outmoded mining robot.

"The ignoramus," a partially repaired chef robot retorted. "I've known smarter vermin-catchers."

"He is heading toward the docking bay," a gold and black interpreter said. He was craning his shiny neck as far as it would go and leaning away from the wall for a better view of the departing customer. "There. Out of sight. Fortunate riddance."

The other robots moved away from the wall and started chatting to themselves and Amalk. Some were incapable of human speech and simply chirped and hooted and hummed. The chef-robot ran through the ingredients it needed from the commons for Amalk's dinner.

"Fortunate riddance to that customer," the gold and black interpreter repeated. "This planet will be better for his departure."

Amalk quietly regarded his chattering metal friends.

"Oh, to be rid of him finally! Bad loco-mechanism indeed! I have no such thing!" the silver sand-pitted robot said. "I had quite my fill of working for that boorish man. Occasional dealings with Dakfars, he claims! Hah! He works for the pirates all the time, and he is leaving now for a rendezvous with a Dakfar captain. They use him, though he does not realize it. He does not see how truly evil the Dakfars are. Some engineer you are, old one. Bad loco-mechanism indeed!"

"I know there's nothing really wrong with you," Amalk said. "Except for the dust."

"Then why..."

"Because I am very bright," the old repairman returned. "It's a long story, my new friend. You see..."

"Company!" the outmoded mining robot announced.

The gold and black interpreter leaned back against the wall, and his fellows quickly joined him. They pretended to shut themselves off. The handheld units dangling from the ceiling fell silent.

A soft buzz cut through the air as the door opened. Amalk watched a pair of dust-covered grifters trundle inside. They were leading a quartet of battle-damaged road-maintenance robots, one of which was pulling a one-legged black robot that looked most intriguing.

"What will you give us for these?" the taller of the two hooded figures began. "Know they're damaged, but figure you can at least get some parts off 'em."

No questions were asked about where the grifters acquired the robots. A deal was quickly struck, and Amalk passed over a counter, smiling politely as they left.

"Appears to be laser-fire scarring. On all five of them." It was the deep voice of a domestic unit. He stepped close to Amalk's new acquisitions, and his metal shoulders moved in the approximation of a shudder.

"Perhaps. But the scarring has a feathering at the edges, like from a pulse-weapon," added one of the handheld units that hung from the ceiling. "Note the slice along right wheel-mount. And that is likely what sheered off the leg of the black unit and caused the fatigue on the arm. In fact, several times I have witnessed..."

"I agree," interjected the chef-robot. "A pulse-weapon. Why, when I worked in the kitchens of a deep-mining ship in orbit about Eldan, there was an overweight Canadian who... "

"No. Definitely lasers," the mining robot argued. "Laser rifles likely."

* * *

"Laser fire!" Marsh yelled. "Rifles! It's a trap! Fall back to the ship!"

The high-pitched whines of laser rifles cut through the air. Dirt showered up where the bolts missed the Marines and instead hit at their feet. Where the bolts didn't miss, the Marines fell, clutching their legs and chests. The scent of burned cloth and flesh was heavy in the air. A dozen men were on the ground, dead or dying in the passing of a heartbeat.

"Fall back! Now!" The lieutenant pressed himself against the side of a hill. He cursed himself for cutting through the gap. It was a perfect site for an ambush, he realized. Only thing was, the Dakfar pirates weren't supposed to know company was coming. Marsh was right. The tracks had belonged to a scout.

"A couple dozen, El-Tee?" Marsh shot as he scrambled toward his commander. "A couple hundred is closer to the truth."

The lieutenant craned his neck forward, straining to look at the top of the hill across from him, eyes stinging from the dust that was flying everywhere. There! Prone, a few dozen Dakfars. He saw the moonlight glinting off their silver helmets. All armed with laser rifles, looks like, he thought. Probably have pistols for close-in fighting. Probably. The lieutenant knew his men wouldn't be able to scramble up the hillside quick enough to get close and find out. Must be an equal number of Dakfars on the hill above him. A lot more than the Marine Intel report said there would be.

"Can't fall back!" came a cry from somewhere behind the lieutenant. Coming in the gap behind us, boxing us in!"

"How many?" the lieutenant shouted.

"Eighty, best guess! Maybe more!" came the hoarse reply. "Hard to tell. The dust's so thick!"

"Swarming us from the base up ahead! Coming at us on mining rovers!" Marsh hollered to the lieutenant. "I'd say Intel's spies were wrong, El-Tee. I'd say the Dakfar pirates are gonna have us for dinner!"

"No!" the lieutenant screamed. "We're not going down tonight!" He darted away from the slope and hit the ground, rolling and dodging laser fire. He paused only to take a couple of shots at the silver helmet peering over the hilltop, then he kept rolling, not bothering to see if he had hit the pirate. Have to get a look at the other side of the hill, he thought. Just to be sure. Maybe we could charge up that hill, circle round, get back to the ship. Get out of here. Come back with a bigger force to rescue the miners. Maybe...

The keen whine of a tripod-mounted laser-cannon cut through the din. A knifing pain shot up the lieutenant's right leg and into his stomach. Then the lieutenant felt nothing, couldn't move. Dying, he thought, probably lasered my leg off. Can't feel, can't hardly swallow. So cold. "Marsh! Your command now! Get the men out of here!"

"Fall back!" Marsh hollered. "It's suicide heading toward their base." He slung his pulse-carbine over his back and scuttled toward the bulk of his men. He leapt over the body of the lieutenant, registered that at least a third of his force was littering the dusty ground. Should have brought more men, more ships. But this was supposed to be a small operation. Where did all the pirates come from?

Just ahead to his left, three Marines were squeezed together in a niche under a rocky overhang. They were taking turns poking their heads out and shooting at the silver helmets on the opposite ridge.

"Too many of them!" Marsh called as he scampered toward the trio. "Fighting retreat!" He paused when he reached the overhang, slung his carbine off his back again and took aim at a Dakfar descending the opposite slope. His finger pumped the trigger, sending light-blue bolts of energy "kzinging" off the dirt and rocks, finally finding a mark on the enemy's torso. The pirate fell. But there were more coming over the ridge now. "Leave me one of your carbines!" Marsh barked. The Marines complied, then took off running.

"Fall back!" Marsh shouted at more soldiers, as he wedged himself into the niche. He hunkered as close to the ground as he could, and his fingers flew over his own carbine, tugging at the stock, opening the compartment where the energy cells that powered the gun were held, yanking the cells out. He grabbed his spare energy cells from his belt and held them together. Then he fumbled with the carbine strap, used it to bind the cells tight. He grimaced when he saw a half-dozen more of his men fall to enemy laser fire.

"See how you like this," he cursed softly. He heaved the bundled cell pack toward the slope the pirates were climbing down, picked up the borrowed carbine, and fired at the bundle.

An explosion rocked the gap. Dirt and gravel showered the pirates and Marsh. Barely over the rumble, the Texan heard the screams of dying Dakfars. He hoisted the carbine and waited, intending to shoot at the first glint of silver he could spot when the dust settled.

* * *

"Settled in for the evening, Sir?" the domestic robot flipped up the closed sign on Amalk's shop and glanced around to make sure everything was secure. The only light inside was over a worktable where several tools were carefully laid out. Most of the robots had turned themselves off for the evening, simulating human rest. A few were in the back room polishing each other.

"No. Far from settled. I'm going to work late tonight."

"On the units the grifters brought in?"

Amalk nodded. "I'm very interested in that one-legged black unit. I think he might indeed be an interpreter. But I cannot locate a speech-vocalizer. Maybe I just don't know where to look."

"A sleek design, Sir. Nothing I have seen before, and I have seen quite a few come through your shop. Either a very new model I have not spotted in the engineering vids from Earth or a one-of-a-kind design specially commissioned. I suppose he might also be a very old one, an antique that has been kept in good shape and that somehow found his way out here." The domestic cocked his hammered aluminum head. "Good shape except for the missing leg, of course."

"I'll have to use that one." Amalk pointed to an olive-gray leg hanging behind the counter. "At least until I can fashion one to match the rest of his body."

"I am certain some of us could help. Unfortunately, I cannot. Electronics are beyond me. Perhaps I could polish him."

Amalk didn't reply. He was busy carrying the black robot over to his worktable. With the dust brushed off the casings, the robot looked smooth and glossy, with few sharp angles. Nothing marred its metal surface. The old engineer laid it down almost reverently and stared as his reflection in the chestplate.

"I told the grifters I was only buying you for spare parts. Truly thought so at the time," he said to himself. "But maybe I can get you running. You'd be quite the showpiece. Wonder what languages you know? How many? Wonder where you've been. Who built you? Where is your speech-vocalizer?"

"If you do not need me for anything else, Sir, I would like to..."

Amalk waggled his fingers, dismissing the domestic robot. "Hmm. Maybe I could sell you to a wealthy spacer who collects antique or rare robots. Or to a merchant who travels Dakfar raiding routes. You'd make a magnificent informer." He flipped open the chestplate and began humming. Picking through his tools, Amalk began repairing the robot.

"Definitely fixable," he said after a few hours passed, and a thorough circuit flush and memory wipe were finished. "Not in such bad shape after all. No. Not at all. Language boards intact. Ah, there's your vocalizer. The grifters didn't know what they had. All you need now is a new leg and my deeply implanted intelligence program. Undetectable, unflushable. Perfect." He continued to hover over the robot.

"No one will ever learn you're working for Marine Intel. Your light-receptors and audio-receptors will absorb all manner of pirate activity, and you'll report to me whenever you're able to sneak away to download information. Why, maybe I'll even be able to sell you directly to a pirate! Shine you up just right to catch his attention."

Amalk grinned. The old engineer had placed nearly two hundred robots with his unique and complex program seeded deep inside them. They had been sending him information on the Dakfars for more than a year, and he relayed it to Marine Intel—which was quick to act on the knowledge.

He oiled the black robot's gears, then carefully polished the metal plates that covered most of the body. "You are a beauty," he whistled softly. The robot's face was well defined, not unlike the visage of the chef-robot he'd acquired a few weeks ago. But this one was almost handsome, even by human terms. The brow swept back to form a ridge that looked like the rounded knuckles of a closed fist. "Judging by that overlarge motor-mechanism, I'd say you will be able to move quickly. Oil you enough and you'll be quiet, too. You have some interesting attachments and compartments. I'll look those over in the morning."

Amalk pushed himself away from the workbench and retrieved the olive-gray leg. "Hate to put this on you, but I want you up and walking around. Make you a little lopsided, but just for a couple of days. Some of my fellows here will help me craft a new leg for you, all black and shiny, so well-made that no one but me and you—and my fellows, of course—will know it's not your original. There!" He attached the wires from the gray leg to the robot's hip, oiled the joints, and then connected the power unit.

The black robot's eyes glowed white against the inky sockets.

* * *

Marsh stared up at the stars, white pinpricks against the inky sky. Most of the dust had settled, revealing that his makeshift bomb had taken out half the opposing slope—and with it quite a few Dakfars. Their armor-clad bodies were scattered amid the downed Marines, arms and legs at odd angles like broken dolls. So many bodies.

The Texan swallowed hard. He'd been in firefights, but not in any with so many casualties. "Back to the ship!" he called to the remaining Marines. "Move your feet or none of us will be making it off this ball o' dirt!"

There were still several dozen pirates to contend with—easily three times as many as there were Marines still standing. But Marsh trusted that his soldiers were better than the Dakfars. He cocked his head and picked up what sounded like an incessant wail. The mining rovers had reached the far end of the gap. They'd be here in the space of a few heartbeats. The noise was loud, and of varying pitches. Marsh swore under his breath. There were more rovers than he had first guessed.

"Be quick!" he hollered to his men. He squatted amid the bodies between the two hills. He intended to cover the retreating Marines, even though he suspected his heroism would cost him his life. He would take a lot of pirates with him, he knew, and prayed enough soldiers would make it back to the ship so they could get off this rock and report the incident.

"Lying Intel spies," he spat.

Behind him the sound of laser rifles continued. Both sides were firing, he surmised, as the Dakfar rifles had a higher tone to them than the Marines' pulse-carbines. There was another explosion in the distance. Marsh could tell one of his men had fashioned a makeshift bomb out of carbine power cells. Faintly, he heard a victory cry, human. He allowed himself a weak smile.

"Maybe they can make it out of here after all," he whispered. Then the rovers were practically on top of him. "Where did all of these Dakfars come from?" He swiveled his borrowed carbine and began thumbing the trigger. He aimed for the lead rovers' engines, netting two before the Dakfars realized what was happening. The rovers sparked and sputtered and took their hapless riders careening along what was left of the hillside. "Two down, ten to go," he grumbled as he dodged a blast from a rover cannon and saw another vehicle headed straight toward him.

Marsh darted to his right as a cannon blasted the spot he'd been occupying a heartbeat before. He spun about on the balls of his feet, raised his carbine, and felt himself flying forward. A pirate on another rover had passed behind him, ramming the stock of his laser rifle soundly against his skull. The darkness reached up and swallowed him.

*   *   *

"It will be light soon. I need to get some sleep." Amalk backed away from the black robot and ran his fingers through his spiderweb-fine hair. "Been working on you all night." He glanced toward the shop window, where the pink light of dawn was peeking through the darkness. "Yes, get a couple of hours of rest, then give you a good polishing. Put you on display."

He made room for the black interpreter between the other humanoid robots.

"You can stay up if you like," Amalk said to his new acquisition. "Make yourself at home. Think of a name for yourself." He yawned and rubbed his eyes. "See you after a nap."

The robot's bright white eyes watched Amalk shuffle to the back room. His head swiveled silently this way and that, taking in the stock of robots, noting none were active, not even the domestic. But to be certain... The robot glided behind the counter, retrieved a set of thin pliers, and moved from robot to robot, snipping through main power wires that could easily be repaired. Tomorrow.

Finished, it noiselessly moved to the back room, raised its right arm and released a thin laser beam. The old engineer had been pulling down the comforter and was climbing into bed.

"Wha..." Amalk fell to his knees and immediately fumbled in his pocket for his only weapon, a small pulsegun he always kept with him in the event someone tried to rob his shop. He tugged it free and gritted his teeth, turned and fired on his new acquisition.

The pulse beam glanced off the black metal and ricocheted harmlessly away. Amalk fired again and again as the robot walked closer.

"Stop," the robot said.

It was the first word Amalk had heard the construct speak.

"Wh-wh-what are you doing?" the startled engineer stammered. "I've done you no harm. And..."

"My laser," it said. "I will not kill you with it. There would be too many questions." Its angular head swiveled on its neck, its white eyes locked on the vat in which Amalk's robots were dipped for cleaning. "Yes."

Amalk crawled toward the back door, his movements slow from age and pain. The robot followed, stayed him with a strong metal hand on his bony shoulder. The engineer struggled, but the black construct was incredibly strong and held him fast, then lowered a hand to his other shoulder, picked him up effortlessly.

"Wh-wh-what are you?" Amalk stammered.

"Not something to be put on display and sold as an Intel spy." The robot's eyes glowed like white-hot coals. "I already am a spy. And I serve a master far better than you."

"The Dakfar," Amalk said.

The robot cocked its head in affirmation.

"I wiped your memory."

"You thought only a human could create so complex a program, so deep it could not be detected, not be flushed."

"Someone discovered me." Amalk gasped at the realization.

"And is undoing everything you and Intel have done."

The old man sobbed openly. "The Marines. What have I done?"

The robot carried him to the vat, dropped him inside, and held his head above the oily surface for several moments as if it were a bug to be studied. Then it pushed Amalk under. Metal hands held the old man there while he feebly struggled. "The shop's new owner will sell to a different clientele. And it is the Dakfar who will profit from the robot intelligence network this time."

Amalk's struggles stopped, and the robot released the body. It wiped its metal hands on a towel and returned the shop, finding its place in the line of humanoid robots, where it waited.

Buried Treasures

When John Helfers invited me to an anthology about knights, I was quick to accept. I have plenty of books about knights on my shelves...including several my friend Andre Norton sent me. Andre also had a tale in this anthology. Oddly, we both wrote about a Templar Knight, and one reviewer on Amazon confused our stories—though they were very different. "Buried Treasures" appeared in Knights Fantastic, *DAW Books, 2002.*

A pink ropy scar ran from just above where his left eye had been and disappeared beneath a thick, salt-and-pepper beard. The eyelid had been sewn shut, the stitches crude and uneven. There were other disfiguring marks—burns on his forehead and all along his sword arm. And on his back and chest, hidden beneath a threadbare white tabard, were dozens of welts from a harshly wielded whip.

Despite these and other injuries, the knight carried himself proudly, standing at military attention with his unusually short hair carefully combed, his broad shoulders squared, and his angular face a stoic mask hiding the pain he obviously felt. His stiff posture was threatened only for a moment, as the ship he road in the belly of rose with a great swell and then abruptly settled back down.

Leaning on a spear for support, head held high, he made his way across the cabin and to a small table, slowly easing himself onto a stool that had been bolted to the floor. The lantern that hung from the ceiling directly above him highlighted the deep lines on his face and hands, revealing him to be an old man.

"Thirsty, knight?"

"Yes," he replied, gently laying the spear on the floor, then digging into a pouch at his side, withdrawing a battered goblet and placing it on the table in front of him. He smiled slightly when his host filled it with sweet mulled cider, and he was quick to take a deep pull.

"Delicious. Thank you, Captain Rogan," the knight said, the words hoarse, a whisper folded around the edges. When Rogan pushed a wedge of sharp cheese toward him, he quickly accepted it and added, "Thank you for your kindness and generosity."

"You are most welcome, knight. But I am not a kind man, and I'm generous only because you are paying me."

"I thank you anyway."

Captain Rogan was easily half the knight's age, a wiry man with curly black hair framing an unblemished boyish face. Flashing blue eyes took in the knight's tired gray ones, holding them as surely as any vise and measuring the man—and finding one who had been beaten to the point of death physically, but not spiritually, and one who had somehow managed to cling to a sense of duty and chivalry. Rogan took the stool opposite the knight, eyes still locked, still measuring.

"And speaking of payment..." Rogan prompted. "You promised me gold."

Three bites and the cheese was gone. "Payment if you could get my cargo and me safely away, Captain."

"We are well away."

The knight skeptically raised an eyebrow.

"Nearly an hour out and still no sign of pursuit. I've just come from the fo'castle. And my mate in the nest gave the all clear. So I tell you again, knight, there is no sign of pursuit."

"Yet," the knight said. He wrapped his fingers tightly around the goblet and took another swallow. "No sign of pursuit—yet."

Rogan drummed his fingers on the tabletop. "You are safe, knight." There was more than a hint of indignation in the younger man's voice. "Aye, my ship is an old one, but she's seaworthy and fast and..."

"Someone may have seen me get onto your ship, Captain Rogan. And for enough coin they'd be quick to tell Philip's men—who would be just as quick after us. Still..." The knight reached for another pouch, a small one, which he untied from his belt and tossed on the table. "Perhaps you are right. Perhaps I am finally safe. Here is part of your payment."

Rogan grinned wide as he stirred the pouch's contents with a finger. "You lied, knight. You've not paid me with gold. These are diamonds."

"More than enough to buy you a small fleet of ships, Captain. And far more than enough to pay my fare to the island."

Rogan wagged his head as he stuffed the pouch of gems into a deep pocket. "Aye, knight, well more than enough to take you wherever in this world you want to go."

"The narrow island, as I requested when I came on board. And once we reach my destination, I shall pay you more. In maps the likes of which you've never seen. Worth a fortune to a seaman."

Rogan craned his neck to glance at a large, tattered map tacked to the cabin wall. France and a watery-pale rendition of his home—England—dominated it. There were three smaller maps hanging near it, these given to him by the knight and displaying lands and islands he'd never seen, all precisely marked with navigation routes. Rogan gestured at one of them. "Knight, what could you possibly want with that place? So far from France and England? A place unknown, it is. Perhaps not real."

The knight didn't answer, dropping his gaze to the surface of the cider and catching a glimpse of his battered reflection. He frowned at the sight.

"And if it exists, there might be nothing at all there, knight. No people." Rogan closed his eyes, leaned back, and listened to the rhythmic creaking of the timbers and faintly above that the snapping of the sails. "Certainly no Frenchmen. No English. A place unknown." He heard a sailor walk across the deck above, followed by another and another. He heard the bark of his first mate, instructing someone to trim the sail. In the distance was the shrill cry of a seabird. He felt the ship turn gently, heading farther out per his orders. "But that narrow island it is," he said finally. "For God and for these diamonds. And for the promise of these maps you claim you carry and will give me, I'll take you there." Much softer, he added. "If there exists."

The knight raised his head, again meeting Rogan's vise-like eyes. "How long?"

"To get there?" Rogan squinted, studying the maps a while. "The wind is against us. And the distance is considerable. A few months, I'd wager. We'll stop somewhere for a hold full of supplies before we head out across the ocean sea. And I'll have to come up with a tale for my men about where we're going and why—or they'll get restless. Good that they are all English and are loyal to me, and that most have a sense of adventure about them." Rogan paused. "But I'm curious, knight. Just what is your cargo? What is it you possess that would cause you to run to an island so very, very far from home?"

The knight shook his head and turned to study the maps.

"For that matter, knight, what would cause the Pope to order all the Templars hunted down and prompt King Philip to torture the lot of you?" Rogan's eyes drifted from the maps to three large satchels that rested in the corner of his stateroom. The Knight had brought them. Atop one satchel was folded a black and white silk flag, what Rogan recognized as the Templar's battle banner.

The knight's face took on a hardness that held a warning. "you've been paid well, Captain. That is my order's treasure."

"Aye, sir knight. I am an opportunist, and a merchantman, and occasionally I raid an enemy ship. But I am not an outright thief. I am a God-fearing man, a Christian, so you've no worry that I'll take your..."

"Holy relics," the knight finished, tipping his head back to gesture at the satchels. "I've brought onto your ship the greatest of all the Templar treasures."

Rogan's eyes gleamed and his eyebrows rose in question.

The knight let out a deep sigh, the sound of sand blown by a gust of hot wind. "Silver chalices from long-abandoned churches, golden crosses studded with emeralds and rubies, strings of rare black pearls, bejeweled brooches and rings once owned by a French queen. There is a singular topaz, the size of my fist. And more, much more. If you've a need, you may look at them."

Rogan shook his head. "I am a merchantman. I am a Christian," he repeated firmly. "I said I'd take no interest in your treasures. But I truly don't need to be tempted." He pointed to the knight's tabard, eyes lingering on the eight-pointed red cross, the symbol of the Templar Knights. The stitches around one edge of it had become loose and so it flapped down. "But I am also a curious man. All that wealth, knight, and you wear a rag."

The knight stiffened, the motion causing him pain and making him flinch. "I wear only the garb of my order."

"And with silver chalices in your satchels, you drink from an old wooden one."

"The silver chalices belong to my order. They are not for my personal use."

"And you carry an old spear for a weapon."

"Philip's men took my sword, a beautiful longblade given to me by Grand Master de Molay himself. Fortunate I was able to acquire a weapon at all when I fled."

"And your armor? I've never seen a Templar knight without armor."

"They took that, too. They took everything I owned."

"Why? Why all of it?" Despite the question, Rogan didn't give the knight a chance to answer. "It was the treasure, wasn't it? You Templars hoarding gold, amassing a fortune to rival any king's. That's why they brought you down. You were too wealthy. They couldn't stomach someone having greater riches than themselves."

"That's not entirely the reason. We had loaned Philip money. And we knew it wouldn't be repaid. We saved his life when the mobs of Paris struck." The knight let out a clipped laugh. "He owed us. But it was power, more than wealth, I believe, that caused our persecution. And his debt to us did nothing to soften his attitude. King Philip feared my Knighthood's increasing influence."

"Feared the power of a band of warrior-monks?"

"And hated the rejection. He asked, once, to join the Order."

"And the Order refused."

The knight ran his fingers along the edge of the goblet, staring at the cider but seeing something far beyond it and the confines of Captain Rogan's cabin.

"The Poor Knights of the Temple of Solomon," Rogan continued. "You should have stayed poor, should have stayed away from kings and governments, relegated yourselves to only protecting Christian travelers to the Holy Land. That's what you did in the beginning, didn't you? Before you gained vast holdings of land all across the face of France and the rest of Europe. Before you accumulated so much wealth during the time of the Crusades and collected far more than what...nine thousand...

manses and castles. You should have stayed poor. You would have stayed safe that way, wouldn't've you?"

A shrug.

"So why all of it? Why were you such a threat to their authority? Were you too popular with the people? Why exactly did the king go after you?"

Another shrug, then a sigh. "Grand Master de Molay said Philip went to Rome and managed to convince Pope Clement that we were not defenders of God's faith, but were—in our rituals and secret meetings—working to destroy it. King Philip must have been convincing, for the Pope ordered him to arrest all of the Templar Knights in France."

"Ah, the start of Philip's holy Inquisition," Rogan supplied. "On Friday the thirteenth. But the king didn't get quite all of you."

"Though he tried. We had warning and were ahead of Philip," the knight continued. "When Philip's men arrived in force at the Templar castles, he found most of them abandoned. A week earlier our brethren had managed to get a few large wagons out of the country."

Rogan slammed his fist on the table. "Ha! And so that's why the rest of you went to Philip like sheep to the slaughter! Your surrender distracted Philip from the wagons spotted leaving the Paris Commanderie. So consumed with his Templar prisoners, he didn't pursue the wagons. Ah, but they must have been filed with things of incredible value for your fellow knights to face torture and death."

"They were."

"Rumors are you knights possessed religious artifacts. The Shroud of Turin."

"The shroud is safely away, well beyond Philip's grasp."

The admonition startled Rogan. "Word is you possessed much more."

No answer.

"And these wagons? Where did they go?"

"To the port. The treasure was divided and taken out on ships."

"Explaining why your naval force in La Rochelle set sail."

The knight gave a nod. "They sailed away with the wealth we had accumulated through the decades, all tucked safely in the holds. Holy relics Philip wanted more for their monetary value than their divine significance. But only two dozen of my brethren escaped on those ships."

"With all of the rest of you tried and found guilty by Philip and Rome."

"Guilty of sins against God," the knight finished with a sad shake of his head. He drained the remainder of the cider and nudged the goblet forward, silently requesting more. "I watched many of my brethren tortured by Philip's decree, and watched too many of them die."

"You nearly died as well from the looks of you," Rogan said. "I'm surprised you managed to escape from Philip's dungeon."

The knight smiled again when Rogan poured more cider. "I am surprised too," he admitted. "But the hand of God intervened. A devoutly Christian jailer helped me escape. And so I was able to return home, recover these relics I'd carefully hidden and that I hadn't been able to get to the wagons before my arrest."

"And you were able to make your way to the docks before Philip and his men noticed your absence."

Another nod.

"Where by chance you found my ship ready to cast off."

"Yes."

"Perhaps the hand of God led you to me." Rogan again looked at the satchels. "And now you want to go to an island across the ocean sea, an island off the coast of a land I didn't know existed. That perhaps might not exist."

"To the narrow island in the north to bury the treasure," the knight said.

Rogan shook his head and made a *tsk-tsking* sound. "A shame. All that wealth to be hidden a world away like a forgotten, nameless corpse. All that wealth you accumulated in the name of God. But God doesn't need it."

"And Philip doesn't deserve it." The knight leaned on the spear and rose from the stool. He drained the last of the cider and replaced the goblet in his pouch, then smoothed at a wrinkle in his tabard. "I wish to go on deck, Captain Rogan."

Rogan stood and gestured to the door, taking one last look at the satchels before climbing the stairs behind the knight.

Above, the wind struck them, brisk and strong and biting with the scent of salt. The knight turned his face into it and relished the fresh air, wanting it to chase the last of the dungeon's staleness from his lungs. There were seabirds in the distance, circling something, white slashes against a dark blue late October sky. He could hear them, oh-so-faintly, and imagined that they must be causing a ruckus that would be annoying much closer. They dove and climbed, and he found himself mesmerized, roused only when he heard a shout from the crow's nest.

"Ship, Cap'n!"

Narrowing his eye to a thin slit, the knight saw just what the birds were circling. A sail as white as the birds came into focus. The ship had been turned so the mast and sail were needle-thin, almost invisible.

"She's got speed!" the mate continued.

There were murmurs on deck—speculations that the ship was nothing, another merchantman heading out on the trade route. But as the minutes passed and the sail grew larger, there were also speculations that it was a military vessel, one pursuing the Templar who had come aboard in such a hurry, fleeing King Philip's men. Speculations that the Templar had brought danger on his heels.

From over his shoulder the knight heard the first mate, the whispers barely carrying over the shush of the waves against the hull and the flap of the sails. "Cap'n, the Templar's sicced bad luck on us. That ship's on an arrow course." After several more minutes had passed, he added "She flies Philip's colors. We've no business stirring trouble with France."

"Tack into the wind," Captain Rogan replied. "Bring her to starboard and we'll outrun our shadow. We've a fast ship."

But it wasn't fast enough. And in less than two hours Philip's ship had closed to the point Rogan could clearly see the men on the deck. Philip's ship was larger, though the crew looked scant compared to its size, assembled in a hurry, he suspected.

"They'll ram us, Cap'n!" this from the first mate. "Give 'em the Templar and we might get out of this. Can't afford to make an enemy of the French."

Rogan defiantly shook his head. He looked to the knight, who was standing at the rail, shoulders square and still leaning on the spear for support, eyes trained on the French ship. "they'll not ram us," Rogan said. They'll not risk our sinking, sending the Templar's holy treasure to the bottom, he thought. "I swear to you they'll not ram us. And I swear we'll not surrender the knight."

The first mate cursed and relayed a string of orders to the men, one last attempt to outrun the other ship. Several minutes later and he was ordering the men to gather crossbows and swords. Indeed, it looked like the French ship wouldn't ram them. But it was turning to pull alongside, and Philip's men were readying grapples and crossbows.

"One knight ain't worth it, Cap'n!" the first mate cried, as he snapped up a crossbow and took aim. "Ain't worth us dyin' for!" Near him a man fell to a French bolt.

"Aye," Rogan admitted too softly for the first mate to hear. "The knight's not worth dying for. But his treasure is. And it's ours if he dies defending it." He clenched his teeth as the sound of wood scraping against wood cut through the air. The thunk of the grapples digging into his ship's deck came next, the repeated "thwuck" of crossbows being fired as Philip's men began to come aboard. Rogan tugged his sword free from his belt, set his feet, and made ready.

The Frenchmen were practiced at boarding, one rank continuing to use their crossbows to help cover the men climbing across to the English ship and to keep Rogan's men from crossing onto theirs.

A half-dozen of Rogan's men were dead to the quarrels before the French had secured the two ships together. Another half-dozen were down to sword blows. Rogan's first mate had waded into the thick of the fight, cursing the

Templar as he went, howling that the French were welcome to take the crippled old knight.

And the knight? Rogan caught sight of him just as a Frenchman darted in and slashed, the blade dancing off his own. The knight was surrounded by Philip's men, who were alternately slashing at him and parrying the thrusts of his spear. Though the Templar was outnumbered, he was not outskilled. He drove the spear forward, skewering one man. At the same time, he brought his leg up and around, sending another man to the deck.

The Templar shoved the speared man forward, pitching him over the side of the ship. Without pause, he brought the spear around, swinging it to keep Philip's men at bay, using it alternately as a staff, thwacking opponents behind him with the butt of it, while jabbing at those in front. Within the span of a few heartbeats, eight men lay dead at his feet, and another three had been knocked over the side. Philip's men were beginning to give him a wider berth, one waving his hand and calling for the crossbowmen to target the Templar. They did, though each bolt miraculously missed, some striking Frenchmen, most biting into the deck.

Rogan watched all of this as he continued to struggle with two foes now. "God-touched," he breathed, as he spied the knight slay another one and then another, bat away crossbow bolts, and send swords flying from the Frenchmen's hands. "Twice my age and twice the warrior." Rogan had downed only one man in the time the old Templar had slain a dozen.

"The Templar!" Someone from Philip's ship hollered. "Everyone at him!"

Everyone, to Rogan's eyes, appeared to be two dozen men, the rest of those on the deck of the French ship. They dropped their crossbows and began to clamber over. Rogan's sword arm worked faster, parrying one blow, then slicing in to cut through the man in front of him.

"Two down," Rogan sneered. "Too many to go." He continued to fight, three men in front of him now. He could no longer keep his eyes on the knight, and he had only a brief moment to glance about at the rest of men to see how they were faring.

The deck was red with blood and littered with bodies, an equal number of French and English. The first mate was among Rogan's casualties, going down still cursing the Templar. Rogan shouted his own curses, all these directed at the French and meant to bolster his men's spirits.

"Surrender!" Someone hollered, by the accent one of Philip's men.

"Should we?" Came an English voice behind Rogan.

Rogan shook his head, not knowing if the mate saw him. The French would slaughter them if they surrendered, no witnesses to their taking of the Templar's treasure. Philip would brook no wagging tongues.

"Die!" Rogan shouted to the largest of his opponents. "Die!" His blade flashed in the afternoon sun, an arc of scarlet following it. His arm throbbed from the constant swinging, and his chest ached from the exertion. The largest Frenchman indeed fell, but there were two more to take his place, and Rogan knew it would be himself that would be dying soon.

"Never should have brought you on my ship, Templar," he said, as he drove his blade down, then dropped beneath the swing of an especially adept Frenchman. "Never should have been tempted by your treasure. Never should have..." His mutterings were interrupted by a cheer—his men hollering.

Rogan pushed forward, knocking one of his opponents back and buying him a moment to get his bearings. "Templar..."

The old knight had a dozen dead around him, had waded over the bodies and was slaying man after man with that spear, the weapon giving him a reach that was turning the tide. The French couldn't get close enough to him—he was running them through as they darted forward. One after another. The cheering grew, and Rogan found himself whooping, too.

"You surrender!" One of Rogan's mates called to the French. "You give!"

But the French continued to fight, and the old knight continued to drop one after the next, moving from one English sailor to the next, aiding Rogan's men and dropping their foes. Within moments he was at Rogan's side, driving the captain's opponents back, slipping in the blood and staggering with the sway of the ship, but never falling and never faltering.

"Templar," Rogan managed as he caught his breath. "My thanks."

The knight didn't reply, he merely continued to worry at Philip's men. Rogan's sailors picked up the infectious energy and surged forward, driving the French back, the survivors scrambling onto the deck of the larger ship and working to separate the vessels.

"Let them go!" the Templar hollered, waving for the men to regroup around him.

"We can take them, Cap'n!" the bossun cried. "We can scuttle their ship."

"No more dying," the Templar said.

"But if they make it back to port," Rogan posed, "Philip will know for sure you've escaped. He'll know you've treasure for certain."

The Templar smiled.

* * *

In the days that followed three more French ships came after them, each larger than the first and each repelled when the Templar took command of Rogan's men. There were no fatalities on the English side.

"A miracle," the bossun pronounced.

"Perhaps," Rogan said. The captain banished all thoughts of taking the Templar's treasure. The diamonds are enough, he told himself, though he continued to eye the satchels that rested in his stateroom. The diamonds and the promise of the maps.

There were no more attacks when they were well out on the ocean sea, away from any hint of land and traveling on waters Rogan was certain no Englishman had sailed. He studied the maps each day, and he headed the ship north, where the wind blew cold and sent his men deep into the folds of their coats and blankets.

The old knight refused the comfort of additional clothing, insisting he would wear only the "garb of my order."

And Rogan was not surprised when the knight paid the price for his stubbornness.

"Pneumonia," Rogan told him one evening.

The knight was stretched out on the floor of the captain's cabin, refusing to take Rogan's bunk—despite the Englishman making offers repeatedly.

"You've got pneumonia, my friend." Rogan paused, touching the knight's fiery forehead. Friend. Indeed they'd become friends in the three months since they'd sailed from the French port. They'd spent their evenings discussing religion, sometimes praying together, spent their mornings on deck—as the knight wanted to familiarize himself with the operations of the ship.

"Pneumonia," the knight acknowledged. "A bad thing for an old man like myself."

"We shouldn't keep sailing north," Rogan said. "Too cold. And the cold's not good for you." Not good for any of us, he added to himself. He hadn't been warm for weeks.

"To the narrow island," the knight insisted. "The one on the northern map. I paid you well enough."

"Aye," Rogan said with a nod. Aye, you stubborn old man, I'll take you to the island.

* * *

It was in the heart of February that they arrived, at an island no more than a mile long and a half-mile across, all covered with oak trees and blanketed with snow. The Templar had managed to hang on until they neared the shore. He was on deck, still refusing to wear anything over his tabard. It wasn't that he didn't like coats, he had explained earlier to Rogan. But there were no Templar coats aboard. And he'd vowed to wear nothing that was not of his order.

"The treasure is to be buried here," the knight said, leaning heavily on the spear and the railing for support. He pointed to the southern end of the island.

"There will do, beneath that one very large oak, I think." The Templar turned to Rogan, a restful expression on his lined face. "Will you see to it? Bury it deep, where Philip or no man can reach it. Bury it as I've instructed?"

Rogan nodded.

"And see to my burial as well? On the opposite side of the island, somewhere in that stand of trees. I would fancy that."

Another nod.

"Bury the spear with me, Captain. And the goblet."

"Aye, my friend. I'll bury your treasures."

The knight died less than an hour later.

It was a simple ceremony, but one that had considerable work behind it. The ground was frozen, and it took days to bury the knight deep in it, spear at his side, goblet clutched to his chest.

The English sailors waited another month offshore, subsisting on fish that were abundant in the area. Then the air started to warm, and with it the ground. They could dig much deeper now, on the southern part of the island. They buried the satchels filled with silver chalices and bejeweled brooches, golden crosses and a topaz the size of a large man's fist. They retrieved the maps the knight had promised them, along with one strand of black pearls—wanting something of the Templar horde. They took nothing else.

Then they stocked up on fish and sailed east, certain the Templar's maps would return them to England.

* * *

"Cap'n?" It was the bossun. He edged into Rogan's cabin and found the captain studying one of the wondrous maps.

"D'ya think anyone'll ever find the Templar treasure?"

Rogan looked up, a crooked smile on his face. "Perhaps," he said. "And perhaps the knight intends someone to. Some day. If they find the things that sparkle, they'll stop looking for the things that matter."

"All them gems," the bossun mused. "They'd matter a lot to me."

"Not the real treasure," Rogan said.

The bossun cocked his head.

"That, we buried with our friend. In an unmarked grave."

"Couldn't mark it. Didn't know his name," the bossun admitted.

"I never asked him it, and he never volunteered it," Rogan said. "All that wealth to be hidden a world away with a forgotten, nameless corpse."

"Sir?"

"Never mind." Rogan dismissed the man with a wave of his hand. When he was gone, the captain breathed deep and leaned back in his chair. "All that wealth. The Grail."

One day he'd gotten a good look at the battered wooden goblet the knight kept close to him, at the bloodstain at its bottom, realizing its significance. The spear he wielded against the French. The spear of Longinus that pierced Christ's side. The Holy Lance. He'd gotten a good look at that old spear, too, and by the bloodstains and by the aura he felt, and by the way the knight never let go of it, Rogan had realized just what it was. Holy relics the Templar hid in plain sight and demanded be buried with him. "Buried. With a forgotten, nameless corpse," Rogan sighed. "The real buried treasure."

Notes about the Templars: Some scholars are certain the Knights Templar were the guardians of religious relics such as the Shroud of Turin, the Holy Grail, and the spear of Longinus. Too, some believe that the Templars buried their greatest treasures on Oak Island, a small island off the coast of Nova Scotia. Treasure hunters continue to this day to search for it on that island, which is roughly a half-mile wide by a mile long.

King Philip's hostility toward the Templars reached fever pitch when he was refused admission to the Order. He mounted false charges against the knights, and on Friday, October 13, 1307, he directed his armies to attack the Templar headquarters. Hundreds of Templar knights were arrested and tortured. Historians believe Philip's true target was the Templar treasure, which had been carted away on wagons to the port of La Rochelle. The treasure was placed aboard the Templar ships, and the fleet disappeared.

Among the Templar's treasures were said to be exceptional maps and navigational charts.

Suede this Time

Once again I had an opportunity to write a cat story—the instructions being that said cat needed to come from a fairy tale. Puss 'N Boots leapt into my head. What more famous cat could there be? This was before Shrek 2 *came along and used the character. I'd like to think my take on the kitty was more interesting. "Suede this Time" appeared in* Magical Tails, *DAW Books, 2005.*

Prince wasn't charming.

Not as far as I was concerned.

He stood in the middle of the castle drawbridge, his wheat-blond hair a mass of tangles, his jowls sagging, and his vacuous black eyes fixed unblinkingly on me. As I returned his stare, a thick strand of drool spilled over his lower lip and stretched down to pool between his front paws. A threatening growl rumbled up from his barrel-shaped chest, and he tipped his snout to display his sharp teeth.

No, Prince wasn't charming at all.

Though I was several yards away, on the far bank of the moat, I could smell him. The early morning breeze pummeled me with the redolence of whatever long-dead thing he'd found to roll in. I could well imagine he had fleas—a burgeoning colony of them—as when he wasn't watching me, he was usually scratching at himself with his hind legs or vigorously rubbing his rump against a post. He probably had mange, too.

It was my master who named the wretch "Prince," just three weeks past—the day he spied the grubby mongrel looking so apparently hungry and forlorn and whimpering so damn theatrically.

How my master could find this creature even remotely "adorable and oh-so-cute" was a mystery.

How he could take this insidious cur into our magnificent castle...

How he could let this filthy animal sleep at the foot of his bed...

How he could feed this...thing...choice bits from the table...

And how he could fashion a collar of the finest leather and the most exquisite sapphires for the beast's thick neck (the jewels being the only princely aspect of the fiend)...

...was well and truly beyond the scope of my considerable intelligence to grasp.

The worst of it—Prince wasn't even a dog.

Oh, he certainly looked like a dog, even to my keenly perceptive eyes, a wavy-coated retriever of some sort or an overgrown water spaniel with a fanciful plumy tail. He could bark with the best of them, shake "hands," roll over, even play "fetch" when the mood struck him. And he was quite practiced at passing wind under the dining room table when guests were present, and hiking his leg against the castle's walls when none of the guards were watching.

But to call him a dog would be an insult to lowly canines everywhere.

"Prince" was an ogre.

I accidentally discovered his dark secret late last night. And mere minutes later—before I could reveal him for the monster he is—he chased me out of the castle just as the drawbridge was raising, forcing me to spend the night beyond the moat on this chill, damp ground. When the bridge was lowered just an hour ago to greet the dawn, he immediately sidled out, no doubt to keep me from getting back in and warning my master about him. You see, I can speak the human tongue when I've a wont to. And the moment I tell my master the truth about his dear "Prince," he will order the ogre captured and slain.

I would attend to the killing myself. Unfortunately, "Prince" is a tad smarter than his departed brother was. I dealt with that particular ogre a few years ago.

I suppose I should explain.

I am Minew Milakye, a chartreux of some distinction. For those of you regrettably unknowledgeable about the finer points of cats, the chartreux is an ancient and esteemed breed that originated in France and was raised into numbers by a sect of Carthusian monks. All of my kind are known for our splendid and wooly slate-blue coats, bright orange eyes, even temperaments, and sharp wits. My wit is sharper than most.

It was my dear mother who named me Minew.

It was my master who drolly and fondly dubbed me Puss, as in "Puss 'N Boots." My good friend Charles Perrault reasonably accurately penned the story of how I came into my master's company—a far better telling, I might say, than he rendered of the sagas of that cinder girl and the child who looked quite silly in the vermilion ridinghood.

The curtailed version of my story: I "belonged" to a miller who died. The miller's will made provisions for his eldest son to receive the mill, his middle son to acquire the donkey, and his youngest son to be given me.

The youngest son struck off, saddened by his lot and unappreciative of my company until I revealed that I could speak his simple language. I took pity on him, and so I promised that I would make him rich—if he would buy me a fine cloak, a velvet hat, a small bag, and a pair of shiny black leather boots for my back paws (on occasion I enjoy walking on two legs). He was reasonably quick to attend to my requests, and I was quick about my schemes.

Decked out quite nicely, I presented the nearest king with various sundries, claiming them all to be gifts from my master the handsome and noble Marquis de Carabas. (What a grandiose title I created for the lad!) When the King's curiosity was suitably piqued, and when he began toying with the notion of arranging a marriage between his beautiful daughter and the mysterious Marquis de Carabas, I invited the royal family to visit my master in his castle.

Now my master didn't have a castle, but I'd heard tell of an ogre who owned a magnificent one. All I had to do was take the castle away from the brute. So I paid a visit to the ogre, a quite magical if dim-witted creature, and I told him that I'd heard he had great arcane powers.

"Yep, I sure do," the ogre replied. "I can change into things...a lion...an elephant...ya know, things."

"That's wonderful!" I played along. "But you're so tall! I bet you can't turn into something tiny." I furrowed my brow. "Say...a blackbird. Or even more difficult...a mouse. That would be impossible even for one of your magical talent, wouldn't it?"

"Nope. Not impossible," he shot back. "I can do a mouse. Watch this."

On the spot the fool cast a spell and transformed himself into a little gray one, which I snapped up, chomped the head off, and swallowed.

Before the hapless beast had a chance to give me indigestion, the "marquis" had a magnificent castle to show off to the king and the princess. And, soon after, the "marquis" had a beautiful royal wife and was able to attract a staff of servants and two dozen well armed and armored guards.

It looked like the lot of us would live happily ever after.

That is until three weeks past when my master brought "Prince" into the castle, and until late last night when I accidentally caught "Prince" prowling through the kitchen for a late-night snack. "Prince" was walking on two olive-tinged legs the size of tree-trunks and had shed all of his doggy-hair in favor of his natural warty ogre hide. No wonder the dog had smelled odd, not like other canines I'd been downwind of. Unfortunately, "Prince" spotted me, and because of that I'm standing here on this chill, damp ground rather than lounging on a pillow high in the castle waiting for breakfast to be served.

How was I to know the ogre whose head I bit off had a brother?

How was I to anticipate that said brother would use magic to show up at the castle looking like some overgrown, sad-eyed water spaniel? And that he would be standing guard on the drawbridge at this very moment, turning the pool of drool at his feet into a veritable lake?

How was I to know?

Quick-witted though I am, do not expect me to be omniscient. So of course I couldn't have known about "Prince." Still, I felt some responsibility to warn the marquis about the detestable creature. I had put the Marquis de Carabas in the castle after all.

I glided closer to the drawbridge, trying to gauge whether I might be able to race past "Prince" and into the castle proper before he could catch me. The beast's eyes lost their empty look and glimmered darkly.

"Ya ain't comin' in, cat," he whispered just loud enough for me to hear. His voice sounded like bits of gravel jostling around inside a bucket. "I heard whatcha did to my brother. Word gets 'round ya know. So ya ain't never comin' back in. This's my castle now." He punctuated the sentiment with a loud dog-belch that added to the evil smells assaulting me.

"Your castle?"

"Yeah. I inherited it. From my brother who you killed."

"Inherited. Big word for an ogre."

He growled and scratched at a plank.

"Fine. Your castle," I hissed. "Then I suppose I have no alternative but to leave." I turned tail and sauntered into the bushes. To myself, I added: "But it is not your castle. There is no way you're claiming the place with the marquis, his royal wife, and all those guards traipsing around. Ogres are powerful. But not powerful enough to deal with that many people."

Still...ogres live a very long time. Perhaps the lout was going to remain a dog for the next several decades, waiting until my master grew old and died and the castle was abandoned—provided the princess did not produce an heir to pass the castle along to. Or perhaps the ogre intended to remain a dog forever. Maybe he found the ghastly form an improvement over his natural one. Maybe he liked sleeping at my master's feet. Maybe he liked the princess cooing over him and scratching his ears, maybe he liked hiking his...

Maybe he had something sinister planned.

I needed to get inside and talk to the marquis. I knew the marquis' brother was coming to visit today—the middle son who had inherited the donkey. Perhaps I could sneak in with him, hop into a pack or something. But he might not arrive until the afternoon, and I didn't want to wait that long.

Neither did I want to wait out the ogre-dog, hoping he'd grow bored of standing on the drawbridge and go elsewhere, giving me an easy way in.

No, I couldn't afford to wait. And so I decided to make an arduous sacrifice. I drifted deeper into the foliage and began circling the castle wall, paralleling the moat. I breathed deep and steadied myself for what I had to do. I located a suitable spreading fern, and beneath it I carefully placed my boots, cloak, hat, and bag for safekeeping. Then I continued on my route until I was behind the castle, where "Prince" couldn't see me.

I padded to the moat's edge. The breeze sent faint ripples across the water, making my reflection shimmer and dance and seem somehow mystical on this early morning. Water—the thought of it made my throat instantly dry. A shiver raced down my spine as I urged myself into it. Some say the part of the cat that hesitates is the paws. Especially over the prospect of getting wet. But I know it is essentially the whole of the cat. Every inch of me wanted to stay on this dry, chill ground. Every inch except one very small and persistent part that made me again pity the young man I'd turned into a marquis. And it made me want to warn him.

"No recourse," I said as I somehow found the water lapping over my toes, then against my stomach, as I somehow found myself practically submerged and swimming oh-so-quietly toward the rear of the wall that circled the castle. I felt something brush against my side, and for an instant I wondered if there were foul beasts lairing in this foul water. But nothing grabbed me, no toothed snout appeared, and no carnivorous fish dared to strike at my churning legs. And so, moments later, I found myself on the opposite bank, wet, cold, wet, thoroughly miserable, and thoroughly drenched. I started to rub against the tall grass that grew against the castle wall, then quickly stopped myself when I recalled where "Prince" tended to relieve himself. I most certainly would rather be wet and miserable than...

I glanced up at the crenellated wall. Though I'd lived inside the place for the past few years, I'd never appreciated just how imposing that wall was. Thick and impossibly tall, ogre-sized naturally—likely constructed to keep out whatever huge creatures might threaten ogres (never mind keeping out small clever cats).

"No recourse," I repeated, as I stretched against the wall and began climbing, claws digging into the hardened mud mortar between the blocks of stone. My muscles were screaming in protest before I'd reached the halfway point, and my chest felt like a fire being stoked. The small part of me that had urged me into the moat was delighting in this. For too long I'd been sedentary, enjoying the pampering of the marquis and the princess and the servants. My walks were brief ones, my lounging considerable, and my food heavy on the tasty aspect and light on nutrition. Often someone carried me up and down the stairs.

I should be carried up and down the stairs, I told myself. I should be pampered. "Why ever am I doing this? Why? Why? Why?" I hesitated, clinging fast and working hard to catch my breath. I'm doing this so I can be carried up and down the stairs, I decided. I'm doing this to oust "Prince."

I don't know how long I hung there, waiting for the fire within my chest to die down just a bit. It seemed like an eternity, my paws aching fiercely, but I knew it was only minutes. By the time I resumed my climb, and by the time I'd made it to the top, my fur was still dripping.

The small part of me that had impelled me up the wall rejoiced in the exertion. The rest of me simply rejoiced in the view. It was all so amazing from the top of the wall, the lush greens of the woods and meadows spreading away in all directions, the water of the moat looking like a silver ribbon festooned with beads of sunlight. The breeze carried the scent of wildflowers, the small fragrant ones that hung on at the close of summer, and I could hear the faint twitter-song of swallows. Turning inward, I could see the castle and the service buildings around it—the stable, blacksmith's stall, and the barracks. Workers busied themselves scurrying about while the guards stood like statues—two on either side of the archway that led to the moat, two on either side of the castle door, two more on parapets. The castle itself stood in the midst of it all, made of white granite shot through with glistening veins of black, a turret rising above this wall with a pointed conical roof looking like a spear jutting into the cloudless sky. There was a window high in the turret, and I'd never thought to perch in it before and absorb the view.

I would now, after "Prince" was dealt with and I'd retrieved my clothes and boots. I'd make that windowsill my favorite spot, and from it I would survey this glorious countryside—after I climbed the stairs to reach it, of course, making sure that small part of me was satisfied that I'd gotten some exercise. An ogre did not deserve such a magnificent place, and could not appreciate the beauty of the land. An ogre would not enjoy the view. So the ogre had to go... now.

The castle was trimmed around the windows and balconies in pale blue, the marquis' favorite color. But the trim had been burnt orange and was chipping dreadfully when I'd acquired the place from "Prince's" brother. The ogre hadn't done much to keep the place up. His brother would do no better job. I felt bile rising in my throat as I continued to think of the ogre-dog that was likely still on the drawbridge.

I started down the other side of the wall, using the cover of the castle to hide my presence. It was a little easier climbing down, and easier still to rush across the ground and dart inside the kitchen door that was timely being opened by a cook.

"Puss!" she said, as I shot past. She'd made a motion to pet me, but I hadn't the time for such pleasantries. "Where's your hat and..."

I was well beyond her and her trivial prattle, through the dining room and into the gallery before I came to a stop behind a suit of decorative plate armor. Here I listened for the beat of the place. Every castle has a heart, sometimes it's a strong one—like those great ancient edifices belonging to important kings. Sometimes it's a small and feeble one, like a few places I'd slipped into during my kitten days, pretentious castles built for men who have titles but lack the miens and brains for leadership. This castle, I'd learned shortly after its previous owner's demise, had a dark heart. Its beat was hard to hear, but if you were a chartreux and if you listened for it, you could manage.

Its steady thrum spoke of its long decades on this land, of its deep foundation filled with dungeons and treasure chambers, of the bloodstained floors in its secret rooms. It beat with the brush strokes of paintings stolen from merchant caravans, with the stitches of great tapestries fashioned by human slaves, with the last gasps of the lives lost to the ogre who once held sway here. And it pulsed with the presence of the damnable ogre-dog.

Why couldn't he have stayed on the drawbridge?

I could hear the beast in the room beyond, nails clicking rhythmically over the stone floor, breath coming short and even. He must have come in from the drawbridge shortly after I'd given up that route, and was now patrolling the main room and the winding stairway that lead up to the chambers where the marquis was most likely to be found.

His ogre-heart beat in time with the castle's, not as strong, but darker, I sensed. The marquis would deal with the monster today, I vowed. Then perhaps the beat of the castle's dark heart would be silenced and a new heart would replace it—one that beat in time with mine.

I slipped back into the kitchen and made my way up the narrow stairs that lead to the cook's room. Faintly, from below, I heard the clacking of the ogre-dog's nails. Could he sense me as I sensed him? Could he smell my pleasant musky odor as I was forced to stomach the stench of him?

I moved faster, darting beneath the cook's bed while I listened more carefully. The clacking was coming up the stairs.

Faster still and I was out of the meager room and into the hall beyond, rushing toward a wider staircase that would lead to the sitting room the young marquis and his princess favored. My sides were aching from the exertion of the swim across the moat, from climbing the wall, from now climbing these stairs. The small part of me that was oh-so-proud at my efforts would be prouder still when the ogre met his demise.

Faster.

"Puss!" the princess exclaimed as I slipped into the massive sitting room filled with stolen paintings and slave-made tapestries, scented tapers and the soft glow spilling in from high narrow windows. "Puss, you're wet! And you've lost your cloak and boots!"

The clacking was louder, the beast closing.

I glanced about for the marquis-I'd-made. I'd never spoken to the princess, only to my young master. Speaking to her now—and about a horrid ogre—would yield nothing but a shocked look on her pretty face. She'd hear my words but she wouldn't listen to what I had to say.

The clacking and...

Humming! The young marquis was humming in the room beyond, the music room he called it, a polished marble place filled with poorly-strung harps and ill-tuned lyres. I was a blue-gray streak past the princess and into the next room, a chartreux blur heading straight toward my master sitting on a plush velvet chair, a skidding mass of fur as I scrambled to come to a stop.

"Puss!" he exclaimed. "You've been out all night! You're wet!" His tone became playfully scolding. "You've lost your cloak and boots. I'll have to buy you new and..."

"No." It was the only word I could manage at the moment, and it wasn't in reference to his offer of new attire. "No." The word was directed at what was swirling around his feet. There were puppies, eight of them—writhing balls of golden hair and shiny black noses, wagging plumy tails and merry yappings. "No. No. No."

"So you don't want to wear clothes any more?" He reached down and picked up one of the pups, cradled it in his lap and twirled his long fingers around its ears.

They weren't puppies. I could sense it as I could sense the castle's heartbeat. Ogres, all of them.

"They're not puppies," I started. The words were coming fast now. "I never told you the whole story of how I got this castle for you. There was an ogre..."

"Yes, yes," he said. "I remember. You somehow managed to slay the vile monster after a fierce battle."

I inwardly groaned. I never told the Marquis de Carabas the truth, that I'd tricked the brute into transforming himself into a mouse. The slay-the-vile-creature-after-a-fierce-battle-story seemed much more glamorous at the time. The marquis didn't know that ogres could magically assume different shapes. Didn't know about the mouse. Didn't know about the true nature of the dog he'd brought into the castle. I'd only told the true story to Charles Perrault and a few stray cats, all good friends.

"Ogres are magical creatures," I began, deciding there wasn't time to explain everything. I was listening for the clacking of Prince's nails, but I couldn't hear it anymore. My heart was pounding too loudly.

"Not so magical as you," he kindly returned.

Much more magical, actually, I thought. Aloud, I said: "They can turn into things."

He cocked his head in polite curiosity and reached down to pick up a second pup.

"Things like dogs and puppies," I continued. "Those aren't real puppies. They're ogres. All eight of them. And Prince is an ogre, too. Last night..."

The marquis laughed then, loud and long, throwing back his head and cackling upward so his voice bounced off the ceiling. When the mirthful cacophony finally subsided, he fixed his eyes on mine. "You're clever, Puss, trying to make me think these delightful creatures are ogres. You probably want me to toss them out of the castle."

"That wouldn't be good enough," I said. "They'd come back. How'd they get here to begin with?"

"The pups? They came in yesterday late in a farmer's cart. He was as surprised as the cooks that they were hiding behind the bushels of potatoes. Aren't they...charming?"

"They're ogres," I repeated. "You'll need to drown them. Or behead them. Skewer them with a long spear and..."

He laughed again, but curtly this time. "I know cats don't care for dogs, Puss, but you're being a little ridiculous." One of the pups stretched up and licked his chin. Another, between his legs and where he couldn't see, raised its lip in a silent snarl directed at me.

I snorted. "Ridiculous? I'm being realistic. They're ogres, the pups and Prince—warty green-skinned smelly monsters that will find a way to..."

He drew his eyebrows together and studied me.

"That will find a way to..." I so hated to talk in front of the ogres, but what alternative did I have? "...to get rid of the guards and deal with the servants, chase you out of this wonderful castle. Kill you maybe. Probably. Ogres kill people." The heart of the castle beat with the last gasps of dozens of humans the previous ogre-owner had slain. Perhaps the heart was too dark to change.

"They're puppies, Puss, charming, adorable puppies." He offered me a slight smile. "And they're staying. The princess and I discussed it, and we've agreed to keep them all."

"You can't, you..."

"And you'll have to accept them."

I shook my head, droplets of moat water flying away from me. "I can't. I won't. They're ogres and..."

"Then you'll have to leave."

What? I stared at him incredulously. What did he say?

"If you can't accept the pups and Prince, you'll just have to find a home elsewhere."

I heard the clacking again, glanced over my shoulder and saw "Prince" standing in the doorway behind me. He was looking at the marquis, tail wagging a greeting.

"There's my good boy," the marquis gushed. "Prince" trotted over and settled in next to his chair.

I needed time. I had to think. There must be a way to get the marquis alone. Perhaps I could again catch "Prince" prowling in the pantry late at night, get my master to see the monster for its true self. But there were nine ogres now, a formidable force. Nine ogres would be more than enough to handle the servants. But nine ogres might not be enough to tackle the marquis' armed and armored guards. There was still time to deal with this threat, especially if the ogres were attacked while in pup form. Kill them as I had swallowed the mouse. Still time and...

"Dear!" The princesses' lilting voice carried in from the sitting room. "One of the maids says she's found more puppies—a half dozen. Isn't that wonderful!"

"No." I had to think. I whirled and bolted from the room, a blur of blue-gray that was in an instant beyond the princess and out onto the landing, was racing up steep stone steps that added to the ache in my sides.

"Puss?" the princess called.

"Leave him be." This from the marquis. Though I was putting distance between myself and the lot of them, my hearing was acute enough to pick up the conversation. "Puss doesn't like the pups. But he'll get used to them. He'll have to."

"He'll have to if he wants to stay here," the Princess finished. "The pups are...charming."

Charming. The word rattled 'round inside my head. Charming. Perhaps that was it! Perhaps the oh-so-magical ogres had cast a charm spell on the marquis and the princess. Perhaps that was why my master wouldn't listen to reason, he couldn't listen to reason, couldn't see the pups for what they really are.

How could I get my master alone? Or at least catch him when none of the ogres were around. Six more of them! Fifteen in all. I skidded to a stop on a higher landing. Fifteen ogres could defeat my master's armed and armored guards. Fifteen ogres would be enough to take back this castle. To wipe out the servants. To kill the marquis and the princess.

I sensed the castle's dark heart beating more strongly, even as my own heart hammered wildly in my chest. It was no longer a matter of dealing with the ogres. It was a matter of getting my master and his wife and as many others as possible out of the castle before the ogres made their move. I turned to retrace my steps, deciding to make another attempt at reaching the marquis-I'd-made, when I saw a ball of golden fur bounding up the stairs toward me. The pup's expression was pure malevolence, and I wasted no time in heading back up the stairs.

How was I to know that the ogre whose head I bit off had a brother?

And that the brother had fourteen ogre-friends?

Before I reached the next landing, even the small part of me that had been delighting in all this exercise was complaining. My lungs burned, my chest heaved, my head pounded, and my legs throbbed. I wanted desperately to stop, to lay down somewhere and rest. But I forced myself on, and at a faster pace still, as the ogre-pup that chased me was far from winded.

The stairs were narrowing now, as we were in the narrowing turret, and they were becoming increasingly steeper. While at first I considered that an advantage, as my agile cat legs could better handle them than awkward pup feet, a look behind sent my head to pounding more. The pup had cast a spell and transformed itself into a dog, one similar to "Prince," though even uglier. Within moments, I suspected it would be on me. It would chomp my head off and devour me. It would reclaim this castle before my body had a chance to give the monster indigestion.

"Faster!" I shouted, and somehow my legs complied. "Move!"

Then I was at the highest landing, through a narrow door, and up on that very high windowsill that provided a glorious view of the countryside. I had no time to absorb the splendor, however, as the ogre-dog burst into the small, round room, snarling and snapping and dribbling saliva on the floor.

Though the sill was oddly high, he could perhaps reach it—barely—if he stretched up on his hind legs. I would go out the window, climb down the stone. In fact, I started to do just that—until I spied three sleek-coated pointers far beneath me. I couldn't smell them, but I was certain they were ogres, too. I spun and looked about the room. There was an iron chandelier hanging from the ceiling, and if I sprang just right I could catch it, pull myself up and get beyond the ogre-dog's...

I bunched my leg muscles and prepared to leap, then I stopped myself when his ugly eyes caught and held mine.

"Ya talk too much, cat," the dog said. Twin strands of drool spilled from his mouth. "Ya shouldn't've went blathering like ya did to the marquis. Shouldn't've exposed our secret, not that he believed ya. Shouldn't've suggested he drown us. Wasn't polite, cat. An' here I surmised that you were a critter with some brains. "

Blathering. Surmised. Big words for an ogre, I thought. Perhaps they weren't all so utterly stupid as the one whose head I...

"Them stray cats we caught a month or so back, they seemed pretty smart—and real tasty. 'Fore we ate 'em, they talked to us 'bout how you killed the ogre what used to live here. Ya shouldn't've told them cats 'bout it."

No, I shouldn't have, I agreed. I risked another glance at the chandelier. It was higher than I'd ever jumped before, but perhaps I could...

"If ya had kept your mouth shut, we wouldn't've known. Grizwald wouldn't've learned ya ate his brother, my second cousin once removed and Ratigan's and Zebedee's best friend. Griz wouldn't've got us all together and had us come here. Should've kept your mouth shut, cat. 'Cause now I'm gonna see if you're tasty, too."

"I guarantee you I'm all gristle," I replied. If I missed the chandelier, I'd fall right in front of him. There had to be another way out...

The dog sat back on his haunches, watching me. "Should've kept your mouth shut," he repeated. "At least the Marquis didn't swallow a word ya said. At least..."

"What are you going to do to him?" Despite my master's unwillingness to believe me, I held a fondness for him.

The dog made an exaggerated gesture that approximated a shrug. "Griz... Prince...likes the marquis well enough. So we probably won't kill him. Probably keep the human tied up in the dungeon. Bring him out and set him to waving at merchant wagons to lure 'em in."

"And everyone else?"

Another shrug. "Once upon a time we ogres was peaceable sorts."

Not any longer, I knew.

"So I 'spose we'll kill 'em. Maybe we'll keep the princess and one or two others around to cook for us. Maybe we won't. Ratigan can cook when he puts his mind to it."

The dog's tongue lolled out, and his eyes took on a hungry gleam. As I contemplated my options—either the chandelier or climbing out of the window, both bad options—I saw him change. The fur melted off him like butter, seeping into the cracks of the stone floor and disappearing. The skin beneath was a pale green, dotted with warts and festering boils. There were muscles, and they were growing as I gaped. The entire dog was growing, and its limbs were changing, becoming manlike and thick and long. Arms extended and front paws turned into massive hands with fingers ending in ugly, cracked nails. The chest became defined and impressive, and the head became hideous. The ogre's face was shaped like an egg, hairless save for a dozen uneven strands that jutted from the top. His eyes were crooked, the right being slightly higher and larger than the left, and the nose was wide and puglike, looking as if it might have been broken a few times. The lips were large and bulbous, licked by a wide black tongue.

"I like gristle," he said, in a sonorous voice that echoed off the walls.

He gave a chuckle then and reached for me, and in that instant I abandoned the chandelier notion and leapt from the windowsill and into the room. In a heartbeat I was through his legs, speeding across the floor and out the door, scrambling over the landing and down the stairs. I was a blue-gray blur heading toward the music room, intent on trying one final time to get the marquis to listen.

"Puss!" the princess exclaimed as I ran past her. She was still ensconced in the sitting room, a half-dozen golden-furred ogre-puppies around her dainty slippered feet. "Dear kitty, have you..."

I barreled into the next room, my clawed feet skittering over the polished floor and taking me to my master.

"Father's cat!" A sneeze. "You still have father's cat."

My master had company, the new voice belonging to the middle brother. The man was sitting several feet away from the marquis, leaning against an enormous harp and sniffling into a handkerchief.

"Yes, Puss is still with me, and..."

"Listen," I blurted, eyes darting from one pup to the next to "Prince," who had taken a discreet position behind the marquis. "You have to listen to me!"

"Father's cat talks?" Another sneeze. And another.

"Yes, brother, and sometimes he..."

"Listen! They're ogres. All of the pups are ogres. And if you and the princess and your brother and the servants and the armed and armored guards don't leave, you all could be dead by nightfall."

The marquis didn't laugh this time, and I for a moment I thought I'd reached him. That notion vanished, however, when his eyes narrowed to thin slits.

"You listen to me, Puss."

The brother sneezed quite loudly this time.

"And you listen good. I like these pups. I like Prince. I like them better than you."

What? His words were daggers, and I heard them well, just as I heard the castle's dark heart beat faster and stronger, just as I smelled the stench of the ogre-pups. I was reeling from all of it.

"I never liked you, Puss. I only tolerated you because my father liked you. Then I tolerated you because you got me this castle and the princess."

The brother sneezed again and again.

"I don't like any cats, Puss. Never did. In fact, I hate cats. They're too aloof. They're too independent. Can't stand the hairballs and the finicky behavior. Dogs, Puss. I like dogs. No. I love dogs. All of these pups and Prince are staying, and..."

"Ahhhhhhhhh-choooooooooooooo!" The brother was caught up in a sneezing fit.

"...and you're leaving, Puss," the marquis continued, raising his voice. "You're leaving right this very instant."

"I'm leaving, too, I'm afraid." The brother stood, handkerchief over his nose. "I can't sit here another moment. I am so allergic to dog fur." His eyes watered as if he'd been to his best friend's funeral. "I can take the cat with me if you'd like. I rather fancy the notion of having a talking cat."

"The pups," I tried one final time, catching the angry gaze of the marquis. "They're ogres. They're going to..." Then I felt myself being lifted and held beneath the middle brother's arm. He stuffed the handkerchief in his pocket, sneezed again, and petted me with his free hand.

"You're damp," he said to me, as he carried me out of the music room and paused in the sitting room to bow to the princess. "However did you get so damp?" he continued, as he started down the stairs. "And you're out of breath. I bet those pups were chasing you."

"Yes, chasing," I said.

"No pups will chase you in my house," he returned. "It's a good house, sturdy and small, nothing like this castle. But you'll like it."

"No dogs," I said.

"No. No dogs. I'm so terribly allergic to them. I've a donkey, though. He doesn't talk, but you'll like him."

"I'm sure I will," I replied, as he carried me out of the castle's front door, strode to the stables, and deposited me on the donkey's saddle.

"Your paws!" he exclaimed, taking note of the rest of my condition. "You've got a few broken claws, and your pads are bleeding."

All the running, I thought, the climbing up and down the wall, the scrabbling up the stairs. I wasn't used to it, and my paws were paying the price.

"Perhaps I should buy you some boots," he continued, as he led the donkey across the drawbridge.

Behind us I could hear the playful yip of the fourteen puppies and the loud bark of "Prince." Fifteen ogres. Eighteen if the three pointers outside the window were ogres, too. A veritable force of monsters! The marquis' guards couldn't possibly...

Then my breath caught, as on the grounds beyond the moat I saw seven more dogs, a motley looking crew—terriers, shepherds, and a one-eared shaggy sheepdog. They smelled just like "Prince." Thankfully they waited until we were over the drawbridge and headed away from the marquis' lands before they scampered across and hurried to join the other ogres. The marquis would be going to the dogs, all right. I fervently hoped at least some of the people within the castle walls could find their way free before...

"Did you hear me, Puss?"

"Minew, my name's Minew Milakye."

"Would you like some boots, sweet Minew?"

My eyes took on a faraway look as I thought of the fine cloak and hat, bag and boots I'd lost beneath the spreading fern.

"Yes," I answered with fervor. "I indeed would fancy a new pair of boots. Suede this time."

Pleading the Fourth

When my husband and I took a trip to the Smithsonian, I lingered at the cases of Civil War weapons and took lots of notes about which soldiers owned what weapons and how they were fired. Then when I sent this story off to a long-running science-fiction magazine, the editor sent me back a terse rejection note saying that I didn't know anything about Civil War weapons, so they would not publish my tale. Oh, how could the Smithsonian have been so wrong? Fortunately, the folks at Peanut Press realized the weapons in my story were indeed correct. "Pleading the Fourth" originally appeared in the Ghosts *anthology by Peanut Press, 2001.*

The air made them choke. Filled with the acrid stench of blood and gunpowder, it seeped into their clothes and settled deep in their lungs, burning their throats and making each breath seem an effort.

It was decorated with a low-hanging fog, a bit of early-morning finery that—despite the warmth of this Kentucky October day—refused to burn off the land and was managing instead to burn their eyes. The fog was manmade, a cloud filled with the smoke of rifles and muskets and from the flying battery, the horse-drawn cannon that whipped along the battle front and fired at the greatest concentration of the enemy.

The air was filled with sounds, too, mostly the "cracks" of weapon fire, the "boom" of the cannon—and the brief and far too numerous screams of the dying. The latter was the worst, giving some of the men pause as they pressed on Stanford, sending the graybacks farther from Louisville. From time to time it was also filled with the calls of Union soldiers searching for their fellows, the shouts of "lice!" to indicate someone had spotted a few lagging Confederates, the clipped orders of their commander—Lieutenant Colonel Robert Minty.

"Move you Sunday soldiers! Kid glove boys!" Minty hollered. He rarely so insulted his men, but he was driven this day. The thought of pushing back the Confederate soldiers of the famous John Hunt Morgan, and of hopefully capturing Morgan, was keen in his mind. "You're acting like fresh fish!" he called to a line advancing near the edge of an orchard. "And I know damn well that you're not raw recruits! So move!"

Morgan threw himself into the thick of it, dismounting from his horse and entrusting the animal to his aide-de-camp. He threaded his way through the men, leading with his sword and intent on reaching the front to watch the action up-close.

This *coup de main* would be successful; he could feel it in his gut. They had thoroughly surprised the bulk of Morgan's men, striking quick—like lightning,

Minty mused. And they continued their assault most vigorously. Despite Morgan's numbers, the Union would have this day!

From reports of spies, Minty knew that Morgan had nearly 2,500 men stationed with him—and two pieces of large artillery. But a good amount of those men had scattered when the Fourth Cavalry came upon them in a wedge and began firing. Minty's cavalry was comprised of fully armed and equipped men recruited from throughout the great state of Michigan and mustered into the service of the United States in late August. In a little more than two months, Minty had them hundreds of miles from home, working like a well-trained team of horses. And they were besting Morgan's forces!

"A glorious day," Minty hushed as he stepped over a body, glancing down to sadly note it was one of his corporals. "Frank," he said softly. He frowned and paused, knelt to close the man's eyes. "Perhaps I'll be joining you soon, old friend. The life of a soldier isn't a long one." Frank had been a barber in Detroit and regularly gave Minty and some of the other officers haircuts on the march.

"A glorious day for the living," Minty corrected when he shook off his melancholy and continued on to where the fighting was more intense.

Three of his men were firing into a rifle pit. It was shallow, one of many the Confederates had dug in the Kentucky countryside. It didn't allow the men inside much protection, and—essentially trapped—they fell quickly to the pepperbox pistols. He nodded to the trio, as much as telling them "good job," then hurried his pace. Minty wanted to catch sight of Morgan.

Things were almost going too fast for Minty. He'd thought the rout would last longer, a fight to savor that would stretch late into the afternoon and produce innumerable campfire tales. There were clearly far more Confederates littering the ground then Union men. Even some of the South's mules and horses had fallen victim to the zealous Michigan men, so well-planned had been their strike. He suspected that within another hour, perhaps two, matters for the most part would be settled here.

Out of the corner of his eye, Minty spotted one of his lieutenants directing some of the soldiers to buck and gag nearly a dozen Confederates that had been captured. Usually only drunkards and shirkers were so humiliatingly held, but the lieutenant obviously didn't want to worry about these men. There was very little chance they could work free of these bonds.

Ahead, Minty watched a Confederate major throw up his arms in surrender. A Union soldier, practically still a boy, raised a pepperbox, meaning to outright kill the man. "No! Take him alive!" Minty sputtered, cursing the sounds of the guns, the screams of the dying. He knew the youth could not hear him over the ruckus. "No! Stop!" he hollered anyway.

He breathed a sigh of relief when he saw a sergeant knock the young soldier's arm, making the shot go wild. A heartbeat later, the major was being ushered toward the other prisoners and the young soldier was getting a sound tongue-lashing from the sergeant.

Minty grinned. "A glorious day indeed."

"Here! Over here Colonel!"

Minty whirled. Kenneth Whit, a giant of a man, one whose arms and legs were too long for his uniform, was beckoning. Minty grumbled. He wanted Morgan, not a distraction. But he knew Whit was a fine scout and a reliable soldier, so it must be important. He turned and made his way toward the man.

"Colonel Minty, sir! Look!" Whit, working to keep a lopsided grin from finding its way across his ashen face, was pointing at the ground a few yards away. "I tried to take him prisoner, Sir. I really did. But he wouldn't have it, spoutin' off about the glory 'o the South an' such."

Minty scowled. Dead at the base of a willow birch was one of Morgan's lieutenant colonels. He was a fine prize, even though he was no longer breathing. But alive, he could have provided important information about Confederate positions and plans.

"Sorry Colonel Minty, sir. He very truly didn't give me much choice."

Minty meant to chastise the man, but finally Whit's complexion registered. The giant's dark blue jacket was slick with blood, evidence the lieutenant colonel had shot him in the side, a wound that would have downed practically any other man. Minty gestured toward a tree. "Sit over there, soldier. Someone'll be over right quick to take a look at you. We'll find the sawbones to dig that bullet." He added a nod, his trademarked unspoken "good job," then he was off again to the front of the battle, flagging a sergeant to get one of the medics.

"Move!" Minty hollered, waving his rifle for added effect as he resumed his press to the front of the fighting. "Move, you parlor soldiers! Movemovemove!"

A wave of blue continued to push across the Kentucky soil, spilling blood as it went, taking more prisoners, capturing mules and supplies. For the briefest of moments, Minty was certain he glimpsed Morgan. Too far away to see any insignia on the gray uniform, he nonetheless spotted the short-cropped beard and the long mustache, waxed so it would stand down and away from his handsome face—a perpetual painted-on frown.

"Morgan," Minty breathed. "I shall have you." He sped toward the spot, weaving through his own men, stepping over the bodies of dead and dying Confederates, tripping when his foot found a gopher hole. His sword went flying, and he hit the ground hard, the air rushing from his lungs. The smoke from the weapons was heaviest right above the earth, and Minty's eyes watered fiercely. He struggled to his feet, nearly losing his footing again, the ground here so slick from blood.

"Morgan!" he spat, as he hurried on his way again, tugging a gun from his holster. It was loaded with grape shot, used for close-quarters fighting and known for its effectiveness—and its gruesome results. But this time Minty could not spot that face and had to settle for shooting a few of Morgan's soldiers who were foolishly standing their ground. They hadn't been much of a threat, armed with buck and ball muskets that were inaccurate.

"Colonel Minty!" It was one of his lieutenants bellowing this time, the one who'd been overseeing the captured Confederates. "We've got them all skedaddling! The day is ours!"

"Yes. Yes, indeed it is," Minty replied, his voice even and lacking the spark that often accompanies victory. He was still scanning the field for Morgan. "Let's continue to push them, lieutenant, shall we?"

"Yes, sir!"

And he continued to search for his foe. He saw him occasionally and fleetingly but never getting close enough, always losing sight of him in the press of gray- and blue-clad bodies. Minty's men drove the Confederates as far as Crab Orchard before he gave up on finding Morgan and considering the objective achieved. They marched back to Mumford, where they were praised and decorated. "A most successful endeavor," Minty had pronounced, silently adding to himself, a disappointing one without the apprehension of John Hunt Morgan.

This was not to be their first clash with Morgan's forces. At the beginning of November, Minty took more than five hundred of his men and marched via Bowling Green, South Union, Springfield, and Mitchellville, all the way to Galatin, Tennessee. From there they crossed the Cumberland River and drove back Morgan's pickets. Then it was on to Lebanon, once more forcing back the Southern's pickets, routing this time a force of seven hundred and fifty. They managed to capture an artillery piece, a fine Napoleon cannon, a 1857 gun howitzer made of bronze and capable of dealing out considerable destruction. And they claimed prisoners, mules, clothing, weapons, and a considerable stash of commissary stores.

"A most successful endeavor," Minty pronounced again and again.

It was early December now. He and three hundred and some of his men were moving out of Nashville. The soldiers were cold, though they did not complain about it to the officers—only amongst themselves, and this usually when they jokingly suggested the Confederates be pushed all the way to New Orleans, where it was sure to be warm and sunny. Many of the men wore heavy shirts and long underwear beneath their uniforms. Even Whit was bundled up. The chill air kept them moving quickly, their arms swinging rhythmically at their sides, their breath feathering in lacy fans away from their faces. But the cold did not seem to bother Colonel Minty. Indeed, he considered Tennessee downright balmy compared to the snow-packed Michigan he called home and thought of often.

They were on a reconnaissance mission this time, heading toward Franklin. They hadn't expected to find Confederate pickets so soon, but they did—eight miles outside of Nashville. Minty, truly seasoned now, barked one order after the next, his men toeing the mark and driving the graybacks to Wilson Creek and Franklin Pikes, then advancing toward where he was certain a significant force of Confederates was encamped. Minty decided to have his men spread out and approach the enemy quietly in the morning—make their observations, and then get back the regiment. But now it was time to rest, save for two scouts he would send out to make sure no Confederates were moving at night.

Minty directed the men into bivouac in a glade ringed by ash and oak trees. It was an idyllic place, drenched in the light of the rising moon and looking so peaceful that the men with their rifles and knives and talk of killing the enemy seemed starkly out of place. They set about hacking branches from pines and building lean-tos, spreading blankets on the ground and settling in. There would be no fires for fear Confederate patrols or partisan rangers might spot them, and conversations would be kept to whispers.

As the night deepened, the men dug into their knapsacks for sheet-iron crackers and dried beef. Whit had some candy he'd been guarding, the expensive kind that he had whispered to Minty was as scarce as hen's teeth. Minty politely refused the rare treat, but his lieutenant, a man named Connor who strained the seams of his uniform, was quick to take Whit's offer. The pair of them were chatting now in hushed tones, sharing war stories while one of the sentries paced alertly just behind them.

Minty was hungry. His stomach growled so loud he wondered if the men could hear it. Still, he wasn't in the mood for food. Too preoccupied. He was thinking, already planning tomorrow's reconnaissance work, hoping that through some miracle he might find a great nest of graybacks, perhaps Morgan—even though he'd heard reports that the Confederate commander had returned to Kentucky. There was always the chance the information was wrong.

He padded from the glade and leaned against a thick ginko, inhaling deep of the chill air—so fresh, it was heady, and scented by a cluster of pine trees that towered above and behind him. Minty mused that he could have truly appreciated this place were it not for the war. The variety of trees, the quiet, the soft chitter of birds from somewhere nearby. From here, through a clump of spindly dogwoods, he could have his privacy and watch the men. He reached into his knapsack, gloved fingers closing about a metal flask. Nokum stiff, he called the stuff, strong liquor that he drank sparingly. It warmed his throat and struck his empty belly, making it rumble even more.

He slid down the trunk, settling his rump comfortably between a pair of knobby roots, his back straight against the tree. Craning his neck to make certain he could still see the sentries and the center of the camp, he took another pull on the flask. There was a mist rising from the ground around the lean-tos, looking like the smoke that always clung foglike to the battlefield. It was birthed by the air, he decided, which was turning colder against the warmer ground, and it didn't carry the acrid scent of gunpowder that he'd become so used to.

He fancied that the mist looked like pale ghosts slowly dancing among his men. The mist hadn't yet spread out to where he was. But then perhaps it had, and he just couldn't see it. The moonlight wasn't so bright here, filtered out by tree branches overhead. Still, there was just enough light so Minty could catch a glimpse of himself in the polished metal of the liquor flask.

He wasn't a handsome man, like he considered John Hunt Morgan. But he thought of himself as better-than-passable and able to draw a few looks from the women back home. He had a high, proud forehead and eyes his mother called kind. His beard was full and bristly and tinged with bits of gray around his jawbone, unlike the smooth and gently curling dark hair that fell to halfway down his ears. He'd look better, he suspected, if Frank were alive to give him a trim.

He'd lost so many friends to this war.

Minty let out a deep sigh. He was exhausted, having pushed himself and his men perhaps harder than he should have. Again, he fought against the notion of digging in his haversack for something to eat. A few hours of sleep was what he so desperately needed, he told himself. Then he'd have something for breakfast. One more swallow of the liquor, then he put the flask away, leaned his head against the tree and closed his eyes.

A heartbeat later they were wide open and staring up—into the heart-shaped face of a beautiful young woman.

He cursed himself for being so tired he hadn't heard her approach, then cursed his sentries for being lax, too. If she'd been a Confederate agent, he'd be dead now. But she hadn't a weapon on her, nor from her gauzy clothes could she have been concealing one. She was wearing what he guessed was a nightgown, with a filmy petal-pink wrap over it. There was a French word for the garment. *Peignoir*? He'd bought his sister something like it—though not so revealing—a few Christmases ago, having found it on sale in a Detroit clothing store.

"Who?" he heard himself asking as he clumsily got to his feet. He knew he should call for the sentries or drag her into camp. Instead he just looked at her. "Who are you?" His words were thick, tainted from the alcohol, and he moved a little sluggishly.

She smiled thinly but didn't answer, so he repeated the question, this time loud enough so he was certain one of the sentries should have heard him.

"Sherrie," she answered. Her voice sweet and velvety.

"Where?" he ventured, knowing instead he should have been a gentleman and asked if she was cold, offered her his jacket. Again he told himself that he should take her into the camp. "We didn't see any houses or..."

She drew a slender finger to her lips. She was pale, and she most certainly must have been cold, yet her skin wasn't dotted with goosebumps as his was. He didn't see her shiver.

"Where did you come from?"

She gestured with her hand toward the clearing, where the fog had grown thicker around the lean-tos. Minty could tell that nearly all the men were sleeping. A sentry passed by the treeline, glancing Minty's way and continuing on. Hadn't the man seen her? He shook his head. Perhaps she was standing so that the dogwoods concealed her.

"Here," she stated finally. "I live here."

"Here?"

She nodded. Her dark brown hair was in loose curls that fluttered around her shoulders. Her hair—or perhaps it was simply all of her—smelled faintly of peach blossoms. "Here," she said again. It finally registered that it was a Southern voice, a soft and preciously brittle one. "You've come upon my home, Robert Minty."

He sputtered in surprise. "You know me? How? Who?"

"Sherrie," she repeated. "Sherrie Eloise Morgan."

"Connor!" Morgan hollered. Through the tendrils of fog he thought he saw the lieutenant stir, and he opened his mouth to holler again. But she thrust her finger against his lips this time. So cold, her finger was like an icicle and momentarily shocked him into silence. And though there was no strength behind her gesture it held him rooted to the spot.

"You're not real," he breathed after a few moments had passed. He blinked furiously. She was a product of too many swallows of nokum stiff on an empty stomach, he decided. Or a comely vision brought on by his exhaustion. He had indeed pushed himself too hard. She wasn't real, he repeated, but there was no sound to the words this time. An angelic hallucination. Perhaps he was dreaming, had never opened his eyes and was still sound asleep propped up against the ginko a few yards beyond the glade. But the scent of peach blossoms was even stronger now, cutting the odor of the pines that towered above and behind him. Did one smell in one's sleep he wondered?

"You've come upon my home, Colonel Robert Minty." This time her words were not so delicate. There was an edge to them, the hint of a threat. Her eyes narrowed. They were dark and sparkling, laced with anger, and he found himself staring into their depths.

You're not real.

"And you've spilt too much blood on Tennessee soil."

What? He mouthed.

"So much Southern blood. It runs deep into the earth."

"I..."

"Have killed so many young men. I hate this war, Colonel Robert Minty!" Her voice was rising, filled with ire. "And I hate you! All of you!"

Minty glanced beyond her. The sentry continued his routine, passing only several yards away, seemingly oblivious to her. The men slumbered. Her tirade had caught the notice of none of them.

"You're not real."

"You steal the lives of babes," she continued. "They've barely left their mothers. Never to have a wife. A life. Their bodies rot beneath the earth. This war!"

"Ma'am," he tried. "We're soldiers. We've no choice but to fight the war." A part of him wondered why he was talking to her, why he didn't take her into the glade.

"And the war has taken my kin. Some buried, others still fighting."

"John Morgan."

"My dear, dear cousin," she returned.

Another glance to the camp, this time accompanied by a wave. The sentry acknowledged Minty's gesture with a smile. He continued his walk. Why didn't he come out here? Surely he had to be curious about the woman. Or had he still not seen her?

"I can't help that there's a war, ma'am."

"I want John to come home."

Minty thought, *And I want nothing more than to capture him.*

Had he said the words aloud? She was scowling, as if she'd heard him. He shook his head. She wasn't real. This wasn't real. He was dreaming.

"Dreaming," he stated.

"You'll not take him," she curtly returned. "You'll leave him alone, Colonel Robert Minty, or you'll bring him back to me."

He laughed then, a deep chuckle meant to chase away his delirium.

"And you'll not mock me."

He gave her a sober look, or imagined that his dream-self was trying to put on a serious face before the beautiful apparition.

"I cannot help the war," he said again.

"Then I must." She put her hands on her hips. Her eyes were wide now, cold and cunning—like a look he'd glimpsed once on John Morgan's face. Was she truly related to the famous Southerner? "I am tired of the blood, Colonel Robert Minty. I am tired of the death and of this war that takes my kin away."

"You're not real."

"And you shall pay, sir." The word sounded like "suh," thickly Southern. "You shall pay for not believing in me and for waging a war against my cousin John Hunt. You shall pay for all the lives you have cut down without a thought. Pay with that which you hold dear, sir."

He reached out a hand, deciding to take her by the arm into the glade. But his fingers closed on nothing. She was gone. He blinked furiously and glanced down. There were no depressions in the grass to indicate someone had been standing there. The scent of peach blossoms was gone. He reached to his haversack, searching for the liquor flask, then deciding he didn't need it—it was probably responsible for the woman.

"Connor!" This time the lieutenant shook off his sleep and unwrapped himself from his blanket. A few moments later, he and a sentry were at the base of the ginko, curiously eyeing their commander.

"Did you see her?"

Connor cocked his head. "Sir?"

The sentry scratched at his beard and glanced around.

"The woman?"

In unison they answered no.

"I was dreaming," he told them. "She was beautiful."

"Wish I had that kind of dream," Connor muttered as he returned to the skimpy shelter of his lean-to. The sentry resumed his path around the camp.

Minty stared at the ground. The mist had reached him, making it impossible for him to find any footprints the woman might have left. Still... He knelt and took off his gloves, gently prodded the ground around him. There were depressions, the size that could have been made by feet. Not his, these didn't have the hard outlines of bootheels. Of course, they could have been the natural contours of the soil he was feeling.

"Whit," he said softly. Whit was a tracker. The big man would be able to tell if these were footprints. Minty stood and carefully picked his way around the dogwoods, making sure he didn't step where the woman had been.

"Whit," he said louder as he stepped into the mist-filled glade and nearly ran into another sentry.

"Sir, the scouts you sent haven't returned."

They should have been back more than an hour ago, Minty knew. But perhaps they'd found something worth investigating. He would let himself become concerned if another hour passed. Nodding to the sentry, he continued onto Whit's lean-to. The big man didn't fit under it, and his legs stuck out.

"Whit, I need your help. Whit? Sleeping like a log." Minty reprimanded himself for marching the men for so long these past few days. Exhaustion had taken over all of them. He nudged Whit gently with the toe of his boot. "I need your skills, soldier. I need you to..."

He stared at the big form and tugged the blanket free. Whit was dead.

"Connor! Over here!"

Minty heard the lieutenant grumble in reply, heard the rustling of blankets, then he heard his lieutenant approach and gasp when he spotted Whit. The big man's face was as pale as the mist, and it was covered with boils.

"Oh my God," was all Connor could manage. "I was talking to him not more than a few hours ago, Sir."

Minty tugged the blanket to cover Kenneth Whit's face. "A disease of some kind," he said evenly, trying to show no emotion in his voice. "A pox or fever."

The camp was waking up, and men were shuffling around and in hushed voices asking what was going on. There were whispered speculations of poison, which made Connor nervous over the shared candy, of Confederate spies who had slipped in through the mist. Someone wondered if Whit hadn't fully recovered from being shot two months back.

Then someone hollered that two more men were dead. Their skin, too, was covered with boils and lesions. Conversations were no longer quiet.

"Break camp!" Minty ordered.

"I'll arrange a burial detail, Sir," Connor volunteered.

Minty shook his head. "No time. If there's something in the clearing... some plant...something...we need to leave. A pox or a fever, most likely. But just in case... Gather their weapons and ammo. Cover them." Then louder, and to the men, "Move, you Sunday soldiers! Movemovemove."

A flurry of activity followed, and the questions continued. Minty did nothing to quiet the men, he was too preoccupied.

"Sir?" It was the lanky sentry again. "Still no sign of the scouts."

"We move out!" Minty barked. "They'll find us. There are enough of us that we'll leave a trail whether we want to. Move!"

The formed rows, buttoning their uniforms and checking their weapons. There were several glances over their shoulders to where the bodies of their three comrades lay. The mist wrapped around the blanketed forms.

Minty raised his sword, the edge shining bright in the light of the moon. Then he pointed it forward, a signal to march.

Fatigued, the men managed to press on through what was left of the night, not stopping for rest until dawn painted the Tennessee horizon with a warm rosy glow. Minty would have ordered the men to continue for another hour or more, had not two dropped from exhaustion. And had he not spotted boils appearing on the face of two more young men. The soldiers noticed it, too, kept their distance while offering nervous words of encouragement to their stricken fellows. There were whispers of leaving the unit, and these Minty squashed with clipped orders and a stern look.

Barely able to stay awake, he addressed the men, talking of the Confederate encampments they were charged with finding, of all the important work they had to do so the full regiment could come in and drive the enemy back.

The two young men died before the sun had climbed halfway into the sky, and Minty and his men forced themselves another few miles just to put some distance between themselves and the bodies.

"Sir?"

Minty acknowledged Connor with a terse smile.

"How long...?"

"We'll rest here a few hours."

"Shall I name sentries and...?"

Minty waved a hand. "All of the men need to rest. Then we'll move again."

They awoke in the late afternoon to find eleven more men had succumbed to the mysterious disease.

"Move!" Minty snapped. And the men did, most out of fear that if they stayed put they might catch the malady.

When they changed direction just before sunset, Connor boldly questioned if Minty was indeed following the orders he talked about.

The Colonel was too tired to reprimand him for his audacity. Indeed, he barely heard his lieutenant. He was thinking of the woman near the Tennessee glade. "Pay with that which you hold dear, sir," she had said.

"She was real," he whispered.

"Sir?"

"Nothing, Connor. We're going back to Kentucky."

"Sir, I thought our orders were to..."

"We're going to find John Hunt Morgan, lieutenant. Do you have a problem with that?"

The lieutenant didn't argue. He was staring at the back of his hands. There were blisters covering them. A dozen more fell before dusk, including Connor, another three before they stopped late that night and Minty directed them to bivouac. There were no conversations, only stares, and they didn't bother with sentries.

Minty sat alone, several yards from the camp, his back against the tree. He was staring at his right hand, where he'd noticed a small boil. Perhaps the start of the disease. Perhaps his imagination. Perhaps the woman.

Dawn found them into Kentucky, another eight men down.

At the edge of their vision was a low-hanging fog. The hint of gunpowder was in the air. Faintly they could hear the crack of rifles and the shouts of men.

Minty considered avoiding the battle, wondering if he should risk exposing other soldiers to his men. Boils covered the hands and faces of another dozen of his charges, and their breathing was ragged.

"Perhaps there's a medic, sir?"

Jones? Minty thought. Yes, the young soldier's name was Jones. The man didn't have a trace of the disease yet. Minty's had progressed. There were boils on his arms, and his legs ached.

"A medic could treat us, sir." There was a suggestion of a question in Jones' voice. "Certainly a medic would know what this is. Scarlet fever...?"

Minty made a move to touch the young soldier, but the man recoiled, eyes locked on the boils that covered the colonel's hands. "Come with me, Jones," Minty said. Then he pointed to three more men, all so far free of the mysterious illness. "Move."

He turned and headed toward the battle fog, not waiting to see if his soldiers complied. Only Jones had. Staying low, they skirted the field, relying on scrub and small trees for cover. The air was thick with the smell of blood and filled with the cries of the dying. An occasional order pierced it—in a voice Minty recognized.

Was it fate that had led him here? Blind chance that had caused him to stumble upon John Hunt Morgan's forces? Or was there something else involved?

Breathing was an effort, because of the smoke and because of his condition. It would be so easy to stop. For just a moment, he thought. A brief rest. But he didn't know how many moments he had left. A glance over his shoulder. Jones was still behind him.

This way, Minty mouthed. They continued to circle the field until they were beyond the Union soldiers, who were winning the day. And they came onto the ground occupied by the retreating Confederates. Jones was clearly perplexed, but he said nothing, continuing to toe the mark and follow his diseased commander. A little farther, soldier. Just a little...

A rifle in the back of Jones held the young man in place. Minty was stopped when a musket was shoved in his face.

"Don't touch me," he said, wanting to warn the graybacks of his disease. But they didn't heed him. Men grabbed him up under each arm, likewise rough-handling Jones, taking their weapons and hauling them east, in the direction the unit was retreating.

Within moments, they were thrown at the feet of John Morgan.

"A fine prize," the southern general declared. "Colonel Robert Minty. Of Minnesota, I believe."

Minty didn't correct him. "Please," was all he managed.

"Oh, I'll not kill you, sir." It sounded like "suh," the way the woman had said it, that gentle southern dialect. "You're my prisoner. A fine prize most certainly! You'll tell me where your regiment is, sir. And much, much more. These men we were fighting don't belong to you. Where are your men? What are your orders?"

Words poured from Minty's lips. Not of positions or numbers or battle plans, but of a moonlit glade in Tennessee and a woman who claimed Morgan was her kin.

"Sherrie?" He stroked his short beard, and a finger drifted up to touch the down-turned mustache. "I had a favorite cousin Sherrie. But she died very early in the war, sir. Shot by mistake, I was told, by one of your Union soldiers."

Minty argued that he'd seen her and she looked quite healthy, long brown hair smelling of peach blossoms, cunning eyes. Jones stared in disbelief as Minty prattled on about the disease his men were falling to—that he, himself was dying of—and that he believed Morgan's cousin was responsible for.

"She was real," he said, as he watched Morgan send his men away. The southern general faced Minty alone now. "And she wants you to come home."

Morgan laughed then, loud and long. "Kentucky is my home." Softer, he admitted that her family lived in Tennessee.

"You'll go see her?" Minty was pleading. "For my men? They're dying." Not a soldier's death, he added to himself. "Please save my men."

Chuckling, Morgan paced in front of his foe. "For a price, I will humor you, sir." He bent in front of Minty, locked eyes with him. "For a price."

"Anything for my men."

"You will not go against my forces again, Colonel Minty. Direct your ire, sir, at Davis instead—provided you live past this day. He's on my side. But I've no love for him." After a moment, Morgan added, "And he's not my kin."

Then he left Minty and Jones, his forces moving back as the Union soldiers continued their assault. The two found their way back to their own unit, where four more had died to the malady.

* * *

John Hunt Morgan was bathed in the pale moonlight of a Tennessee glade. A mist swirled around his feet and clung to the trunks of the ash and oak trees that ringed the clearing.

"Cousin." She approached him, dressed in pale pink nightclothes, brown hair swirling around her shoulders in the slight breeze. "He bade you come home."

Her touch was cold, and her eyes darkly captivating.

"I can't stay," he told her. "I've only stopped for a visit." He wanted to ask her how she managed to recover, as he was certain the reports of her being shot were true.

"I didn't," she said.

Had she answered him? Or had he only imagined the words?

"Stay a while, cousin John."

"I can't," he repeated. "The war."

A nod. "You're a soldier. Meant to spill blood on Tennessee soil."

* * *

It was early May of 1865, more than two years after Minty and the remainder of his men had miraculously recovered from the disease. He was in Georgia now, Irwin County, his men picketing the Ocmulgee River to keep Jefferson Davis from escaping. Minty took a hundred and fifty-three of his best men, Jones among them, and followed the river. For some reason he opted to follow a bridle path through the woods toward Irwinsville.

"Fate," he whispered. Or perhaps blind luck. He led his men toward a camp made in a thick pine forest. And there they surprised and captured Davis and his family.

In Quest of the Beast

I like to read mythologies, and when I find snippets that are particularly interesting, I save them in a file folder for future inspiration. When Denise Little invited me to an anthology about mythological creatures, I pulled out that file and discovered my questing beast. This story originally appeared in Creature Fantastic, *DAW Books, 2001.*

Clare couldn't afford to be the last one to leave tonight, so she relegated Stewart to finish the Society for Creative Anachronism display. She passed him the permit that allowed them to be in the student union after hours, slipped into her Madison Muskies jacket, and slung her new backpack over her shoulder.

She'd been the last one to leave the past three nights, taking on the proverbial lion's share of the work on the overly elaborate and very time-consuming project—which was only right, Stewart had repeatedly pointed out.

"Your idea. Your responsibility. Your thing," he was fond of saying. Last night he had added: "Besides, you're the ranking SCA member at the college for crissakes. And you're sleeping with the guy who's gonna be the region's next seneschal." Stewart had more than hinted that all of this was to impress her Milwaukee boyfriend, who would be visiting next weekend. Though she scoffed at his comments and said it was only to help with SCA recruitment, Stewart hadn't been entirely wrong.

I should stay and help him finish, she thought, noting, however, that the display was looking very good, and that Stewart should have it done in another two hours or so. He was normally so very much like his SCA persona, only interested in fighting and jousts, a jock in any era. But he'd been a relatively good sport about this.

In fact, she had offered to stay, she reminded herself, though there hadn't been any strength to her words—and Stewart knew it. Stewart poignantly played the martyr, shaking his head, and raising a hand, fluttering his long, skinny fingers toward the elevator in a dismissive shooing motion.

"Go already. I thought you said you have a big mid-term tomorrow? The Quest for King Arthur's Camelot or some such fusty fictional nonsense." He paused and gave her a lopsided grin. "Just because a moistened tart lobbed a scimitar at young Pendragon was no basis for a form of government." Stewart never correctly quoted Monty Python. "Go."

"Yeah, I've gotta go," she told him, padding down the hall and stopping at the elevator. She gave Stewart a last glance. "Gotta study. Hard. Very hard. I should've been hitting it all week. And I shouldn't've stayed here this late."

Go, go, go, he mouthed to her like a mantra.

She groaned at the prospect of her impending all-night-all-morning session and punched her thumb against the down button several times, as if that act might speed the elevator's arrival and get her deep into her textbook faster. Clare loved the subject, but she hated the Camelot course because she hated the professor—with all his winks and innuendos and blatant suggestions that she should come over to his condo when his wife wasn't home for—how did the slug put it—"mulled elderberry wine and much more detailed and comfortable research." She would've gladly dropped the course by the end of the fifth week—when courses were still dropable without affecting one's grades. But her upcoming Master's Thesis was on Sir Thomas Mallory and his *Le Morte D'Arthur* as the source of Arthurian legends, and so the Camelot course could be useful. And she might actually learn something from the old lecherous, beady-eyed dirtbag. But once this semester was over and she had her "A," or at the very worst her "B" in hand, and when the next semester had safely started, she intended to file a scathing sexual harassment report with the liberal arts dean about the slug. At the very least she'd get him fired.

"Professor Mides. Professor Creep," she said, as the elevator finally chimed and the doors hissed open. "Professor Slimeball." She stepped inside and stabbed several times at the "1" button. Clare groaned again when the elevator dropped to the ground floor and stopped, doors defiantly remaining closed. She balled her fist and struck the doors in the center, as she always did when she lazily rode the thing instead of walking down the four flights. One more properly applied fist-pounding and they opened with a protesting hiss. She escaped into the empty lobby.

It was just past midnight, the union closed to the general student body, and only a few lights were on, reflecting off the myriad of tall windows and casting a ghostly glow against the polished tile floor. She hurried outside, the Wisconsin fall wind forcing her to zip up her jacket, and whipping her hair so wildly across her face that her eyes stung.

"Wonderful."

There was a single loud crack of thunder and she looked up into a black sky that was shot through with bands of thick gray clouds. A heartbeat later she felt the first drop of rain plop on her cheek.

"Truly wonderful."

Clare glanced back at the student union. The front door had of course closed and locked securely behind her, and Stewart and any janitors who were about wouldn't be able to hear her shouting to let her back inside. This late, the Madison city bus came by only on the hour.

Her watch proclaimed it ten past midnight. She wasn't about to wait fifty minutes for the next bus. And she wasn't about to walk a block to the nearest payphone to call a cab that she would have to wait God-knew-how-long for and would take her only nine blocks more, charging her what she'd rather spend on lunch tomorrow. So...

"Time to hoof it," she told herself just as the sky opened up.

The rain was cold and came at her sideways, driven by the wind, the drops hard like tiny darts—angry insects biting her face and hands. She pulled the collar of her jacket up and held the tips together under her chin, and she started to jog across the campus, heels clicking rhythmically against the concrete sidewalk.

I'll bet Sir Thomas Malory was never caught in weather like this, she thought. But he would've never been caught dead in Wisconsin. Knight, prisoner, scholar, he finished his eight tales of Arthur during the ninth year of King Edward IV's reign in an England that in the early fall was assuredly beset by fog and drizzle—but not the Badger State's bone-chilling cold rain. *Ah, to be in England,* she mused. *Sir Thomas' land.* She intended to use her thesis as an excuse to join a student trip to London next summer. She might actually even study something when she was there, visit Sir Thomas' grave.

Sir Thomas loved hunting and knightly tournaments, embraced chivalry—and it was said he thoroughly immersed himself in his readings of Arthurian romance. *Tristan, Quest de Saint Graal, Mort Artu,* she'd read all of Mallory's works more than once and looked forward to tackling them again.

However, Clare was not looking forward to immersing herself in the lecherous slug's Camelot textbook that was laying open on her desk, a seven-hundred-page monstrosity he'd required all his students to buy so he could impress them while earning hefty royalties. The professor's view of the Arthurian legend paralleled Mallory's for the most part, at least from what she'd read so far of the text. But in her mind it diverged considerably in a few critical spots, which made the course—though certainly not the slimy instructor—interesting. The test tomorrow would focus mainly on Pellinore, perhaps the foremost knight at King Arthur's round table, and on Morgawse.

Morgawse, Clare concentrated on that woman to take her mind off the weather. Morgawse was said to have come to King Arthur as a messenger—though in truth she was a clever spy and Igraine's daughter, and thus Arthur's sister. Beautiful, she coerced the king into her bed and later gave birth to Mordred—the man who was both Arthur's nephew and his son. Incest. Clare shivered at the thought and from the cold. Morgawse. Clare shivered again, recalling that the lecherous dirtbag told her just last week that she was "as lovely as Ingraine's favored child."

She was soaked before she reached the next corner, the streetlight illuminating the sheet-like rain that was striking the pavement ever harder—and bouncing back. Tat-tat-tat, it sounded harshly against the storm grate and the metal lamppost. From somewhere nearby a dog howled mournfully. Tat-tat-tat.

Hail? Clare stared. It was starting to hail.

"Well and truly wonderful."

She sped her pace, crossing the street and jogging down a poorly lit service road that ran behind the liberal arts building. It was a shortcut she'd discovered a few weeks after she moved here. Her heels clicked faster, sounding syncopated now with the ice pellets that were pummeling the road and her, that were bouncing everywhere and performing a stentorian rat-a-tat-tat off a collection of big garbage cans. The dog continued to howl. Closer now, she decided it sounded like there were a couple of them—probably chasing a cat that was every bit as wet and unhappy as she was.

She could've taken her "beater" today, but that would've entailed parking it on the other side of campus during her afternoon classes and trying to find a closer spot when she went to the union. And parking near the union in the middle of the week wasn't likely to happen, unless one was lucky enough to find a place right out front on the street and was willing to feed the meter until well past dark.

So what's a dozen quarters compared to getting chilled to the bone? she grumped.

She found herself wishing she would've stayed to help Stewart, at least for fifty more minutes. That would've put her late enough for the one a.m. bus that would have picked her up just across the street from the union, and which would have—after a meandering few-mile course—spit her out within a hundred yards of her place.

What would the fifty minutes have hurt, since I'd stayed so blasted late anyway?

"Nothing," she answered aloud. It wouldn't have hurt anything. It would have saved her time, actually. Now she would be arriving home thoroughly cold and thoroughly drenched and in need of a hot bath and a hot cup of chocolate that would keep her from the dirtbag's Camelot for at least another hour.

"Three blocks down," she muttered. "Six to go." Clare felt around behind her to make sure her backpack was tied shut. It was dyed-green leather, a gift from the soon-to-be-seneschal, and was probably getting ruined because she hadn't been willing to spend the quarters at the meters out front or the blasted fifty minutes to help Stewart.

"Fifty goddamn minutes. I should've stayed in the union," she said as she passed the far corner of the liberal arts building, where she would be taking her Camelot test in just under ten hours. Light spilled out from a second-floor window. Some professor working late, she thought, someone who had a car conveniently parked right in this lot that she was now crossing.

There was only the one car, she noted, and the hail was loudly tat-a-tat-tatting off it and probably scratching the glossy black paint that had been applied in a German factory. Looked expensive.

Clare hadn't bothered to glance up into the window, nor had she registered just what window it was. And so she hadn't seen the professor watching her. He craned his neck to follow her progress across the lot and past his car, and he opened the window so he could hear the hail and the sound of the hounds, the latter most pleasing and familiar. He smiled. It wouldn't be long now.

She darted onto the next street, cutting down a long alley that led past a squat brick apartment building. She had briefly considered renting there three years ago because of its proximity to the liberal arts building, where most of her classes were. But the rooms had been far too small, and her SCA friends rented at a slightly more upscale place that she was now practically running all-out toward.

It was darker away from the campus, but the alley was blacktopped. And slick with water and icy shards, it gleamed in the lights that spilled out the squat apartment building's windows. *Students in their microscopic rooms either studying or partying,* Clare thought—probably the former, as she didn't hear any obnoxiously loud music drifting out.

Only the constant and annoying tat-a-tat-tat and the howling dogs.

"Five blocks down. Five to go." Clare stopped at the end of the alley and cocked her head, listening to the hail pound the metal roof of a garden shed behind an old Victorian, strike the street that T'd in front of her, patter off her probably-ruined leather backpack. The top of her head was sore from the onslaught. She'd need aspirins with that hot cocoa now.

Those dogs were still howling, even louder it seemed, not caring about the weather and still after that unfortunate cat. There must be an entire pack of them, Clare guessed, as she headed east through an aging residential neighborhood, slowing her pace now because the walk was completely icing up. Everyone was asleep, the windows all dark, the only light coming from the lampposts that were being tat-tat-tat-tatted against on every corner.

So loud—the hail and the dogs. Were they after something else?

Something niggled at her brain, then, about the dogs. Something she'd read recently from the slug's textbook and long ago from Mallory's writings.

Something about the howling. About Morgawse and Pellinore and Arthur.

A shiver raced down her spine. She'd definitely been reading too much lately—especially about King Arthur and medieval England and France, about the legends and...

So loud.

Reading too much and sleeping too little. Spending too much time on SCA and too many weekends with her boyfriend.

She urged herself faster despite the ice, her feet slipping and slapping against the sidewalk, her eyes darting to the houses, halfway hoping there would be a light on in one of them to signal that someone else was still awake at this hour.

The dogs were certainly baying loud enough to wake up the entire neighborhood—to wake up all of Madison for that matter. They sounded close. Too close. Her breath caught at the notion that perhaps they were chasing her.

"God, I should've stayed with Stewart," she said. Then she laughed at her nerves and again slowed to a walk, as if her pace would make her calm down and realize how silly she was being. She grabbed her side, which was aching from her run, and she continued to scan the block for even a front porch light. Ah, there was a light, on a second floor about two blocks down. Another light flicked on a few houses closer, perhaps someone wanting to see what all the barking was about. Maybe they wouldn't mind if she stood on their porch, just to get out of the hail for a few moments and to let the dogs pass.

The howling was so terribly loud now, much louder than the hail, and so wrongfully out of place. Dogs didn't run in packs in the city limits of Madison. It was Wisconsin, so it was hunting season for something. But not in the streets. So close, they sounded. Close enough that she should be able to see them. Clare threw her hands over her ears and spun around, nearly losing her balance on the slick pavement. Where are the dogs?

Nothing. She saw nothing but the hail and the dark houses, the lampposts still being tat-tat-tat-tatted against. And in the distance she saw a soft glow, which was coming from the myriad of streetlights on the campus.

Where are the dogs?

There had to be a few dozen of them, she thought by the racket they were making. Thirty? Forty?

Forty. Another shiver shot down her back.

Maybe they were in someone's backyard, she thought, giving herself a slight measure of relief that they wouldn't venture onto the street. Maybe they'd treed the cat and would stay put, would not come out where she could see them and make her feel like she was their target. She laughed again, the sound brittle this time. The dogs—however many there were and no matter where they were—would most certainly leave her alone, she told herself. This was middle-of- the-road, middle-of-the-state Madison, Wisconsin. She was near the university. She was in a peaceful and quiet residential neighborhood a couple of blocks from her apartment. Weird things like hunting dogs going after people didn't happen here. Maybe she should just start running toward home again. Maybe...

"What is that?" She hadn't meant to voice the words, or the one following. "Omigod." Her mouth dropped open as her mind tried to put a name to the thing she saw. It was at the edge of her vision, cutting across the old Victorian's front yard and not close enough to truly make out. But it was large, she could tell that, and it moved quickly, gracefully, seemingly heedless of the hail and seemingly heading straight toward her.

As it passed beneath the streetlight, Clare screamed—her cry of terror drowned out by the hail and the howling—the pack-of-dogs sound which was coming from the one creature.

"It can't be. It's n-n-not possible. It's n-n-not real!" It never existed, she told herself as she turned and ran, prized leather backpack slipping from her shoulder and hitting the pavement with a "smack!" "Not real!" she cried as her feet struck against the sidewalk in time with her rapidly pounding heart, then struck against the street as she darted across it and toward the closest house with a light on. She took in great gulps of air, held her side, and forced herself to move faster still. Someone was up and would let her inside where she'd be safe from the beast.

The beast that lived only in the pages written by Sir Thomas Mallory, T.H. White, and a few others.

The creature was a thing of fiction, her mind screamed, as the beast screamed—the baying of forty hounds echoing off the homes in the night-dark Madison neighborhood.

A risked glance over her shoulder. "No!" The creature was indeed closing and was better revealed in the spotlight of the streetlight she'd just passed. Her feet were instantly anchors, her fear holding her in place.

The beast certainly didn't look real, though it was clearly moving and breathing. Nothing that looked like that could be real, her mind argued. It couldn't exist.

The nightmare creature was at the same time magnificent and horrifying. It was longer than a car, its body that of a leopard, coat slick from the rain and hail, sleek muscles rippling under the glow of the streetlight. From its shoulders sprouted the head of an impossibly large snake, green and brown scales glistening, dark eyes sparkling, blood-red forked tongue flicking out. Its maw open, the frightening sound of forty hounds that seemed to rumble about in thing's gut was even more clearly heard. The creature slowed its pace to practically a crawl, "clacking" as it neared Clare, deerlike hooves striking against the pavement, lion's hindquarters quivering. It was stalking her.

"The Questing Beast," Clare whispered.

In response to her soft words, the snakehead cocked and raised, its thick lizard tail twitched making it seem catlike.

She'd seen the creature, or rather renderings of it, depicted in paintings and drawings as described by Mallory several times in his *Le Morte D'Arthur.* A symbol of incest, it was said to be, and its varying parts symbolizing chaos and anarchy. It was birthed by the devil upon a princess who unjustly accused her handsome brother of rape. Her brother hadn't touched her, rejecting her advances. But he died to the beast. Hundreds of years ago.

How could it be here?

Arthur was said to have seen it, according to Mallory. After laying with Morgawse, the king had a dream that all of his people were killed by griffons and great serpents. And when he awoke from the dream he and some of his knights went hunting. Arthur followed an impressive stag, chasing it until his horse died from exertion and he summoned another. While he waited at a fountain, still determined to pursue the stag, a strange creature came to drink. It was the Questing Beast. Pellinore brought the fresh horse and saw the creature, too. Then Pellinore pursued it, never able to catch it. And after his death Sir Palamides, the Saracen knight, chased it. Hundreds of years ago.

"You're not real," she told it. "Not at all."

For the briefest of moments Clare decided that it truly wasn't—that she was dreaming. That she'd fallen asleep in the student union and that Stewart would wake her soon and she would wait for the bus and then would go home and study for the damnable slug's Camelot test. That she would be safe.

The creature's tongue flitted out again, teasing the air. Its dark eyes were locked onto hers, holding her in place as surely as any vise. It crept closer, muscles bunching and releasing, every movement liquid.

"Beautiful," she hissed. Transfixed, she found herself admiring the thing, her mind replaying all the tales of it she'd read and reread. French folklore claimed it was birthed by a woman torn apart by hounds. It was called *Beste Glatissant,* or the barking beast. In White's *Once and Future King,* the creature was pitiful and misunderstood. There was no good reason for Pellinore to hunt it, and the knight doing so pointed out that chivalry was often meaningless. But Clare tended to think Mallory was right, that the creature was called into being by the devil and by a sister who'd been spurned by her brother.

The creature stopped a few yards from her, perhaps studying Clare as she was studying it. The hail continued to pelt both of them, and the sound of the baying hounds continued to issue from the Questing Beast's belly.

A light flicked on behind her, and she faintly heard the sound of a door creaking open.

"What's all the racket about?" It was a man's voice.

The Questing Beast cocked its head and snarled. The muscles of its back legs gathered themselves.

"No!" Clare screamed as she swung about and bounded down the sidewalk and then up the steps of the house behind her and right into the path of a startled old man.

He was dressed in a rumpled bathrobe, his face creased from sleep, and he held the door handle firmly.

"See here, young woman. You can take your dogs and..." He paused and narrowed his eyes, trying to look past her.

The sound of the hounds had stopped. Clare glanced over her shoulder. The Questing Beast was gone. Perhaps it had never been there.

"I'm s-s-sorry," she stammered. "I was just walking home from the student union and...," she searched for the words. "And this thing started chasing me."

The man shook his head. "I don't see anything. Heard some dogs, though."

"It wasn't a dog." The words came quick now. "It was a creature. The Questing Beast. It was part leopard and snake, and it was making the baying sound you heard. I think it was after me, but..."

"Drugs," the man cut back. "College students and drugs. You get outta here or I'm going to call the cops on you."

Clare tried to insinuate herself in the doorway, but he closed the door to a crack.

"Get out of here, now."

"No. You don't understand," she pleaded. "Could I come in. Just for a moment. I'll call a cab and..."

"I'm calling the cops." The door slammed, and she heard a bolt fall into place.

She turned and sagged against the side of the house. "Gone." The creature really was gone. "Dreaming," she said with a sigh of relief. Clare tromped down the stairs and started home again.

"Three blocks to go," she grumbled. "Ah..." she remembered her dropped backpack, and headed out into the street, intending to get it. She stopped when she heard a dog bark. Then another barked, and another.

The baying resumed, and from behind a parked pickup truck came the Questing Beast.

She ran, faster than she believed possible, the ache in her side a memory as her feet churned over the sidewalk then over the curb. She was running in the center of the street now, where the pavement was flat and where she could see better. Her heels click-clacked, just as she heard the hooves of the creature flying along behind her.

"Why are you after me?" she screamed. "Why me?"

The beast didn't answer, it simply bore down on her, leaping with its front legs extended, deer hooves striking her back and sending the wind from her burning lungs.

Clare screamed as she was driven forward and down, her head hitting the icy street and momentarily stunning her. The baying continued, mixed with an odd wuffling sound as if the creature were sniffing her. It pawed at her, turning her over while at the same time she fought the wooziness and tried to get to her feet.

She managed only to make it to her knees, putting her eye-to-eye with the thing. It looked at her sadly, if it was possible for a monstrosity such as it to show an expression of remorse. White was indeed wrong, she vaguely registered. The Questing Beast was not misunderstood and was not a thing to be pitied. It was to be feared and hated.

"Why?" she breathed.

A heartbeat later she had her answer. The creature edged forward, dark eyes wide and so mirrorlike shiny. Reflected in them was a visage, not hers, but a man she knew. Her professor.

She opened her mouth to scream again, but the beast's snakelike maw snapped opened and shot forward, needle teeth piercing her flesh and ending her life.

And all the while it bayed like a pack of forty hounds.

* * *

There was a polite knock. "Professor Mides?" Another knock. "Professor Mides, this is the police. We'd like to speak with you."

The man who opened his door for the officers was distinguished looking, markedly handsome and with a complexion that was sun-bronzed, though it was well into fall. He gestured the two officers inside. Both were plainclothes, marking them as detectives.

The woman officer flipped open her badge holder. "Lieutenant Anders," she said as way of introduction. "And this is my partner Lieutenant Hoskins."

The professor nodded to each and spread his hands. "I was just on my way to my class. I've a mid-term I'm giving at ten."

Lieutenant Anders thrust out her chin. "One of your students was killed last night, professor, a Clare Kinsley."

He scowled and put on a saddened face. "A good student," he said. "Majoring in medieval studies, I believe."

"Seems she was torn apart by some wild animal," the lieutenant continued. "Less than a mile from here."

The professor *tsked.* "Sorry to hear that. The class will be devastated."

"We'd like to ask you a few questions about Clare and you."

He raised an eyebrow.

"Where you were late last night?"

"Here," he said, gesturing to a desk filled with opened books and curling papers. "Until after two or so." He cleared his throat. "Why? If a wild animal..."

"Professor, it was last year about this time another young woman was killed."

He stroked his chin. "Ah, I seem to remember something about that."

"She was one of your students, too."

"Kathy Wilkers," he said. "Kathy studied from other professors. So did Clare."

"So did Ellen and Mary Hammerlund," Lieutenant Anders added, checking her notebook. That twin murder dated back four years, to his first at the university.

A shrug. "A coincidence."

"I don't believe in coincidences," the lieutenant replied.

"And what do you believe in, Lieutenant Anders?"

She laughed, the sound pleasant, like crystal windchimes. "King Arthur and Camelot? I don't believe in those either, Professor. But I believe in finding out what or who killed your students."

"You did admit they studied under other professors, too." Mides puffed out his chest. "They weren't just my students."

"But you're the one constant. The one thread in common to all of them."

"You can't possibly believe I was involved with Miss Kinsley's death? And with the deaths of those other women?" He put on his best shocked expression.

Lieutenant Anders answered with a shrug and scribbled a few notes in her book. "Do you own any pets, Professor Mides?"

"A few calico orandas. They're goldfish," he answered. "And actually they belong to my son."

She scribbled a few more notes. "We'll be back, Professor." She turned to leave.

"Has anyone ever told you that you're beautiful, Lieutenant Anders?" After she was well down the hall, he added, "As beautiful as Igraine's treasured daughter."

Mides glided to his desk, to the ancient books there written in Old English and French. He turned a page. There was a woodcut, of King Arthur resting against a willow tree, which was shading a fountain. Drinking from the basin was a singular creature. It had a snake's head and a leopard's body, the hooves of a deer and the hindquarters of a lion. He traced the outline of the thing with his index finger.

"They call you the Questing Beast because you are sought after. After and after and never caught." He sighed and closed the book. "I can't catch you. But I can summon you, and you can be controlled."

Just as his knightly ancestor Palomides sought the creature and discovered that while he could not catch it, in making a dark pact he could control it.

"Just as my son will someday use you, too." The professor reverently placed the thick tome on the shelf, and followed it with the others he'd used last night to call forth the beast and to send it after the comely young woman who had spurned all his advances. His distant relative.

Perhaps, he mused, if Lieutenant Anders was clever enough she might discover that he was vaguely related to Clare, a tenuous family-tree thread that could at best be called "shirt-tailed cousins." But it was a thread nonetheless, the suggestion of improper love and incest. And it ran to Kathy Wilkers and Mary and Ellen Hammerlund. It ran to a freshman whom he would convince to take his Camelot course next year. The men in his family had been guilty of several extra-marital transgressions, making the family tree a veritable forest.

The thread did not run to Lieutenant Anders, not that he knew of anyway. But he would consult his genealogy texts to be certain. Perhaps he could find her in the family forest. However, if he could find no thread, perhaps the Questing Beast could be persuaded to hunt her anyway.

Mides smiled slyly and headed out the door, stack of tests in hand.

Through his still-opened window, he heard the bark of a dog.

Hat for a Sail

Okay, so I like the Civil War era. I'm eager to write short stories in that period, particularly if they involve the military. When I was invited to write for the "First to Fight" series, provided that I write about a submarine, I was quick to say "Yes, sir, and I'll make my tale about the Hunley. *I have the distinction of being the first woman author in that anthology series. "Hat for a Sail" originally appeared in* Crash Dive, *published by Jove in 2003.*

Miller suspected dying would feel just like this. He could scarcely breathe, his chest so tight he swore a mule was sitting squarely on it. What little air he managed to take in was uncomfortably warm and heavy with the stink of men gone too long without a bath. Sweat rolled down his face and into his mouth, soaked his clothes and added to his misery. His eyes burned terribly, and he blinked to bring tears—quite an effort, it seemed, considering his state.

It was dark. The flame of a stubby candle flickered several feet away, but it was too feeble to chase away the shadows. Couldn't really see anything by it, not anymore. Miller had been watching the candle for...how long? One hour? Two? An eternity, most likely. The flame was much taller at the beginning, somehow comforting in its dance and letting him see the weathered face of Arnold Becker, the man sitting next to him, and—if he leaned forward a bit—James Wicks, who sat just past that. But now the flame was little more than a glow, and he couldn't see Becker at all—though he could plainly hear the man gasping.

Miller heard a lot of things.

There was a somewhat steady "plinking," which would be Wicks, who broke his precious pocket watch on the last outing and was now futilely trying to keep track of time. A harsh wheezing, this undoubtedly coming from an older man named Simkins, who would likely spread his cold to all of them—if they survived. There was the soft rustle of clothes, someone moving his arms. The "thunk" of a boot heel. Above all of that, almost painfully loud, was a quick, rhythmic pounding, which Miller realized was the beating of his own heart.

Miller stared at the candle more intently, as if by focusing on that little piece of fire he could will it to burn brighter or, at the very least, force it to take his mind off all the irritating noise and the ache in his lungs. When that didn't work he glanced away, blinking furiously now and seeing tiny motes of white behind his lids, the "stars" that he'd come to learn signaled the last of the air going away. Then out of the corner of his eye he saw the candle wink out, plunging him into a blackest black. In response, his chest tightened even more, Wicks' "plinking" stopped, and Becker's gasps became thin and strangled.

"Up," Miller heard Wicks croak. "Up."

"Up," Becker echoed.

Miller tried to say the word, too, but found his throat too dry and his tongue too unwieldy to cooperate. He tried to work up some saliva.

"Up," someone else managed, Simkins from the sound of it.

"Up."

"Up."

Amid puffing sounds and the rustling of shirtsleeves, Miller summoned what was left of his strength and fumbled forward with his hands, finding a section of the metal bar in front of him. The bar ran the entire length of the submarine they were sitting in. Miller wrapped his sweat-slick fingers around his portion of it.

"Up," Becker said.

He felt the bar move a little, and he threw his back into it, helping to push it forward and down, pulling it toward him and up and around and over again, as if he was operating the cantankerous hand-pump on his uncle's old well. Becker was at it, too, as was Wicks and Simkins and the rest, all in the cadence of desperation. The bar was one big crank, and it manually operated the submarine's propeller.

"Up." Miller finally found his voice. *Please,* he added to himself, as he inhaled once more. *Please hurry.* Then he worked faster, in time with his panicked fellows, seeing the "stars" winking in and out of the blackness with more frequency, his head growing light and bobbing forward, his lungs holding fast to that last breath he'd impossibly been able to suck in.

After several revolutions of the bar, there was a lurching sensation, and Miller's hands accidentally slipped off. His arms felt like lead weights, but he reached deep inside and somehow found the energy to raise them. The bar was turning 'round without him, propelled by the other men at their stations. In the absolute darkness, it painfully struck his searching fingers and caused him to expel the precious air. But a moment more and he'd locked a grip again and was helping to push the bar forward and down, up and over, forward and...

"Up," he heard Wicks say with more conviction.

God! Miller's mind screamed. There's no air. I'm dying! He sucked in nothingness.

They hadn't gone deep this time, no more than four fathoms, and so there was little pressure on Miller's ears. Still, he could tell that the damnable submarine they were squeezed inside was rising. Compared to his on-fire lungs and everything else going on around him, it was a rather subtle sensation, but

Miller had taken a half-dozen rides in the thing and so could recognize the perception of going up.

But would they reach the surface in time?

He doubted it—not soon enough this time. In their pride and foolishness they'd tarried too long on the bottom of the river. Miller felt like he was sinking into oblivion.

"Up!" Becker and Wicks whispered in unison.

Dying does indeed feel like this, Miller thought. *Dying and...*

Then suddenly and blessedly shades of gray intruded as the submarine came toward the surface. Light streamed in through small windows near the fore and aft hatches. Miller closed his eyes as he heard Simkins working a valve and felt the wondrous stir of fresh air. He and the others started gulping it in—long-starving men at a sumptuous feast—leaning away from the bar and shaking out their fingers. Becker leaned back a little too quickly and "thunked" his head soundly against the curved metal wall at his back.

Miller scarcely heard the man's cursing over his own ragged breath.

"Two hours and thirty-one minutes," Lieutenant George Dixon announced after a few minutes had passed—and he'd had time to catch his own wind. "A record, gentlemen. Congratulations."

There were no whoops of victory. There hadn't been any yesterday either, when they'd stayed down for two hours and twenty minutes, and the day before that when they'd stayed down for two. There was only the sucking in of blessed air.

Please not tomorrow, too, Miller thought, as he continued to gulp it in. *Please let this be the last test of this damnable contraption.* Then he was rubbing his face into his shoulder, futilely trying to wipe the sweat off, opening his eyes and breathing deeper still in an effort to shut down the furnace his chest had become.

"Well, boy," Becker said as he slapped Miller on the knee. "We made it! Stonewall Jackson'd be rightfully proud of all of us."

Wicks chimed in: "Stonewall'd be rightfully prouder if we won the war with this infernal thing, eh Miller? Quite a damn fine machine this *Hunley* is!"

Miller didn't reply. He just rolled his shoulders, as much as the cramped confines allowed, and started working the crank again. Lieutenant Dixon was consulting the compass, looking through the small windows, and directing the men to head for shore.

Becker nudged Wicks, and the two men started a tune in time with their cranking. Simkins joined in on the second verse:

> Come, stack arms, men pile on the rails,
> Stir up the campfire bright;

No matter if the canteen fails,
We'll make a roaring night.
Here Shenandoah brawls along,
Here burly Blue Ridge echoes strong,
To swell the Brigade's rousing song
of Stonewall Jackson's way.

We see him now—the old slouched hat
Cocked o'er his eye askew.
The shrewd, dry smile, the speech so pat,
So calm, so blunt, so true;
The "Blue Light Elder" knows 'em well:
Says he, "That's Banks, he's fond of shell;
Lord, save his soul! we'll give him—" well
That's Stonewall Jackson's way.

An hour later Becker was singing the same song again, the song he sang at least a few times every day—the only one Miller swore the man seemed to know. But this time he was singing it in the shade of a thick red oak several yards back from the shore of the Cooper River and the dock, where the submarine *H.L. Hunley* was moored.

"That's Stonewall Jackson's way," Miller muttered as Becker began to repeat the tune for the God-only-knew-how-many-hundreth time.

Silence! Ground arms! Kneel all! Caps off!
Old "Blue Light's" going to pray;
Strangle the fool that dares to scoff!
Attention! It's his way!
Appealing from his native sod,
"Hear us, Almighty God!
Lay bare Thine arm, stretch forth Thy rod,
Amen!" That's Stonewall Jackson's way.

"Becker, stop that ruckus! You sound like a cat getting squeezed to death. Miller, on your feet! Come grab a root with us!" Wicks was waving and gesturing toward the cookfire on the bank, where Simkins and a few others were roasting potatoes and passing around some of the pickled beef they called salt horse.

Becker was quick to stop singing and jump up. "Comin', boy?"

Miller shook his head. "Maybe later, Beck."

"Won't be any of the good stuff left, Too Tall," Becker *tsked* as he hurried to join the men. "Nothing but sheet iron crackers for you if you don't skedaddle, boy."

Another shake. "Thanks, though." Miller was stretched out, legs pointed toward the river, leaning back on his elbows, and face pitched toward the clear, early November sky. He was a lanky, beanpole of a man—nicknamed Too Tall by some of the others—and though he was young and nimble, sitting hunkered inside that submarine for hours made him stiff and set his knees to throbbing. He intended to sprawl here an hour or so with no walls and nothing but fresh air around him. Then he'd walk into town and get a bath and a change of clothes so he could stomach himself. He'd probably head over to Willum's and order something tasty for supper, then get him some nokum stiff to chase away the memories of this morning and the one before.

Would Lieutenant Dixon see how long they could stay down tomorrow? What would satisfy the man? Would he make them stay down until they died? Despite the day's heat, a shiver raced down Miller's spine.

"Damnable submarine," he cursed to himself. Miller propped himself up a little higher so he could see it, tied to the dock, the top of it showing above the water, all black and ugly and glistening, looking like a giant, bloated bullhead a fisherman had tugged in and left there, forgotten. "Damnedest thing, that is."

Miller continued to stare at the *Hunley* as he caught a whiff of a potato burning, the smell settling sour in his mouth and making his nose wrinkle.

"That's foul," he said, purposely loud enough for the others to hear. But he knew it wasn't near so foul as the odor of himself and the smells that always hung inside the submarine. He hated that—the stink of the men so cramped up in that thing, the stink of the piss jug that was passed down the line whenever someone called for it. Yesterday Wicks vomited early on and Lieutenant Dixon didn't bring the submarine up for more than an hour after that. It all had to bother the other men as much as it did himself. But no one said anything, least not so Lieutenant Dixon could hear. It was like torture being in the *Hunley's* crew, Miller decided, like wallowing in a slop trough.

Maybe I shouldn't come back after Willum's, he thought. Maybe I should just head on home and stay out of the war. It'd make my father happy.

At sixteen (though he told the Lieutenant he was three years older than that), Miller was the youngest member of the *Hunley*'s eight-man crew, and the only one not in the military. He would have joined up to fight the North, signed on with the Army or the Navy, despite his father's protests to stay on the ranch and stay safe. But if he had joined up, he might have been sent out of South Carolina, and he didn't want that. The *Hunley* was moored on the Cooper River, across from the eastern end of Drum Island and within shouting distance of Charleston. He was already farther from home than he'd ever been, his family's small ranch sitting to the southwest near the Georgia border.

And if he had joined up, he was certain he never would have been a part of this damnable submarine's crew. No chance to serve Alabama engineering officer Lieutenant George Dixon. And no chance to die in a slop trough at the bottom of the river.

And if Lieutenant Dixon sent them down tomorrow—to see if they could go beyond two hours and thirty-one minutes, Miller felt in his gut that he'd surely not be coming back up. It was Dixon's rule that the men were to holler "up" when they believed they would pass out from lack of air. But Miller had his pride and would not let himself be the first to give in. In fact, he was usually the last to say the word.

"Lord, but I don't want to die in that thing," he whispered. "Maybe I won't come back after Willum's. Maybe I'll just go home. Yes, sir, I'll just go home."

* * *

Miller was back shortly after dawn, feeling clean and refreshed. He strode toward the bank, past a pair of tents where Army men slept when they weren't guarding the *Hunley* or waiting anxiously for it to surface after another one of its tests. The *Hunley*'s crew had the luxury of staying in town. Miller nodded to a pair of sentries and stepped onto the dock, absently whistling Becker's favorite tune and heading to the submarine. He'd brought with him cleaning rags and lye soap, and a pitted wooden bucket.

In the early morning light, his face reflected back ghostly from the river's smooth surface. Miller had to admit that he didn't at all look nineteen. He looked like a boy, though at six-foot-four a tall one, freckle-faced and with wheat-blond hair that never laid flat. His nose was a little too long and hawkish to please him, and his chin had a deep dimple in the middle of it. Lieutenant Dixon had to know he wasn't nineteen. Miller grinned wide at the notion that he'd been accepted despite the obvious lie. He dipped the bucket in the river, chasing away his reflection, then was quick to the task of scrubbing the hatch covers of the submarine. He didn't have to do it, had never been assigned the job. But he was by nature fastidious, and when he was cleaning the *Hunley,* he had the submarine all to himself.

Miller was at the same time fascinated and frightened by the *Hunley,* and he was certain it would put him in newspaper articles and in history books—and somewhere in there make his father proud.

It had taken quite a bit of persuading to get Lieutenant Dixon to take Miller aboard. At the onset, Dixon already had a full crew—seven volunteers, six Army men and one from the Navy. Six of them were needed to turn the hand-cranked propeller, and one steered the contraption. Dixon kept watch on the compass and depth gauge and attended to other business. Not one more man could fit inside the submarine, and so Miller had spent days on the dock, glumly watching the *Hunley* sail down the Cooper River and disappear beneath the surface. Always without him.

But when one of the men was transferred—it happened three and-a-half weeks past—Miller dogged the Lieutenant even worse. Eventually his persistence landed him the open spot, and his chest had been swelling with pride ever since. He'd never considered himself happier. Still...sometimes...like yesterday afternoon when there was no air—and the day before, Miller cursed himself for wanting to be a part of all of this.

He opened the fore hatch and climbed inside, almost tipping the bucket as he held it above his head. The opening was only fourteen inches across, and so he even though he drew his shoulders together he always scraped his arms and wore at his shirts. Miller had to crouch and crawl inside, for while the *Hunley* looked impressive and weighed a hair better than four thousand pounds, it was actually quite small.

It was less than five feet wide and roughly twenty-five feet long, a deepened, cylindrical iron steam boiler that had been hammered to give it tapered ends and that was held together by rivets and iron strips. Lateral fins were part of a shaft attached to the submarine, and these were moved by a lever inside the *Hunley,* and helped the submarine to maneuver underwater. Lieutenant Dixon usually operated the rudder, which was moved by turning an iron wheel. When the entire crew was inside, there was very little room to move, and the air was very close and often stale.

The submarine had been fitted with a seacock and opposing ballast tanks, and Miller was trying his best to understand just how it all worked. He'd never been "book smart," as his father used the phrase. But Miller didn't consider himself stupid. He was certain Lieutenant Dixon didn't either, as the man had been patient with him, explaining that the tanks could be flooded when the valves were turned. Miller'd been set at one end two days past and given a chance to operate a tank, helping to send them to the bottom, then pumping the tanks dry so they could thankfully rise again. There was additional ballast—a fancy name for weights as far as Miller was concerned. And this was simply iron pieces that had been bolted to the bottom of the hull. Miller'd been taught that if the submarine had to surface quickly, Lieutenant Dixon would order the man assigned the wrench to unscrew a few bolts, which would drop the iron pieces.

"Damnedest thing ever made," Miller whistled appreciatively, as he started scrubbing the floor. "Damnedest thing, this submarine."

Miller had trouble reading, but he'd saved every newspaper clipping about the *Hunley* and her predecessors, fascinated by the Confederate submarines. Some of the stories he'd practically memorized, and his favorites he carried carefully-folded in his back pocket. First came the steam-driven *Davids.* Actually, Miller knew only one had been named *David,* this after her contracting engineer—David Chenowith Ebaugh, or perhaps after the David in David versus Goliath. In any event, everyone just called all of them *David* after that. The three-man *Pioneer* was born going on two years ago, christened in Louisiana's Lake Ponchartrain, and sunk to keep out of the Union's clutches. The *American Diver* came right after that, and it unfortunately sank during a storm at the mouth of Mobile Bay early this past February.

They and the *Davids* were smaller than the *Hunley,* and none of them had been very useful to this point, from what Miller could tell. They hadn't sank anything, which he considered the entire purpose of building such a thing as a submarine, though they had damaged a few Union boats. And the *Davids* couldn't wholly submerge because of their smokestacks and breathing tubes, which always stuck above the water.

From what Miller had read, the *Hunley* was privately built in Alabama and brought by rail to Charleston. And it seemed the *Hunley* was not so much an improvement on the Army-built *David,* as it had been an improvement on something built almost ninety years ago. That had been the *Turtle,* a one-man bulb-shaped boat that was hand-cranked like the *Hunley.* The *Turtle* hadn't done anything to the English back in 1776, but without it, perhaps the Confederates wouldn't have built the *Davids* or the *Pioneer,* the *American Diver* or the *Hunley.*

And had that been the case, Miller would have stayed out of the war and not risked suffocation in the belly of an iron boiler in his effort to be a part of the South's history.

When they were testing the very first *David,* it sank and suffocated its crew. The first crew had likewise died in earlier trials of the *Hunley,* and the submarine was hauled back up, inspected and fiddled with, and sent back down. The second crew died, too—even old H.L. himself died in the thing he had helped to finance and had named after him. All those deaths and his father's sharp words almost kept Miller from dogging Lieutenant Dixon into accepting him in this crew.

"Almost. But not quite." Miller shook his head and increased his efforts, rubbing at the seats now and deciding he'd clean the propeller crank next. He started humming "Stonewall Jackson's Way," unable to get Becker's tune out of his head. An hour later he was lightly polishing the mercury gauge, which would show how deep they were. The gauge went to ten fathoms, but Lieutenant Dixon claimed the submarine could go deeper than that.

"War makes men geniuses," Miller mused. It was only when times were dark, such as now between the North and the South, did men toil so hard to create such wonders as the *Hunley*. "And it makes boys like me foolish."

And just how deep could this wonder go with him inside it? Would Dixon take them all to the bottom of the ocean? Or would he simply try to exceed two hours and thirty-one minutes today?

Miller shuddered as he gathered his cleaning supplies and squeezed out the aft hatch, rubbing at a few spots on the small windows and checking the watertight rubber gaskets before he pronounced his morning project done. He spotted Lieutenant Dixon near the tents, talking to a handful of Army men. Wicks was there, too, and Simkins was approaching from behind the big red oak. As Miller hurried toward them, he saw Becker appear, in uniform save for a very Stonewall-like slouch hat. Becker scowled and dug the ball of his foot into the dirt, and Miller listened hard as he ran, trying to pick up on what the men were saying.

"Come back when the sun's setting, gentlemen," Dixon said. "Pass the word to the others. We'll be going out then, and it will be a late night. Make sure you get plenty of rest first."

"Where are we going?" Miller asked, his eyes falling on a dozen candles the Lieutenant had stuffed in his pockets.

Dixon narrowed his eyes.

"Where are we going...Sir?" Miller amended.

"Out," Dixon said after a fashion. The lieutenant's gaze drifted past the men and to the *Hunley*, seeing something very far beyond the submarine and the Cooper River.

"Another test, Sir?" Simkins risked.

Dixon slowly nodded. "You could say that, I suppose."

"What's it about...Sir?" Miller cut in. He was afraid Lieutenant Dixon would be sending them down at night to go past two hours and thirty-one minutes—when no one would be watching and no one would know they'd all suffocated.

"Guns, Too Tall. It's about General P.T. Beauregard and guns."

"I don't have a gun, Sir."

"You won't be needing one, Too Tall. If things go well, none of us will. But you can all bring full canteens, and a spare shirt and socks if you've a mind to."

* * *

Lieutenant Dixon had a pepperbox strapped to his hip, as did Becker and Wicks and Simkins, by the time the first rays of the setting sun hit the Cooper River. The water sparkled orange and gold like a tawdry lady's dress, with flashes of silver looking like glass beads. Miller always liked to stare at the river this time of the day, watching for jumping fish to set the colors to stirring. But Miller gave the Cooper only a passing glance now, as he squeezed through the aft hatch of the submarine, a second shirt folded tight under his arm. He and Lieutenant Dixon were the last two in this time, Dixon telling Miller he could work the ballast tanks tonight.

There was only a handful of Army men on the shore when the *Hunley* eased away from the dock and headed past Drum Island and toward Castle Pinckney across from Charleston proper. Becker started singing again, the song's rhythm setting the pace for the men to crank the propeller.

> He's in the saddle now! Fall in!
> Steady! The whole brigade!
> Hill's at the ford, cut off—we'll win
> His way out, ball and blade!
> What matter if our shoes are worn?
> What matter if our feet are torn?
> "Quick-step! We're with him before dawn!"
> That's Stonewall Jackson's way.

They submerged before they pulled even with the castle, Becker softly speculating that Dixon didn't want anyone in town to see the *Hunley* heading out. They surfaced again when they were beyond the city and steering roughly between Fort Moultrie on the northern shore and Fort Johnson to the south.

"Maybe whatever test General P.T. Beauregard has in mind tonight is a secret," Becker wondered aloud. "Maybe General Beauregard don't want no Northern sympathizers watching us and telling their kin." Already quite a bit of word had leaked out about the *Hunley* and the *Davids,* and there were reports the Union ships blockading the harbor were keeping a close watch for the submarines.

Becker wriggled himself a few more inches of space and made a show of managing to wedge his Stonewall slouch hat behind his neck. He'd been making sure everyone saw his hat and was clearly disappointed that no one had spoken of it. "Maybe Beauregard is done testing the *Hunley.* Maybe he's given us something to do."

The crew knew Beauregard had been cautiously overseeing the *Hunley,* not sure if the submarine was a good idea, but listening to Dixon's and his men's arguments that the *H.L. Hunley* could make a difference in the war.

"Maybe we're going to finally use the torpedo," Becker pressed. A pause. "Are we, Lieutenant?" It was usually always Becker who asked the questions everyone else was thinking. No use more than one man provoking the Dixon's ire.

Miller and the others looked to Lieutenant Dixon, waiting for an answer. The submarine had been fitted with the torpedo sometime during the afternoon. This consisted of a barrel-like copper cylinder filled with powder explosives. It was attached to the rear of the submarine by a twenty-foot thin line, and through the windows of the aft hatch Simkins nervously reported seeing it bob along. Becker had asked Dixon about the torpedo before climbing in the submarine, but Dixon hadn't answered then.

In the light of the candle, Lieutenant Dixon's face displayed a faint sheen of sweat. He was staring at a small map spread across his knees.

"Are we, Lieutenant?" Becker repeated with a little more volume—just in case Dixon hadn't heard him the first two times. "Are we going to use the torpedo against the Union?"

After a few moments Dixon raised his head. His eyes looked like dark pits and his face took on an uncharacteristically pensive expression that made Becker swallow the rest of his questions. Dixon tugged two candles from his pocket and set them on the narrow shelf next to the burning one. Then he folded the map and placed it in his front pocket.

"Faster," Dixon said.

"Aye, Sir!" Wicks said, putting more muscle into the task and starting to sing once more.

The sun's bright lances rout the mists
Of morning, and, by George!
Here's Longstreet struggling in the lists,
Hemmed in an ugly gorge.
Pope and his Yankees, whipped before,
"Bayonets and grape!" Hear Stonewall roar;
"Charge, Stuart! Pay off Ashby's score!"
Is Stonewall Jackson's way.

Ah, maiden, wait, and watch, and yearn
For news of Stonewall's band!
Ah, Widow, read, with eyes that burn...

"Faster," Lieutenant Dixon demanded. "And without that damn caterwauling. I think we've all had enough of that song, Mister Simkins."

They continued in relative silence for a while, submerging again when they were at Cummings Point and then beyond Morris Island, cranking the propeller until their arms were numb. The candle provided an eerie light, and at the same time its flame let them know the air was going.

"Up," Lieutenant Dixon said. He studied the map again and then consulted the compass. He made a rudder adjustment and stood so he could look out the hatch windows.

"Dark outside," Simkins announced. He was looking out the aft windows. The moon was only a sliver, and so there wasn't much light. But he was using what little there was, while craning his neck this way and that until he could see the torpedo. "Still there," he said, then sneezed.

Wicks rubbed at his nose and coughed just loud enough to let Simkins know he'd caught the older man's cold. "This *Hunley's* somethin'," he said to no one in particular. "But give me a real boat where you're sittin' up top and can see things. Don't like this, not seein' things."

"Doesn't matter," Miller whispered. "Dark up there. Dark down here. What's the difference?"

"Difference is," Wicks cut in, "if we were on a real boat there'd be things we could see."

Dixon tucked his head down. "There are several 'boats' up there, Wicks."

"The blockade." This from Becker.

Dixon nodded and took his seat. He used the stub of the first candle to light the next. "Yes, gentlemen, the Union blockade." A wave of the lieutenant's hand kept Becker from starting his questions again. "I've always contended this submarine could help the war," he began. "The tests have shown she's a worthy vessel. And General Beauregard has given us permission to strike a blow for our cause."

"We're going to use the torpedo on one of them Union ships," Simkins whistled. He finally ducked down from the aft hatch. "I see three of them, Lieutenant."

"There are five, gentlemen, one ironclad, four wood. Five Union ships keeping much-needed supplies from entering our fair harbor." The blockade had been in place for the past two years, since 1861. That first year only about one in a dozen ships attempting to run the blockade had been snared. Last year it was one in eight, as the Union had been building more ships. This year... Dixon told his men it was one in four. The blockade ran along four thousand miles of coastline, and it was because the divided nation's Secretary of State called it a blockade that the Confederate states could be declared a belligerent status and could welcome foreign profiteers brave enough to run the Union ships.

"We only got one torpedo," Simkins said. He was looking out the aft hatch windows again, eyes on the copper barrel of explosives. "Don't think that's going to be enough, Sir. Not against five of them."

"It'll have to be enough."

"But..."

"And you all will have to keep your voices down. We cannot afford to be heard, gentlemen."

"Or spotted," Wicks said in a hush. "Their canons could sink us."

Miller immediately thought of the first *David,* and the *Pioneer,* the *American Diver,* and even two previous crews worth of this *Hunley.* All sank. His chest started to feel tight, like a mule was slowly easing its weight down on him.

"Oh, I'm sure they'll see us all right," Lieutenant Dixon returned, his voice a conspiratorial whisper. "After we use our torpedo on one of them. But we don't want them to see us just yet." His orders were soft now, the men straining to hear each word and trying ever-so-hard to keep the rustling of their shirtsleeves and the cranking noise of the propeller to a minimum.

Dixon's eyes were moving constantly, from the compass to the map, to the men—all of them were sweating now from the heat and their nerves. Then he was looking through the hatch windows at the Union ships, then slowly and oh-so-quietly easing the hatch open so he could get his shoulders through it and get a better look.

The sound of the waves lapping against the *Hunley* reached the ears of the men. The sloshing was as rhythmical as their cranking of the propeller. There was something else, too...music, they decided after a moment. From somewhere outside the submarine, men were singing.

Becker cursed under his breath—it was a Union tune, something about sending all the Graybacks and Stonewall Jackson to their graves.

"A little farther men," Dixon urged as he climbed back down. "Just a..."

There was a grinding sound and the *Hunley* reeled and then stopped, the submarine's propeller refusing to be cranked. The submarine listed starboard.

Wicks growled and redoubled his efforts, nudging the men on either side to work their parts of the bar harder. Simkins nearly lost his balance at the aft hatch when the *Hunley* moved another two feet forward, then listed a little more and stopped again.

"What?" Dixon quietly demanded.

Wicks and the rest tried once more to work the propeller. "C'mon," he whispered. "We can..."

"Stop it," Dixon said. He held up the candle so he could better see Simkins. "What's going on out there?"

The older man drew down and faced Dixon, peering through the poor light. He pulled his lips into a thin line and shook his head. "That wondrous torpedo we been hauling...its line's fouled in the propeller, Sir. Almost sure of it. Has to be it. Can't see the torpedo now." He turned and looked through the aft hatch windows again. "Got to be it, Lieutenant Dixon. We ain't going anywhere. Maybe I can get out there and cut it loose. If it bumps up against us..." Simkins sneezed and drug his shirtsleeve under his nose, shuffled around to face Dixon again.

The lieutenant was stroking at his chin, the way a man might who had a beard. Some of the darkness had seeped from his eyes. "I suppose you'll have to do that," he said after only a moment's thought.

"I'm the better swimmer." Becker had been quiet for some time, and his voice startled Dixon.

Dixon offered him a sour grin and a single headshake.

Becker sat in the middle of the *Hunley,* and the only way he would get out of the hatch was if three men preceded him.

"No. I think I am the better swimmer, Sir." Miller looked up at Dixon and dropped his hand to the knife on his belt. "And my Arkansas toothpick's awfully sharp."

Dixon nodded at this notion, and Miller managed to tug off his boots. The lieutenant squeezed back against the submarine wall as with some effort Miller wormed his way past and up the hatch.

"You be careful, Too Tall," Wicks offered.

"I'm always careful," Miller replied, too soft for Wicks to hear.

Then Dixon was following Miller up, stopping when his shoulders cleared the hatch and watching the young man crawl along the top of the listing *Hunley.* "Wait, Miller..."

He turned and tried to read Lieutenant Dixon's face, fearful the man would call him back and he'd lose a chance to get a page in some history book all to himself.

Dixon kept his voice low. "You say you can swim well, Too Tall. Can you also swim far?"

Miller gave a boyish grin and nodded, catching onto Lieutenant Dixon's cobbled-together plan. "I can do it, Sir. It's not too far after all."

"Good man, Miller."

Miller crawled to the aft hatch, noting that Simkins had his face pressed against the windows. He was careful not to crack his knees against anything and make a noise that might alert the Union soldiers. He could hear them, singing off-key, and he thought that Becker's voice wasn't so bad after all.

The faint breeze was salty and fresh, and it felt cold against his sweat-beaded skin. It was just strong enough to cause the canvas of a lowered sail to flap on the nearest wooden ship.

Miller could see all of the ships from here, the four wood and the single ironclad, which was thankfully the farthest away and which was definitely not something he wanted to see up-close. In the light of the moon sliver, the Union ship's masts looked like blackened sticks, tall pines caught in a forest fire. Picking through the shadows, he could see men moving on the decks of the closest two ships. Maybe a dozen on one, and none of them were walking about with any real purpose as far as he could tell.

Careless, Miller decided, definitely. They're all so confident and... Then he quickly changed his opinion. The nearest ship had men in the rigging, with spyglasses trained toward the open sea. And when he squinted and looked past that closest ship and to the next, he saw another man high on the mast. They were being diligent about the blockade after all. He prayed that the *Hunley,* so low in the water, would remain unnoticed.

Miller climbed to the far side of the aft hatch, dipping his head to grin at Simkins before he slipped into the water. It felt slightly warmer than the air, and it smelled strongly of salt. A river boy, Miller had never been out to sea, and the taste of the water in his mouth almost made him gag. He tugged the knife from his belt and placed it between his teeth, then he swam to the rear of the *Hunley* and sucked in a breath. The line dragging the torpedo indeed had become wrapped in the propeller. The thin rope was tangled badly and chewed, and Miller knew it wouldn't take too much work to cut it away. The problem was, it had pulled the torpedo to within a few feet of the submarine, and the waves were bringing it dangerously closer.

Miller treaded water, one hand touching the *Hunley.* He glanced over his shoulder, toward the fore hatch, from his vantage point seeing only the silhouetted head and shoulders of Lieutenant Dixon. He couldn't see the man's face, and he couldn't risk calling to him asking for advice. He could swim to the fore section of the submarine and whisper. But that would take precious moments, and the waves were still nudging the torpedo.

Could Lieutenant Miller see what was happening? What would he want me to do? Didn't matter, Miller instantly decided, interposing himself more firmly between the torpedo and the aft end of the *Hunley,* the tangled rope brushing against his left arm, the torpedo being nudged toward his chest now. That mule was sitting squarely on him again, hurtfully so and making it hard to breathe—even though there were no walls and no flickering candle, plenty of air everywhere.

God, it felt like he was suffocating all over again!

He could make out no details on the torpedo, but he'd seen it this afternoon. It looked like a small water barrel, though made of hammered copper. One end was tapered, and there was some mechanism on this end, near the rope, with prongs sticking out of it. Simkins had explained that if the prongs connected with something hard, they'd depress, setting off the charge of explosives. Ninety pounds of explosives. The intent had been to drag the torpedo close to a ship, submerge beneath, and let the explosives catch against the enemy's side and detonate.

Biting down hard on the knife blade and feeling its edge against his tongue, Miller stretched out his right arm, just below the surface of the water. He slammed his eyes shut, prayed to God, and waited.

What would it feel like? Being blown to pieces by the explosives that were crammed in that copper barrel? Would he feel anything? Would the torpedo kill the men inside the *Hunley,* too?

A moment later he felt the underside of the torpedo bump against his palm and he felt the furnace in his chest being rapidly stoked. His breath was ragged, and despite the coolness of the breeze against his face he was sweating furiously. He stopped treading and felt himself sinking.

"Miller?" The word was a whisper, barely heard. "You be quick about this, then come back to us. Miller?"

"M' all right," he answered, a little louder than he intended. He opened his eyes and started moving his legs again to keep himself afloat, the material in his trousers threatening to tangle him like the rope had tangled up the propeller. Miller tried to calm himself and slow his breathing, neither effort being successful.

With his right hand still against the torpedo, cupping it just under what he considered its nose—inches from where the mechanism would be—he held it an arm's length from the *Hunley.*

"M' all right," he whispered to himself. "All right. All right. All right for the moment anyway." He brought his left hand up until it wrapped around the rope. Then he slowly turned, until the torpedo was against his right shoulder and that hand was free. How close was his shoulder to that mechanism? And if the prongs brushed against him, was he a hard enough object to set off the charge? Miller suddenly felt much older than his sixteen years, older than the nineteen he'd lied about to the lieutenant. He took the knife from his mouth and tried once more to futilely stop his heart from hammering so. "M' all right."

"Miller?"

"You can toe the mark, Too Tall," he whispered to himself. "You ain't no Sunday Soldier, no kid-glove boy." In fact, there wasn't any boy left in him. He was as much of a man as any one of the soldiers sitting inside the *Hunley.* "You can do this." A deep breath and he started carefully cutting the line, each slice oddly in time with the shushing of the waves and the beat of the Union men's song, and each so slight and gentle so as not to jostle the torpedo and risk striking the mechanism. He was cutting the tangle of line free from the propeller first, making sure all of the rope was away from the blades, then nudging the blades to make sure they could turn. Then he worked on the last snag, trying to leave some rope still attached to the torpedo.

"Miller?" Lieutenant Dixon's whisper again.

"Fine," he said softly. "But them damn Mudsills won't be much longer if I have anything to do about it." Miller contorted around so he could sheath his knife, keeping his left hand firmly around the length of rope still tied to the torpedo. The remaining rope was little more than two feet long, not near long enough to suit him. He swam slowly and awkwardly with it, and figured he looked a bit like a frog. He didn't glance over his shoulder to the *Hunley,* though he wanted to know if Lieutenant Dixon was still watching or if he was moving the submarine farther away. He couldn't hear Dixon or his fellows. All he heard was the Union men singing and the sloshing of the water. And all he could do was pray that the torpedo would not blow up while he was attached to it.

Miller wasn't sure how long it took him to frog-swim from the *Hunley* to the nearest Union ship. It was long enough that his legs and arms felt on fire from the effort, and that he was breathing so deeply that he feared the men on deck would hear him. They weren't singing anymore, but they were talking. He could pick out only a few scattered words: "Charleston," "wallpapered," and "greenbacks." And after a few minutes: "Tom caught the quick-step." He faintly heard the creak of the deck, someone walking across it, and the groan of wood from the mast.

Then he was up against the hull, laying the torpedo parallel to it—not having the courage or a large enough dose of foolishness to ram the mechanism against the ship and destroy it and kill himself in the process. Lieutenant Dixon had told him to come back to them, after all. Sixteen years was not old enough to die, he thought.

But how old were the men on that ship?

Miller thrust that thought from his mind. He didn't know all the intricacies of the war—what precisely had started it, what all was being fought over. And he wasn't sure he wanted to know. It was more than about slaves and about this blockade, and maybe one day he would study about it. He'd only involved himself because of this submarine. He was more caught up in the inventions of the war...the *Davids,* the *Pioneer,* the *American Diver* and his precious *Hunley*...the North's hot air balloons...and even the North's pitiful attempt at their own submarine. The *Alligator* they called it, Miller remembered from some obscure newspaper clipping. Men were at their best inventing things, he knew, when they were on their worst behavior by waging war against each other.

Miller realized he was at his best, too, finding courage he didn't know he had and volunteering to do this damn fool thing. He'd pushed off from the Union ship, swimming quickly and not worrying about any splashing he might make. He wanted only to be away from the torpedo, which the waves were forcing up against the enemy's hull. Miller barely spotted the *Hunley,* so low in the water and black against the dark water. The sliver of moonlight briefly revealed the silhouette of Lieutenant Dixon. Every muscle screamed for rest, but Miller picked up his pace, pushing the ache in his limbs to the back of his mind and focusing only on that silhouette.

With every stroke he expected to be discovered and to hear an explosion. Neither happened, not even by the time he reached the *Hunley* and had to be practically pulled up its side by Dixon. He felt like a discarded rag doll, but the lieutenant slapped him on the back—that lone gesture giving him the strength to follow Dixon inside. The submarine was no longer listing.

The men were congratulating him, Becker's voice the loudest. Miller nodded politely, as he folded himself onto his seat.

"I don't understand, Sir," Miller said, waving his fellows to silence. "I put that torpedo against that ship. All of that bumping with the waves...I thought it would have exploded by now. How could..."

Dixon didn't reply, raising himself again through the fore hatch and peering at the closest Union ship, then returning below. "There's British ships nearby, so Beauregard's sources say. That's why we're out here. They're sitting somewhere out there and waiting for a break in the blockade. And I told Beauregard we'd give them that break. It's all about guns, gentlemen. Those ships are bringing guns that we need, and we're to give them the cotton that they treasure and make their captains rich men."

"I'm sorry, Sir," Miller began. "I should've shoved that torpedo against that ship. I should've..."

"You did more than I expected," Lieutenant Dixon cut back. "The torpedo just hasn't hit the hull at the right angle, that's all. Maybe all we have to do is get that ship to turn."

"And how can we do that?" This from Wicks, who was waving for the piss jug.

In the light of a new candle, Dixon gave his men a rare smile. "Why, we get that ship to notice us, gentlemen. We get her to turn and chase us. Then we'll see if we can get that torpedo to work."

"Too dark," Miller said. Those two words threatened to erase Dixon's smile. "This submarine sits so low in the water. Everything's too dark. I could hardly see the *Hunley,* Sir. And that was only 'cause I knew where to look. I could barely see you. We ain't got a sail or anything to catch their notice."

Lieutenant Dixon stroked his chin and glanced down the row at each of his men. His eyes came to rest on Becker. "Your slouch hat, Arnold."

"Sir?"

"We'll use it for our sail." Dixon waggled his fingers at the man.

With a frown and a shrug Becker reached behind him, tugging free his "Stonewall" hat and passing it down the line to the Lieutenant.

"That long wrench, Wicks."

Wicks was quick to comply.

Then the lieutenant was up the fore hatch again, raising his arm high—the wrench held in it and the slouch hat on top of that. "Sing, Becker!" Dixon hollered. "Sing as loud as you can. And get your hands on the bar, gentlemen. We'll be needing to move quickly."

In the belly of the Hunley Becker cleared his throat and tapped his fingers on the bar to set the rhythm.

> Away from Mississippi's vale
> With my ol' hat there for a sail
> I crossed upon a cotton bale
> To the Rose of Alabamy.
>
> Oh brown Rosie
> Rose of Alabamy!
> That sweet tobacco posey
> Is the Rose of Alabamy.

The Rose of Alabamy? Miller thought. Becker knows more than one song after all. He coughed to clear his lungs of the salt water he'd gulped down, then he joined in:

> Away from Mississippi's vale
> With my ol' hat there for a sail

"Louder!" Dixon ordered. "Sing it much, much louder!"

The men complied, their craggy voices bouncing off the iron walls of the *Hunley* and finding their way outside the submarine and drifting with the breeze.

"It's working!" Dixon shouted. He was waving the wrench, slouch hat catching the scant moonlight and catching the attention of the men on the deck of the Union ship. "Louder!"

A flapping sound faintly registered, and Dixon said it was sails being raised. "She's coming at us, gentlemen!"

"Bully!" Becker cheered.

Dixon was ducking down, Simkins, too, both men sealing the hatches.

"Miller?"

The young man was quick to work the ballast tanks. "Taking the *Hunley* down, Sir!"

The submarine hadn't wholly submerged when it was pitched wildly by an explosion.

"Bully!" Becker and Wicks shouted in unison.

Dixon stood and peered through the window. "I see fire, gentlemen. Good work, Miller. Good work, indeed!"

They took the *Hunley* farther out to sea, past the blockade, then brought her up so they could better see the carnage.

The night was lit up by the burning ship, and the air was filled with the desperate cries of men. The Union vessel was listing dangerously, and after a few minutes Dixon announced that it had begun to sink.

"That's what submarines were made for," Miller said. "To sink ships."

"Stonewall Jackson'd be right proud of us!" Becker said.

"Yes, indeed," Wicks chimed in. "Stonewall'd be right proud."

The other Union ships were moving closer and searching the water, looking for whatever had brought down the doom, and looking for men who'd jumped overboard. It would be days before Dixon and his men learned that in the commotion two big British ships were able to slip past the distracted blockade, riding low in the water because of the guns, ammunition, and other much-needed supplies riding heavy in their holds. And no one would ever know the *Hunley* was responsible, General P.T. Beauregard wanting to keep this night's activities quiet so the ploy could be used again.

The *Hunley* waited at a safe distance, cloaked by the black water, Dixon and Simkins describing the ship slipping below the water and the efforts of the Union men to save as many of their brethren as possible.

"Sir?" Miller asked after several minutes. "I was wondering if..." The rest of his words were drowned by a yawn.

"How do we return to the Cooper now?" Becker finished for him. "They'll be watching."

"We don't go back." The smile spread clear across Dixon's face now. "At least not for a while. That's why I asked you to bring an extra shirt, gentlemen. We're going south, along the Georgia coast. Slip in and get some more torpedoes, see if we can break another part of the blockade. Though we'll see if we can use the torpedoes properly this time. Then we'll come back home and see what else General Beauregard has planned."

And then I'll go home and visit my father, Miller thought, tell him what I did. I think—like Stonewall Jackson—he'd be right proud of me.

Excerpts from the songs "Stonewall Jackson's Way" and "The Rose of Alabamy," were used in this tale. Although this story of the Hunley's *exploits is fictional, on February, 17th, 1864, the real* H.L. Hunley *became the first submarine to sink an enemy ship. She rammed her spar torpedo into the Union sloop* Housatonic, *an ironclad. The* Hunley, *herself, was believed to have sunk shortly thereafter, perhaps damaged in the blast and unable to surface. Divers and archeologists are currently working with the crew's and the submarine's remains.*

History books show her crew consisted of Lieutenant George Dixon of the Company E 21st Alabama Volunteers; James A. Wicks; C.F. Carlson; Arnold Becker; F. Collins; C. Simkins; Ridgeway of the Confederate Navy; and Miller.

Heat

I attended an annual dinner for my husband's Water Utility one fall. And since I didn't know many people there, and since I was a tad...uhm, bored...I spent some time studying the program lying on the table. There were wonderfully interesting names listed under the various recognition categories, and so I borrowed a few, my favorite of which appears here—Manni Rizzo. Because I love museums, I decided to set this tale in one, and the Field came to mind. It bothered me that they stuck a McDonald's fast-food restaurant in it, and so I had to put in my proverbial two cents. I thought the neon golden arches took away from the class of the place. "Heat" was originally published in The Repentant, *DAW Books, 2003.*

The beads of sweat were thick on Street's face, running into his eyes and down his neck and forming—he was certain—a veritable river that coursed along his spine and spread out at the waistband of his favorite jeans. It didn't help that he was wearing mostly black, a well-lined leather jacket he'd lifted from The Alley on Clark last week, and under that a black T-shirt, long-sleeved. On his feet were leather Reeboks, also taken from The Alley, though these from a visit two months or so back—he'd had plenty of time to break them in. A snug cap, grabbed from a store in the HIP, kept his hair from hanging loose, but the cap was wool and at the moment only contributed to his discomfort. He felt thoroughly sodden in the clothes, his chest tight from the dry air and the painful cocooning warmth, his nerves on edge. It hurt to breathe.

He glanced down, seeing, in the gray half-light spilling in through the cracks in the vent, that even the backs of his hands were slick with sweat. Should've waited 'til the summer. Damn fool thing to do this now. Summer would've been the time.

In the summer the air conditioning would be on, rather than the furnace—which on this late December evening was steadily spewing a stream of hot air through the aluminum duct into which Street and his friend had carefully and oh-so-quietly wedged themselves.

You'd think they would've turned back the heat when everybody left and they locked up—which was an hour ago by Street's reckoning. But the furnace was still making the occasional and almost melodic popping sounds that drifted his way.

He blinked the sweat clear from his eyes, stared at his watch and pushed the stem—it was one of those cheap Timex's he wouldn't have normally lowered himself to pinch. But he'd taken this one because the face glowed green so you could see what time it was if you were in a dark movie theater. *Or,* he thought, *in a frigging hot air duct in the men's bathroom of the Field Museum.*

Aloud, Street whispered: "We'll wait another couple of minutes, Manni. Just to be on the safe side."

"Safe? We ain't safe. We gonna die in here, Street," came a gravely voice from just behind him.

Street kicked at Manni's face to shut him up, the tip of his shoe instead hitting the duct wall and making a loud "thrum."

"Shit."

"Street..."

"Another couple of minutes, I said." Or maybe more now because of the noise he'd just made. "Another couple of minutes, Manni. Keep your mouth shut forgodssake."

It was actually closer to a half-hour before Street popped the vent cover off and eased himself to the floor below, taking in great gulps of the cooler air as he helped Manni and his pillowcases out. Then he replaced the cover without making a sound and held his finger to his lips to keep Manni quiet. Manni retaliated with a different finger gesture, then was quick to use the facilities.

"Manni. Hurry up."

"Hurry? You kept us in the damn vent for hours," Manni shot back. "You can gimme a minute. Ain't never stuck with you in a vent for that long, Street. Ain't never gonna do it again."

Street shook his head and looked out the narrow window. It was snowing outside—hard—and the flakes hitting the glass melted, sliding snakelike down and picking up the lights of passing cars and looking neon against the backdrop darkness. He pressed his face to the glass, which helped to cool him a little. Then he almost reluctantly turned away and caught a glimpse of himself in a long mirror. The overhead light sputtered and tinted everything a dingy yellow. He squared his shoulders and grabbed for a paper towel, dabbing at the sweat on his face.

Street considered himself a handsome man, his smooth skin the color of the Irish Cream Coffee he favored at the Starbucks across from his flat. His six-foot frame was lean and straight, slightly muscular from working out, and with broad shoulders that gave his shadow the appearance of a dagger stuck into the bathroom's tiled floor.

Manni Rizzo was another matter. At least a head shorter than Street, he was winter pale, with a shock of chestnut-colored hair that was perpetually uneven and that never lay right. He looked unhealthily thin, save for an odd little paunch of a belly that was usually accentuated because of the tight-fitting shirts he insisted on wearing.

"Ready, Manni?" Street glided toward the door and listened. No clicking of night watchmen heels. Nothing. "C'mon. And stay quiet."

Manni grumbled and grabbed for the paper towels, wiping at the sweat, then discarding them and quickly following Street out into the first floor of the museum proper.

To Street's right, he could see the hazy amber glow from the muted counter lights in the McDonald's. It didn't seem right, there being a McDonald's in the Field Museum. Street figured a modern fast-food restaurant had no call to be in a place filled with antiques and long-dead things. Should be some old sidewalk cafe you might find in nineteenth-century Germany or France, or better yet a replica of Chicago's first hotdog stand serving up something smothered in sauerkraut and onions, something of historical significance to the city. No place for a friggin' Big Mac and fries, he thought. He could faintly smell the grease from the place.

"Hey, Street." Manni edged by him, tapped his toe and looked skittishly around. "Street..."

Street ignored him, turning away from the McDonald's and craning his neck around a pole. He was listening intently, making sure they were alone, and getting his bearings in a museum made ghostly by the dimmed lighting. *At least they're conserving on electricity,* he thought. *But it could be pitch black in here for all I care. I could still find my way.* Indeed, Street knew his way around the place well, having visited it every other day for the past three weeks, staying for hours, scoping out everything. Before that, he hadn't set foot in the place since he was a kid dragged here by his mother—who insisted history was good for him.

He knew where the security cameras were, not positioned near as well as they could be—and thus giving him and Manni paths they could take without risk of showing up on some television monitor. These paths he'd committed to memory, of course. He also knew which stairs to use, and how far up to go, knew where the loading dock exits were, and the back door in particular by which he planned to leave. Cut across a stretch of parking lot, across a field and to his car parked a few blocks away. He knew that a window in a far lecture hall on the ground floor had loose panes and would provide a secondary way out if something prevented him from getting to the loading dock.

He'd thoroughly cased the place, more diligently than any store he and Manni had robbed in the past several years. Only difference was this wasn't a store. It was the frigging Field Museum, a veritable Chicago landmark. And they weren't after money or Rolexes or electronics, CDs or Nikes or designer clothes this time.

This was the Big Time.

Street knew precisely what he wanted. It was two floors up and all the way to the back, in the Special Exhibits Gallery. It was only going to be here another few weeks, which is why he and Manni had to do this now. In the summer there might be another special exhibit worth a second visit—provided this one went without a hitch. It would be a cooler trip. But it wouldn't be any easier than it was tonight. Street suspected that right now there would be fewer guards on duty than usual—two days before New Year's there had to be extra guys on vacation. A skeleton crew to contend with.

"'M Still hot," Manni whispered. He pulled his collar away from his neck and fanned his hand in front of his face. "Ain't doin' no more ducts with you in the winter, Street. Should just bust in a back door."

Street didn't reply. But he unzipped his jacket and gained some more relief from the heat for himself. He touched the T-shirt beneath to discover it was as wet as if he'd just washed it in the sink. Sticky. When he put it on late this afternoon and slipped out of the apartment, Leena asked where he was going "dressed so dark and all."

"Me and Manni got some business, Lee," was all he told her. "Be back before midnight."

Good thing he'd glanced through *The Reader* Leena'd brought home last month. Good thing he saw the notice about the museum exhibit. Good thing she made some sort of snide comment about why didn't he rip off something valuable like this rather than the crap he'd been bringing home and fencing. Should've been Big Time ten years ago.

"Hey, Street." Tap, tap, tap.

Street roused himself from his musings and motioned for his friend to follow, gliding down one wide corridor, sticking to the south wall, taking a jog and squeezing past Bushman, the huge stuffed gorilla which in life had been on exhibit at the Lincoln Park Zoo.

"Street."

He slipped past a room marked the Sea Mammals Black Box Theater and then cut by the Kid's Field Trip Store.

"Street," Manni repeated a little louder. Tap, tap, tap with his foot. "Ebenezeer."

Street stopped, whirled, and glared. He hated being called by his given name—Ebeneezer. Ebeneezer St. Peter, as in Saint Peter, a moniker that had been passed down by his father and grandfather. He didn't like it, instead accepting the nicknames he'd picked up from Leena and friends and enemies, and the aliases he'd created, among them: Christmas, The Christmas Man, 'Neeze, 'Neezer, Scrooge, The Saint of Rush Street, Saint E, E-Pete, E. Z. Street, and his favorite, just Street.

"Manni, keep it quiet, I said," Street hissed. "Quiet and stay behind me."

"I'm thirsty, Street. Can't cool off. Got so hot in that duct, I..." Manni gestured past the Field Trip Store and to an arched doorway. The light from a pair of vending machines reflected off the polished floor. Manni swallowed and stared, a deer caught in headlights, Street likened him to.

Street tugged on his friend's arm and pointed to the stairwell at the back. They took the steps two at a time, quiet in their sweat-slippery shoes. Street imagined he heard the squish-squish of his socks against the insoles and felt blisters being born. On the next level he pressed his ear to the door. "Gotta take a different stairway now," he whispered to Manni, nodding with his head to show a surveillance camera up on the wall a few feet that would pick them up if they climbed this one to the next level.

Manni nodded and followed Street out into a main exhibit hall, hugging a pillar to stay out of sight of another slowly swiveling camera. There was an eerie stillness to this hall that chased a shiver down Street's back. It was the intenseness of the quiet, perhaps, that had finally settled in and decided to bother him. He'd noticed the quiet on the first floor, too, but his ire over the McDonald's, coupled with his nerves at stepping up to Big Time, had kept him occupied, kept the quiet from niggling at his craw. Like a tomb, he thought. Quiet like the mausoleum where his grandfather's ashes were kept. Quiet like the stores they'd robbed after hours. But this quiet was more serious, and inside the thick walls of the museum, they didn't hear the traffic that must be zooming by outside. The other places they'd robbed were up against sidewalks, and the noise of hookers and their marks, sometimes of bums and gang members, intruded—and there was always the sound of the traffic. But not here. Nothing intruded except the sound of their own breathing. Like a tomb. Best finish this job and get out of here—out to the cold air and the city noise.

"Geeze, Street. Take a look at that!" Manni broke the uneasy quiet, forgetting himself and practically shouting.

Street elbowed him in the side and instantly regretted taking his friend on this job. Small Time was probably better suited to Manni Rizzo. Radio Shacks didn't pose the threat getting caught in this place did. Street had no intention of doing time in Stateville because of Manni's big mouth.

"Look at that, Street." The words a faint whisper now.

"It's Sue."

Manni cocked his head and strained to hear Street's soft voice.

"Sue. The T-Rex skeleton. It was in the paper. Don't you read? They called it Sue after some farmer's wife." Street had seen the colossal thing every other day for the past three weeks. The towering monstrosity gazed down at them through empty sockets, the silence wrapped tightly around the thing and stretching out to Street. The shadow it cast in the dim light wavered.

Another shiver, then Street thrust his nervousness aside. Just bones. Not even bones, actually. No big deal. He thought he should have been impressed by Sue. But it was just a collection of fossils, he told himself, just dead matter. It wasn't even the dinosaur's real head that was poised above them. It was a plaster replica. The real thing was on the next floor up, along with a printed explanation that it was too heavy to set on the skeleton.

Manni was watching the surveillance camera, then without warning skidded out after it swung to the left, darted onto the display and knelt at Sue's foot.

"Manni!" a whispered shout from Street. "What the hell are you doing? We ain't here to mess with the dinosaur."

"A souvenir," Manni shot back. "I'm gonna give this to my old man. Late Christmas present. Pappa Rizzo'll love this."

"Forgodssake, Manni."

"Just a foot bone's all," came the muted reply. "Ain't no one in the museum gonna miss it." Then he was back at Street's side, clinging to the pillar and holding up his prize.

"What if that thing had tipped over?"

Manni shrugged and put the fossil in his pocket. "Thing wasn't gonna tip over, Street. Really had to work at it to get it, though. All wired up. Had to cut it and..."

Street glared at him.

"We should get goin', Street, I think I hear somethin'. Maybe a guard."

Street tugged Manni through the North American Birds exhibit, then turned and cut down through the World of Animals display. Out of the corner of his eye, he saw a night watchman, uniform pressed, ID clipped to his pocket, flashlight held out and beam bouncing ahead of him, soles clicking rhythmically against the floor.

Must've heard Manni's *Look at that.* "Shit," Street hissed.

The watchman angled the light through the bird exhibit, and he paused, as if he was debating whether to go down the aisle for a looksee. He trained the light on the floor, and Street sucked in his breath. The beam didn't quite reach to where they were. Had the watchman indeed heard Manni? Or had they dropped something along the way? A pillowcase? No. Manni had both of them tucked under his belt. Maybe the sweat. All that sweat, maybe some had run off, leaving a trail on the tile.

But after a moment the watchman retreated, heels clicking away, light bobbing and then disappearing. Street and Manni let out a collective deep breath, and Manni looked innocently away to avoid his friend's icy stare.

Then Street was heading south, past a display of stuffed lions, one standing and the other lying on a rock. The Lions of Tsavo, there were called, subject of a movie Street remembered seeing quite a few years back—*The Ghost and the Darkness* with Michael Douglas. Male lions, it didn't seem right to Street that they didn't have their manes on. A McDonald's, and male lions that looked like female ones, Street mused. And a dinosaur with a plaster head rather than the real one. Museum's got some problems. Well, it's gonna have another one 'fore the night's out—it's gonna be minus some real expensive stuff.

Street gestured with his head and Manni kept up with him, passing the Africa exhibit and the African Resource Center, then cutting through the Ancient Egypt Display.

"Street!" Manni hushed. "Look at this!"

Hadn't the man ever been to a museum before? Street groaned as Manni skidded past him. Now this place really did look like a tomb—moreso now with the dimmed lighting then when Street had been through it during the day. The quiet was thick here, too, the soft slapping of Manni's tennis shoes echoing eerily. Street let out a deep sigh, this sound, too, unnerving.

"Hate the quiet and the heat," Street whispered.

The heat was oppressive in this exhibit—and dry, a condition he'd noted here during the day, probably to preserve everything or to make the patrons feel like they were in an Egyptian desert. *I'll give you one minute, Manni,* he thought. *One minute, then we're upstairs. And no more Big Time jobs for you, Manni Rizzo. Better enjoy tonight.*

Manni was struggling to take it all in—the images of bronze and stone, a funerary boat that Street knew from a previous visit belonged to Senwosret III. There were two chapel rooms from the tombs of Unis-ankh and Netcher-user, and fortunately Manni wasn't interested in these. He was heading straight to a sarcophagus, making oohing and ahhing sounds as he made a move to touch the thing inside. Street shot forward, his hand grabbing Manni's just in time.

"Motion sensor," Street said.

Manni shook his head. "Already looked. There isn't a motion sensor on anything in here."

"You're an idiot, Manni. You wanna see the mummies? You come back during regular hours. Take a tour or something. Understand? Stare at Sue and the Bushman and anything else you want to. I ain't gonna do no time 'cause you're making like a school boy." Street shook his head for emphasis and paced in front of a catlike statue, the ears of which were badly chipped. It was said to be one of the finest Egyptian representations of a cat ever found, a scarab set on its forehead, a sacred eye appearing on its chest. Street thought it was ugly. "You gotta be taking this serious, Manni."

Manni nodded and ground the ball of his foot against the tile floor. "'M sorry, Street. Let's go get the jewels and get out of here." Behind Street's back, he dug his penknife into the cat statue's head, retrieved the scarab and thrust it in his pocket. "Merry Christmas Pappa Rizzo," Manni whispered.

They cut across Stanley Field Hall and slipped into the display on Ancient North America and Mesoamerica. Street lost Manni for a moment—he'd jimmied the door on the Filed Museum Store, rushed in and retrieved a denim

"Eye of Horus" baseball cap, a Sue keychain, and a pen with a rubber lizard on the top.

"Dammit, Manni."

Manni grinned sheepishly and plowed ahead, through the Yates Exhibition Center and...paused when he heard music. "Street..." he whispered.

"I hear it."

"Boz Skaggs. Lido Shuffle."

Street pressed his friend up against a wall and stepped past, craning his neck around a corner and seeing a small room where a light bulb hung down over a small wooden table. There was a radio, a deck of cards, and two guards drinking Dr. Pepper and chatting.

"Trib says Jordan's thinking about coming back," the one with his back to the doorway said.

The other shook his head, his policeman-like hat almost falling off. "Speculation. Just something to sell papers. Jordan ain't coming back. And the Bulls ain't never going to be great again. Your deal, Mick."

Street recognized the one named Mick when the fellow turned to grab the deck. He'd been the one with the flashlight, the one that had almost caught them by the North American Birds.

Mick called one-eyed jacks wild and took a pull on the soda. "Be good, though, it would, if Jordan did come back."

Street stared at the men, certain they couldn't see him from his shadowy vantage point. A moment more, then he backtracked, Manni on his heels, until they were at the Museum Store again.

"Now what?" Manni said. "The stairs are past that room, you said. And to get to the jewels we gotta..."

"Take a different way," Street cut in. On his previous trips to the museum the door had been closed to that little room, and Street hadn't realized guards would be there now—or that they'd have left the door open. Shouldn't they be patrolling? Shouldn't they be protecting the museum from folks like him and Manni? Well, mark up another thing to complain to the alderman about—lax museum guards. Probably getting twelve bucks an hour to play poker and listen to the Boz. If he ran the museum, things would be different.

"There's more stairs back here, Manni. C'mon."

Manni adjusted the brim on his new hat and gestured for Street to lead the way. Through the Eskimos and Northwest Coast Indians section they went, pausing at a temporary exhibit—Kachinas: Gifts from the Spirit Messengers. Arrayed in glass cases were colorful carved wooden figurines. Kachinas, Street had learned when he read the signs last week. They were supposed to symbolize spirit messengers and act as intermediaries between the Hopi Indians and the supernatural realm. Thought to provide rain and improve crops in a harsh desert land, the dolls were often given to children and women to strengthen their religious beliefs. On the spur of the moment, Street decided these had to be valuable.

"This case, Manni. Don't see any motion sensors."

Manni concurred, thoroughly examining the case and the floor around it before pulling out his penknife and wires and going to work. A few heartbeats later a dozen of the figures were inside one of the pillowcases. "Papa Rizzo'll..."

"Go to our fence if he wants one of these, Manni. The damn dinosaur bone's enough."

"Street..."

Street gave his friend a baleful look.

"It ain't about gettin' presents for my dad."

Street turned away, but Manni tapped on his shoulder. "Street..."

A raised eyebrow, still the glare.

"Street, I think I heard something. One o' them watchmen. Listen."

Street did, picking through the still-unnerving silence and detecting a repeated "shush." He slipped back down the corridor to the guardroom. Mick and his friend were just finishing a hand. Street listened again. The "shush" was slightly louder, closer. He turned and practically ran back to Manni.

"It's another guard. I knew they'd have more than two," Street said, his voice so soft Manni couldn't catch all the words. "A smart guard. No leather heels. Don't think he has a flashlight either. I didn't see him. But I'm sure he didn't see me either."

Manni snatched up another doll, and looked to Street for advice. Into the pillowcase with it, then the last two from the shelf joined it. "You want we should find a place to hide?"

Street drew his lips into a thin line and pointed to the far corner, where a faint light glowed from behind a glass panel on a metal door. "Service stairs," he mouthed. "Move."

Manni did, trying to be quiet, but the dolls softly clacked together in the pillowcase. Then more noise intruded on the otherwise silence of the museum, the creak of the doorknob being turned by Manni's sweaty fingers, the metal groan the door made when Manni tugged it open.

"Quiet!" Street hushed, knowing Manni couldn't do anything about the dolls or the door, and why had they stopped for the damned Hopi trinkets to begin with. It hadn't been in Street's original plan. "Move. Up the stairs." He heard a "shush" before he fell in behind Manni and closed the door behind him. His fingers fumbled for a moment, trying to find a lock. There wasn't one. So Street pressed his ear to the door, feeling the cool metal against his face. He didn't hear anything beyond it.

A glance through the window panel. Nothing. No movement. No flashlight beam. There was only the dim light in this stairwell, and only the soft clacking the dolls made as Manni hurried up the steps.

The dolls. They weren't part of the plan, Street cursed. Maybe there was a motion sensor after all. Maybe there was some silent alarm that was triggered when they busted into the case. Maybe the dolls were so valuable that something had been rigged to them to alert a guard.

He took the stairs three at a time, wondering if they should leave at this moment, be content with the Hopi spirit dolls. But there was Leena to consider, and the jewels upstairs. This was the Big Time, Street knew. And if he was going to be Big Time from here on out he better follow through with the job.

Upstairs, Manni was waiting for him. He took off the ball cap and jacket, stuffing both in the pillowcase. "To keep the dolls quiet," he mouthed.

Street's expression didn't soften, and Manni looked nervously at him. Then the pair was moving away from the door, through the Life Over Time section and past the McDonald's Fossil Preparation Lab. Sue's head came into focus to their right, the dimmed lighting playing over the massive skull. Nothing should be that big, Street mused.

The quiet had returned in force, at the same time relaxing Street and setting him to sweating again. Manni was moving ahead of him now, past a kiosk that said something about Tibet, past The Art Lacquer of Japan, around the corner and through a Maori Meeting House, which seemed unreal in the darkness and the quiet.

The quiet broken by the softly groaning metal of the opening stairwell door.

"Street..."

Waggling fingers encouraged his friend to move faster.

They were into the Marae Gallery now, the Pacific Spirits section to their right.

"Shush" Street heard. "Shush, shush, shush, shush." Regular, coming from somewhere behind him. Manni heard it, too, and he almost dropped the pillowcase with the Hopi dolls.

"A guard's coming. Street..."

Street circled round and entered the Tibet gallery, Manni so close behind him he imagined he could feel the shorter man's breath on his back.

"Shush, shush, shush, shush."

"What the hell is that?" Street whispered, not intending to speak the words aloud. Regular, like footsteps, but different. He'd decided the "shushing" pace seemed too slow for a guard, and there was no flashlight. He pushed Manni up against a corner, his dagger-eyes telling his friend to stay put.

Then he was edging out into the main gallery, looking, listening, seeing a shadow pass by the Art Lacquer of Japan store. Too short for a guard—unless the dimness distorted the figure. An odd thought crossed Street's mind. Another thief? Someone who'd gotten the idea to break into the museum this night, too? Anger grabbed him, and he headed toward where he last saw the figure. Street spun around the corner, intending to confront his competition. Feet flying across the tile, sweat dripping from his face, he closed the distance.

Shush, shush, shush. The figure stopped and turned, stepped away from a partition perhaps so it could better see in the dim light. Or perhaps so it could better be seen.

Street swallowed hard and felt his heart hammer in his chest. A dozen things assailed him, all terrifying. The silence of the place settled in again, more profound than ever before. And the heat assaulted him. It was the heat he'd noticed in the Egyptian display, the dry heat he thought would either preserve the antiquities kept there or make the patrons think they were in the desert. The heat emanated from the creature.

Manni, Street meant to say. But nothing came out. The heat of the desert had settled in his throat, and he couldn't work up enough saliva for even one word.

Shush, shush, shush. The creature came closer. It was a mummy, not so physically impressive as the ones on the movie screen, but one terrifying because it was real. No more than five feet tall, and slight, the thing shambled forward, just as Street managed to find the will to take a few steps back.

With it came the heat, and an odor of chemicals and age and death and things Street couldn't put a name to. The shushing sound came from its bandaged feet moving across the tiled floor. The creature seemed not able to pick its feet up, but to shuffle along on straight legs, straight arms held out to its sides. Perhaps it couldn't bend them because the wrappings were so tight, Street wondered. Or perhaps its limbs had been locked in place by whatever ancient man embalmed it.

After a moment more, Street tried to tell himself the thing was not to be feared. It was slow, small, and without a weapon. Its face was bandaged and so couldn't really see. Maybe it followed Street by smell, like some bloodhound. Maybe it was the mummy Manni had tried to touch, and had inadvertently disturbed.

"S-s-sorry," Street managed when he worked up some spit. "Didn't mean to disturb you." He backed away as the mummy shushed forward. Then he took in a great gulp of air and spun on the balls of his feet, finding the courage—or more likely propelled by the fear—to get back to Manni's side.

Shush, shush, shush, came the soft sound from behind him.

Damn dead thing's slow, Street realized by the time he'd found Manni, who had edged away from the corner despite Street's instructions. *Can't keep up with us. Gotta get out of here. Can't catch us, so slow.*

"Street?"

"It's not a guard," Street said, the words coming hard, as his throat was still desert dry.

"What..."

"You don't want to know, and I haven't the time to tell you. Gotta get out of here, Manni." He wasn't whispering any more, wasn't worried about someone hearing him.

"The jewels."

"Forget the jewels. We got dolls and..."

Manni vehemently shook his head and brushed by Street, heading to the back of the hall where the Special Exhibit Gallery stretched. Even in the muted light, Manni could see the sign: Kremlin Gold—One Thousand Years of Russian Gems and Jewels. "If there ain't no guard, I ain't leavin'. Look at this!"

On display were thousand-year-old icons excavated on the Kremlin grounds. Behind glass cases were diamond- and sapphire-bejeweled crowns of the tsars. Manni pointed toward a separate case, one clearly attached to motion sensors. Inside was a pair of Imperial Faberge eggs.

"This is what we came for, Street. This was your idea." Manni knelt by the egg case, tugging free his knife and wires, setting to work on the motion detector. "I'm gonna show one o' these to Papa Rizzo 'fore we hock 'em."

Shush, shush, shush.

Over the pounding of his heart and his labored breathing, over Manni's incessant prattle, Street heard the damn shushing. No wonder the guards were playing cards, he thought. Why'd they need to patrol this place when they had a mummy to do it for them? And why did he go through the Egyptian exhibit? He could've taken Manni another way, though longer. Had he wanted to impress Manni by taking him past the various exhibits?

And how could a mummy be walking around in the museum? He knew better than to tell himself it was a security man dressed up. The heat that pulsed from the thing, that he was feeling now, the scent that came with it, the way it moved. It was real. Why was it after them?

Shush, shush, shush.

"Manni!"

"Got past the sensor. Got the case open," Manni reported. He reached inside and carefully retrieved an egg.

"Manni, did you take anything from the Egyptian display?"

He retrieved the second egg. "And if I did? If I did I ain't splittin' it with you. We'll split the jewels and the dolls. I just picked up a little souvenir for Papa Rizzo."

Street felt his stomach rise up into his chest. "You took something."

He didn't see Manni nod and shrug, didn't see him move to another case and set to work on that motion sensor. But he heard the shush, shush, shush, felt the heat becoming more intense, saw the mummy come from around the corner.

No eyes? It had eyes, Street discovered. A hellish green glow came from behind the bandages on its face.

All of your organs are removed, Street mentally told it. He'd read all about embalming on one of his numerous trips to the museum. *They're sitting in some jar somewhere. You can't move without organs. You can't move 'cause you're dead. Dead, dead, dead.*

Shush, shush, shush.

"Manni! Forgodssake, Manni!"

His friend turned, sapphire crown in hand. "Gotta be quiet, Street. Gotta be..." The crown slipped from his fingers, striking the tile. The bag with the eggs followed. And then the bag with the Hopi dolls. Manni's fingers trembled and grabbed at the air.

"What'd you take?" Street was practically shouting. "What'd you take from downstairs?" He tried to say more, but his throat was desert-dry, his tongue swollen and filling his mouth. Sweat poured down his forehead and into his eyes.

Manni's fingers fumbled in his pockets, eyes wide and locked onto the hellish green ones of the mummy. "That's real, ain't it, Street? That's..." Then Manni's words were gone, too, swallowed up by the heat that pulsated from the closing mummy. His fingers touched the scarab, the one he'd pried from the cat statue. He pulled it out and held it as the mummy passed by Street, bringing the unbearable heat with it.

Here, Manni tried to say, thrusting the scarab at the creature, which clumsily held out a bandaged hand. *Take it.*

The creature did, but continued on, forcing Manni back against a display case that held a ruby-encrusted necklace. It pressed its chest against Manni's and the heat became an overwhelming force, wrapping around Manni tighter than the bandages that were around the creature.

Manni gasped, his legs buckling. He couldn't fall, the mummy held him in place, the green eyes boring into his. *Street,* he tried to say. *Street!*

Street was there, having found the will to move his feet. He grabbed at the mummy's shoulder, intending to pull it away from his friend. But he quickly withdrew his fingers. Scalding hot, the surface of the mummy was. His fingertips were blistered.

"Manni...omigod, Manni."

Street stared as blisters formed on Manni's face, the kind you'd get from being too long under a desert sun. Manni's too-pale skin was bright red and peeling, his lips were deeply cracked, his eyes fixed on the mummy.

"Manni..."

The mummy stepped back, and Manni fell to the floor. He was still alive, Street could tell, his chest rising and falling and his fingers twitching. But he wouldn't be able to go anywhere soon.

The green glow of eyes caught Street.

"No." Street whirled, feet flying over the tiled floor, as he dashed toward the service stairwell. There were cameras, and he raced by them, not caring if his image was picked up. Hoping his image would indeed be picked up. "No, no, no."

Shush, shush, shush, he heard coming from behind him—and from in front of him.

Another one? Street's mind cried in disbelief. There, at the stairwell doorway, was another mummy. This one slightly taller than the other, and not so well preserved. It was missing its left hand and the bandages were dark at its abdomen, as if something had gone awry in the embalming stage. It generated the same heat, which came at Street like a fist.

He gasped as the force of the heat struck him from the front, crumpled when the heat came at him from behind, completely cocooning him. For only an instant the coolness of the tile floor registered against his back, then the heat overwhelmed him.

"Suffocating..." he gasped before his words were taken again. The mummies looked down at him, green eyes glowing through the gauze. Shush, shush, shush. They stepped back.

Street heard a clicking now, rhythmic and getting louder. Someone was coming up the stairs. A flicker of light bouncing through the window and against the ceiling signaled the approach of a night watchman. It was the one called Mick.

The watchman didn't give the mummies a second glance, seeming far more interested in Street.

"Thought someone was prowling around," Mick said, staring down at Street and shaking his head. Mick made a *tsk-tsking* noise.

Street tried to say something, but his tongue filled his mouth and wouldn't cooperate.

"We'll get you an ambulance," Mick said. "After I get these fellows back to the Egyptian exhibit."

Street managed to raise an eyebrow, the gesture painful on his sunburnt face.

"From the Fifth Dynasty," Mick explained. There was some amount of pride in the night watchman's voice. "Don't know their names. But they were Unas's guards. Don't have anything of Unas's on display downstairs. See...the guards were lax in life, let some thieves slip in and steal all of the pharaoh's riches. So they're making up for it all in death, their repentance so to speak. Their way of trying to pave themselves a path to the afterlife." The guard slapped the taller mummy on the back. "They guard the museum's treasures right well. And we don't have to worry about them killing anyone. See, I think they want to keep thieves alive to give 'em a chance to repent, too."

Mick voiced a clipped laugh and the mummies' eyes seemed to glow a little brighter.

Street closed his eyes and surrendered himself to the heat.

Rag-Tags & Crumbled Leaves

I didn't write this story for any particular reason. Just had an idea about beggars and magic, and threw the words together. Peanut Press was gracious enough to pick it up for their Witches *anthology in 2001.*

The beggar settled himself on a corner at the edge of a small merchant district, not far from the harbor. From here, if he craned his neck at just the right angle, he could watch the ships approaching Cavan Oak Pier, their sails billowing with the early summer breeze. He could see the midmorning sun paint the Bay of Elsbeth with flecks of gold that were sometimes so bright they made him squint, like they were doing now. And he could count the Lord's Knights that came and went from the wharves—though he almost always got mixed up when the number surpassed twenty.

Across from a flower shop, the air was always pleasantly scented on this corner, his corner he called it, better and sweeter than just about anywhere else in the sprawling city of Mollybindor. He breathed deep and held the fragrance in his lungs while he tried to determine the mix of flowers for sale today. Lilacs and Hollow Ridge roses, he decided after a moment, staring at the window to make sure his nose was correct.

The shop almost always had lilacs this time of year—violet and pink and white ones that had pale yellow centers the color of a pair of wool socks he found nearly a decade ago and still wore on special occasions. And there was something else a bit exotic mixed in the bouquet this morning that he couldn't put a name to but that smelled truly... "Dwonderful," he pronounced after a second deep breath. Must be those bright orange blooms that in a fashion resembled the heads of big parrots.

He grinned wide at the lovely lass arranging the flowers and waved to her. She offered him a scowl and a toss of her head. She always scowled at him, but he didn't mind. He thought she looked beautiful anyway.

A massive, colorful skirt swished by, sending the dust on the street into a tizzy and temporarily blocking the beggar's view of the flower shop. It was followed by two smaller and equally colorful skirts—a thickset woman and her two dutiful daughters. They always made their way down this street this time of day without so much of a greeting. He knew better than to hold out his hat to them; their eyes exhibited no trace of charity. Ah, but the man that was following several steps behind. Now he had a congenial face—and thick gold rings on nearly every finger.

"Dow do you do?" the beggar asked, his eyes twinkling merrily.

The man stopped and glanced down, wrinkled his nose and fished about in the pocket of his immaculately pressed pants. "I'd say I'm doing better than you, my little fellow," he returned.

The beggar cocked his head and offered an affable smile that spread to the corners of his careworn face. Three copper coins dropped into his hat. "Materialism is da bane of a doble society," the beggar said in his thick, nasally voice. "Charity marks da spirit of a drue gentleman."

"Well, yes, I suppose," the man said, taken a bit aback by the beggar's philosophical spoutings. "Perhaps you can buy yourself some new clothes and several good meals," he suggested, as he added a fourth copper coin. Then he was on his way, polished leather heels clicking rhythmically on the cobblestones.

The beggar glanced at himself in a nearby window, the image blinking back at him. He was a Rock Hill gnome, a diminutive, fleshy soul, who though certainly not the brightest being on the street, was usually the cheeriest. He had a bulbous nose, sun-weathered skin, and saucer-shaped blue eyes that absorbed—though did not comprehend—everything, and that flashed with a myriad of emotions depending on the circumstance. Now they reflected contentedness, as it was, after all, a most delightful morning.

His clothes were a raggedy mix. His pants at one time had belonged to a human and had been cut off at the knees—ankles to the beggar—and belted with a frayed cord found on the docks. They were an olive green, what one could see of them, though a brighter shade along the seams hinted that they had been more colorful some years ago. There were a profusion of small blue, gray, and brown patches sewn on them here and there, but mostly congregated on the seat, which was always getting worn from his sitting on Mollybindor's cobblestone corners.

The ochre shirt had belonged to a stout human child and was just about a size too small, fastening nicely at the neck and the waist but straining the buttons in the middle. At his elbows there were holes that he hadn't bothered to patch—not this time of year anyway. And this time of year he didn't wear shoes, so the breeze could circulate around his tanned toes.

His red hat completed the outfit. It was a grand and recent acquisition, given to him by a shopkeeper in Mollybindor's wharf district. One side had become so faded in the window, practically pink, that no one would buy it. The beggar happily accepted it, though, as he was certain it would keep his head warm in the coming winter and it was deep enough to hold lots of coins.

He pulled the four copper coins from the hat, thrust them in his pocket, then offered a "Dow do you do?" to a well dressed woman headed toward the flower shop. She smiled and dropped a few coins inside, then made her way across the street. The beggar knew that people who could afford flowers had money to spare. "If you dink domeone is following you, dook over your shoulder!" The beggar loved to cite his particular words of wisdom—he believed in giving the people something for their coins. Most people anyway.

A Lord's Knight officer strode by, coin purse bulging and clinking invitingly at his hip. The beggar's deceptively lightning quick fingers reached up, a thin blade concealed in his palm. With a swift gesture, the thong holding the purse was cut and the bag fell into the beggar's lap. The knight continued down the street unaware.

The beggar stole only once more this morning, and that was from another passing knight. He'd made it a practice not to steal from other folks. The two purses found their way into the deep pockets of his pants, while more offered coins continued to clink into his hat.

"Your generosity is dood for da both of us!" he chirped. "Da sun shines brighter on dose who give!"

When his stomach and the sun directly overhead told him it was noon, he glanced across to the flower shop. Right on time. The lovely lass came out, broom in hand.

"Get out of here, you little rag-tag!" she scolded. "You've dawdled long enough!"

He smiled warmly at her and sauntered away. Sometimes he got to spend the better part of the day on his corner, when she was so busy with customers and arranging flowers that she couldn't take time to shoo him off. But usually the lass—or some other merchant—tolerated him only until lunchtime. The beggar didn't mind. He had places to go and people to meet. And he didn't mind if another beggar settled down on his corner for the afternoon. He glanced over his shoulder and spotted a gangly looking human sit in his spot—Sam. The man had introduced himself two weeks ago.

The gnome felt sorry for Sam, who was new to Mollybindor and who wasn't very good at spotting generous faces. He hoped that he would remember tomorrow to give Sam a few coins, and maybe a few lessons. Sam certainly needed the help.

The diminutive beggar walked slowly down the street, so the bags of coins in his pockets wouldn't jangle overmuch. Hat held out in front of him in case anyone he passed felt in a beneficent mood, he ogled the city's old buildings—all well kept up in this area, with freshly painted eaves and shutters.

He paused in front of a baker, waiting until the man came out and offered him a sandwich. Thin roast beef, the beggar's favorite. He grinned warmly. "Danks," he said. "If you love a puppy, drub his dummy." He moved on, collecting a cup of lemonade from a sidewalk vendor, and a piece of peppermint candy from a sugar shop. "Witches and their spells dwill defeat da evil Lord's Dights."

His path took him down one of the central spokes in the city's wheel-like formation. It cut through the main merchant district, the artisan's section, and the slums, and ended at the busy and impressive Molly Gardens. But the beggar stopped just short of the gardens, perpetually thick with the Lord's Knight guards. Instead, he turned down a circular street that ringed the gardens and the courthouse and that cut between the Lord's Manor, which made him involuntarily shiver. The beggar paused in front of a temple and bowed his head, offering a silent prayer to whatever god was honored there.

He happily accepted a few coins from an obviously wealthy old man, who was also regarding the temple. "Two birds ding much louder than one!" Then he continued past the knights' barracks, and found himself on a side street that took him by a small park and an abandoned warehouse. A dozen more steps and he was in an area that was a mix of residences and small businesses.

"Dow do you do!" he called to a pair of raggedy dressed plains gnomes perched across from an establishment called Crumbled Leaves.

"Hi Migiligin!" the smaller of the two happily returned. The youth waved exaggeratedly, shooing away a cloud of gnats.

Migiligin hurried toward his friends, chinking loudly with the hidden coin purses. "Drancis," he nodded to the smaller plains gnome. "Argatroit," to the slightly larger.

The plains gnomes were dressed no better than Migiligin, though they were certainly more garish. Mismatched colors warred on their tiny frames. Each had a large floppy hat that had a smattering of patches on the outside and copper coins on the inside. They had more coins, as indicated by their bulging pockets, but they never let the passersby see that they'd already collected a substantial amount.

"Is he din there?"Migiligin asked.

Francis nodded.

"Dwhat's he doing?"

"Something with witchcraft," Francis replied. "He's always doing something with witchcraft. I can tell."

The three beggars studied the shop, trying to peer through a window that was streaked with grime—or magical powder, Francis insisted. The shop had little on display in the window—tins of tea leaves. The placard advertising it as Crumbled Leaves was small and weathered and not easy to notice.

Francis had found his way inside the shop once, discovering all manner of things other than tea—unusual spices, powders, dried animal parts, roots, and more. There were scrolls and carved sticks just out of his reach that he was certain were wands, elaborate staves that the young gnome was doubly certain were strongly enchanted, and a broom he suspected could fly. The proprietor, a hawk-nosed man on the distant side of middle age, rushed him out before he could investigate further.

Sometimes the man poked his head out the door and glared at the gnomes, but he never shooed them away. Francis claimed the man didn't want to leave his shop and all its arcane treasures.

The gnomes fared well across from Crumbled Leaves, as the sparse and interesting clientele had considerable coin and frequently shared it. Of course, there were other establishments on this block, and the shoppers that frequented them were also targeted by the gnomes. There was a scribner's and a mapmaker's, and the folks who visited these places had to have coins. But it was Crumbled Leaves that always had the most fascinating patrons.

"There he is again," Argatroit whispered, as he pointed a diminutive finger toward the shop door. "The one with all the money."

A tall, reed-thin human with a shock of dark red hair exited and made his way toward the trio. His green eyes narrowed as he scrutinized each beggar in turn, and his long, birdlike fingers reached into a green velvet coinpurse at his side and tugged free three gold coins—one for each of their hats.

"Da frog dat croaks at high tide croaks da best," Migiligin told the man.

The trio had been begging on this corner for the better part of four months, ever since Francis decided it was a witch's shop and snuck the look inside. And for the past three months, they saw this willowy man leave the shop once a week, though they never saw him enter. And he always gave them each a gold coin.

"And his bag is always the same size," Francis whispered when the stranger glided out of earshot. "Like he always has the same number of coins in it. I know it's magic."

"Dould just be full," Migiligin suggested. "Dould be dat it's always full 'cause he deeps filling it every day."

The young plains gnome shook his head. "You just wait. Wait until next week and take a good look at it then. It's witchcraft, I tell you. Bet he bought it in that shop." Francis' eyes looked dreamily at the weathered door and his jaw worked as he imagined the wonders inside.

A week later seemed to prove the young gnome right. The willowy man with the green velvet purse emerged and deposited a gold coin in each of their hats. The purse looked to be stuffed just the same as the previous week.

Surprisingly, Migiligin saw the man a week later exit the flower shop as he perched on his favorite corner. He couldn't remember seeing the man enter it. The tall human carefully regarded the hill gnome, giving him no coins in the morning, but giving the trio each one when he left Crumbled Leaves that afternoon.

"Wonder how he gets inside places," Francis whispered, as he ran his little fingers over the coins in his hat. "All we ever do is see him leave."

Migiligin shrugged. "Dust matters dat he has money."

Argatroit simply grimaced and announced that it was time to go home for dinner and count their earnings for the day.

They didn't see the moneyman for the next two weeks, and this worried only Francis, who speculated that he might have fallen ill. But the week after that, Migiligin spotted him leaving the flower shop again, a large bouquet of snapdragons in hand. He walked right past the beggar. And for the first time in his life, Migiligin did something he had vowed never to do—he stole from someone other than a Lord's Knight. A flick of his wrist and his hidden blade had sliced through the cord of the green velvet bag. The bag felt soft, and it tingled against his fingers as he stuffed it inside a deep trouser pocket. Migiligin didn't intend to share this acquisition with his rag-tag gnome friends—not just yet. Not until he was certain it was magic. Feeling especially guilty over the theft, he gave several copper coins to Sam, who came to take his spot for the afternoon.

"Dungry?" Migiligin asked Sam.

Sam nodded.

"Come with me." Migiligin's course took him by the sandwich shop, the lemonade stand, and the candy maker's, Sam happily wolfing down the offered treats. Sam even bowed his head reverently outside the temple. But Migiligin had trouble praying today, and so did not tarry. The velvet bag tingled against his leg and kept him from concentrating.

"Dow do you do!" he called to his friends, as he led Sam down the street and nodded for him to sit across from Crumbled Leaves.

Argatroit looked up suspiciously. Francis smiled cordially.

"Dis's my friend Sam," Migiligin began. "De's lonely," he attempted to whisper. "And hungry. Dike you were when I met you."

Argatroit's expression softened a little. "Hope he doesn't eat too much."

"He hasn't come out yet," Francis interrupted, gesturing at the shop.

Sam cocked his head.

"The tall, thin human. The moneyman," the little gnome explained. "The one with the green bag who visits the witch who runs the shop. Today's his day to come out of the shop and give us gold coins. He's late."

And when he didn't come out when the shop closed at sunset, Francis twiddled his thumbs. Migiligin opened his mouth, about to tell his friends that he'd saw the willowy human earlier today at the flower shop. And that he had stolen the green bag. It continued to tingle against his leg, and he cast his head around nervously, half expecting the man to show up and demand the coin purse. "Dime do go home," was all that came out.

"C'mon, Sam!" Francis chirped. "We'll find you a place to sleep."

The foursome wended their way down the street, stopping here and there to look at pottery and paintings in a few shop windows and to admire the residences that seemed to be more artfully trimmed in this part of the city. Then they found themselves at the city's outer wall. They paralleled the wall until they reached Lord's Road, and took it north toward the Molly Gardens. Several minutes later they were standing outside an abandoned warehouse.

"Home," Migiligin told Sam, as the hill gnome turned a board that on the surface looked securely nailed to a side door, but that merely camouflaged the fact that the bottom half had been sawed through to allow entrance. The three little beggars had no trouble squeezing inside, but Sam had to work at it, practically folding himself in half.

"Home of the rag-tags!" Francis echoed, as he found Sam's hand in the darkness. He tugged the human toward the center of the warehouse, while Argatroit and Migiligin secured the door. Then the young gnome bumped into a collection of crates, dropped Sam's hand, and fumbled about. A heartbeat later, a large lantern was lit.

Sam stared slack-jawed.

The light didn't reach into the corners—the warehouse was too big for that. But what it did manage to reveal was amazing. Furniture was strewn everywhere—none of it in good repair, but all of it useable. There were three beds with linens and comforters; an assortment of other beds propped against a wall; chairs, with and without stuffing on the seats; tables, some with missing legs; and curio cabinets that held a variety of valuable-looking knickknacks. Shadowy shapes hinted at still more furniture, and Francis explained that the big pieces were dragged in at night and through a hinged panel on the far walls.

There were oil lamps, some hammered bronze and crystal, others rusted and with more dents than smooth surfaces. And there were weapons hanging on hooks.

"From da evil Lord's Dights," Migiligin volunteered, pointing at a row of swords.

"A dozen of 'em got suspicious of us 'cause we beg all the time," Francis added. "They snuck in here thinking we had lots and lots of gold and were up to something!"

"We dealt with them easily enough," Argatroit concluded. "Kept their weapons as souvenirs." He gestured Sam over to a bed leaning against the wall, and the two of them righted it. Francis rummaged through a listing cabinet for some not-too-worn sheets and a light blanket.

"Don't have any extra pillows," Argatroit stated.

"He can dorrow one of mine." Migiligin fluffed one and tossed it on Sam's bed. "Welcome do da rag-tags."

Sam cocked his head.

"Rag-tags. Da people in da shops named us dat."

"Welcome to the rag-tags," Argatroit said grudgingly. "I'll get us something to eat, then we turn in. Long day tomorrow, and you'll have to find yourself a street corner to call your own in the morning."

"In da afternoon we go to da Crumbled Leaves," Migiligin said. The hill gnome was standing in front of a mirror, inspecting his face and hands. His skin had begun to itch, and he suspected the tingling bag was doing it. He yawned and made his way toward his bed, waving away Argatroit's offered dinner of pears and dried turkey. Migiligin wanted everyone to go to bed and turn out the lights so he could privately examine the bag.

"Why Crumbled Leaves?" The first words they'd heard Sam speak.

"It's a witch's shop. And one of the customers has a magic bag," the young gnome continued. "He gives us money from it every week. 'Cept he wasn't there today."

Migiligin pulled the sheet over his head and tugged free the velvet bag. It was full to bursting, but he waited until his friends finally blew out the lantern before he opened it and began to count. There were forty-eight coins in the bag, all gold ones from the feel of them. He slipped them all inside a slit in his mattress and waited to see if the bag refilled itself. However, his eyes would not stay open and he dozed, the now softly tingling bag held firmly in his fingers. Migiligin snored, as did the plains gnomes.

But Sam didn't. He wasn't sleeping.

The raggedy human threw back the sheet and stretched his legs, then rose and glided silently through the warehouse. It was dark like a cave. Only in one corner did any light creep in, and that was where a section of the roof was cracked and a bit of starlight filtered through. It was plenty enough light for Sam to see by. He paused in front of a curio cabinet and eased the door open. His fingers fluttered over the small figurines inside, tarrying on a collection of golden thimbles.

Next, he went to the wall where swords, daggers, and a pair of ornate hand axes were displayed. Then to a chest, which opened only on his second try, the lid heavy, and the hinges stiff. Inside were vases padded by moth-eaten blankets. Most were old and of little value, but two were made of the finest crystal, handblown and shaped like swans, necks straight and beaks open to accept flowers.

"Interesting," Sam whispered, as he gently lowered the lid and looked about for more chests, which he was certain had to contain coins. After all, the beggars took in coins every day, and it was obvious they weren't spending all of it on clothes or food.

Two more chests, one of them empty, the other filled with bronze candlesticks. Sam made sure everything stayed as he found it, and he moved on to a seriously tilting wardrobe and tugged the door open. There were cloaks inside, all of them human-sized and quite old. On first glance none of them looked valuable. But perhaps... Sam's fingers separated each one and dipped into pockets.

"No money," he whispered. "What are they doing with...what?"

Suddenly, a dark brown cloak came to life, whipping about his arms. Another fluttered off a hanger and snaked around his legs.

Migiligin yawned, awakened by the sound of the flapping. "Dorning already?" No. It was still dark. He grinned wide when he felt the bag. There was something inside it. Eight gold coins. "Da purse is magic." He pulled the coins out and stuck them in the slit in his mattress. He vowed to present it all to Francis in the morning.

There was another sound, like a gale makes when it tosses the trees on the far north point of the harbor. A loud swishing followed by a string of muffled curse words and stomping. Migiligin sat bolt upright.

The large lantern was lit by Argatroit, casting a dim glow over their guest, who was wrapped up in several cloaks and was furiously worming his fingers free.

"Rats to you, Migiligin!" Argatroit barked. "You've brought in another ringer. Bet this one's a Lord's Knight, too!" The grumpy gnome scurried to the weapon wall and tugged down one of the hand axes.

Francis was wide awake, staring at what used to be Sam.

The beggar had grown quite a bit taller, his new form stretching the cloaks and making it easier for him to force his hands out.

"The man with the green velvet bag!" Francis squeaked.

"Fools!" the man spat, as he wheeled on the young gnome.

Francis backed up, bumping into a charging Argatroit and spilling both of them to the ground. Behind them, Migiligin crawled out of bed, hiding the bag beneath the sheet.

The human's fingers were glowing, and within a heartbeat the glow was spreading up his arms, melting the entangling cloaks as if they were butter. The glow brightened, from a pale yellow that reminded Migiligin of the lilac centers and his old socks to an intense orange the shade of dying embers. The glow crackled and raced away from his long fingers, arcing across the warehouse and striking Migiligin solidly in the chest, pitching him back onto the bed.

"No!" Francis hollered. "Migiligin!" The young plains gnome scrabbled to his feet and twirled his fingers in the air, creating his own glow that was a pale blue and not near so impressive as the stranger's. Francis's face was drawn together, his eyes squinted so tight it looked painful. The tiny fingers worked fast, and the glow spread from them and to the wardrobe and the remaining cloaks there. The remaining garments came to life and whipped out like tendrils, wrapping about the stranger and pinning his arms to the side.

At the same time, the orange glow was working its way up the human's arms again, melting the fabric—but not before a scarf leapt from the wardrobe and wrapped around his head, pulling him into the closet. The doors slammed shut, just as Argatroit raced toward it. The gnome barreled into the wardrobe with all of his strength, knocking it backward. Without pause, he jumped up on it and sat, keeping the doors closed.

"Let me out of here!" came the cry from inside the cabinet.

There was a muffled thumping coming from inside the cabinet, and the wood groaned, but Argatroit refused to budge and shook his head. "You all right Migiligin?" He gripped the hand axe so tight his knuckles turned white.

"Let me out of here!"

"Migiligin?" Argatroit persisted.

A whimper came from the bed. "I duess so," came a soft answer. "Durts a lot." Migiligin eased himself to the floor and slowly approached the overturned wardrobe, rubbing his chest the whole way. The ochre shirt was burned in the center, and the buttons were charred.

"Let me out of here! Let me out or so help me I'll bring this warehouse down around your dirty little ears." The wardrobe glowed orange, and smoke drifted up from the hinges.

"Do it!" This from Francis. "Whoever's in there is really powerful. Maybe if we let him out, things'll..."

"Now, you damnable little rag-tags! Let me out!"

Argatroit slid off the wardrobe, patting his smoldering pants as he went. The wardrobe doors flew open and scarves and cloaks and a showy shower of sparks erupted. When everything had settled, a different man emerged, a middle-aged hawk-nosed one, face pinched in rage.

"It's the witch," Francis said softly.

"Who?" Argatroit risked. "What happened to the moneyman?" He was backing toward the weapon wall. "Who?"

"The man in Crumbled Leaves. The one who chased me out. The proprietor. He's a witch."

"Warlock," the man corrected.

Migiligin scratched his head. "What dappened do Sam?"

"There never was a Sam," the warlock spat. "Or a Hershal."

"Who?" Argatroit repeated. Just a few more steps. There were a few daggers hanging there somewhere.

"Hershal. The man with the green velvet bag. The moneyman as you call him."

"Why did you come here? Why deceive us?" Francis took a step toward him.

"Because I was curious," he answered, his face relaxing only the slightest bit. "Everyday you're on my corner, begging. On other corners. Begging. All those coins. You had to be spending them on something. I was curious."

"Last year da Lord's Dights thought we were spending dit to fight them." Much softer, Migiligin added, "And Drancis dealt with da dights."

"We're saving the coins," Francis told the warlock.

Argatroit's fingers found one dagger on the wall, which he thrust in the back of his belt. Now for another one.

"Saving them," he parroted. "For what?"

The young gnome ground the ball of his foot against the floor. "For Crumbled Leaves. I want to be a witch or a warlock or whatever you call them. There's some of the craft in me. I can make cloth come alive. And some other things. But I want to know how to do more. A lot more. So when I visited your shop to see if you'd teach me some...I heard you telling a customer how expensive it was to study witchcraft...well, you shooed me out. I figured it was 'cause I didn't have enough money. We've been begging so I'll have enough to learn real witchcraft."

Three daggers now, all concealed. Argatroit edged to the center of the warehouse. He wrapped his fingers around one, steadied it, and dropped it with an "ouch!" as the handle grew too hot for him to touch. He tugged the others free and patted at the back of his pants. Then he and the warlock glared at each other.

"My velvet bag..."

Migiligin spun on his calloused heels and retrieved it from his bed. He held it out to the human. "Dorry."

The warlock's face looked almost kind now, as he stepped away from the wardrobe and sat on a crate. "Witchcraft isn't this expensive," he said, gesturing at the sprawling collection.

Francis padded forward.

"My real name is Krolnish Greenleaves," he said, looking directly into the young gnome's eyes. "You can call me Master Greenleaves. I am indeed a warlock, one of the most powerful in this country. And in all my years, I have never encountered anyone the likes of you three."

"Will you teach me?" Francis asked, his voice cracking with nervousness.

The warlock nodded.

"I don't understand. Dwat happened do Sam?"

* * *

Migiligan settled himself on his corner across from the flower shop and craned his neck so he could watch the ships approaching the pier. The midmorning sun painted the bay with flecks of gold so bright he had to squint. A few Lord's Knights were making their way up from the wharves, and he cut the purse strings of the one that lagged behind.

He inhaled deep. "Dilacs and carnations," he pronounced, just as the thickset woman and her two daughters strode by.

The pretty flower lass didn't chase him away until well after noon. A sandwich and a glass of lemonade later found him perched with Argatroit across from Crumbled Leaves.

"Francis's inside," the gnome told him. "Been there since dawn. That warlock's teaching him." Argatroit's face took on a sad expression. "Hope Francis doesn't forget us when he's a powerful warlock, too."

Migiligin shook his head. "Dwon't happen," he said knowingly. "Drancis'll always be a rag-tag." The Rock Hill gnome held out his hat as a rotund man passed by. A few coins clinked off the brim and fell into the bottom. Then he glanced at Argatroit. "I'm saving up," he explained, as he shook his earnings. "In case I dee Sam. He might deed some money."

Salvor's Pearls

I have a couple of books about underwater archeology and wrecked ships off Pearl Harbor. I find it all very fascinating, and I wondered what underwater archeology might be like in the future. Brian Thomsen invited me to one of his science-fiction anthologies, and so I had the chance to speculate. This story originally appeared in Oceans of Space, *DAW Books, 2002.*

One-hundred-and-twenty meters down, the alien sea looked like an unending blanket of fog—a green-gray murkiness that extended away from the broken spaceship. There was a hint of brightness directly overhead, a faint cerulean blue that registered on the salvors' visors and that was cut through by a black wedge, the *Mary Carleton* that hovered above the waves. But where the salvors worked in the thermocline against the shattered asteroid reef, where the spaceship had tightly wedged itself, was a place filled with shadows. It was eerie and still, haunting and yet somehow familiar.

Worlds differed more on the surface, the salvors knew. The oceans and the wrecks they contained tended to be much the same.

"Captain Kilian." The tenor voice belonged to Pug Willum, the latest addition to the crew who was picked up on the Neptune colony four months back. "I've found somethin' a bit unusual, Ma'am. Captain. You might want to come take a look." Willum was the farthest from the crashed ship, capturing images of the entire scene. It was standard practice for the *Mary Carleton* to keep a visual log, and Willum was trying to document the angle the wounded vessel had entered the sea and where it broke up against the reef. This allowed them to retrace the spaceship's path, determine where it entered the planet's atmosphere, and discern if anything valuable was jettisoned along the way.

A dozen salvors crawled about the wreck in yellow skintight suits that managed to keep them dry and warm and easy to spot against their dark surroundings. Their slightly bulbous helmets, lighted along the crown, and the small turtle shell-shaped rebreather tanks on their backs, made them look like overlarge crustaceans involved in some hunting ritual.

One figure separated itself and moved silently toward Willum, propelled by small thrusters on her belt. It was the same thrusters they used when working on repairs on the *Mary Carleton*'s hull in space, just fixed to different settings. The captain was economical where equipment was concerned.

"This better be good, Rook," came the whisper-hoarse voice over the com. Rix Kilian referred to anyone who served under her for less than a year as a rookie.

Willum was pointing to something at his feet.

It was a humanoid skull, though obviously not human, coral growths thick around its long, pointed jaw and under its double-ridged eye sockets. There were other bones nearby, amid rotted planks of wood and a twisted fluke anchor. Looking closely, almost an entire skeleton could be seen halfway buried in the silt. The being who had died here would have been a little more than eight feet tall in life and would have had feet resembling horse hooves. There was flesh remaining on its breastbone, exposed ribs, and one thighbone.

"I figure, ma'am, that when that ship hit the asteroid reef over there," Willum was now pointing back at the spaceship lodged in the fissure it had created, his eyes following the form of a slight yellow-suited salvor who slipped inside the hull breech, "I figure the impact stirred up the silt all the way over here and exposed this old wreck and these bones. Should I get some sifters over here, Ma'am? Captain?" He returned his attention to her, trying to pick through the lights on her helmet to get a good look at her face, read her reaction. But the water and the lights distorted everything, and he all he caught was his own gawky reflection in her visor.

She didn't answer him, as she was studying the skeleton.

"Ma'am," he risked repeating. "Captain? Should I get some men over here? See if there's somethin' valuable? Might be ancient. A real sailing vessel. Rigging and all. Maybe better'n what you sent us down here after. "'Sides, Ma'am, the land above ain't inhabited anymore, records say the beings who lived here blew themselves up in a fusion war a few decades back. This ship's gotta predate that war. By a lot. Really ancient."

Rix was still staring at the skeleton.

"Not ancient, Rook," she said finally. "Definitely worth taking a look at, though. Old, quite a bit before the war certainly. But not that old. Can't be. Pearls for eyes."

"Captain?"

She knelt and ran a gloved finger around an eye socket.

> Full fathom five thy father lies;
> Of his bones are coral made
> Those are pearls that were his eyes;
> Nothing of his that doth fade
> But doth suffer a sea-change
> Into something rich and strange."

Willum glided over to stand even with her. "That's pretty Ma'am. Captain." He corrected himself again. "Did you write that?"

She shook her head, the light from her helmet bouncing off a half-buried bell and making the shadows dance wildly. "It's from *The Tempest.* Shakespear wrote it, Rook."

"Who?"

"Someone truly ancient. Someone who lived on Earth well more than a thousand years ago." She stood and faced him, stared through his visor at eyes that seemed to small for his wide, boyish face. "I'd say what you found maybe goes back six or seven decades." She gestured at the bits of wood and the anchor. "You don't find remains on wrecks that are much older than six or seven decades."

Willum cocked his head.

"The sea eats them, Rook. The fish. The scavengers. The only creatures that survived this planet's war. What are they teaching in the science academies these days?" She let out a sigh, a fine stream of bubbles escaping from a thin tube at the back of her neck, catching the light from her helmet and looking like sparkling gems rising to the surface. "But we might have gotten lucky. It is cold here, and the cold tends to preserve things. Maybe what you found is older than I first thought, near a century dead maybe. Or more. We finish with the spaceship over there, and we'll take a look around here. In the meantime, disturb nothing." Rix was looking at the coral-encrusted skull again. "On second thought."

Then she was gliding toward the downed spaceship, directing her people to stop what they were doing and to move to the older wooden wreck, calling her own ship. The *Mary Carleton* eased into the water above Willum, moving so slowly so as to carefully displace the water and stir up as little silt as possible, its sleek lines making it look like a huge Earth reef ray. Sound reached the salvors, through their helmets, a groaning noise the ship always made in dives, but that the crew never seemed to hear in space. Rix jokingly told her men it was ghosts in the hull. They were protesting the change in environment, fearing the ship might become one of the undersea wrecks that its crew sought and salvaged for a living.

At least this wasn't a deep dive. The gravity around objects in space was one thing, but the pressure of various worlds' oceans was often times worse. *Mary Carleton*'s hull, though specifically designed to withstand all the rigors of underwater work, was still suffering some of the effects from last week's deep salvaging foray into the Antarean Cluster ocean worlds.

"We'll take the old sailing ship first," Rix decided. "Be careful around it, you picaroons. It's a fragile one."

Minutes later, her crew was swarming over the find, collecting brass decorations from old firearms, the wood of which had long-since rotted away, gold fingerbars, neckchains, and pottery jars—one containing a trace of mercury—an intact fragile goblet, the pale color of which was impossible to visually determine at the moment, a large cylinder that Rix pronounced as a wrought-iron breech-loading gun, and more. They were all things reminiscent of Old Earth, the sixteen to seventeen hundreds when pirates sailed the seas.

Willum swam above it all. An underwater archeologist who specialized in primitive rim world surface cultures, he made meticulous recordings of what little of the exposed structure of the sailing ship they found—aided by a network of frames and underpinned strakes offloaded from the *Mary Carleton.* All of it was to gather information, which in some circles was as valuable a commodity as the objects that were being floated into the *Mary Carleton*'s hold.

Among other things, the information would show how the sailing ship had been constructed and what its purpose had been. They didn't need to go to such elaborate work on the wrecks they normally sought—those wrecks were space-going vessels, and computer logs provided all of that information.

Tubes were dropped so silt could be uplifted, revealing more of the old vessel, and in the process stirring up the sand and making everything seem murkier.

"Rix?" A salvor swam from the *Mary Carleton*'s hold, straightlining toward the captain. "Rix?"

The captain nodded without looking at her first mate. Though all the salvors tended to look the same in their yellow suits, he stood out. He was tall and had the broad shoulders and wide chest of a miner. "What is it, Dalan?"

"What are we doing here, Rix? We should be working the Leerkan vessel that plowed into that asteroid reef. You were damn lucky to pick this system and by chance make the find. We should be working it."

"I'm always lucky, Dalan. And we will work it."

"Look at it over there. Couldn't have crashed more than a month ago—in a cold sea on a backwater world where nobody lives and where probably no one on any nearby worlds noticed. No record of any other salvor activity here. It was a fast freighter, and that means she was probably carrying something important. Should be a good haul. All ours."

"She might have been a pirate ship." Rix was staring instead at the scattered remains of the old sailing ship the crew continued to pick its way around, her eyes locked onto what might have been part of a mast, a line still intact and now floating free when more of the silt was moved. "I named the *Mary Carleton* after a pirate, you know, one of the most famous female swashbucklers ever to sail the Caribbean back on Old Earth. Sixteen or seventeen hundreds, if I recall my ancient history correctly. Mary might have had a ship like this one."

Her first mate rolled his eyes.

"I fancy myself a pirate sometimes, Dalan. We're stealing—from the rim worlds' seas and from the dead, plundering their riches and making them our own. What treasures will we find here?"

"Treasures? Ha! Broken trinkets of a dead planet." Dalan shook his head. "And this work for what? Only a few eccentric historians will buy whatever we dredge up from here, Rix. You know that. Or maybe you can get some antiquated spacer to pick up a couple of baubles to set on his desk. We'll get more money from that Leerkan vessel. Worlds more."

"I imagine she was indeed a pirate ship." Rix was still staring at the mast, as if she hadn't heard Dalan. A pinstriped fish swam by, intrigued by the floating line. It made a strike at it, then finding it inedible, streaked away. "Had the weapons for it, she did. See? So primitive. There's another breech-loader. But we'll know for sure what the ship was in the weeks to come, when we carefully study the evidence we're taking into the hold, piece together the past." She let out a deep sigh, more bubble-gems floating the surface.

A pair of salvors freed the bell, turning it and noticing the engraving. The words were in an alien script, but Rix's microcomputer zoomed in and translated some of it, displaying it on the inside of her helmet. The *Dauntless.* A press of a button and her visor was clear again.

"You can tell quite a lot about the people and the time from a ship. It's all frozen here in front of us, Dalan. The ship, the crew, fashions, politics, what they considered valuable, what they loved, the whole of their lives and their alien culture—everything held in stasis by this cold, cold sea, frozen at the moment of its sinking. A salvor's dream, Dalan. The skeletons will tell us if the beings of the time were healthy, if their teeth were intact, if their bones were straight and strong. The armaments, how advanced they were. Did a fight bring them to the sea floor, as it did the Leerkan spaceship? A storm? It's all a window."

"Rix?"

"This wreck, Dalan. It's a window to the past." Another sigh. "The Leerkan ship is too recent to be a window. It's simply a door to wealth. And one that we'll open when we're done here."

Dalan returned to the *Mary Carleton,* knowing the captain had made up her mind. Twice before in the five years he'd sailed the space lanes with Rix Kilian, she accidentally came across old wrecks and lost herself in them. "You're mad, Rix," he breathed. "Always knew you were."

Eight days later he returned with the rotated crew, this time to work on the Leerkan spaceship, all that had been practical to salvage from the wooden vessel locked away in the *Mary Carleton*'s reserve hold. Dalan was pleased that at least Rix had a smattering of sense to keep the large hold for the space vessel's cache. He watched Rix float into the lower hatch of the *Mary Carleton,* the black wedge swallowing her along with the last of the crated antiques and eight crewmen. All of them looking the same in the suits, like a school of big yellow fish.

"Yo ho ho. At least she had the presence to let me take over on this one," he mused. The muscular salvor moved to the recent wreck, the numbers TRG-237 barely discernable because of the color used—blue, black or green likely—against a hull that also one of those shades. In water certain colors were almost indistinguishable from each other and hard to see in anything but the most crystal-clear of seas.

From his experience he could tell that the spaceship had been under power when it made planetfall, but not under control, else the crew would have brought it down on one of the large landmasses and not smashed it against the submerged asteroid reef. He pictured the vessel slicing into the water, ramming into this asteroid reef and embedding itself there, offering the crew little chance of escape and at the same time ruining what was left of this dead world's ecosystem in the immediate vicinity. The fuel tanks had ruptured and had spilled whatever they had left inside along the reef. Most of the coral was dead as a result, no creatures crawled over the ridge, and only an occasional fish swam by.

The hull was breeched in two places from the impact, but as he looked more closely he spotted three other areas where the hull was ripped open from weapons' fire.

"No chance of escape," he whispered.

As he floated along the ship he saw traces of scoring at the bottom of the mid and aft sections and a spot where a plate had buckled, not from water pressure and not by dropping from space unexpectedly into the planet's gravity, but from a sanz-torpedo.

"Pirates," he chuckled. Only privateer ships skirting the rim's merchant lanes carried those kinds of torpedoes anymore, unavailable in most mercenary circles, and largely unwanted because they were not always precise. But they were cheap and the staple of black market weapons' dealers who operated in the far reaches, and when they hit they did their job.

"So you didn't run afoul of some interplanetary government. You probably didn't steal your cargo and find yourselves chased across half of known space by its former owners. Pirates came after you, TRG-two three seven. But you fell into the water before the pirates could plunder you." Another chuckle as he headed toward the largest breech. "Yo ho ho. All the better for us."

His com crackled, interrupting his musings.

"Twenty-eight bodies, no survivors. All of them Entirians."

"Leave them for the fish," Dalan cut back. Had Rix been here, she would have at the least told the salvors to lash the corpses together and weight them down—her version of a burial at sea. And she would have demanded their records be pulled from the computer so their kin could be tracked down on whatever world they lived and properly notified. That still might happen, Dalan thought, if the records were in the chips that were being pulled from the bridge.

"Captain's log recovered."

"Good work," he replied over his com. He was about to slip into the breech for a look himself.

"Debris cleared away. We're at the main hold, opening it now."

Dalan growled from deep in his throat. In some respects he was like Rix, caught up in the discovery of something, wanting to be the first to see it—before the crew had a chance to disturb anything. He'd told them to wait. Why hadn't they listened?

"I told you to..."

An explosion rocked the vessel, propelling Dalan away from the breech and into the asteroid reef. The wind rushed from his lungs, and he gasped for air, instantly sputtering when he inhaled water. The impact had cracked his rebreather, and dead coral had sliced through his suit. He felt the warmth of blood along the back of his leg and the icy cold of the alien sea.

Without a second thought, he pushed away from the ridge, flicking on his thrusters and aiming for the *Mary Carleton.* He didn't look back to check on the crew, he didn't have to. His com crackled with a half-dozen voices, some of them screams, all of them in a panic. Dalan heard Mitchell trying to restore calm, access the damage, but Mitchell's voice cut out, only to be replaced by rapid breathing. At least two were dead, the hysterical voices told him that, another two injured—one with a vent pipe lanced through his gut by the concussive force of the blast.

Dalan balled his fists in frustration. He couldn't do anything about them—couldn't help them, couldn't even reply to the cries over the com, couldn't risk expelling his last precious breath. He kicked his feet, hoping the added momentum might get him to the ship faster. Then he could do something, after he put on a new suit. His teeth chattered and he felt his fingers grow numb, nothing to keep out the terrible cold of the sea now. How cold were his fellow salvors in the wreck below?

Dalan reached the hatch, just as he felt himself blacking out, his body involuntarily inhaling and drawing more of the icy water inside his lungs. It was several moments later before he came to, the *Mary Carleton*'s lone medic working over him. Around him a half-dozen salvors from the previous shift were scrambling into suits, attaching rebreathers to each others' backs, not bothering to check their instruments before setting their weight belts and dropping through the hatch.

"I need a new suit," he told the medic. Dalan tugged his belt off and tossed it near his helmet. He stared—the back of the helmet was covered with spiderweb fine cracks. He was lucky it hadn't shattered. "Gotta go back."

"You're not going anywhere," the medic corrected. She pointed a doughy finger at Dalan's leg, which was stretched out in a pool of blood. "You got yourself cut up good." Then without another word she was running a pack over the wound, sealing the flesh while at the same time cleaning and disinfecting it.

"Have to see Rix."

The medic shook her head. "Missed her. She just went down."

"There was an explosion."

"No kidding, Dalan." Then she was helping him up and gesturing. "Move. To your quarters. In a minute I'm going to have seriously injured people to deal with—one of them a Rizer, and I don't have any of his blood cloned for a transfusion. I'll check on you later."

* * *

Dalan knocked before entering the captain's cabin.

She looked old, outside of her yellow diving suit, and small—not more than five feet tall. The soft light of the cabin revealed a myriad of wrinkles around her watery-blue eyes and lips, wisps of gray-tinged brown hair that danced in the breeze of the air recycler. Rix was sixty-eight, and she had done nothing with cosmetics or nanites to ease the years. She'd never had surgery and she resisted cloning technology. She believed her age gave her a visual edge on the younger crew.

Dalan, who was a little less than half her age, believed the alcohol and the hard life she'd chosen made her appear even a decade older.

"Mum?" she asked.

He shook his head, and ran his fingers through his close-cropped black hair. Dalan detested the stuff, a mix of wheat and barley malts flavored with herbs and sweetened, brewed by the chef at Rix's precise instructions, approximating a seventeenth-century strong ale favored by pirates and the men who hunted them.

She poured him a mug anyway. He noticed she was drinking from the goblet they'd recovered from the old wreck. It was pale blue etched glass, looking like a piece of carved ice, and looking like it belonged in her small, age-spotted hand. He discovered that he was admiring it in spite of himself.

"Thanks," he said, as he uncomfortably settled his bulky frame into a narrow chair across the table from her and took a sip of the stuff. At least mum was better than the captain's other drink of choice—flip, this also a seventeenth-century concoction made of watered beer and flavored brandy. She was born about fifteen hundred years too late, he thought. "Mitchell?" he asked.

"Still dicey. Doc says not much brain activity, but she hasn't given up yet. Cameron and Juth reported back to duty this morning. And our Rizer's coming along."

"Three dead."

Rix nodded.

"The cargo hatch on the spaceship was booby-trapped."

Another nod.

"My fault," Dalan said after a moment, drawing his lips into a thin line. "I didn't have them use sensors on it, even though I saw the sanz-torpedo evidence. Didn't think the Leerkan crew would do something like that to their own ship."

"The Entirian captain feared they would be boarded by the pirates." She nudged a green chip across the table until it touched his fingers. "It's in his log, already translated. He was ready to destroy the whole ship to keep them from taking it and the cargo. A proud man."

"A foolish one," Dalan breathed.

She shrugged. "Everything logged?"

Dalan shook his head, his dark eyes dancing. "Took only one day to recover what we could of the cargo—a fraction of the time you spent on that old sailing ship. But we're still inventorying everything."

Rix raised an eyebrow.

"Despite what was lost to the explosion, it's still quite a haul. The ansally-sealed crates to the back weren't harmed, just knocked clear. I told the men to double-check everything. I want them to be exact.

"And..."

Dalan offered her a rare smile. "So far we've logged irichium ore capsules, two thousand of them, all nice and labeled and packaged. Bet they were destined for a rim energy weapons' plant. Maybe the planet Delkin or Rauk. Bolts of natural fabric, figured we could keep a few of those. A ton of dehydrated orinthris roots from the Ordis Colony, and half that much again of Rel spices—which will bring a small fortune if we unload them in the right port. Here's the partial inventory." He dropped a small black chip next to her goblet. "Yo ho ho. We should celebrate."

"After we mourn our fallen."

It was Dalan's turn to nod. "Still, you should be pleased."

Rix raised the goblet and offered a silent toast, then ran her index finger around the edge of the glass until it hummed. "Real crystal. I am pleased."

'Best haul we've made in past four months." Despite the loss of men, Dalan couldn't hide his enthusiasm.

"Indeed. A marvelous haul."

It took Dalan a moment to realize they were talking about two different ships.

She nodded to a shelf above her narrow bed. On it were a few of the objects taken from the *Dauntless.* Dalan recognized a sextant, a piece that might actually bring some money if it was sold at a military space station. He knew the rest of the objects were still in the smaller hold, in containers of seawater. Incomplete or damaged by barnacles and other alien growths, they would have to be restored or preserved before they could be brought into the open air.

Dalan took a long pull from the mug, the liquid stinging his throat. "You've a port in mind? I have all the documentation from the frigate, TRG-two three seven is the call number. It's a clean find. No one will contest us. And it crashed on an open space planet. Any relatives and creditors are out of luck."

She was staring at her reflection in the liquid. "A few minutes ago I gave the coordinates to the helmsman. We'll sell in the Wauk Colonies. Another few days and our holds will be empty again. And we'll be richer." She paused, clinking her nails against the goblet stem. "We'll take on some crew replacements, and then we'll head for the Dener System. I've a strange feeling we'll find another wreck or two there."

"Somehow, I've a feeling you'll be right." Dalan rose and left his half-finished mug on the table. He hadn't quite made it to the door when the claxon sounded. The *Mary Carleton* rocked, and Dalan grabbed the edge of the doorframe.

"No!" Rix's goblet jangled against the table, and she tried to snatch it. But it slipped through her fingers and struck the tile floor, shattering and sending mum flying. Behind her, the sextant slipped off the shelf and fell harmlessly onto her bed. She steadied herself against the table and then impatiently waved Dalan into the hall.

Moments later both were on what amounted to the *Mary Carleton*'s bridge. It was a small room, wedge-shaped like the ship. Rix settled herself in the chair at the point and peered out a viewscreen that wrapped itself around half the room and displayed nothing but winking stars and a distant comet.

"They're behind us." This from her helmsman, who Dalan was leaning over. Both men's fingers flew over switches and panels. "One large ship. A smaller trailing it."

"No markings. They're not responding to the hail." Dalan let out a deep breath, the air whistling through his clenched teeth.

The *Mary Carleton* shook again, and the main grid lit up with damage reports.

"Sanz-torpedo strike! Rear crew quarters. No one there. No casualties," Dalan reported with some measure of relief in his voice. "Damn it all. We're being chased by pirates."

"Again," the helmsman said softly.

The *Mary Carleton* was built for deep space and oceans, not speed. And despite the best efforts of the helmsman and Dalan, she couldn't outrun the unnamed pirate vessel. Laser fire scored her outer hull, but did not breech it.

"Either we're lucky, or they're lousy shots," the helmsman muttered.

"I'd say neither," Dalan quietly returned.

The air crackled with a burst of static, then a tinny voice cut through. "*Mary Carleton,* this is the cruiser *Sabrewind,* Commander Ormane. Prepare to be boarded. Or prepare to die." There was another burst of static, then silence. The handful of men looked to Captain Kilian.

Rix was leaning forward, punching rapidly at an instrument panel. "Slow to a third," she snapped. "Swing her around. We'll let them through the aft docking hatch." Her shoulders slumped, and she ran the back of her hand across her sweat-slick forehead. Her fingers trembled in time with her lower lip.

"Would we had some decent explosives," Dalan said, his voice barely above a whisper. "I'd rig the cargo doors and give them a taste of what TRG gave us. I've plenty of pride, too."

Rix brushed by him. "Take my chair. Unfortunately, I'm going to greet our...guests."

* * *

She was sipping mum again, this time from a mug. Dalan was glad there wasn't a spare mug in sight for her to offer him some.

Rix looked up as he entered, Willum was behind him, furtively looking around. She raised an eyebrow at the rookie's presence.

"They didn't take everything we had," Dalan began, "the pirates."

She shook her head and stirred her drink with a slender finger. "No. Half the irichium, all of the spice. It could have been worse. Much."

"Odd that it wasn't."

"Seems their hold was already pretty full," she sharply returned. "They didn't have room to take on any more."

"Just like the last time," Dalan cut in. "You know, Rix, you're pretty convincing. Going through the motions, trying to elude the pirates, sweating, looking all frazzled. Letting them damage our ship—but not damage it too much. My compliments."

She pushed the mug away and steepled her fingers.

"Rix...why?" Dalan's angular faced was etched with bewilderment. "Why are you in bed with pirates?"

She laughed softly, the sound of windchimes filling the small cabin. "You're smart, Dalan. More wits than I gave you credit for."

"That's why you hired me. For the big brain inside the big body, you told me."

A pout overtook her lips. "Still, I thought things—the raids—were spaced far enough that even you wouldn't be suspicious."

"It was the same ship that came after us two months ago." Dalan edged closer. "Why?" he repeated.

She looked up, the lines on her face more pronounced, the gray in her hair shining in the cabin's muted light. "It was a *charte-partie* I signed."

He cocked his head.

"A charter party, a freebooter covenant. It was drawn up years ago between their pirate commander and myself. It delineates the division of spoils from the ships they notify us of."

"Yo ho ho." Dalan whistled and shifted back and forth on the balls of his feet. ATRG. The pirates told you where it was? Didn't they?"

A nod. "And several others over the past several years. The ships that they downed and that went into the seas."

"Where they couldn't get them, because their own ships weren't equipped for oceans."

"But the Mary Carleton could. And could do it legally. I guess I'm fortunate you didn't figure it out before now." She paused. "Not a bad arrangement, actually. We both come out ahead—we finding wrecks we likely wouldn't otherwise, getting a share of them, the pirates getting part of the booty they'd went after. I'll have to cut you in now, it seems."

Dalan paced in a tight line, the cabin too small for him to move much. "But why, Rix? We didn't need to. We've been making a good living salvaging legitimate wrecks." He stopped and met her stare. "Just how many of them have been legitimate finds?"

She smiled. "About half."

"A living. A good one. Better than most salvors, in fact."

She shrugged. "But not a fine living. And not an exciting one. Besides, Dalan, I told you I considered myself a pirate at heart."

"Then why not tell the crew about your...charter party? Most of 'em would've gone along with you. They're mercenary enough."

She wrinkled her nose. "Then I'd have no secrets. Besides, would you have gone along with it?"

He didn't answer.

Rix reached for her mug of mum and he moved—fast and catching her off-guard. Dalan grabbed her arm, knocking the mug from it and spinning her around, clamping her hands behind her back. He expected her to struggle, she was a fit woman despite her age. She should have at least cried out. But she didn't put up a fight and she didn't offer an argument. Not even as he and Willum led her through an empty hallway and to the aft docking hatch airlock.

"A mutiny, Dalan? Rook?"

Dalan didn't answer at first. "I guess you could call it that."

"Fitting," she judged. "So you'll have me walk the plank, return the *Mary Carleton* to strictly honest work."

"Ah, the *Mary Carleton.* The ship you named after a famous woman pirate." Dalan chuckled. "*Mary Carleton* wasn't a pirate, Rix. I know my Earth history, too. But *Mary Carleton* knew more than a few of the pirates. She was undoubtedly the most celebrated whore in Old Port, Jamaica. Some called her the German Princess. They hanged her in sixteen seventy-three in Tyburn. I looked it up."

He opened the hatch and shoved her into the airlock, swinging the door shut and flipping the lever that jettisoned her into space.

"Pearls for your eyes, Rix," he said.

"Sorry ma'am," Willum offered.

Willum followed Dalan silently back to the captain's cabin. "I should bring your things here?" he asked after Dalan had settled himself at the table.

"Yes, First Mate Willum," Dalan answered. "But not until tomorrow."

He returned to the bridge, finding the captain's wide chair comfortable and to his liking. The stars spread out before him, winking at him. He wasn't sure how long he'd sat staring before a gentle tap on his shoulder interrupted his thoughts.

It was the crew's only Rizer, a being who looked wholly human save for his pale green skin.

"Sir?"

Dalan nodded, pleased that the ship's medic had patched the Rizer up like new. He was a good salvor.

"Some bad news, sir." The Rizer's voice was halting.

"Go on..."

"It seems there was an accident in the reserve cargo hold. Captain Kilian must have been restoring some of the things recovered from that old sailing ship. She hadn't properly secured the airlock when she flushed the sea water from a couple of the crates."

Dalan stared incredulously.

"She's gone, sir."

He swallowed hard, forcing a tear to his eye as the Rizer explained that Dalan was the captain now, the ship his as Kilian had no relatives and no will.

Dalan wiped at the tear and took a deep breath. He looked suitably sad and made his lower lip tremble.

"Sir?" the Rizer seemed to need direction.

"Notify the officials in the Marsh system," Dalan cut back. It was his first order as captain of the *Mary Carleton.* "Rix might not have had any family, but she had friends there, and an ex-husband if I recall. But first notify the crew. We'll have a service for her at the end of this shift."

"Yessir."

Then the Rizer was padding away and Dalan was staring at the stars again. He was silent for several long minutes, squeezing the bridge of his nose and shaking his head in feigned grief. It was an act he thought Rix would have been proud of.

"Helmsman," he said finally, his voice a gasp, "take us to the Galitor Quadrant. I've a hunch we'll find some choice wrecks to salvage there."

He leaned back in the chair and tugged a red chip from his pocket. It was his own charter party.

In a secret communique between him and Commander Ormane a few days ago, the pirate told Dalan he'd downed two merchant haulers in that quadrant, both slipping into a deep ocean. "There will be others, too," Ormane had said. "This is just the beginning."

Fifty-fifty on everything, the arrangement between the two had been sealed, a little better than what Rix had offered Ormane. But it was more than enough to please Dalan. At least for now.

"And this is just the beginning," Dalan whispered. "Yo ho ho."

The Walnut-Hued Man of Sutton Passeys

I thought the sheriff of Nottingham deserved more screen time in the various Robin Hood movies I watched as a kid. I thought he had a far snappier outfit than any of the Merry Men, and he seemed to be the better swordsman. This anthology presented the opportunity to let the sheriff shine...at least for a time. "Walnut-Hued" originally appeared in Warrior Fantastic, *DAW Books, 2000.*

His dreams rode on the exquisite blade that shimmered in the light of the full moon. He put all of his strength and skill behind the weapon, his years of careful study. He imagined the point crying out for blood, aimed straight at the heart of his most-hated enemy. The keen edge sparkled, like his eyes sparkled in morbid anticipation. He lunged so fast that he was certain he heard the weapon whistling as it drove faultlessly through the air, forward and true and...

...missed.

"Not this night, My Lord Sheriff!" his enemy taunted, grinning mischievously and springing back a heartbeat before the blade would have connected.

Another leap and the outlaw was beyond his second swing, and his third—which was clearly awkward in his desperation. The fourth was worse, so clumsy now that he caught his own cloak, slicing through a voluminous fold and drawing the hissing snickers of the townsfolk who'd come out of their cozy homes to watch.

"Damn you Robin of Locksley!" the sheriff hollered, rushing forward and slashing furiously again and again, missing his agile foe each time by inches. "To the pit with you, I say!" The sheriff knew he needed to compose himself, needed to drown the ire that made him woefully inept in the presence of Sherwood's famous outlaw. He silently shouted at himself to relax and focus—but the doing of it was not within his capabilities. At least not this night.

Despite the ungainly way he was wielding the weapon, the sheriff was an accomplished swordsman, riding with the king a few years past on one of his all-important crusades. In his reasonably short life he'd cut down dozens of skilled warriors, perhaps hundreds. But he could not put more than a scratch on this one despicable foe—no matter the weapon he chose to use. This night, it was a heavy Mascaron sword, embossed with gold on the crosspiece, an expensive gift from a visiting Spanish noble.

His collection of bladed weapons included the finest—Damascan steel, one with a basket hilt layered with silver and bronze; folded blades from unpronounceable far-eastern villages; an elegant Italian malchus; a singular French rapier said to have belonged to a prince; a silver-edged Moorish three-point; an ancient parazonium (that he flaunted on his hip, but never used for fear it would break); a broadsword taken from a Saracen chief; and more. He practiced daily, save during tax weeks, and no man in the castle could last more than a few minutes with him in a sparring session.

But this man...this one very arrogant and insolent man. This man was truly beyond him.

Why had Robin Hood come to Nottinghamshire this evening? Supplies for his Merry Men most likely, as the sheriff's guards spotted him skirting a wall in the merchants' quarter. The guards were assembling a force to take him, but the sheriff bid them to keep their place, intending to take Robin Hood alone and claim all the glory and notoriety for himself. It was not the first time the sheriff had tried this stunt, and the way the duel was going now, he was certain it would not be the last. Clearly if he had gathered enough guards and soldiers, Robin would be captured and on his way to the dungeon at this very moment. But the victory that he so profoundly craved...no, the victory he so desperately needed...would not be his. He must take the man alone.

Robin said something, but the sheriff didn't catch it, too deeply lost in his musings. The daring outlaw was several feet away, clearly illuminated in the moonlight, dressed in greens the color of wet fern leaves. His long brown hair fluttered about his shoulders in the slight breeze, and his mustache curled up on the edges as his smile grew wider. Robin was a handsome man, only a year or two younger than the sheriff, and the sheriff yearned intensely to deeply scar that pretty, unblemished face.

The sheriff spat—this, too, missing the outlaw. Through clenched teeth he cursed his foe again. "Damn you, Robin Hood!"

"It is not your place to damn me, my good sheriff. Only God can do that." Robin feinted to his left, the sheriff following him, sword leading and jabbing and missing wide when the outlaw unexpectedly pivoted to the right. "And I'd like to think God is on my side, Philip Mark. The good friar prays for me every night—right after dinner, you know."

The sheriff tried a feint, too, a move that did not catch the outlaw off guard. It only made Robin laugh louder. The outlaw was quick, spinning to the left again, darting right, his own blade flicking out like a striking serpent. It caught the sheriff's tunic, slicing through the laces and causing the growing crowd to cheer. Another deft flick and he'd cut through the cord that held the sheriff's cloak. For a moment the black velvet hung suspended like a giant bat, then it fluttered to rest around his ankles.

"In need of a new tailor, my Lord Sheriff?" Robin's mocking voice was musical and light. "I could recommend one." The outlaw danced forward then, suddenly slashing with a speed that made his inferior blade sing.

Startled, the sheriff stepped back, his feet becoming tangled in his cloak. His sword flew from his fingers as he fell to his rump, and Robin thrust forward, skewering the sheriff's hat. Then the outlaw continued on his way, flicking the hat to one of the onlookers, grabbing up the sheriff's lost sword. He bowed and twirled in front of a comely young woman as if he were at a dance, then he effortlessly hurdled a horse trough.

By the time the sheriff had picked himself up, Robin had melted into the shadows and was no doubt out the gate or over the wall. Heading back to the refuge of his blessed Sherwood Forest.

The townsfolk were murmuring, casting amused glances at the sheriff as they returned to their homes.

"Aye, not this night," the sheriff whispered, recalling the outlaw's words. "But soon, Robin Hood. I shall have you very soon."

He grabbed up his cloak, tossing it over his shoulder, not wanting to leave it on the street as physical evidence of tonight's debacle. The sheriff drew his tunic together, lamented the loss of an expensive, unique blade, and strode purposefully toward the castle.

* * *

"Eustace!" the sheriff stormed into the great hall, brushing by a pair of guards and dismissing them with an angry wave. He slammed the door shut behind him and glanced up the staircase. "Eustace!"

It was late, only a few candles flickered in the room and caused ghostly shadows to cavort along the walls. Did even the specters of Nottinghamshire mock him? he wondered.

"Eustace!" he bellowed once more. "Come down here at once!"

Heart hammering wildly in wrathful indignation, the sheriff dropped his ruined cloak on the table and tugged free the tunic. He turned to stare up into the mirror that hung above the mantle. "Why can't I beat him?" he moaned. The image that looked back had no answers. The sheriff's ropy muscles gleamed with sweat, his chest rose and fell rapidly. He ran his fingers over his taut stomach and up to his face, which was angular and darkened by a hint of stubble. There was a thick scar leading from his jaw to just above his ear, the end disappearing in his jet-black hair—Robin Hood had given him that memento early last year.

"Eustace!"

There were hurried footfalls in the stairwell beyond, accompanied by the soft swish of fabric.

"Yes, my Lord Sheriff."

"Eustace of Lowdham, if you manage to get any slower I will..."

"I was sound asleep, Philip. One of your guards just roused me..."

Philip Mark glared at his deputy.

"...and told me what happened near the merchant district. Robin Hood again. Pity."

Philip's eyes narrowed.

"You can't beat him, Philip. Not alone. You should have called the guards. They would have caught his sorry carcass." Eustace glided farther into the room, the hem of his robe dragging on the floor behind him. He was quite a bit smaller than the sheriff, and the overlarge garment made him look frail. "All you need is the element of surprise and enough men," he continued. "In fact, Philip, if you had..."

The sheriff moved quickly, reaching Eustace in two steps and bringing his hand up to the man's throat, pushing him back until he hit the wall. The smaller man's skin blanched and his eyes grew wide like a frightened doe's.

"You...will...not...talk...to...me...that...way!" The sheriff spat each word for emphasis. "You are my deputy, Eustace of Lowdham, serving at my behest, and I'll warrant that if your tongue wags with such insolence again you'll be on the first ship headed toward..."

"I'm sorry, Philip," Eustace gasped. "Truly sorry." The smaller man's eyes successfully pleaded with the sheriff to relax his grip. Eustace sagged against the wall and rubbed at his throat. "Forgive me. I wasn't thinking."

Philip Mark paced in front of him. "A favor to your family. That's why I selected you. That and your knowledge of all the villages that litter this land. You're an expert in intrigue, my good little Eustace. And you've a remarkable memory. People don't consider you a threat, and so they aren't very careful with their secrets when you move about them."

Some of the color was returning to Eustace's face. "Secrets? What secrets do you concern yourself with so late this evening?"

The sheriff seemed not to have heard him. "A favor to your family. And now you'll do a favor for me." He stopped in front of his deputy, noting that the smaller man seemed more than a bit nervous by the closeness. It brought a faint smile to Philip's lips that he could so intimidate Eustace of Lowdham.

"You have a Yorkshire connection."

Eustace nodded.

"And you're well known in the Barnsdale area. And throughout Derbyshire for that matter."

Another nod.

"You know of the swordsmen there."

"You are an excellent swordsman, My Lord Sheriff. Certainly one of the best in..."

"The swordsmen there," Phillip repeated through clenched teeth.

"There are several My Lord..."

"The very best swordsmen. Someone better than me, far better than the men in my service. Someone even better than that damnable Robin Hood."

Eustace studied the sheriff, trying to figure out precisely what he was up to. The shadows continued to dance around the room for several silent moments, occasionally teasing the sheriff's sweat-slick face. Finally, Eustace took a deep breath and spoke. "There are a few legendary swordsmen in Nottinghamshire, men who rode with the king a long time ago, and some of whom you know. Local heroes, I suppose you could call them."

"I don't want a local hero! I want someone relatively obscure. A very private man. Not one of the wizened old fools who can't even lift a weapon anymore. And not one of those braggarts whom every night wraps his hands around a tankard of mead instead of the pommel of a sword. I want the very best, Eustace. Do you understand?"

Eustace cleared his throat and gestured to the table. Phillip nodded, and the two of them selected seats opposite each other. They lowered their voices, talking in hushed whispers more because whispers were the stuff of conspiracies rather than because they did not want any passing guards to overhear them.

Eustace suggested swordsman after swordsman, Phillip rejecting them all as either too celebrated or not good enough. "Someone who is not known to any of the nobility of Nottinghamshire. Someone whom I have not heard of. Someone who keeps to his little village and keeps to himself. Surely there must be such a swordsman. Someone who has fallen out of memory," Phillip hissed. "This is a very private thing."

The deputy sheriff sat back in the chair, running his fingers through his hair as if he were trying to stir up some recondite recollection. The sheriff drummed his fingers on the table and waited.

"There is a man in Sutton Passeys," Eustace began. "I believe he is still alive." He leaned forward until he was practically forehead to forehead with the sheriff. "He is an old man, but not so ancient as to be infirm. Keeps to himself—now. But two decades or so past he was with the king on one of those years-long crusades. I believe his name is Aruze."

"An unusual name. What one might call a cat or a dog."

Eustace steepled his fingers. "It is what the villagers call him, in any event. But those outside the village refer to him as the Walnut-Hued Man. And those in Nottingham proper know nothing of him."

Phillip cocked his head. "This Walnut-Hued Man. Is he a Moor? In Sutton Passeys?"

Eustace shrugged. "I've never met him, only seen him once or twice as I passed through collecting taxes. He looked a little exotic. Definitely a foreigner."

The sheriff crooked his finger, indicating he wanted more information.

"I've heard tales about the man, from the more talkative folks in Sutton Passeys. Seems they all welcomed this stranger into their midst several years ago, even though he lives in a shack alone. And if half the tales are true, he was indeed a formidable swordsman years back. Tends livestock now with the rest of them, sheep and..."

"Take me to him in the morning."

Eustace let out a deep breath, the sound of leaves rustling across the ground. "My Lord Sheriff, sometime tomorrow the Courtneys..."

"...will be coming to Nottinghamshire," Phillip finished. "Yes, I know." His voice was so soft now that Eustace had to strain to hear him. "There are plenty of people in this castle to entertain the old man and his sons and that hawk-nosed daughter of his. Enough people to keep up appearances. And we should be back well before nightfall, in plenty of time for the feast. Besides, we will be made more important to the Courtneys by our tardiness."

Eustace yawned and pushed himself away from the table, stood and brushed at a wrinkle in his robe. "At first light then, My Lord Sheriff." He waited for Philip to wave his hand, officially dismissing him. But the sheriff's gaze was locked on a whorl in the tabletop, concentrating on something far from this room. "My Lord Sheriff?" Louder: "Philip?"

The sheriff waggled his fingers. "All right, go. But be ready at first light."

Eustace glided toward the stairs and caught up the hem of his robe. "Phillip?"

The sheriff almost reluctantly raised his head.

"This trip will be for folly, you must realize. The Walnut-Hued Man will not fight Robin Hood for you. No matter that he rode with the king. Or that he might have been noble in whatever country he's originally from. He's one of the common people now, whom we tax to death. His sympathies most assuredly will be on the side of the outlaw. If you want a swordsman who will face Robin alone, I can..."

Philip Mark smiled. It was a wicked-looking expression that held all manner of maliciousness within it and sent shivers down Eustace's back. "I don't want him to fight Robin Hood, my dear Eustace of Lowdham. I want him to teach me. And I don't care what side his sympathies are on. He will teach me. Of that you can be confident. I can buy his sympathies. Every man has a price."

* * *

"Teach you? The likes o' you? Teach the Sheriff of Nottinghamshire how to use a sword?"

"I know how to use a sword," Phillip Mark returned tersely. From the back of his horse, he looked down at the old man and thumped his fingers on the basket hilt of a long sword that had been specially made for him. "I can use any blade quite well. I merely wish to improve on the skills I already possess."

"Me? Teach the Lord Sheriff?"

The man was dark-skinned, though not near so dark as to be considered a Moor. His skin was more the shade of walnut shells, free of wrinkles despite his years. Perhaps he was from Italy or lands to the east of it, Philip mused. His head was shaved, like a man from the Orient or from a reclusive order of monks. The sheriff looked closer and shuddered, discovering no hair on the back of the man's hands or forearms or on his face, as if a horrible disease rather than a religious sect had robbed him of it. Age had certainly robbed the man of his posture. He walked stooped over, one shoulder slightly below the other, and one foot turned in. His clothes were in tatters, though reasonably clean and a shade or two darker than his skin. He looked up at the sheriff, squinting into the sun.

"Me? Teach you?" He let out a clipped laugh. "I haven't heard somethin' so silly in all o' my days." His voice sounded like gravel bumping around in a bucket. He looked over his shoulder. A few villagers milled about, kept far enough back by Eustace and the guards that they couldn't hear all of what was being said, but desperate to at least see what was transpiring. Whispers of "more taxes" passed from one man to the next. The old man nodded to them, offering them some measure of reassurance that he wasn't going to be carted off to the dungeon for some silly offense.

"I guess I was mistaken that you could teach me anything," Philip Mark stated evenly, turning his horse so his back was to the rabble, yet so that he could still watch the old man. "I had heard that at one time you were an expert swordsman."

But the shriveled wreck before him was far from a swordsman, the sheriff could see that. The dark-skinned old man would be hard-pressed to even make a worthy peasant. And Eustace would find himself entertaining the Courtney woman this evening for mentioning this walnut-hued lout and dragging him out here so early in the day.

"It would seem that I am looking for someone else. Someone named Aruze. Someone who once rode with the king."

The dark-skinned man returned his attention to the sheriff, his eyes needlelike slits.

"I am Aruze," he said, after a fashion opening his eyes wider. "But I'm a shepherd, not a warrior."

The sheriff would have left then, thankfully abandoned this quaint village that smelled strongly of sheep dung and poverty. Indeed, he was looking forward to watching Eustace squirm before that ghastly Courtney woman. But there was something about the old man's eyes that held him like a vise. A cunning intelligence flickered in them, something that the years and the harsh conditions of this life couldn't chase away and that the sheriff found fascinating and hypnotizing. Philip's hands tightened on the reins. He should leave now, but...

"I used to be a swordsman," the man finally acknowledged. "It was a long time ago. And many miles from here."

"And so you've forgotten those skills," the sheriff baited, his eyes still captured by the old man's. A small part of Philip's mind again told him to leave, screamed that he should not waste another minute of his precious time chatting with a dirty commoner who did not even address him as "Sir" or "My Lord Sheriff." Why, if Philip were home in the castle right now, he would have servants trimming his hair and measuring him for new clothes. And the hawk-nosed Courtney daughter would be fawning over Eustace, throwing herself at the smaller man and making everyone quite nauseous. Did she still marinade herself in sickeningly sweet perfume? "What was I possibly thinking...Aruze... that one such as you might..."

"I've forgotten nothin'." The man made an effort of straightening himself.

Philip Mark slid from his horse's back, his eyes still not leaving the peasant's. Closer to the old man, he could smell him. There was a sharp, musky fragrance to him, no doubt from spending his days and nights with sheep. "Forgotten nothing? Then teach me what you know."

"Why?"

"Does it matter?"

Aruze dug the ball of his good foot into the ground and slowly shook his head. "I've schooled many a man in the blade. Here, and in my homeland. But I'll not teach the likes o' you." Then the old man dropped his gaze to the toes of his worn boots, releasing Philip's eyes.

The sheriff blinked to clear his head. He should have the man whipped for refusing. No. Not enough. He should have him hung or drawn and quartered. Then he should find a swordsman not as old or as crippled, but every bit as obscure. He should get back on his horse right now and...

"Teach me," Philip found himself saying. "I will make it worth your while old man."

Aruze spat at the sheriff's feet. "I don't like you. I don't like your kind. Nothin' you could do would make it worth my while to help you. Nothin'."

The sheriff spun, looking across the rundown village to the men and women kept back by the guards. They were a pitiful lot, all poor and broken and dirty.

"I'll not tax Sutton Passeys for two months."

Aruze raised his head, again meeting the sheriff's gaze. He drew his lips into a thin line, as if considering the offer. "No."

"Three."

"Five months."

"Done."

"Not quite." The old man smiled thinly and his dark eyes sparkled. "Five months worth o' tax money you will return to this village before we begin."

Philip clenched his fists. It was his turn to refuse.

"And you'll not tell a single soul that it's for swordplay lessons. You'll say all o' that taxin' was a mistake. You simply took too much. The people here were over burdened. And you'll say you're sorry for it."

Philip vehemently shook his head.

"I don't like you, Sheriff o' Nottinghamshire. And I don't trust you. If I teach you for a month, you might well turn around and start taxin' us again."

The sheriff forced himself to relax and offered the man a slight nod in appreciation. Taxing them again was indeed what he would have done.

"So you'll return five months worth o' tax money. If you want me to teach you."

Words flitted through the sheriff's mind. He should call this man an impudent cur, should throw him in the dungeon, increase Sutton Passeys taxes for spite—though he was certain from the looks of these indigent folks he wasn't likely to get more than another coin or two.

"Very well," Philip said softly. "We shall start tomorrow. I shall bring the tax money with me."

"And..."

The sheriff cocked his head, anger glimmering in his eyes.

"You'll bring me a sword. A fine one, as good as what you're totin' on your hip."

"That I won't agree to."

"Then we don't have a deal."

Philip balled his fists and set them on his waist. "I am being more than generous as it is, old man."

"Swordplay lessons are expensive. And the time of even someone like me has value." Aruze smiled, showing a row of yellow-brown teeth. "Besides, I don't have a sword, My Lord Sheriff. And I'll need one to teach you...Sir." The words showed contempt, not respect. "I was forced to sell my favorite sword last year to pay your taxes."

"A sword, then."

"As fine o' one as that." He pointed to the sheriff's long sword.

"Tomorrow morning."

Aruze shook his head and dropped his voice to a harsh whisper. "Tomorrow night. There is an old stable a few miles south, down this road. It has no roof and is barely standin'. But it will do. Come there. Bad enough that I will teach you my craft. I cannot let my fellows here know what I am doin'. It wouldn't do at all to let them know I've sold my soul for tax money and a fine blade."

The sheriff clenched his jaw tight to keep from smiling. No tales of this endeavor would be spread! The foreigner was ashamed at this bargain. "Tomorrow night, Mister Aruze." Then he was quick on his horse and riding hard from Sutton Passeys. Eustace and the guards hurried to catch up.

* * *

Philip was tired, the ordeal with the Courtney nobles had lasted well into the early morning hours, and a noon meeting with the Merchants' Guild prevented him from sleeping late. He had considered sending Eustace to find the barn and tell the old man he would meet him in a few days. He should have, he told himself.

But here he was, alone and yawning and traveling south from Sutton Passeys. The horse's saddlebags chinked with coins, and he halfway worried that Robin Hood and his men might rob him. They might have, had he been dressed properly. But he was wearing commoner's clothes that Eustace had fetched for him, drab garb that kept the people of Nottinghamshire from recognizing him as he rode out the gates on an aging, sway-backed mare.

The barn loomed ahead, and he pulled on the reins, stopping well short of it. "What am I doing?" he whispered. "All of this skullduggery because I wish to best one man."

Perhaps Eustace of Lowdham was right, this was for folly and he should simply summon plenty of guards and soldiers when he caught sight of the outlaw. "But for pride and my obsession," he said, as he slid from the horse's back and led the animal to the barn.

He had expected it to be dark inside, but with no roof the moon shone in. There were gaps in the walls, and Philip wondered if a strong breeze would topple the thing. The old man was there, standing crookedly in the center, carefully regarding him. "I didn't expect you'd show," he said, the gravelly voice still sounding unpleasant to the sheriff's ears.

"Neither did I." Philip dropped the reins and fumbled about on the saddle, tugging free the tax money and tossing it to the ground. "Your fee."

"And..."

He retrieved a rolled blanket, and from it he pulled a sword. It was an unusually thick-bladed rapier with a steel hilt, one embossed with brass designs. Near the half-basket the sword was scalloped, and the indentations were edged in silver and bronze. The moon caught the sword and made it gleam, as the old man's eyes were gleaming.

"A very fine blade," Aruze said, a hint of awe in his rough voice. "A most superb weapon."

"Worth more than the five months of taxes collected from your village," the sheriff added, as he tossed it to him. Worth far more than your sorry hide, he added to himself. The old man caught the sack of coins and continued to admire the sword, which was one of the lesser pieces in the sheriff's collection. "I trust, Mister Aruze, that this sword will..."

"More than suffice, My Lord Sheriff." Respect in the voice this time. "My thanks to you. And I trust you will not be disappointed with my tutelage."

"Let us hope not," the sheriff swore under his breath.

As the night wore on, the sheriff discovered that the bent and crippled man still possessed a considerable measure of grace, and that he moved with a speed belaying his years. There was an awkwardness about him because of his crooked foot and dropped shoulder, but it was evident that the man had adapted to his deteriorating condition and had compensated with other moves. Philip suspected that Aruze had been a masterful warrior in his youth, one the king was proud to have with him—no matter from what foreign land he came from.

The sheriff found himself struggling to keep pace with Aruze, finding that it took all of his effort just to parry the old man's blows. There was little strength behind Aruze's swings, but they were accurate, aimed at vital organs and stopping short just in time. The sheriff inwardly beamed when as the evening grew older the peasant praised his techniques. And he surprised himself when he did not get angry when the old man in turn said he had a long way to go to match him.

Eventually the old man tired, announcing an end to the first lesson. He carefully placed the rapier on the ground, then he sat next to it, this move taking a bit of work because of his misshapen foot. He let out a great sigh and looked up at Philip, who'd led his horse to the door. Then he dropped his gaze to the sword and reached a finger out to caress the crosspiece.

"My Lord Sheriff, you are a passable swordsman."

Philip nodded.

"So I am curious why you have a need to be better. And why you came to me."

No answer.

"I am no one, My Lord Sheriff. No songs are sung of my deeds. Few know of my talent with a sword."

"There are a few tales," Philip said.

"So I am still curious. Why do you need to be better? Do you fear someone from within the castle? The king did and so became more skilled."

"You taught him, Aruze?"

No answer. Instead, another question. "Is it your deputy? The young fancy man from Lowdham. Does he want your position? Some lesser noble scrabblin' up the Nottinghamshire ladder? There is always intrigue among your kind. Plottin' and schemin' and..."

"I want Robin Hood."

Aruze wiped at something on his tattered pants. "The outlaw?"

A nod.

"He's good. Very good with a sword and very good for the common folk."

Philip instantly cursed himself for telling the old peasant the truth. He could have easily fabricated something, went along with the notion that Eustace of Lowdham was out to get his title.

"But I don't like him," the old man continued. "Good that I know who you plan to face, My Lord Sheriff."

Philip cocked his head in a question.

"Makes the lessons different." There was still a question on the sheriff's face, and so the old man went on. "Saw Robin Hood once, fightin' some o' your soldiers on the road near Sutton Passeys. He fights from his heart, doesn't use any techniques taught by any masters. Taught anywhere for that matter. He's unpredictable. And he taunts those he fights, his words workin' as a second sword that pricks at their hearts."

Philip found himself agreeing.

"So we will have to make you unpredictable, too. And, o' course, we will teach you to close your ears to his babble."

The sheriff gave the old man a genuine smile. "You say Robin Hood is good for the commoners, yet you'll help me best him. Why?"

Aruze looked at his beautiful sword. "It is wrong, all this stealin' he does. I'll make you better than him."

"How long shall that take?"

The old man shrugged, the motion exaggerated because of his bent body. "Depends on you, my Lord Sheriff. How quick o' a learner are you?"

"Tomorrow night, then?"

Aruze nodded. "And can you bring some wine?"

The nights blurred, and in them Philip learned to improvise and to anticipate the unexpected. He discovered that by studying an opponent's eyes he could judge where the man's sword would lead. He forced himself to shut out his opponent's words, be they hurtful or filled with pleas for mercy. And all those steps and thrusts he studied from his youth, he hid away in the back of his mind and instead relied on what the Walnut-Hued Man taught him.

When nearly three months had passed, the old man announced there was no more he could pass on to Philip Mark—though he could always learn more by finding an even better instructor. There existed a hint of friendship between the student and teacher, one that was guarded by the difference in their stations. Still, they had closed each session with fellowship by drinking wine and feasting on whatever the sheriff brought; this last night he offered up the very finest from his cellar. Aruze would recount a battle or two from the crusades or from a duel he fought in his faraway home, and Philip would tell of some of the goings-on in Nottingham Castle, though he never spoke of the more nefarious activities. This last night the sheriff even told Aruze of his many losses to Robin Hood.

"I don't like the man," Aruze admitted again. "But I like life. A part o' me regrets givin' you the skills to kill him."

"Everyone dies," Philip said evenly, his tongue thick from the alcohol they'd been sharing. "I only intend to hurry his death along." He noticed a sadness in the old man's eyes, and he cursed himself for feeling compassion for a mere peasant. "But I will make it quick," he added for consolation.

Aruze offered his hand.

And the sheriff almost took it.

* * *

Four nights later, Philip Mark found his green-clad foe at the edge of the merchants' quarter. Robin had been skulking, hood pulled tight over his head and keeping close to the shadows. His bags were filled with goods he'd either stolen or purchased with ill-gotten gold, and he barely had time to drop them and pull his sword before the sheriff was on him.

Philip was using the Saracen chief's blade this night, finding the balance perfect now that he had more strength in his arm. This night when he lunged, Robin wasn't able to so easily dance away. Indeed, the outlaw struggled to keep pace with the sheriff, and the merchants who climbed out of their cozy beds and opened the shutters were quiet as the men traded blows.

The sheriff tried a feint, one the old man taught him early in their sessions. It caught Robin off guard, and Philip spun to his right, slashing and cutting Robin's cloak. He could have run him through, but he needed to prolong this fight, he needed to relish his victory, and he needed more witnesses.

"It is you, perhaps, who is in need of the tailor now, Robin Hood!" The sheriff swung again, and a thin line of red appeared across Robin's arm.

Robin didn't offer a reply, putting his effort instead into parrying the sheriff's expert swings. The duel took them past the merchants' businesses and into a courtyard near the front gates, where the moon shone down unobstructed. The guards turned from their posts to watch the display. People were coming out onto the street, some wrapped in blankets, others struggling into cloaks. There were no giggles this time, and no words against the sheriff, only wide-eyed stares of disbelief and gasps of surprise as he forced the outlaw to defend himself.

As the fight continued, there were murmured speculations that the sheriff for once in his life would indeed defeat Sherwood's favorite son. Robin's leggings were slashed, the moon showing that the sheriff had drawn more blood.

"No," the sheriff told him. "On second thought, you won't be needing a tailor this night. You'll be needing a priest. To pray over your grave."

Philip's swings grew bolder and wilder, the moonlight flashing along the edge of the blade as it clashed against Robin Hood's sword. Then the moonlight caught the outlaw's weapon, just as Robin began to vary his thrusts.

It was a fine and unusually thick-bladed rapier the outlaw was wielding, one with a steel hilt embossed with bronze. There were scallops near the half-basket, edged in silver and brass that sparkled like the stars.

"It can't be!" Philip hollered, as with that realization he now found himself working to parry Robin Hood's blows. "It is not possible!"

The moonlight showed no hair on the back of Robin's hand, and when the outlaw lunged, his hood flew back, showing a shaved head.

"By all that's holy, no!"

"By all that's holy, yes," Robin returned.

There was no stoop in the posture, no dropped shoulder or crooked foot. But the eyes were the same, glimmering with a cunning intelligence. Robin rained a series of blows against the sheriff's heavier weapon. Then he darted in and jabbed at his thigh.

"Why?" Philip gasped. "Why the game? Why teach me?"

"I needed a better sparring partner," the outlaw continued. "One worthy of my efforts. And I thank you for providing me with one."

"How?" But in the back of Philip's mind, he began to answer that question. Robin had stooped his posture and turned in his foot, shaved himself. But darkening the skin?

Philip's musings stopped when Robin further increased the tempo of his swings, the tip of his rapier catching the basket of the sheriff's sword and sending it flying from his grasp. Robin darted forward again, slashing at the laces on the sheriff's tunic, again cutting the cord that held his cape. The garment fluttered to the ground. "We must do this again sometime, eh, my Lord Sheriff?"

Then the outlaw was scampering toward the gate, catching the pulley rope and hauling himself up it. Before the sheriff and the guards could react, he was over the wall and on his way to Sherwood.

Philip turned and retrieved his cloak. Then he headed toward the castle.

* * *

"Eustace!"

The sheriff slammed the door shut behind him, dismissed the guards with a wave and tromped into the great hall.

"Eustace of Lowdham if you..."

The deputy sheriff was scrambling down the stairs, the hem of his robe gathered in trembling fingers.

"My Lord Sheriff?"

Philip glared, clenching and unclenching his fists, taking a step toward Eustace, then stopping himself.

"Robin Hood?" Eustace risked.

The sheriff nodded. "Indeed. Robin Hood."

Several moments of silence passed between the two, the flickering candles sending shadows dancing across the walls, specters to mock the Sheriff of Nottinghamshire.

"I will have him, Eustace. I will have him twitching on the end of my sword. There will be no force of guards to take him. I won't use soldiers. I will take him. Alone!"

"Philip, I..."

"To my last breath, I will work. Do you understand? He can't kill me, Eustace. He wouldn't dare kill the Sheriff of Nottinghamshire. And so I am safe. But not him. I will have him!"

"Philip, perhaps I..."

"Swordsmen, Eustace, you will find me the very best. I don't care if they're known. I don't care where you get them. Tomorrow at first light, you will..."

"Philip, I..."

"But this time you will make sure that they are indeed who they claim to be. No imposters, or I will find myself a new deputy sheriff and I will send you on the first ship to..." The sheriff glanced up into the mirror that hung over the mantle. His face was red from ire and exertion, his chest rose and fell rapidly, and he could feel his heart hammering in his chest. Through the gap in his tunic, his broad chest gleamed, and the outline of the muscles in his sword arm rippled. He had to admit he was better and stronger. But he was not yet good enough.

"The Walnut-Hued Man, Philip..."

"Was Robin Hood," the sheriff spat, returning his attention to his deputy. "In disguise. Aruze, Eustace. Aruze! He was in deed a ruse. And I—with your eager help—played right into his hands. But I will have him. You will find me a better teacher. And I will have him very soon."

The sheriff strode from the great hall, brushing by Eustace and nearly knocking the slighter man over.

"My Lord Sheriff..." Eustace began. "The Walnut-Hued Man is real. I saw him in Sutton Passeys. He can't have been Robin Hood. The tales..." But the deputy sheriff's words were lost in the shadows. Philip Mark was on his way to his armory to practice with his swords.

* * *

An old man walked south on the road past Sutton Passeys. His skin was dark, branding him a Moor, not painted on from the juice of crushed walnuts—as Robin Hood's complexion had been. His gait was slow, his foot being turned in and his shoulder dropped from age and injury. Still, it was a determined pace he kept up. The old man knew not to stay in these parts, as the sheriff would be angry at the ruse he and his student Robin Hood had concocted. It had been his idea, in truth, wanting to give the outlaw a more formidable opponent. And when Robin embraced the idea, the old man had volunteered to do the teaching. But Robin wouldn't have it, not wanting to risk the old man's life—and not wanting to risk the possibility that the sheriff might become too skilled. And might possibly defeat him.

And so the old man was headed...somewhere. His purse was heavy with gold coins, payment from Sherwood's beloved outlaw. And on his hip hung a fine Mascaron sword, a singular weapon that a Spanish noble had once gifted to Philip Mark. And a blade that the old man knew how to use very well.

Author's notes: Historians differ on who they believe was the "Sheriff of Nottingham" of Robin Hood fame. One candidate is Philip Mark, who acted as the sheriff of Nottinghamshire and Derbyshire from 1209 to 1224. Another possible candidate is Eustace of Lowdham, who served as Philip's deputy from 1217 to 1224. Eustace, himself, served as the sheriff from 1232 to 1233.

Auriga's Streetcar

Yerkes Observatory used to operate in Williams Bay, WI, but in its last few years it suffered because of the dog track nearby. The track left its parking lot lights on all night, which made it difficulty for the observatory minders to study the stars. Light pollution intrigued me, so I did some reading on it and came up with the idea for this story. "Auriga's Streetcar" was originally published in Space Stations, *DAW Books, 2004.*

It looked wholly unremarkable—this fog-gray box suspended against the glittering darkness of space.

It possessed none of the technological elegance of its kin, none of the graceful butterfly-wing panels or sculpted solar scoops. No gently curving sections contrasted with the sharp angles of its thick hull. No lights—not that Hoshi had expected any, as the station was abandoned more than eight months past. No rotating grav-bands or revolving antenna arrays.

No beauty to it.

Indeed, there was nothing that made this aging space station even the slightest bit interesting to look at. Yet, Hoshi pronounced it...

"Wonderful."

She thumbed the controls of her skimmer, taking the runty craft once around the station, past the large docking bay, then closing on the side facing Earth. Here, she faintly made out *Yerkes-Two* in block black letters that had been pitted by space debris. Though *Yerkes-Two* was the station's official designation, the first team of astronomers serving aboard it referred to it instead as *Auriga's Streetcar,* a name that seemed untoward but that nevertheless stuck.

Hoshi supposed the station had the vague shape of a streetcar—she'd seen one in a California museum more than a few decades ago. But this lacked the riotous color she remembered. Lacked any color—there weren't even shades to the gray.

To her, the space station looked more like a brick, and that is precisely what *Auriga's Streetcar* had become. Its orbit was approaching the final stages of decay, and in a handful of days it would touch the upper limits of Earth's atmosphere, then pass through it and drop like that proverbial brick, breaking into pieces and burning up as it went. The *Streetcar* would be colorful then.

Hoshi told herself she'd timed this visit just right—the station's orbit taking it over Japan, requiring little use of fuel cells and little time to reach it. And there was more than enough time to thoroughly explore every nook and cranny and retrieve its precious antiquities. In truth, she'd hoped to make this trip months ago, but she'd been ill and her ship needed repairs. It was possible other scavengers had already visited the station in the meantime. She sucked in a breath, praying they had not beat her to the *Streetcar.* At her age she had little time for wasted trips.

The University of Chicago last year announced they were abandoning this station. They said its equipment was outdated, that it was too expensive to replace all the telescopes and their housings with the new more powerful refractors being manufactured. Too expensive to send ships and personnel to nudge the station into a higher, stable orbit and to keep it operating—as they had done when they refitted it three times before. Building a new station to study the stars was ultimately more economical now, the university financiers deemed. It was even judged too expensive to send a team of salvagers, not that the university thought there was anything worth retrieving from *Auriga's Streetcar*—not even the largest lenses.

They said to let the whole thing drop into the Atlantic Ocean. The station was simply too old to bother with.

Old.

Hoshi was old.

She brushed at a strand of thin silvery hair as she edged her craft into the small docking bay under the *Yerkes-Two* insignia and locked hatches with the station.

Indeed, she felt very old today, achy and a little out of sorts. It had been quite a while since she felt thoroughly good. She was chilled, despite keeping the temperature well above normal in her craft. Poor circulation, she mused—the years could be cruel to space stations and people. Her limbs were stiff, despite the zero-G. At eighty-four, she was among the senior of her country's independent spacers, and the only one who worked so often and who dealt exclusively in salvaging abandoned in-system stations and satellites. Abandoned—she wasn't a pirate, didn't go after anything that truly belonged to anyone.

Hoshi'd made a very good living at salvaging, and she certainly didn't need to keep at it, didn't need to be here when she was feeling every one of her years. Her grandson frequently begged her to "act her age," to retire and come live inland with him in Yashiro. But she was acting her age, she told him. She so enjoyed piloting and staying busy, finding technological treasures amid things people had unthinkingly left behind. Moreso, she enjoyed the solitude—of being away from the crowded, noisy, light-plagued Earth. And above all of that, she cherished being out where she could see the stars.

Hoshi—the name meant "star."

Slipping into her enviro-suit, she fastened her helmet and flicked on its beam. A few deep breaths and she floated from her skimmer, through the docking hatch, and into the empty *Streetcar.* The beam cast a ghost-light down a narrow corridor with walls as gray as the station's exterior. It was all so still, the only sound her breathing and the soft clicking her helmet made as it bumped against the ceiling. She started humming, faintly, a tune from her youth, as her gloved fingers guided her like a bobbing balloon—past an empty locker, then to a storage room.

A look inside: grav-boots all held neatly on shelves—she made a note to check later if there were any small enough to fit her; cartons of lens cleaners; panels of circuitry. The latter, and the thin layer of film that covered everything, nudged Hoshi's lips into a slight smile. It was obvious no one had been here since the last astronomer left, all the scavengers taking the university's word for it that there was nothing worthwhile remaining. It was all hers. There were other odds and ends in this storage room and the next two, most fastened tight onto shelves, only a few things floated free. Nothing of any particular value or interest, so Hoshi moved on, pausing only when she heard the groan of metal and sensed the station shudder. Perhaps the *Streetcar* didn't have that handful of days.

She passed what served as either a conference room or a cafeteria—wherein hung the only bit of color she'd seen so far—paintings of Earth scenes arranged without any real sense of art. The Golden Gate bridge highlighted by a fiery sunset, the Sydney Harbor filled with sailing boats, London at night, a wide-eyed child looking up at a seated statue of Abraham Lincoln, China's Great Wall. None of the pictures worth taking.

There were crew quarters, these far more spacious than on the other stations Hoshi had explored. There were no bunkbeds or wall-nets. There were real beds with thick mattresses, comfortable-looking chairs, and desks—all bolted to a gray floor. She fumbled at a panel on the wall, and a heartbeat later a section on the ceiling glowed bright enough to light the room. She felt a gradual heaviness, and realized artificial gravity was kicking in. Earth norm from the feel of it. The University of Chicago astronomers had been patricians as far as scientists went—hence the fine room that served as their escape from work and zero-G. They likely had taken all of their meager personal possessions with them, save the snugly fitted sheets and blankets and quilts, the plush pillows tied down with ribbons. Hoshi didn't bother to check the cabinets and closets. Her interests were elsewhere.

It took her nearly an hour to reach the main observatory, which occupied the entire upper level of the *Streetcar.* She had dallied here and there along the way. Incessantly curious, Hoshi inspected everything she passed. And she knew it could take her quite some time to properly inspect this room.

There were banks upon banks of instrumentation, and Hoshi began working controls she recognized—lighting the room so she could turn off her helmet beam, coaxing a livable temperature, bringing a little gravity to the place, though certainly not Earth norm. She felt more comfortable in a near-weightless environment. A slight thrumming indicated she'd found the oxygen system. It would take many long minutes, she guessed, for it to flood this room so she could remove her helmet. The station groaned again and shook.

Hoshi ignored the threat and glided toward an exterior wall, eyes as wide as the child's at Lincoln's feet. Spaced every three meters were telescopes, and she had but to nudge the controls to extend them through the *Streetcar*'s shell and really look at the stars. She nearly did just that, stopping herself halfway there when she spotted the large telescope at the far end of the room. The true prize of *Auriga's Streetcar*—what she had journeyed here for. She felt her heart hammer in her small chest, and she hurried toward the telescope, the chill and ache washing from her body to be replaced with a youthful giddiness.

"How could men of science leave this behind?" she breathed—at once thankful they had so she could claim it, and sad that it meant nothing to them. "So old."

More than two hundred years old to be precise, she knew. Hoshi had studied up on the station and its telescopes when she was younger, and again this year when she'd been ill. The pair of forty-inch polished lenses in this one telescope were fashioned in 1891. Three times the station had been refitted, and each time the lenses were placed in a new telescope. It was out of a sense of nostalgia that the astronomers must have continued to use the lenses—better, smaller ones had been developed in the centuries since and were doubtless in the other telescopes spaced throughout the observatory.

It was because of these antique lenses that the station had been named the *Yerkes-Two.*

It was in October of 1892 that Charles Tyson Yerkes, a wealthy Chicago businessman who owned the North Side Streetcar Company, was asked to donate funds to finance what would be the world's largest telescope. The request wasn't without precedent. In long-ago times Galileo sought the financial support of Cosimo II de' Medici, the grand duke of Tuscany. Yerkes had in a sense been the Duke of Chicago.

Yerkes needed something to elevate himself in the public's eye. In those years he was attacked daily in the newspapers for the way he ran his mass-transit empire and conducted his other business dealings. And so he agreed to this scientific venture, and went on to also fund an observatory in which the mammoth telescope would be housed. Hoshi recalled from her research that it was in October of 1897 that the Yerkes Observatory was officially dedicated. Nestled in quaint Williams Bay, Wisconsin, it fell under the auspices of the University of Chicago. There were other telescopes there, of course, but none so large as the refractor with the forty-inch lenses. It wasn't until 2025 that a larger telescope was built.

Hoshi would have liked to have seen the old telescope that the lenses were originally attached to—it was in a museum somewhere gathering dust. The observatory closed shortly before she was born, history reporting that the lights from a nearby dog racetrack and its parking lot caused so much havoc the stars could no longer properly be viewed.

It was the same all over Earth—years back and moreso to this day. So much light. From the cities and streets and attractions. Lights everywhere to keep the darkness at bay. To keep the stars hidden. When she was a child her parents took her to the top of the Tateyama Mountains. People used to stargaze there. But eventually the lights reached there, too, and the stargazers were relegated to only a few remote patches of desert. And later, they were relegated to...nothing. There was not a spot on Earth where one could stand and view the stars.

So the astronomers built satellites to compensate, the Hubble telescope being the first. This way man could still view the stars, though not firsthand. The Hubble was designed to last only two decades, and—unmanned—it required an extensive number of people and hours to plot each movement of the satellite and its scope. Subsequent satellites had similar limitations, despite the ever-increasing technology. And so the Yerkes-Two was launched, in 2031.

That was why the station was plain, unremarkable. It was among the first several birthed—and the only one designed for stargazing, the only one from its day still in orbit. It was primitive compared to what was crafted in the decades since and certainly compared to the others Hoshi had traipsed through. Primitive, but nonetheless functional, with a full crew of astronomers charting stars that men on Earth could see only in pictures because of the light pollution.

The *Streetcar* shuddered just as Hoshi activated the great telescope. She intended to retrieve these lenses, cut the gravity in the observatory, and maneuver her treasures into the hold of her skimmer. These lenses and the ones from the other telescopes, perhaps a few more trinkets, would be whisked away before *Auriga's Streetcar* plummeted Earthward. She couldn't take much, her ship being so small. But she could take what was historically important, what she would briefly covet and show to close friends, and what antique collectors would pay dearly for.

"Beautiful. Wonderful," she pronounced, as she stared through the scope. Diamonds on black silk, she thought of the stars. So bright and visually intense, hypnotizing. She believed there was nothing more incredible than a vivid starscape. She blinked away tears as she continued to watch—so happy to see such distant systems, so grief-stricken to know that those on the Earth below could never experience this.

She took off her helmet, the air uncomfortably cool but the oxygen content satisfactory now, though traced with the artificial metallic scent that settled distastefully in her mouth. She could see better without her visor in the way, though her breath feathered away from her face in a lacy fan.

Hoshi stared through the scope for what she sensed was hours, as her legs began to cramp and the ache returned to every inch of her body. The chill air that swirled around her face set her teeth to chattering. Couldn't she coax more heat into the room? Later, perhaps. Too much to see to be interrupted.

She fixated on what were considered the constellations of autumn, as would be viewed from the middle north latitudes. Cassiopiea and Perseus. A curved line of stars that made up part of Perseus extended toward Auriga.

"Auriga the Charioteer," Hoshi stated when she took in the large constellation. Auriga was the last of the autumn formations. The stars heralded the approach of winter. Capella, a bright triple star on Auriga's chest glared hotly at her. Capella was sometimes called "The Goat," and near it were a triangle of stars referred to as the kids. She noted several open clusters in the formation, each containing about a hundred stars and—according to the readings on the telescope—sitting nearly three thousand light years away. She could see them plainly when she made a few adjustments. The starlight was intoxicating.

"Auriga's Streetcar." Named for the constellation this telescope was keyed to and for the shape of the station and the business Charles Yerkes had been famous for. "An appropriate name after all," she decided. Auriga the Charioteer that beckoned winter. Hoshi was well into the winter of her life.

She would have watched longer, had the ache in her joints not become a dull, persistent pain she could no longer ignore, had the cold not sunk in to become unbearable and forced her to replace her helmet, had the stationed not groaned and shuddered once more. With a great sigh, she reluctantly edged away from the refractor and busied herself with removing the lenses from two of the smaller telescopes. Were she younger and stronger, she could have taken more this trip.

As she turned to leave, a small telescope on the opposite end of the observatory caught her notice. It looked much newer than everything else. Not an antique, it would be her last priority.

Hoshi patiently made her way back through the narrow gray tunnels and to her skimmer, carefully placing the treasures in her hold and retrieving thick silk padded slipcases that she intended to use for the largest lenses. She tried hard to thrust to the back of her mind the groaning of the station. It moved more this time, slipping in its orbit, causing her to curse her slow, old woman's body. The station hadn't days left, she knew now. It likely had only hours. And she would have to push herself to gain *Yerkes*' antique lenses and more.

A glance through the large refractor when she was again in the observatory. Auriga had moved, or rather, the *Streetcar* had moved significantly. Hoshi worked fast to remove the lenses, a task that should take two or more people, or that should take time and great care—she couldn't afford the time.

Somehow she handled the task. And with the room now at Zero-G, and the lenses protected by the silk, she maneuvered them through the ghost-lit corridors. She would have taken one at a time, Hoshi had the patience for it. It would have been safer for the lenses, easier for her to deal with. But she handled the time limitations presented her, and she fought to keep from crying out as her fingers clamped vise-like around the edges of the slipcases ached so terribly from age that they felt on fire.

"A few minutes more," she told herself. "Just a few more." Then she would be settled in her skimmer and heading toward her Takasago home on the coast, contacting several potential buyers and cherishing her look through the telescope, her oh-so-wonderful view of Auriga's goat and kids. What a story she would tell her grandson.

"No." Her fingers opened in surprise, and she had to struggle to catch the slipcases as they floated upward. "No!" Looking out through the hatch window, Hiroshi could see the stars. But she couldn't see her ship.

Was she at the wrong bay? Had her aging mind taken her down a different corridor and to the bays on the other side of the *Streetcar*? Had she...

Hoshi froze, eyes locked onto a spot below a second-magnitude star. There was her skimmer, drifting free of the *Streetcar*. "How?" her gaze settled on the hatch door. She'd done nothing to release it, nothing to break the lock. "How is it possible?"

Turning and swallowing her fear, she summoned what speed she could and carried the lenses down one corridor and then the next, her helmet beam bouncing light off doorways and protrusions, sending shadows to eerily dancing. Her side burned from exertion by the time she reached the other bays and spied a sleek freighter. Someone else had made the trip to scavenge from the dying station. That someone had released her ship. There were no markings that she could see from this position. What nationality? She quietly made her way to the hatch, worked the controls, and slipped inside the freighter. Empty—of people anyway. It was otherwise filled. A glance through the hold revealed the lenses she had previously stored on her ship. There were also circuitry cards and various other things—all taken in a hurry judging by the way they were strewn about.

"Pirates," she cursed, as she carefully placed the antique lenses alongside the others and backed out the hatch. Well, she could be a pirate, too, take this ship and head home. The station lurched and something popped deep inside a corridor, and for an instant she indeed considered taking the freighter right this instant—not only would she be saving her life, but she'd be saving the valuable, historical lenses. In a sense, she had a duty to save both.

But she'd prefer not to leave someone stranded here. And she was curious about the pirates and what else they might be taking from this place.

"How long?" she wondered, as she made her way through the network of corridors, glancing in rooms and in service-ways and heading toward the observatory, where she was certain the pirates were working to gather the remaining lenses. "How long does the station have?"

She nearly ran into him as she emerged from the last corridor and into the observatory, and he released what he'd been carrying—a spectroscope, a mechanism used to show the spectra of an object being viewed by the telescope it was attached to. The device hovered in the space between them.

"Pirate," she said.

He laughed, the sound odd and echoing in his helmet. It took him a moment to gain his composure.

"Pirate," she repeated.

"Hardly," he returned, his voice rich and deep, matching his youth. He was striking, though she wouldn't call him handsome, with a crooked hawkish nose and an impish grin. A dark lock of hair hung down what she could see of his forehead—skin eggshell white. His brown eyes flashed at her almond-shaped ones. "And you're hardly what I expected. I certainly wouldn't've released your ship if I'd have known that you were such...an old woman."

He looked through her faceplate, seeing her myriad wrinkles and noting her anger. "A very old woman."

She snatched at the spectroscope with a speed that surprised both of them.

"I'm not a pirate."

"A murderer, then," she hissed. "You would have me die, marooning me."

A shrug. "I shouldn't've released your ship. Truly, I'd never done such a thing before. But I'd never been challenged on a find, either. It was impulse."

"I was here first."

"You can travel back on my freighter, old woman. I won't maroon you. But all the finds are mine. Be satisfied you'll have your life."

Hoshi opened her mouth to argue. The antique lenses were hers, this "find" was hers. Would have been hers much earlier had she not been ill, had her ship not needed repairs. They were all hers—every piece in his hold. But she said nothing. There would be time on the trip back to Earth to think, to plan what to say to port authorities. She had a good reputation, and someone would listen to her. The lenses, and anything else she cared to claim from the young man's craft, would be hers.

He was continuing to talk, and she was shutting out his words, craning her neck around him to see the telescopes, several of which had been cruelly dismantled.

"Barbarian."

"I'll settle for that," he said, taking the spectroscope from her. "Keith Polanger," he added as way of introduction.

She did not give him her name.

"You could help, grab some of those fittings—they're made of brass. And I've got a half-dozen lenses loose." He nodded upward, and she saw them resting against the ceiling. "And stay close to me old woman."

It was clear he didn't want her out of his sight, didn't want to risk the chance she might take his freighter and instead maroon him. Two more trips, and Hoshi was moving very slow;u, fatigued despite the weightlessness and despite her simmering ire. She would claim all of his hold, she decided, once they were Earthward. His ship for good measure. And she'd see to it he was sent to prison. With fortune, he would be her age when he got out. Port authorities were hard on pirates.

"Aren't you too old for this?" Keith had been saying other things, all trying to draw her out, some an effort at feigned politeness. "I know there are astronauts your age. But aren't you a little old to be out here on your own?"

She still refused to answer.

This trip to the observatory—what had to be their last judging by the creaking of the station and its shifted position—they worked on the last few larger telescopes. They would leave only a few intact, the smallest and least valuable. He focused his efforts on the newest one, which suited her. She carefully loosened the fittings on her target, several meters away. Lost in thought, she continued to ignore his prattle, until she picked out a few words that piqued her curiosity. She moved aside a miniature driving clock and glided toward him.

"Don't understand this," he was saying. "Doesn't seem to want to give." He was struggling to free what seemed to be the spectroscope. Except it wasn't the spectroscope. It wasn't anything familiar to Hoshi. Her hand on his arm stopped him.

Hoshi leaned close, her face reflecting back at her on the inside of her helmet. The housing for the mechanism was foreign, unlike anything else on the station. And there was no evidence of the film that covered everything else in this place. Whatever the mechanism was, it had been installed less than eight or nine months ago—since the station had been officially abandoned.

"No time to worry over it," he said. It wasn't as interesting as the older telescopes and equipment anyway. "No worry."

But there was worry in his voice, Hoshi could tell. He was fretting over the *Streetcar*'s decaying orbit and imminent demise. "Yes, no time," she said. "We need to be out of here."

Still... She continued to study the new apparatus, and the telescope it was attached to. She peered through the scope—seeing Earth. Fingers playing along the sides of the tube, she magnified the view, seeing past the clouds and finding the Americas, magnifying more and seeing cities, then buildings, then people in offices—things on desks. She heard things, too, a man talking. He was discussing an upcoming anniversary, wondering where to take his wife for dinner.

Hoshi sprang back, the motion propelling her away from the telescope and against Keith Polanger.

"Did you hear?"

A nod. "So the astronomers were studying more than the stars up here, old woman. Maybe doing a little corporate spying. Maybe looking in on government officials. No way for them to detect the spying. Doesn't matter. We need to move."

Hoshi moved closer to the unusual telescope.

"I'll leave you here if you don't hurry old woman."

"Not the astronomers," she told him, holding tight to the scope when a tremor raced through the station. "Not the University of Chicago. Not any university. None of them put this telescope here." What had the telescope been trained on before Keith Polanger began fussing with it? What had someone been watching and listening to? From the associated circuitry, she could tell images and sounds from the scope were being broadcast...somewhere. "Where?"

"Where? I'm leaving to go home," he stated. "With or without you."

A moment more and he did just that. She heard the soft clink of his helmet bouncing against the ceiling, heard the protest of metal as the station's orbit continued to decay, saw him slip through the doorway and disappear down the corridor. She should follow him, but something held her here. She crossed to the status bank and thumbed it to life. A quick check of the station's position showed she still had some time before the orbit completely decayed, though not much.

He might wait for me, she told herself, feel guilty for leaving an "old woman," especially leaving one whose craft he'd released. "The young pirate, he will wait," she said aloud, somehow knowing that he would wait as long as he possibly could. The status bank showed his craft still docked.

Hoshi returned her attention to the unusual telescope, tugged off one of her gloves. The icy air was daggers against her skin, and she cried out, not expecting so intense a cold. When she'd reduced the room's gravity to nothing to aid in transporting the lenses, she also must have reduced the temperature.

Defeating the urge to immediately retreat back into her glove, she tentatively touched the telescope. So cold! It didn't feel like metal. Not like ceramic or plastic either. It didn't feel like anything she could put a name to, and it had a silky softness to it. The glove back on, she turned the telescope's dials this way and that, discovering markings that were not in English—everything else that she'd spotted on the station was in English. The strange symbols were flowing, like her native script, but they were not Japanese or Chinese. They were nothing familiar to her.

A look through it again, changing the focus and the pitch and discovering she was looking at the outside of the British New Parliament House. Another shift and she was peering through a window, seeing faces, men talking. She heard them. Again the sound coming from so very far away, but so clear as if they were in the same room with her.

Another change and she was viewing the Israel Emirates, closer and she keyed in on one small building in the northern hemisphere—someone's house. Someone sleeping, a man important or rich from the look of the surroundings. She heard him snoring, heard the soft muffled whisper of two people outside the door. There was urgency to the whispers.

Hoshi wrapped her arms about the scope as she made a move to refocus the incredible device again. A series of small tremors rocked the station.

"Should go," she told herself. Leave with Keith Polanger and claim his cargo when they touched down. But she should take this telescope with her. It was the smallest of those fitted in the observatory. If she could find a way to free it from the panel—where were the fastenings?—she could maneuver it to Polanger's freighter. Even an old woman could maneuver practically anything in Zero-G. Someone on Earth should know that they were being spied on by... by whom?

Hoshi poked out her bottom lip and ignored another series of tremors, forced out the sounds of metal scraping metal somewhere overhead, concentrated instead on the snoring of the man caught in the view of the telescope, and the whispers of people beyond his room. She worried at the telescope's base and at what should be its drive clock. After a few minutes she managed to loosen both a little.

What do you want?

She turned with a start, seeing no one in the observatory with her. A sigh of relief: the voice was the man's. She glanced in the scope, seeing two men in his room, rousing him from sleep.

President, one was saying. *We have a situation.*

Something needs your attention, the other said. Lights were flicked on and clothes were brought for the man.

The blue suit, he told them. I wore brown yesterday.

Hoshi resumed her work as she felt the panel beneath her fingers tremble. Something crashed in a room below, and the lighting in the observatory flickered. She turned on her helmet beam as a precaution.

"Hurry," she told herself. "Hurry or Keith Polanger will leave."

The station rocked and Hoshi pushed off from the telescope, floating to the status panel. "How much time?" she asked as she ran her gloved fingers over the controls, searching for the *Streetcar*'s orbital status.

What is all the fuss about so early this morning? Morning? It's barely past one.

President, it is a matter of international concern...

"By my father's memory, no." Hoshi's shoulders slumped inside her suit. Polanger's ship was gone. The precious antique lenses were gone, as were her hopes of returning to Earth alive. She felt so cold, and the ache in her limbs—kept at bay by her excitement—settled in again with a vengeance. Too long, she'd waited, caught up in a discovery of...

"Of what?" A telescope meant to study Earth and not the stars. But one she suspected came from the stars. It felt alien, its technology sleek and alluring—alluring enough to cost Hoshi her life. Damn her curiosity. So something alien had placed a scope on an abandoned space station, studying Earth like she might study a dragonfly's wing beneath a microscope. Studying Earth without anyone noticing.

We've detected two ships in orbit, Sir. They're not ours.

China's? Brazil's?

They're not from Earth, Sir.

Are you certain?

When no words immediately followed, Hoshi pictured heads nodding. The station bucked, and Hoshi found herself floating free of the status panel. Red lights were blinking, and she didn't need to read the indicator labels beneath them to know what was happening. The station was falling.

She felt so cold, achy. Lived long enough, she thought. She'd seen plenty of stars, the goat and the kids up close thanks to this station. In truth, she'd seen more than enough—more stars than practically anyone else on Earth would ever see in their lifetimes. She drifted, listening to the voices coming from the telescope, to the station starting to break up around her.

"We're out of time!"

The voice came from beneath her. She turned, head down, feet against the ceiling, seeing Keith Polanger emerge through the doorway, fear splayed across his youthful face. "My ship," he said. "Someone released it from the bay. I thought at first you did it for spite. But I didn't think you were the suicidal type."

They did it, Hoshi thought. The ones who installed the strange telescope. The ones who were in Earth's orbit, that the President of some English-speaking country had been roused from his sleep over. The ones that she and Keith Polanger would now die because of.

"But there's still a way out," he said, reaching up and tugging her down. "I found a pod. They built an escape pod into this place. It's quite small, but I believe it will..."

Hoshi pushed away from him, floating toward the alien telescope and worrying at it again.

"Old woman! I'm getting out of here. Didn't you hear me say there's a pod?"

"We're leaving with this," she said, her voice even and free of the panic so thick in his. One more tug and she had it, or at least a substantial part. She pushed it toward him, and he grabbed it, scowling and shaking his head. "It belongs to...them, the aliens. Someone below needs to see it, Keith Polanger."

"Aliens?"

President, there are three ships now. The words still came, though part of the telescope was free of the fitting and in Keith Polanger's hands. *But reports are they're moving away from Earth now.* Fighter shuttles have been scrambled, but they won't reach the ships in time. We have images, though.

As they have images of Earth, Hoshi thought. Eight months worth of images and sound, things quietly captured from an abandoned fog-gray box called *Auriga's Streetcar. For what purpose had someone...something been watching us?* she wondered, as she followed Keith Polanger through the doorway and down one corridor after the next, to an area she hadn't explored. It contained an egg-shaped pod, just big enough for two. Outside it were several of the lenses she'd recovered, including the large antique ones. So Keith Polanger had meant to take the valuables away in the pod when he discovered his ship gone. But he'd come back for her. Guilt? Too much humanity in his heart?

"So you're not a pirate," she mused, as she watched him float the alien telescope into the pod, followed by some of the smaller lenses. There wouldn't be room for the precious *Yerkes* lenses.

He turned to motion to her, reached out to tug her inside with him. She watched as a mix of horror and surprise flooded his face, saw how quickly his fingers fumbled to reconnect his oxygen tube. She held the other end in her gloved hands.

"So sorry," she told him. "But there is not room for both of us on the pod—and Yerkes' lenses. The lenses and the alien scope must return to Earth."

He flailed about for the tube, which she'd managed to rip free. An old woman could be strong in Zero-G. Fortunate he had not invested in a new suit with wholly internal workings. She probably couldn't have taken him then.

"Sorry," she repeated. So sorry Keith Polanger."

* * *

There was one good telescope remaining on the *Streetcar.* It had not been the best of the lot, and so had escaped the prying fingers of Hoshi and Keith Polanger.

Hoshi was training it now to what she sensed was east of the Perseus constellation. She'd made sure the young man was safely stored aboard the pod, and that the oxygen was flowing freely inside. It would revive him soon. She made sure the lenses were carefully fastened down, and that the alien telescope would be able to weather the brunt of the reentry force. He would have left them behind to save her—a woman well into the winter of her life.

Then she'd released the pod and returned to the observatory, and to this one remaining good telescope.

The lenses were far superior to the pair of old forty-inch ones racing away in the pod, though there was no historical significance to them.

East of Perseus, as seen from the middle-north latitudes of Earth. East and...

"There!" she exclaimed. Auriga the Charioteer. The last of the autumn constellations, as would have been seen from her homeland on Japan's coast—had there not been so much artificial light from the cities to block the stars. Auriga in all his glory. Capella, the bright triple star, the Goat. The kids. The open clusters almost three thousand light years away.

That was where the *Streetcar* was headed, the largest of the three alien ships towing it. The stars twinkling hotly and intensely beautiful all around.

"Wonderful," Hoshi said.

On the Scent of the Witch

Denise Little asked me to send her a story for Familiars Fantastic, *an anthology she was editing. I love working for Denise, so I immediately said yes and started playing on the Internet to find unusual familiars. Oh, I certainly could have made one up on my own, but I was looking for a little inspiration. There were plenty of references to cats and crows, but I wanted to give Denise something different. Besides, I'd already written a couple of cat stories. My surfing led to—of all things—the Salem witch trials. And after a little research, I found my familiar. This tale originally was published by DAW Books in 2002.*

There were lots of smells this bright spring morning—all coming at a wonderful, dizzying pace, all pushed by the strong wind that whipped across the field and fluttered the wildflowers and teased her graying hair.

She breathed deep and held it for as long as she could, picking through all the scents and settling on what had to be her very favorite at this time of year—earth that recently had been turned over. Planting time. Dark with moisture from the rain two days past, it was filled with delightful things—husks of beetles that had died when the cold hit, pieces of rotted cornstalks striped with mold, smears that had been tomatoes, wriggling masses of red worms and more. Oh gloriously more!

Edging forward, she tipped her head this way and that, letting the breeze play across her brow and letting it bring still more smells her way. Something... yes, there was something that stood out from everything, something that caught and held her attention as sure as any vise.

Luck, what amazing luck! She inhaled again and headed toward what must be a most amazing treasure. Closing, as she seemed right on top of it now, she brushed aside one clump of dirt after another and another, moving a few feet and working at it some more, relentlessly, until she discovered part of a rabbit—the plump hindquarters. Indeed, an amazing find! It had been frozen over the winter, but was now nicely and thoroughly thawed. She sniffed at it, tail gently wagging when she noted just how pleasantly pungent it was. Had it been cut in half by a farmer's tool? Had a fox caught it in the fall, taking only what it wanted to eat at the moment and leaving the rest? No matter. Fortune was hers that no one else had come by earlier to claim this!

With a happy yip she fell on what was left of the carcass, rolling and twisting first on her back then on each side to smear the odor deep into her fur. She felt the dampness of the ground against her, bits of cornstalks scratching at her in just the right places. Looking up while she continued her gyrations, she spotted birds flying overhead. Oh, to give chase along the ground! She almost gave into the urge. But she was a smart dog, and she knew that there would be more birds coming along at any minute. There were always more birds. And she was an old dog, one who didn't run much anymore because she tired easily. Besides, she wanted to continue rubbing against the rabbit a little while longer, take as much of the smell away with her as she could, make sure she got it on her rump and legs, a little on her neck and...

She heard another dog bark, concentrating as she rolled more slowly now and trying to picture who was making the racket. Hathorne's dog perhaps? The big black brute was a noisy one, frequently barking only to hear itself. She hoped he wasn't headed this way to steal her treasure. Or maybe it was the sleek-coated yowler living at the bottom of Gallow's Hill. He was always fenced in near the sheep pen. A most friendly dog, he had freedom only when with her help he could work the gate latch open. Or it could be...

With a disappointed whine she stopped her musings, feeling a presence stir at the back of her mind and forcing her to thrust aside all thoughts of the unidentified barker and the pungent rabbit. It was always the same when John intruded this way—a tickling sensation, that despite the number of times and through the number of years he'd done it, still gave her a curious feeling. Not an unpleasant one, and not close to the satisfaction of a good rub behind the ears. But something in between. There was something that was oddly soothing about it, the presence of her man John, who found her as a stray ten winters past and took her into his home and let her sleep on a thick rug by the hearth.

After a moment John took a more prominent position in her mind.

Where are we going? she asked him.

"To the church, Keesh," he answered. Though he spoke the words aloud in his cabin a half-mile away, she heard them as clearly as if he were standing in front of her. "To see what visiting Cotton's up to."

She slowly rolled off the rabbit and shook until a stubborn clump of dirt dropped off her stomach. Then she gave an exaggerated wag of her plumy tail, happy to be doing something important for John. Keesh dutifully headed across the field and to the dirt street that ran through the middle of Salem, adopting a quick pace—or what was relatively fast as far as her advanced years were concerned. She reluctantly passed by the baker's, cocking her head to better pick up the smells of fresh bread and other delicacies.

In his cabin, John Broadmore looked out through the mongrel Keesh's eyes and at the same time inhaled the scents of cinnamon and apricots and melting butter. He concentrated and felt the dirt beneath the dog's paws.

"We will stop back at the bakery later, Keesh," he told her. "And we'll beg for a suitable treat. You're a smart dog. You're a very good dog."

John sat on an old wooden bench in front of a low table that was covered with chicken feathers dipped in fat, sand he had painted various colors, a bowl of dried-out ewe eyeballs, and a jar of whiskey that held the corpse of an unborn piglet. A thick book was in the midst of all of this, opened to the middle where his fingers danced over symbols that none in this town save he could translate. It was an old book, older than John, older than Salem and written long before the first Englishman came to this new world. Passed down from his father and grandfather and great-grandfather—who was said to have obtained it from a clueless Spanish merchant—it was a book of incantations, most of which John had mastered and several of which he indulged in the casting of daily.

John was the only practicing witch in the town, likely in the entire state of Massachusetts, and he'd hoped his work would have gone unnoticed. He had tried to be secretive, his altering the weather in the span of minutes—late at night when most folks were in bed and couldn't see the dry lightning, his causing corn crops to flourish in droughts or to wither unexpectedly in the passing of a day, his tinkering in the lives of neighbors to make them fall in and out of love for his entertainment, his manipulations to make the Newton boy steal and bully his friends.

And all the spells were cast through his familiar Keesh, the mongrel he'd taken such a liking to. "You're a clever dog," John mused. "A smart dog."

And all the spells were cast when John was safely inside his cabin with the doors and shutters locked, as they were now. All of the enchantments coming easier to him with each season. Making him more powerful and tying him more securely to the Art. He didn't even need the book for some of them, so expert he had become. The one that linked himself to the mongrel was second nature, and sometimes he found himself staring out through the dog's eyes without having invoked the spell. Keesh had become an extension of himself, and she was just this moment rounding the corner near the church, heading to the back where there was a stack of boards just under a window. Jumping up on them and peering through streaked glass, Keesh and John watched a florid-faced man scribbling at a desk.

"Cotton Mather," John hissed through tightly clenched teeth. He let a breath escape, sounding like steam rising from a kettle left too long on the fire. "Damn him," he cursed, as his fingers turned one page and then another. His fingers danced faster. "Damn the man to the belly of Hell." John hadn't a spell that would do that, but he sometimes fancied taking a trip south where it was rumored a French woman brewed concoctions that would handle the job. "Vicious Cotton Mather."

Cotton Mather was why John had moved to Salem. Cotton Mather and his own curiosity. Mather was a frequent visitor to the place and had published a book recently, last year or the year before that John believed, 1691 or 1690. No. A few years earlier. It was called *Memorable Providences,* and it dealt with, among other things, an Irish washerwoman who lived in Mather's Boston and was suspected of being a witch. The book was popular and sold well, and John had two copies—one for posterity and one that he had marked up for research.

Mather, an influential Calvinist, took himself much too seriously and believed himself an authority on witches. "A subject which he truly knows nothing about," John said. Nevertheless, there were germs of truth in what Mather penned—undoubtedly lucky speculation, and John decided that this most dangerous man had to stop inciting folks. John just hadn't settled on a way to stop him. Mather should stick to his study of science and his concern for the public health. He should leave the matter of witches alone. It would be healthier for him.

Keesha and John watched Mather for the better part of an hour, then listened intently as a stodgy assistant came in and eased himself into a nearby chair.

"The girls were at it again last night," the newcomer said. "Twitching and running around, hiding under the furniture. The smallest fell into a convulsion, and her father almost called for you. But it subsided soon enough."

Mather put down his quill and shook his head, his mop of curling white hair reminding Keesh of a cloud she spotted earlier. "Witchcraft," Mather pronounced. "No other explanation."

"Same as that child—Betty Parris," the assistant said. "Same as what happened to her this February gone."

Mather nodded and placed his hands on the table. Another shake of his head and he pushed his stool back and stood. "Horrible, Godforsaken witches. We will find them. And we will make them pay. We will chase the Devil out of Salem." As he walked to the window, Keesh scampered away.

John directed the mongrel to take a side street, one that went past the Parris house, where six-year-old Betty—one of Mather's study subjects lived. Indeed the child had suffered a convulsion and acted erratically, as had several other girls in Salem. A few whispered that the children were just trying to get attention or had caught some strange illness, though Mather and his cronies stood by their defense of witchcraft sitting at the heart of it all.

"Mather was right," John said. "Withcraft indeed." He spread some of the green sand and drew a design in it, then sprinkled a line of red sand beneath it. "But Mather will never understand just what it is all about." Keesh had visited Betty's home in February, and the child was quick to come outdoors and play with the friendly mongrel. Through Keesh, John had cast a spell that transferred his own essence, via the dog, into the child. John was experimenting with moving his mind from one body to the next and decided that children were the only vessels to consider at this juncture.

An adult might remember too much about the experience, might see John's face or draw the conclusion between the presence of John's mongrel and the episodes of fits. But a child...a child couldn't be entirely believed. They made up stories. They didn't understand things. To further help cloud the issue, John drew upon a simple incantation that passed the child a mild malady—and hence the brief convulsion. No harm done. No child injured. And John got closer in the process of being able to completely leave his body and enter another. With each passing month, he could do it for greater and greater periods of time.

The transference spell intrigued him, and it was the one he concentrated on above all others. He intended to use it—after he thoroughly mastered it, of course—to get himself a young, healthy body. But that would be a decade or two from now when this one began to ache and his senses began to grow feeble. He could not allow himself to succumb to the pitiful vagaries of old age, and then death, as his father and grandfather and great-grandfather had. There was too much magic to absorb in only one lifetime, and John wanted an opportunity to learn it all.

He shook off his thoughts and gazed through Keesh's eyes, seeing Betty playing in the yard with two other children. John smiled. The Jameson boy. The child was prone to exaggerating anyway. John flipped a page in the book, muttered a series of arcane phrases, and felt his mind pass from his body into Keesh, and then into the little boy.

The body in the cabin slumped forward, head cradled by the book.

The little Jameson boy kicked dirt at Betty and began running with glee. Keesh kept up with him for several minutes, yapping and jumping and delighting in the spring.

The trials started the following week.

* * *

John hadn't intended for anyone to be hurt. He'd not injured a soul with his spells—not physically. And despite rough times, none of those he'd meddled with romantically divorced their spouses.

"No real harm had been done," he told himself. With Keesh curled between his feet, he sat at his table, stirring sand and flipping pages in the book.

In late April. several of the girls John had "borrowed" with his transference spell accused a former Salem minister of witchcraft. John hadn't planted the thought, didn't really know the poor man, and was at a loss to understand the girls' ramblings.

The following month more were arrested—examined and tried and hung.

"For no reason," John said. "Still, there's nothing to be done about it."

What could I do? he repeatedly asked himself. *Tell Old Cotton Mather that those being strung up on Gallows Hill, and that the old man pressed by stones just yesterday, were not witches? That there were no witches in Salem save for himself?* John knew if he confessed, he'd be hung. And there was too much magic in the world to master for that to happen. He couldn't surrender his life—no matter the consequences.

And so he watched the hangings, with Keesh at his side. The dog forlornly saw people who had once showed kindness by petting her drop to their deaths, kicking until the last of their lives trickled away. John explained to the dog, as best he could when they were melded, that matters had gotten out of control. Despite that, he continued to practice his transference spell—though not as frequently as before.

* * *

It was the end of summer when they came for John, on a day when the sun hung high in a cloudless bright sky. Perhaps it was because the previous night dry lightning shot above the town, yellow-gold fingers arrowing away from where his cabin sat. Perhaps he hadn't locked all the shutters. The wind had been fierce that night. Or perhaps it had been the Jameson boy. He'd targeted the child a dozen times and only lately had been worrying that the boy's description of the witch involved in the incidents closely matched his own appearance.

Cotton Mather personally took John away. He locked him in a cell, gave him little to eat and questioned him repeatedly.

"Are you a witch?"

"No," John lied.

"Have you familiarity with the Devil."

John vehemently shook his head.

Mather shook his, too, and trundled away. In the hallway, he announced there would be a trial in the morning—and a hanging before sunset. John heard Mather and his associates discussing the details, and he heard Keesh whimper from beyond the cell window.

"I don't need the book," John said. It had been confiscated. They'd left all the sand and the feathers, every dried animal organ he'd collected and carefully cataloged. They didn't know what to do with it all. But they took the precious book. "I don't need it."

John pressed his face against the wall, just under the window, stretched out with his mind as he muttered a string of incomprehensible words and felt his consciousness slip into the mongrel's body. This time, he pushed the spell to the limits of his ability.

* * *

Keesh woke with a start, lying on a dirt floor inside a cell, lying in an unfamiliar body. With a sniff she knew it was John's body, knew what her man had done—she'd participated in so many of his spells to understand that he had mentally traded places with her. And though she didn't understand why he'd done this, she accepted it. She crawled on all fours to the door and barked, the sound strange coming from John's mouth. Keesh pulled herself up, weaving back and forth on two legs that threatened to crumble beneath her. Four legs were so much better for balance.

She barked again and again until the jailer came, and she kept barking until he opened the cell, frantic at what could be happening to his prisoner. Keesh barked once more as she bolted from the small building, ran across the street and toward John's cabin. Though unused to this form, she quickly mastered it. She was a smart dog. She delighted in its speed and its youth, and she threw back her head and let the breeze play with her hair as she hurried along.

Unfamiliar with fingers, she fumbled at the door for several minutes before she could get everything to cooperate. She shut the door behind her. Then after pacing the room for several minutes, smelling her own scent and John's heavy in the air, she lay down on the rug and slept. It was shortly before midnight that she arose, an idea stirring at the back of her mind. She was a smart dog.

The fingers were easier to manipulate now, and having two feet was posing little problem. Standing on John's toes, Keesh stretched a hand up to a top shelf and began pulling down colored sand and feathers.

She was indeed a very smart dog.

* * *

The gray mongrel had been caught shortly after John's escape from jail. The old dog was headed toward the edge of town, running as fast as it could—which wasn't particularly fast, given its age. Before sunset it was presented to Cotton Mather.

"Witch dog," someone pronounced. "Creature of the Devil."

The mongrel's eyes were wide with fright. From inside the animal's shell, John tried to scream. But only a mournful howl escaped.

"Aye, it is a witch dog," Mather agreed. "A devil dog." He proceeded to go into great detail on how dogs were familiars of witches, agents of the Devil and easily magicked. Since they could not have John Broadmore, they would have his dog.

They hung it the next morning.

* * *

Cotton Mather tended to the ceremony himself, placing the noose about the frightened animal's neck. He thrust out the cries of the children to leave the animal alone. Only the young Jameson boy championed the execution.

When the animal was dead, and when he'd ordered it to be buried, he returned to the church and went straightaway to the back room. There, he dug about in an old chest that was filled with all manner of books and jars and bundled sheets of parchment. He pulled out one book in particular, a very old one filled with symbols that only he could translate. He turned to the transference spell and decided he would use it in another town, one that hadn't had trouble with witches and overzealous Calvinists. He'd find himself a better body, a younger one. Cotton Mather's was too old for his tastes, though he was grateful that Keesh had managed to switch his and Cotton's minds before the execution.

"A good dog," he breathed.

He would have to find himself another one, a mongrel. But before that, he'd end all these witch trials and hangings.

* * *

Keesh stood next to a willow birch at the edge of Salem. She'd watched her dog body being hung, knowing Cotton Mather was deep inside it. The man would trouble no one again. She watched John, in Cotton's form, trundle off to the church. And she'd seen him turn at the last moment, looking to the woods, catching sight of her and smiling.

"You're a smart dog," she saw him mouth. "A very good dog."

Keesh smiled and stretched and turned north, well accustomed to this new two-legged form now. The early fall wind was bringing a myriad of smells her way—damp fallen leaves, a patch of earth covered with thick moss, and something amazing. Weaving through the trunks she strained to catch the odor, frustrated that these senses were not quite as keen as what she'd had before.

No matter, with patience she found it. There, beneath a large oak, was a dead bird—a big crow all swollen. It was not more than a few days dead, and it was pleasantly pungent. She dropped down on it and began to roll.

Historical note: In Salem, Massachusetts, in 1692, a man named John Bradstreet was charged with being a witch. He escaped and hid in the woods, but they caught a dog he supposedly used to give others "the evil eye," and hung it instead.

Wingmen

I'm a WWI aviation buff, relishing trips to the Dayton Air Museum, the Smithsonian's Air and Space Museum, and other venues where I can see the old planes. I have a collection of tapes and DVDs about the Great War, more books about the planes and pilots than I want to count, and games. I'm a fan of an old TSR, Inc. board game called Dawn Patrol, *and I have a roster of pilots for the various planes in the game. I have several aces in the mix, though it's been quite some time since I've "flown" them. I'd previously written a WWI story where I put Merlin in a night bomber over Stonehenge. But I couldn't find that tale on my computer, and elected not to dig out a copy of the anthology and type it in from scratch. "Wingmen," which has a scene with a cat in it, originally appeared in* Slipstreams, *DAW Books, 2006.*

Stapenhorst swore he could taste the oil spitting off the engines, could feel the wind whistling shrilly past his ears, cold as ice so high this late morning in November. If only he could be up there!

He craned his neck farther out the truck's window and tipped his chin back to catch a glimpse of a Fokker barrel-rolling to come behind a Spad. The tiniest sparks of light, the Fokker's machineguns, and the wounded Spad banked away, Stapenhorst's eyes following it.

"Catch him," he breathed. The Fokker pursued, as if following Stapenhorst's orders. "Finish him. Bring him down and...*hurensohn*!" The curse came as the truck Stapenhorst was riding in hit a deep rut, making him momentarily lose track of the two planes.

"My apologies, Leutnant Stapenhorst. The road here is very bad."

"Though not so bad as your driving I think, Feldwebel Gerhtz."

"Luetnant, I..."

Stapenhorst gave the driver a dismissive finger wag and again focused on the aerial battle to the west. Eight pilots from Jasta 11 that he could count. Nine a few moments ago, but one plane spiraled down trailing thick gray smoke and then a puff of white—a parachute.

The Jastas, distinguishable at this distance only by the blush of color and the three wings of their Fokkers, were sparring with a mixed French bag—better than two dozen Spads and Nieuports. The Frogs had wing guns that could flip up and shred the bellies of any Fokkers above them. Probably what had happened to the unfortunate German plane that should be nosing into the ground about now, Stapenhorst thought.

The truck turned left down a narrow and less bumpy road, the new direction giving Stapenhorst a little better view of the dogfight.

"They're outnumbered," the driver offered. "Frightful odds. There'll be more than a few widows tonight, damn the French. The Jasta will certainly need you, Sir. Need more than you to replace all the pilots who will not be coming home."

Stapenhorst watched a pair of Spads sandwich one of the Fokkers, taking top and bottom angles in an effort to shoot out the German plane's engine. A Nieuport was banking in to add to the misery.

Suddenly a lone Fokker came down from the clouds. It sideslipped toward the offending Nieuport and spit slugs in the French's fuselage, sawing the tail off. As that Nieuport spun out of control, the Fokker continued to the high Spad, then, after finishing it, dove on the bottom one to save his wingman. The odds were impossibly altered in but a few heartbeats.

Stapenhorst's breath caught as the rescuing Fokker leafed down on another French plane.

"Richtofen," Stapenhorst said. That able pilot could be none other than the vaunted leader of Jasta 11, Stapenhorst's new commanding officer. Stapenhorst's hand tapped the orders in his pocket, and he allowed himself a satisfied smile.

The truck turned again, now following a tree-lined road that effectively blocked Stapehorst's view of the deadly aerial ballet. He cursed again and pulled his head inside.

* * *

It was more than two hours later that the truck rolled onto a cleared field.

The Fokkers he'd watched in the dogfight had arrived well before him and were spaced evenly in front of a row of large tents. The setting sun was striking the blood-red paint and canvas, making the planes practically glow. The color was said to frighten the allies, particularly the inexperienced ones.

Each triplane had slightly different markings, so the pilots could recognize each other in the air and so that spotters stationed along the German lines could more easily confirm the kills of specific pilots. Mechanics were working on only two of the planes, meaning little damage had been suffered in the dogfight—save the plane Stapenhorst saw going down.

"Leutnant Stapenhorst, this is the Jasta 11 aerodrome. Will you be needing..."

"*Nein.* Nothing else, Feldwebel Gerhtz." Stapenhorst slid out of the truck and shouldered his duffel, slammed the door, then motioned the driver away.

It wasn't what he had expected, this aerodrome. Stapenhorst pictured the famed Jasta 11 having permanent buildings, hangars for the planes and warm quarters with well-stocked bars for the officers. An aerodrome that would be the envy of every German pilot. But there was nothing here save tents—for the planes, and smaller, shabbier looking ones for the men—all of which could be quickly taken down and moved on a moment's notice.

"Of course." Stapenhorst mentally chastised himself. Many Jastas moved often so that the French and English could not easily target the aerodromes. And Jasta 11—fighter squadron *jagdstaffeln* 11—moved in particular. The *Flying Circus,* the unit had been dubbed, because it traveled across the countryside like a German circus—by rail. The planes were carefully dismantled so they could fit on railway wagons. Any observers would think it nothing more than a circus traveling on to the next engagement. The Jasta stayed no more than a few days in any one place, then the planes and the men were loaded onto railway wagons again, always late at night, and taken to another field. Stapenhorst noted there were train tracks nearby.

Since Bloody April, this Jasta had become the most decorated and most successful. Baron Manfred von Richtofen and a few of the other Jasta 11 pilots held the coveted *Pour le Merit,* the Blue Max, for obtaining forty "kills."

Stapenhorst had only two kills to his name, Brits, though he had many commendations for assisting in bringing down enemy planes.

"But I will get many, many more kills on my own serving here," he said. Squaring his shoulders, he headed toward a large tent at the end of the row of planes, his breath in the chill air feathering away from his face. He spotted two pilots duck through the entrance. Tapping the papers in his pocket, he hurried after them.

The men inside were haloed in cigarette smoke, and the smell of beer and of spiced sausage cooking on a small stove hung heavy. Stapenhorst blinked to take some of the sting out of his eyes. Like a dream, the greatest pilots of the Jasta were all gathered here—Hintsch, thin-lipped Festner, Emil Schaefer, Otto Brauneck, Kurt Wolff, Georg Simon—whom Stapenhorst had met a few years back, and who recommended him for this Jasta, Esser, Krefft, Lothar von Richtofen. And in the center, like a king holding court, was Jasta 11's leader—Manfred von Richtofen, the famed Red Baron.

They'd all been talking, and though Stapenhorst was paying only slight attention to the loudest buzz, he could tell they were discussing the late afternoon battle. Someone near the baron was making a toast. "*Der Tog*!" To the day.

Stapenhorst stepped farther inside, and the conversations ceased. All eyes turned to him. Peering through the fog of smoke to get a better look, Stapenhorst was struck with their appearances—all of their faces planes and angles, their pale skin tight across their cheeks and jaws, their eyes dark and unblinking. Every aspect gave them the miens of predators.

One of them finally spoke to him, but he wasn't sure who or what was said, and he cocked his head hoping it would be repeated.

After several beats of silence, he removed the orders from his pocket and walked toward the baron. "Leutnant von Stapenhorst reporting per orders."

The baron, smaller than Stapenhorst thought he looked in photographs, took the papers and idly glanced at them. "You were expected yesterday." The words were smooth and melodic. "We could have used you this afternoon."

"There was no available transportation."

"Always the problem." The Baron handed the papers back. "Welcome to the Circus, Leutnant."

Stapenhorst gave a curt nod. Outward, he presented a stoic mask. But inside, his stomach churned. Face to face with his idol—all of Germany's idol. Inches away. "Where do I..." Stapenhorst glanced at his gear.

"Do not bother to get comfortable." This came from Simon. "We move tonight."

* * *

The railway wagon had benches bolted to the bed. After trying several seats, Stapenhorst decided the benches were all equally uncomfortable. The track was uneven and added to his suffering. The other pilots in the cabin were engaged in hushed conversations and did not think to include him. Two were trading cigarettes and taking turns with a flask of whiskey.

They had all been reasonably polite to him, though they did not go out of their way to make him feel truly welcomed. Perhaps that would have to wait until he became an ace.

Simon told him that would happen soon. All of Jasta 11's pilots—save Stapenhorst—were aces. The Jasta's record was impeccable and incredible. The pilots defied all the desperate odds thrown at them, particularly when they were against French planes.

"Ah, it is heaven to be a part of this," Stapenhorst had told Simon an hour or so earlier.

"Heaven?" Simon shook his head. "Nein. Not even close. But you will see that soon. When you're an ace. You will truly be a part of the Jasta then."

Stapenhorst asked Simon to explain further. But the elder pilot shook his head and instead questioned Stapenhorst.

"Would you do anything for Germany? Anything?"

Stapenhorst nodded.

"I told the baron as much. That is why you were invited to join us. Anything for victory, eh?" Simon smiled grimly and excused himself to another train car.

Stapenhorst watched some of the other pilots leave through the cabin's rear door. The door at the front led to wagons where the planes were kept. After a while he decided to see where the other pilots went.

"Odd." Stapenhorst stood at the head of the next cabin. It was lit only by a pair of oil lanterns. There were benches along the side to his right; the left had bins for storing duffels and supplies. He pressed to the next cabin, also empty, balancing himself as the train rocked back and forth, bracing himself as he stepped on the platform between the cabins and again felt the wintry air.

He paused at the next door, though he couldn't say what held his hand. Nor could he explain why he pressed his ear to it, as he hadn't at the previous cabins. Nothing. Wait. There was something other than the keening of the wind and the ratcheting sound of the railway wheels. Concentrating, he picked out voices, some high-pitched and excited, some deep, one melodic—the baron's. But he could make out none of the words.

Stapenhorst smoothed his uniform and squared his shoulders. He opened the cabin door and quietly stepped inside. It was darker than the other cabins, and longer. Stapenhorst could barely see the silhouettes of the pilots. Everything was indistinct in the light of a lone lantern that had been turned as low as possible. He swallowed to moisten his throat, intending to step forward and offer a greeting—but he stopped himself. For an instant he thought he saw other shapes—small, deformed ones. The lantern flared a little brighter and they were gone.

Simon looked up and spotted Stapenhorst. *When you are an ace,* he mouthed.

* * *

Stapenhorst had flown more than fifty missions, but he'd never flown a tripe before. His was designated Dr. I 144/17. His last plane had been an Albatross DIII, which he found comfortable and responding, if sometimes ponderous. This new Fokker Dreidecker was...snug, and it made him at the same time giddy and nervous. It looked small inside and out, with three wings of descending length, the largest with a span of about thirty meters. He had considered requesting a familiar plane, even an out-dated DII. But he didn't want to ask any favors of the baron. Besides, he told himself, the other Jasta 11 pilots were flying these contraptions.

For a brief moment he recalled the shadows of the previous night, then he focused on the hum of his plane's engine, not so loud as what he was used to.

He nudged the throttle forward. In an instant the plane leapt off the field. Stapenhorst expected the Fokker to drag with its three wings. Instead, they provided an astonishing lift. He was angling upward faster than he had in any other plane. Its engine was a 110 Le Rhone rotary, built and supplied to Germany under license by Thulin, a Swedish firm. The cowling was enclosed to just below the airscrew boss and had two cooling holes. The ribs and leading edges were plywood, everything else fabric-covered, and the trailing edges were wire. Balanced ailerons were fitted to the top wing only, and the center wing had two cutouts. Lightweight, highly manageable, and with exceptional upward visibility—as it lacked the bracing wires that could be shot away on biplanes.

Stapenhorst knew the plane had its champions—Werner Voss last year demonstrated that it was outstanding in a dogfight and that nothing matched its climb rate. It had its detractors, too, as many pilots, including the famous Heinrich Gontermann died from wing failures. He'd heard there'd been structural improvements since those days. He certainly hoped so.

The twin Spandau machineguns were perched in front of him. "Easy to aim," he noted.

He opened the throttle and the plane sped forward, catching up with the rest of the squadron—all on the way to the front for a strafing run. "To slaughter the *frontschwein,*" he said with a smile. The enemy frontline pigs.

The Dr. I was faster than he expected, and the rudder moved effortlessly. He tried a roll, discovering that the ailerons had a stiff feel, and he worried if that could prove a liability.

"Let's try something else," he said, staying at the back of the formation, as the baron had suggested. Richtofen wanted Stapenhorst to experiment with the Dr. I a bit—while still keeping the other Jasta 11 pilots in sight.

He attempted a slight turn, the wings producing still more lift and giving him a quick heading change. He circled the plane back and worked the rudder to keep it from rolling too much. No aircraft could possibly turn better than this! Amazing, he thought, as he adjusted his goggles tighter.

So the ailerons were a bit stiff, so it lost some maneuverability when the tail dropped. Ax-handle-like skids had been added to the lowest wings so if the tail dipped too close to the ground, the plane would not easily crash.

"Heaven!" Stapenhorst was caught up in the speed, the excitement, the glory of flying. Nothing matched the sensation, and the cold could do nothing to trounce his spirits. God bless the war that allowed him to experience this, and to be in the baron's squadron. He opened the throttle wider and followed the others to the front.

The land changed dramatically the farther they flew. Farm fields, barren this time of year, gave way to scabrous, ugly land pockmarked with craters from bombs and artillery fire.

The forward planes angled down, and Stapenhorst matched them, still marveling at how the Dr. I moved.

"Heaven," he repeated.

They paralleled a river, then flew over a ruined bridge. Above the drone of the engines, he could hear the boom of flak canons and the whistle of bombs. An instant more and he could see manmade clouds of weapon-smoke rising into the early-morning sky. The allies were hunkered down in the trench, and the lead Fokkers dove on them, machineguns spewing lead.

The strafing run lasted only minutes, though it felt much longer than that. Time twists during combat, Stapenhorst knew. The Jasta was astonishingly successful in taking out several banks of anti-aircraft guns and well-entrenched machinegun emplacements, and only one plane was damaged in response.

It was unnervingly too easy. But Stapenhorst was an expert pilot, and he was flying among Germany's very best. And so he told himself that skill won the day. He ignored the shiver that danced down his spine, and he somehow managed to set aside any qualms about the victory.

And that night, when Simon and several other pilots retreated to the rear train car, Stapenhorst tried to follow them.

"Nein," Simon scolded. "When you are an ace."

* * *

A few days later, Stapenhorst scored his fourth kill. One more would give him the coveted title and entry into the private gathering at the back of the train. They were getting more dogfight missions close to the front, and tomorrow morning they were going after a French balloon. Just before sunset they would go out again, this time to strike at a French squadron. The squadron seemed to fare the best against the French.

Stapenhorst thought of that fifth, magical kill as he lay in his bunk, cold despite the wool blankets. The Jasta was camped in a clearing near the tracks this night. Winter was deepening, and its winds were chasing away some of the joy he felt at being in midst of these great pilots. Winter and the curiosity of what he would find in the rear cabin when he was invited into their little circle. He shuddered and nestled farther under the covers, and he tried to fall asleep.

He listened to the snores of his fellows, and he heard the rustle of clothes and the grunt of a pilot pulling on his boots. Moments later, he heard the tent flap open and close. There was the sound of boots crunching over gravel and the frozen ground.

Perhaps the pilots were excited about the prospect of flying two missions tomorrow. Couldn't sleep and so they decided to take a walk and perhaps share some whiskey and smoke. Stapenhorst threw off the blankets and struggled into his boots. He would join them. He drew his coat tight around him and stepped outside and glanced across the field, the full moon making it easy for him to see the planes and the other tents—and still more pilots that were striding toward a copse of trees.

Some sensible part of him insisted he go back to bed. But Stapenhorst ignored the warning and started off at a trot.

The trees ahead were a mix of evergreens, looking like black cutouts under the bright moon. He wondered why the pilots would come all the way out here.

The sensible part of him complained louder, but he only picked up his pace, brushing past the first evergreen and knocking frost off its branches, pieces of lace flittering to the ground. Two pilots were just ahead of him, and one of them turned—Festner. Caught in the moonlight, Stapenhorst froze.

Festner motioned for him to come closer.

There was no threat in the gesture. Indeed, Festner was smiling. But the smile didn't reach his eyes.

"*Nein,*" Stapenhorst said. "I think it is too cold out here tonight."

"You are persistent," came a voice from behind him. "But in a little while you won't be minding the cold." Simon prodded Stapenhorst forward. "We were waiting for you to become an ace before we introduced you. That's been our custom. But I suspect you'll get your fifth kill tomorrow, all the action we'll be seeing. So we might as well introduce you now and settle your curiosity."

There was a campfire burning merrily just past a column of tall pines. Esser, Wolff, Krefft and Richtofen were the highest ranking of the eight seated around the fire. Simon prodded again, and Stapenhorst complied, finding a spot next to Esser. Simon sat to his left.

"See? It's not cold around the fire," Simon laughed.

Stapenhorst nodded, feeling his throat constricting and his chest tight. Nerves. He glanced quickly about. There were no cigarettes or flasks of whiskey, none of the trappings of fellowship. The only conversation was between Richtofen and Wolff, and it was soft and in a language Stapenhorst couldn't understand.

Simon slapped him on the back and went to say something else. But he stopped as Krefft stuck his hand in the fire and pulled out a blackened stick. He started tracing a pattern across the hardened ground and mumbled in the language Richtofen and Wolff spoke. Some words had a familiar sound, and Stapenhorst futilely tried to pick through the jumble.

"It is old Norman," Simon finally whispered. "It is a chant that calls them."

Calls who? Stapenhorst mouthed, though instantly he knew the answer. The small shadows he saw in the railway wagon.

"The *lutin.*"

Lutin. Lutin. Lutin. Stapenhorst knew the word, and his mind stretched back to tales of his childhood. Goblins! Mischievous folklore beings who at one instant could be a fully equipped mount, a *Le Cheval Bayard,* and at the next a housecat. Some were said to be good spirits meant to protect German houses and at the worst would twist a child's hair into locks so tangled they had to be cut. But others were of a dark nature, so the tales said.

Lutin here? How could they be real? Not possible!

Simon was saying something else, but Stapenhorst was too lost in thought. It wasn't until the fire flared that his thoughts came back to his surroundings.

The wisps of smoke rising from the flames formed shapes and spun away, coming to ground and circling the pilots and giggling maniacally. There were a dozen, each different. The largest was nearly two meters tall and looked like the misshapen skeleton of a man, red skin pulled close across the bones. Another looked like a small gorilla, fur as scarlet as the flames and eyes solid black. A few were rats, with glowing red fur that melted away to become gray and mangy. They cavorted behind the pilots, making clacking and hooting noises, slapping each other and occasionally wailing like prowling wolves. There was music to their sounds. It had a primal rhythm that was interspersed with complex dissonant rifts. Some of the pilots were swaying to it. Krefft was trying to sing along in the old language.

Despite himself, Stapenhorst found he enjoyed the dance and the melody, closed his eyes and let the sounds overtake him. He felt pleasantly warm and welcomed, and suddenly the hard ground was comfortable.

Then the music stopped and the creatures stood still, forming a circle inside the pilots now. One of the beasts, a large rat, settled itself in front of Stapenhorst and rose on its tiny hindquarters, waving its claws in the air.

With the music gone, Stapenhorst's will was returning. "I-I-I don't think I want to take part in this," he whispered to Simon. "This isn't real."

"Oh, it's very real. And you've no choice, brother." Simon made a *tsk-tsking* sound. "You said you'd do anything for Germany."

"Anything," Stapenhorst admitted.

"This is a small sacrifice, my friend."

Stapenhorst made a move to get up, but Simon slammed a hand on his leg.

"Anything for Germany, you said."

Stapenhorst swallowed hard, but nodded. *Anything,* he mouthed.

"Good. When you joined this very special Jasta, you signed on for this. We're careful who we let into our ranks. I recommended you, remember. Don't disappoint me. Besides, it won't hurt much."

The rat crawled up Stapenhorst's leg, nose quivering and eyes shining. It opened its mouth to reveal snow-white teeth. As he stared at the creature, it appeared slightly fuzzy and out-of-focus.

Around the circle the other creatures were selecting pilots, Richtofen and Wolff each getting two.

"What will happen?" Stapenhorst risked.

"Take off your coat, brother. And unbutton your shirt. As I said, it won't hurt much. And it is the least you can do for the war."

Stapenhorst shook his head, one last, vain attempt at defiance.

"They want our blood. It is a special treat for them." Simon dropped his voice so Stapenhorst had to strain to hear. "In return, they serve as our most valuable wingmen. With them, no odds are too great." Then Simon was doffing his coat and rolling up a sleeve, offering his arm to the creature that had chosen a miniature gorilla form.

Stapenhorst couldn't remember loosening his clothes, but he could tell his chest was bare to the winter air. The rat clung to a fold of his shirt and stared up into his eyes. It chittered something in the old language, then it sunk its tiny teeth into Stapenhorst's breast, and it feasted.

Stapenhorst wanted to know how often this ritual was performed, and how often he would be expected to take part. But he decided those questions would be for another time. So nothing was said during the walk back to the tent, nor at breakfast. Stapenhorst had no scar from the odd encounter, and the only souvenir from the night was the dissonant tune he kept hearing in his head.

They would be running on the French balloon within the hour. It was reported near the front and spotting German gun emplacements. It needed to be brought down quickly to protect the infantry, and Jasta 11 was the closest squadron. They should expect the balloon to be heavily protected—with anti-aircraft guns and machineguns, and of course with planes. Richtofen selected himself and only ten other pilots for the mission...the men who were in the clearing last night.

* * *

Stapenhorst opened the throttle and stayed even with Simon. The plane handled effortlessly this morning, better than ever, perhaps due to the damaged aileron being replaced. They climbed high, nearly to the Fokker's ceiling of more than six thousand meters. It should have been unbearably cold this high up in January, but Stapenhorst felt only the slightest chill.

"Is it the wingmen?" he mused aloud, meaning the *lutin* goblins. "Could they possibly..."

"Yesss." The word was a hiss coming from over his shoulder. "We help you." A rat, Stapenhorst assumed it was the one who fed on him last night, came down his chest and settled in his lap. "We give you warmth. And what you call luck."

It wasn't speaking the old language now. It was crisp German, though the words sounded tinny because of the creature's high-pitched voice.

"And you do all of this—for us and for Germany—for a bit of my blood?" Stapenhorst cursed himself for talking to the thing. He looked away from it and focused on the other planes in the formation. In the distance below, the oblong form of a dirigible was faintly discernible through a thin layer of clouds.

"For that," it replied. "And for a bit more."

Stapenhorst's plane sped up, though he hadn't moved the throttle. The others were moving faster, too, and had started their dives. He double-checked his machineguns and warned himself: *Don't get too close to the top of the balloon, as it could burst into flames and catch me.*

A side shot, he decided, watching Simon barrelroll down with the same intention. Richtofen was diving straight down for the risky shot on the top. Perhaps he had nothing to fear. Perhaps there was a *lutin* in his plane protecting him.

"Closer," the creature urged him. "There. Faster."

Again the plane sped up of its own volition, and Stapenhorst opened fire, the bullets ripping into the silk. He heard machinegun fire all around him—from the other Fokker pilots and from emplacements on the ground. There were rifle shots, too, these coming from the observers in the basket beneath the balloon. It all sounded like he'd swept into the middle of a giant hornet's nest.

And in the background, he heard the dissonant music from the clearing.

"Now onto the other planes," the *lutin* told him. "They're coming up from the ground. There are two British planes with them, but you will not shoot at them. Sometimes the British station pilots at French aerodromes. We did not know they would do so today."

"We?"

"My fellows," the creature sneered. It looked slightly out-of-focus to Stapenhorst.

Indeed there were two British Bristols amid French Breguet fighters. Slower and larger than the Fokker Dr. Is, the Brequets were nevertheless more formidable. They were two-seaters, meaning there could be double the firepower and double the chance of dying to them. There were a couple of Morane-Saulniers in the mix, monoplane two-seaters that were not as maneuverable and that had Hotchkiss machineguns that spit copper bullets.

"I'm not to shoot the British. Why?"

"Because I said so. I say you only shoot Frenchmen today."

Stapenhorst shook his head. "I don't understand."

"You are not meant to," the *lutin* purred. It had become a fuzzy cat, snuggling on Stapenhorst's lap. He studied it, seeing some of its features indistinct. "They have many, many planes up today, the French. But you are not to worry. You will shoot them."

Stapenhorst nosed down to meet the climbing Breguets. Four other Fokkers had broken off from the tattered balloon and were joining him. He was warm, in the high, cold, January air. He was unduly confident. And he was thinking it more than a fair trade for a bit of his blood.

"And a bit of something more." The cat intruded on his thoughts. "Get closer, I say."

Stapenhorst did, though not as fast or as close as Simon had managed.

"Are the others not to shoot the British, too?" As Stapenhorst prepared to take aim on one of the two-seaters, he saw Simon's plane out of the corner of his eye. A small, red gorilla was climbing out of the cockpit and walking along the wing. Then it was spreading its arms and taking flight toward the nearest Breguet, latching onto its wing and scrambling toward the fuselage. It was clear the French pilots didn't see the *lutin,* which was climbing in with the observer now and dismantling his twin machineguns. A moment more, and it was headed for the pilot's guns.

"My God," Stapenhorst whistled. No wonder the Jastas had few fatalities and little damage to their planes. The creatures disarmed their opponents. "The French can't see you, can they?"

"*Nein,*" the cat said in thick German. "Not unless we wish it."

"And you do this all the time? Ruin their guns?"

"Break their spars and poke at their engines. Shred their canvas and steal their breath."

"For the glory of Germany."

"For the glory of Germany," it parroted snidely. "For the glory of Jasta 11."

"And all for a bit of my blood? And a bit of something else?"

"A bit of your soul. The small piece you keep for yourself. That piece that hasn't been given to the Fatherland."

The warmth fled Stapenhorst's body and he pulled back hard on the stick, taking his Fokker higher, narrowly missing Wolff's wing.

"A piece of my soul."

"You won't miss it."

A lump formed in his stomach, and he took his plane higher still, past what was left of the balloon that was being winched down.

"A small price to pay for the glory of Jasta 11." The cat started kneeding his leg. "Now return to the battle. I'll make you an ace today. Isn't that what you wanted?" The cat gestured with a paw. "The pilot in the Morane-Saulnier there, and his observer. Their guns are useless now. An easy kill, Ace Stapenhorst."

"But what about the Bristols?" The dissonant music of the clearing became loud in Stapenhorst's ears, competing with the sound of machinegun fire.

"You ask too many questions," the *lutin* grumbled. "Pilots who ask too many questions do not fly long. We have not taken enough of your blood, Stapenhorst. We have left you with too much will."

"What do you..."

"The day you joined the Jasta. Do you remember it?" The *lutin* didn't wait for a reply. "The Jasta lost a pilot that very morning. He asked too many questions. He was too willful. Like you." The *lutin* became a rat again and wriggled its nose at Stapenhorst. "That Morane. Dive on it and become an ace."

"Anything for Germany," he whispered.

But he would have to talk to someone tonight, Simon or Richtofen. Winning this way wasn't settling right with him. And why wasn't he to fire on the Bristols? Why couldn't...

"*Nein. Nein. Nein.*" tittered the rat. "You will talk to no one. And you will stop asking questions."

"Get out!" Stapenhorst shouted. "I will talk to anyone I please. Get out of my plane!"

"Perhaps Simon was wrong to request you in this squadron. None of the others have complained of our tactics. All they think about are the kills and the medals." The rat yawned and scratched its nose. "I think you are too much of a risk."

Stapenhorst stared at it, seeing nothing else and all at once seeing something truly fuzzy about the creature. It opened its eyes wide in surprise.

"What...are...you?"

"Pity you look so close," the creature taunted. "So few of you Germans have the presence to truly see us. We should have taken much more of your blood last night."

"Get out!"

"If you insist Leutnant Stapenhorst."

"Get...out...now...you...little...demon."

The creature complied, scurrying up his chest and onto his shoulder, then around to the back of his collar, where it began digging into the parachute. Stapenhorst tried to grab it, but the feat proved impossible while still flying.

The parachute destroyed, the rat scurried out onto the fuselage. It seemed the creature had no fear of speed or height or gravity. It crawled down the nose and starting scratching at the engine casing. It turned back, once, to glare at Stapenhorst. Then it proceeded to dismantle a piece of his plane's engine. When it was finished, it turned into a childlike creature with pastel wings.

"Not a *lutin,*" Stapenhorst breathed.

It shook its head and grinned, somehow looking innocent and mischievous at the same time. "Unfortunate that you looked so close. And now you'll join the few others who saw us for what we really are."

"Fey."

The child-creature nodded. "From the Unseelie Court. We take a bit of your soul, and we let you think you are winning for Germany. But we are stealing your secrets and we are using you, paying you back for the Saxon invasion."

"And using us to kill the French."

"We never liked the French," the fey smiled. Then it leapt into the air and disappeared.

Stapenhorst threw all of his being into leafing the plane down with a dead engine. Had the plane not been so lightweight, and had he not been such a gifted pilot, he would have drove into the earth.

He had just enough lift to get him well behind the front—and into British territory, where he suspected there would be fey waiting.

Leutnant von Stapenhorst of Jasta 11 was captured January 13, 1918, when he was forced down in allied territory. His Fokker Dr. I 144/17 was the first intact plane of its kind captured by the British.

Mineral Spirits

I had one of those proverbial wild hares...or is that hairs...when I wrote this, a mix of the Old West with an odd bent to it. I sent it off to an anthology that was collecting Weird West stories. The editor sent me back a lovely note, saying that while he enjoyed this tale, he'd received far too many submissions about otherworldly mines. Go figure. This is the first publication of "Mineral Spirits." I even managed to stick a reference to a cat in it.

The Missouri Fox Trotter looked out of place in the rugged hills of the southern Nevada Territory.

Nearly sixteen hands high and roan red, the show horse had a narrow blaze as white as a newly painted gospel mill, running from between her ears to the tip of her muzzle. Her eyes, large and inky and expressive—coupled with half a bottle of Irish whiskey—had caused Wilford to part with all his worldly wealth to buy her two years past when he was in Eagle Station.

Wilford led her under a rocky outcropping where the shadows would grow longer as the morning progressed. He tugged a wooden bowl from her saddle and filled it to the brim from a large canteen. Then he tied her to a metal spike he'd driven into the rock on the last trip here, making sure she couldn't get loose and yet could reach the water.

"Shouldn't be gone too long, Princess." He gestured toward the entrance to a mine a dozen yards away, then wiped at the sweat beading thick on his face. "It's as hot as a whorehouse on nickel night, and I reckon it'll only get worse. Old Nate, he doesn't take this heat none too well and..."

"Quit jawin' to that damn crowbait and get a wiggle on!" Nate pulled off his shirt and folded it at the mine entrance and sat a rock on it to keep it from blowing away in the event a wind kicked up. His ribs gleamed with sweat, and Wilford swore the old man was so lean that if he didn't start eating more his bones were going to burst through his skin.

"I'll be along directly, Nate. Have to see to Princess first."

"Damn crowbait."

Wilford gathered his face into a point, then his expression softened when he scratched at a spot between his horse's eyes. "Now don't you be insulting her, Nathaniel Smith. Princess is a far piece better'n what you ride."

Nate hadn't tethered his swaybacked packhorse to anything, expecting—as usual—for it to be waiting for him when he was finished.

"Get a wiggle on, I say again! I'll be as ornery as a fried toad if I have to wait another minute for you!" The old man was studying the dirt around the mine entrance, one hand on the revolver holstered on his hip. On the way here he'd stopped every few minutes and studied the ground, brow furrowed and lips working the entire time. "Don't see no boot tracks. Some funny marks here, though." He pointed to narrow ruts that looked like something a heavy snake could leave behind. "I want to be sure no one's claim jumping on me, gettin' gold that tain't theirs."

Last night a granger from Dutch Flats said he saw lights coming from high in the hills and later around Nate's mine when he drove some cows past. The granger said he'd also heard an odd howling noise: woooooooooooooo. The report was enough to send the old man out to the mine this morning, despite the oppressive heat, dragging Wilford with him.

"Maybe that granger only thought he saw something, Nate. Maybe he was half seas over, full as a tick." Wilford rested his hand against a beam while he waited for Nate to light a lantern. He stared out the mine entrance and across the uncompromising land. On a low hill in the distance stood a large Joshua tree. Closer were clusters of creosote, saltbushes, and yucca, all looking brittle. "Whiskey can make a man see things, you know."

"You should well know that. It can make a man spend too much on a red crowbait," Nate growled. "Now bring that other lantern. Maybe there's no boot tracks out here on account of them claim jumpers covered them up. Maybe there's tracks inside."

Wilford reluctantly lit the second lantern and followed the old man, hearing Princess nickering, and then nothing but the click and "shush" of his boot heels against rock and stretches of dirt.

"We ain't gonna be down here too long, are we Nate? It's real hot this morning, and you know I don't like to leave Princess..."

"Hobble your lip about that horse, Wilford." The old man stopped and held the lantern close to a patch of dirt. "More of 'em, see? Wigglin' lookin' marks. Just like on the outside. T'weren't here before, none of 'em. My bones may be old, Wilford, but my eyes are in apple pie order. Might be drag marks. Might be they found some gold and drug it out of my mine." He resumed his pace, the shaft going down at a steeper angle now.

"You been working this mine for what...three years? You ain't found no gold in it. How's anybody else in these parts gonna find..."

Nate snorted. "There's gold here, all right. Somewhere." The old man raised his lantern, squinting as he studied a gouge in the stone near the roof of the shaft. It was sharp-edged and deep, looking like the tracks he'd found in the dirt. "This wasn't here before neither."

The air wasn't as dry where the shaft angled to the west and went deeper still. It didn't smell like dust and stone, it smelled like something neither man could put a name to, and it overpowered the odor of their sweat. It wasn't a pleasant or unpleasant odor, but it hung heavy and settled strongly on Wilford's tongue.

"Princess, she don't like the heat, Nate. She's a right pretty horse. How long you think we're gonna..."

"Shut your bazoo!" Nate made a fist with his free hand and waved it. "I think I hear somethin' other than your jaw flappin'."

Wilford cocked his head. "I hear something, too."

It was like whistling, a sound the wind might make whipping through breaks in the hills. But the air remained still, and so no wind could be responsible for it. The sound changed pitch as they stood and listened, coming lower now. Then the ground beneath their feet started vibrating, and stone dust filtered down from the ceiling. Wilford stretched an arm to the nearest beam and felt the wood trembling.

"Maybe we should come back later," Wilford suggested, his voice little more than a whisper. "I'll ride Princess over to Old Man Simpkins' place, get him and his hands to come back here with us."

"Ya got no sand, boy," Nate shot back. His free hand pulled the gun from its holster. "Wish you was heeled."

"Ain't never carried no gun, Nate. Don't think I'd know how to..."

Suddenly light spilled from around the corner, pale blue like the color of fog that wraps around the yucca on early autumn mornings. The light grew brighter, and the whistling louder.

"Th-th-the light the granger said he saw," Wilford stammered.

"Probably the same."

"And th-th-the noise he heard."

"Probably the same."

"We should leave, Nate, like I said. Skedaddle back to your ranch and get some other fellers to come with us. I'm a might nervous 'bout this. Worse than a cat in a roomful of rockers. Don't know what might be 'round that corner."

"Claim jumpers is what's around that corner, boy. And they's doing something to make this mine tremble like a frightened babe."

"Can't be claim jumpers," Wilford countered. "Ain't no horses outside 'cept ours. Ain't nobody would walk here in this heat. Too far from anywhere. Don't know what might be around that corner, and..."

"I thought you'd be someone to ride the river with, Wilford," Nate growled, as he edged toward the bend, steadying himself against a beam as the ground shook a little harder.

"I'm not afraid," Wilford returned, working up some spittle and failing in his attempt to sound brave. "I'm just thinking there might be ghosts down there."

"Ghosts?" The word was like a piece of spoiled meat the old man spit out.

"Yeah, that woooooooooo wooooooooo sound. Ain't natural. Sounds spooky, like ghosts."

Nate drew the hammer back and edged forward, revolver leading. "Tain't no such thing as ghosts, Wilford."

"Ain't true, Nate. Some o' them little places up north, they're starting to call them ghost towns."

"This is a mine, Wilford, not a town. And there tain't no ghosts. Just claim jumpers. Bet they got dynamite."

"L-l-look! Th-th-that ain't no claim jumper, Nate!"

Nate had nearly reached the corner when something stepped out to meet him. Small, it had the shape of a man, though it wasn't a man. Its legs and arms were even thinner than Nate's, elbows and knees exaggerated. Its fingers—three of them on each hand—were long and ended in nails that glimmered liquid gold in the odd, blue light; matching nails were on its three toes.

"Them's what made the marks," Nate said, pointing to the thing's feet and fingers.

The old man did not seem flustered by the creature's appearance. He appeared angry.

Its head looked overlarge for its child-size body, bald with the tiniest of ears. Its eyes glistened saucer-wide, gold, and devoid of pupils. It didn't seem to be wearing clothes, as all over it was shiny, as if it had been dipped in molten silver.

"N-n-nate, I think that there's a ghost." Wilford took a step back and motioned for Nate to follow. But Nate's eyes were narrowed and locked onto the creature, and he didn't see his young companion. "We gotta get out of here, Nate. I gotta see to Princess."

Nate aimed the revolver at the glimmering apparition. It regarded him almost curiously and opened its little mouth. The woooooooo woooooooo sound came out.

"Told you it's a ghost, Nate." Wilford took another step back and then another, wiping furiously at the sweat that was running into his eyes. His chest hurt and his throat felt hot and tight. "I got Princess to think about."

Nate fired, the bullet striking the apparition in the chest. Surprise flashed across its smooth face, and its thin silvery fingers clutched at the hole the bullet made. Something dark green spilled out of the wound, and the little man threw back its overlarge head and howled. Wooooooo ooooooo oooo.

"Tain't a ghost, Wilford. Ghosts don't bleed."

The creature dropped to its knees, then pitched forward with a final woooooooo.

"M-m-maybe it's a special ghost, Nate. See how shiny its skin is? Just like silver from a mine. Its eyes are gold. Maybe it's a mineral ghost."

"A mineral spirit?" Nate said with a chuckle. "C'mon. Let's see if there's more of 'em." Nate disappeared around the corner.

Wilford rubbed at his chest, looked up the shaft behind him, and then cautiously followed the old man, swallowing the dry lump forming in his throat and grabbing a beam when the ground shook beneath him again.

The tunnel widened—as did Wilford's eyes. A cavern loomed down and away, the walls smooth and not worked by man or nature, shot through with veins of gold as thick as a fence post. In the center of the cavern was a great glob of metal, the size of a large chuck wagon but looking like an overturned soup bowl. It was the thing casting off the blue light and by its vibrations causing the ground to shudder. Above it was open sky—a rent in the hill that Nate and Wilford hadn't known was there. And around the glob of metal a dozen of the silvery men worked, all of them woooo wooooing to each other, then suddenly all of them looking at Nate and Wilford. One of them grabbed up something that resembled an anvil, though it had blinking lights and strands of something like horsehair protruding from its top.

"N-n-nate, I think me and you should skedaddle on out o' here and..."

Nate dropped his lantern and aimed his revolver at the one holding the anvil. "Tain't no mineral spirits going to cheat me out of my gold! I reckon this one—whatever it is—has to be the biggest toad in the puddle. He's a little taller than the rest. I take him out an' the others might well skedaddle themselves."

Nate fired twice, the first bullet striking the anvil and sending sparks in all directions. The second caught the silvery creature in the neck and sent it reeling backward, making it drop the device.

The cavern erupted in a cacophony of woooo wooos, screeches, and sputtering crackles, the latter coming from the anvil, which was continuing to spark, and which now had started to glow red-hot. The silvery men were waving their spindly little arms and running—some of them toward their downed fellow, some behind the overturned soup bowl, three toward Nate.

The old man took aim and fired one bullet into each of the three figures charging him. Two were hit in the chest, the third in the center of its face, all of them falling and wooooo wooooing in hurtful high-pitched tones that caused Wilford to drop his lantern and clamp his hands over his ears.

The anvil glowed brighter and the sparks came wilder. The silvery men ran away from the thing now and disappeared into the overturned soup bowl, which was glowing ever harsher. The ground started shaking more fiercely, and Wilford fell, unable to keep his balance.

Nate reloaded and fired at the soup bowl, the bullets bouncing off the metal. Then he, too, was falling—as the cavern bucked and rocked, and cracks split open in the floor. The anvil burst into a shower of ruby-colored stars and then roared like a maddened beast, erupting in flames that whooshed toward Nate and Wilford.

"Princess!" Wilford hollered. "I gotta get to..."

* * *

She was a roan red Missouri Fox Trotter the guide rode, a real show horse. He patted her neck, slid from her saddle, and waited for his tour group to get off their rented horses.

"See that slash in the rocks?" He pointed to the entrance of what had been Nate's mine. A bleached-white horse skull had been nailed above it. "That's one of a half-dozen haunted mines in this area. Played out close to a hundred years ago by prospectors looking for gold and finding nothing but death, the hills so unstable their tunnels collapsed on them. They say on still nights if you go close to the entrance of this particular mine you can hear the spirit of a nag softly nickering and someone desperately calling to her. A few have claimed to hear the cackle of an old man and the sounds of gunfire."

"Do you believe in all of that nonsense?" This came from a middle-aged woman wearing an Astros baseball cap and a sweat-soaked "I Escaped from Area 51" T-shirt.

"Ain't no such thing as ghosts," said her companion. "Now let's get done with this and visit those alien landing sites."

"Do you believe in them?" she persisted to the tour guide. "Ghosts?"

The guide smiled and nodded. "There are lots of spirits and odd-such things in Nevada, ma'am." He ran his fingers through his horse's mane, and she wuffled in pleasure. "C'mon, Princess, we've got more ground to cover with these fine folks before lunch."

Nothing Newsworthy

This is the first cat story I ever wrote. When I was young, and a member of Job's Daughters, I adopted a grandmother at the Rockford Eastern Star Home. Actually, I adopted two. This story was inspired by one of them, Nada Downey, who during one visit told me her name meant "nothing soft" in Spanish. Funny how I remembered that after all these years. "Nothing Newsworthy" first appeared in 100 Crafty Little Cat Crimes *by Barnes & Noble, 2000. My thanks to Marty, who gave me a reason to write it.*

"Gran'ma Nada! Gran'ma Nada!"

She ignored the willowy man who'd just burst in the front door, bringing with him an uninvited flurry of snow and a gust of frigid winter wind. He stomped his feet on the rug and furiously brushed at his coat. "Gran'ma Nada!"

"And you're certain nothing else was taken, ma'am?"

The old woman shook her head, freeing several strands of steel-gray hair from her stumpy braid. "No, Sergeant. Nothing else. I'm certain."

"Gran'ma Nada!"

She sighed and shivered, wrapping her shawl tighter about her shoulders. "In here, Rupert! We're in the library!"

"Always in the library," came Rupert's muffled reply. "Musty old place."

"No jewelry?" The policeman continued.

She shook her head again.

"Money?"

Another shake. "I have a large coin collection, Sergeant. Quite valuable and on display in my study. They left that alone."

"Nothing else?"

"Nothing else."

"Gran'ma Nada!" Rupert tromped into the library, tugged off his gloves and thrust them in his pocket. He smiled tightly when he spotted her. "Are you all right, Gran?"

"Yes, Rupert. Sergeant, this is my great-grandson..."

"Gran, I saw the police cars out front, and I..."

"...was worried something had happened to me?" *Or to your inheritance?* she whispered half under her breath.

"Gran'ma Nada, I..."

"Hush, Rupert. I'm not finished with Sergeant Decker." She returned her attention to the policeman, who was busily scratching notes on a small pad.

Rupert huffed and glanced about, his features drawn together so as to make his rosy face look even more pinched than usual. There were three policemen in the library—the one at Nada's side, who was obviously in charge, and two others dusting shelves for fingerprints. Each gave Rupert a perfunctory nod.

"What was taken, Gran? God...the paintings?"

She continued to ignore her great-grandson, instead chattering animatedly to the sergeant in her tinny, old-woman voice. One of the other officers glanced at Rupert and said "Newspapers," then went back to work.

"Newspapers," Rupert repeated. He let out a deep breath as if in relief. "From the library."

The library was the largest room in the ancient house, up until thirty years ago serving as both a living room and a dining parlor. Then Nada had the intervening wall knocked out and shelves upon shelves upon shelves installed, forcing even guests to eat in the kitchen. A fireplace took up part of the far wall, nestled between overloaded shelves, merrily burning birch logs on this cold February day. Two striped cats, as orange as the flames, were curled up in front of the hearth, Rupert couldn't recall their names. A beefy, plump Siamese, conveniently named Cat, was sleeping on Nada's rocking chair a few feet away. Its tail dangled down to look like an inverted question mark. A fourth cat, one coal black save for the white front paw which gave him the name Boot, was slinking back and forth between the policemen, all the while keeping a protective eye on Nada. And the fifth, an Angora as fluffy and white as the snow outside, was perched on a high shelf where she could regally survey the entire room and hiss at Rupert when he looked her way.

"Cats and shelves," Rupert softly growled. "Shelves upon shelves upon shelves."

Covered by stacks upon stacks of newspapers.

Oh, there were some books in the mix, Rupert noted, a half-dozen early Ed McBain's and the latest Tony Hillerman. There were two first printings of Edgar Rice Burroughs' *Tarzan and The City of Gold,* one of them supposedly personally autographed to Nada—Rupert had never bothered looking to confirm his great-grandmother's boast. A well worn southwestern chili cookbook. And there was a thick pictorial tribute to the Texan cowboy. A rumpled copy of a Lillian Jackson Braun paperback. An early Joe Haldeman. The books were difficult to spot amid the thousands of newspapers.

"Just newspapers?" Rupert asked. "Nothing else was taken?"

The sergeant raised an eyebrow to the old woman.

"Nothing," Nada repeated to them both. She looked so small standing between the men. Stoop-shouldered from age and from leaning on a three-pronged cane, she barely came up to their chests. Her sadness made her seem smaller still. "Nothing but some of my greatest treasures. Months of my life. Stolen."

"Sergeant Decker!" A fourth policeman came into the library. Boot slipped toward him and rubbed against his legs. "Checked all the windows 'n doors, Sir. No obvious signs of forced entry, but the locks are old. Some barely catch." He lowered his voice. "A halfway decent thief coulda picked his way in without leavin' a clue. You need better locks, ma'am. Deadbolts all the way aroun'. A security system'd be a good idea, too. Looks like you've got plenty of valuable things you should be protectin'."

"Original paintings," Rupert volunteered. "A pen and ink Picasso—which thank the Lord they didn't spot. A Diego Rivera. A Max Beckmann. Coins. Jewelry and pocket watches and...

Your precious inheritance, Nada mouthed.

"...some unique military memorabilia from her first late husband. Depression glass. Cut crystal vases. No, wait, the vases were taken in a burglary last year."

Sergeant Decker raised an eyebrow again.

"I didn't report that one," Nada explained.

"Her gardner," Rupert cut in.

"He was poor. Had medical bills from his wife. Trimmed the hedges really nice before he left."

"Stole her entire collection of vases and vanished. Year before that, or maybe it was two, a burglar broke in and took two sets of silver and all of her Rosewood bowls."

"That one I reported," she said smugly.

"Gran, at least only newspapers were taken this time. But next time..."

"My newspapers," she said wistfully. "Months of my life. Gone."

Sergeant Decker stared at his feet. Boot was rubbing against his ankles now, signaling that the policeman had been accepted.

"Were they valuable? The newspapers?" Decker scratched some more notes when she answered "Yes, very valuable."

The old woman shuffled away from the pair and toward the east shelves, pausing in front of the fire a moment to warm herself and acknowledge the orange cats. Newspapers, all folded neatly, stretched from the floor to the ceiling on nearly every shelf. Only one shelf was bare, and that was by the door. Nada explained that was for the newspapers yet to come.

"Months of newspapers stolen. Taken yesterday, maybe three months ago."

"So you're uncertain of the exact time of the theft." Decker took more notes.

"Sometime in the late fall or early winter, Sergeant. I didn't notice them missing until just before breakfast today when I wanted to read again about Woodrow Wilson's term winding down. Wilson had a cat, you know. So did McKinley. Abraham Lincoln had the first cat in the White House. But I'm not so old as to have newspapers about those men." She leaned heavily against the cane, drawing her free hand up to the shelf at shoulder level. Her age spotted fingers tugged free a newspaper, and then another. "It was December of 1920, the *Detroit Free Press* was what I was looking for. Good paper. Good article on Wilson. When I couldn't find it, I poked around and noticed half of December of that year was missing. Five weeks out of 1932 are gone, too. And four or five each out of 1941 and 1944. Some from 1948. Months all together. Probably a year's worth."

"If only you didn't have so many," Rupert said.

Sergeant Decker scribbled furiously, recording the strings of missing weeks and the names of the newspapers.

Nada shuffled along the shelves and tugged free another paper, then another and another. She continued her work until she had more than a dozen papers tucked under her arm and was struggling with the burden. Then she went to the north row of shelves, her eyes scanning the newspapers there and the dates scrawled in marker on the wood beneath the stacks. "This one." She pulled free one more. "Sergeant, the head reference librarian comes out here once in a while to look at my collection. Says my library is more complete than the one in town. She borrows a few from time to time to take back with her and put on microfilm. Ones of special interest to the town. So everyone can read them."

"Gran, perhaps the librarian didn't return some of your newspapers," Rupert suggested. "You've called these policemen out here for..."

She shook her head. "I called Louise at the library to check. Just before I reached Sergeant Decker." Nada shuffled to the rocking chair and tapped her cane. Cat slowly raised his head, then reluctantly uncurled himself and plopped to the floor. She took his place, commenting on the propitiousness of having Cat around—he kept her seat toasty warm. The Siamese curled at her feet, narrowing his blue eyes to take in Nada's great-grandson.

Rupert raised his lip to sneer at the creature. "If you had a dog, Gran, a big one, he would've barked at the thief, maybe chased him away."

"I like cats." She reached a hand down and scratched Cat's ears. Boot sauntered over, and she scratched his ears, too.

"You were saying the newspapers were valuable," Decker prompted.

Nada adjusted the papers on her lap and pointed to the one on top. "I really like the *Detroit Free Press.*"

April 20, 1912. The headline read: BLAME OF *TITANIC* TRAGEDY IS FALLING ON J.B. ISMAY. A secondary head proclaimed: *TITANIC'S* LIVING ARE ALL TENDERLY CARED FOR IN NEW YORK CITY. "This one's worth about three hundred dollars," she said. "Would be worth more if I stored them properly, hanging them from bamboo poles and keeping them in plastic in a moisture-proof room. Too hard to read them that way, though. The fire plays havoc with the papers, too, drying them out, yellowing them. It's this Wisconsin weather, really, that's to blame."

She dropped the paper on the floor and pointed to the next. The *Cleveland News,* August 6, 1945. The headline read: U.S. ATOMIC BOMB RIPS JAPAN, GREATEST WEAPON IN HISTORY. "Sixty to seventy dollars," she pronounced.

The next was another edition of the *Detroit Free Press,* May 24, 1931: WARSHIP *BISMARCK* IS FIGHTING FOR LIFE AGAINST OVERWHELMING ODDS, NAZIS ADMIT. "Probably seventy, more to a World War II buff. All of these are valuable," she added, stabbing a now-ink-stained finger at her stack. "None worth less than ten or twenty dollars. A few worth maybe a thousand."

The *New York Times,* October 2, 1921: YANKS WIN 1921 PENNANT. Pictures of Babe Ruth and Frank Frisch stared up from the brittle page.

The *Los Angeles Times,* May 18, 1935: LAWRENCE OF ARABIA NEAR DEATH. Another, from April 24, 1936: HOUDINI WIDOW PLANS SEANCE.

There were other headlines: CHURCHILL RESIGNS, VICTORY PARADE FOR IKE, PATTON TO BE BURIED IN LUXEMBOURG.

"This is one of my favorites, though not so old." It was an edition of the *Chicago Sun-Times,* Thursday, July 17, 1980. Ronald and Nancy Reagan smiled from the lefthand side of the front page. The banner read: IT'S REAGAN AND FORD, FORMER PRESIDENT AGREES TO VP DEAL. "Bad journalism," she observed. "Picked it up when I was visiting a friend in the suburbs. The paper jumped the gun and printed that Ford would run with Reagan. Ford was thinking about it, that was common knowledge. But he declined. The papers were pulled from the newsstands, but not before some of them were snapped up. Like Dewey wins." She wrinkled her nose and made a *tsk-tsking* sound. "Reagan."

"Didn't care for him?" Decker asked.

"A good enough president," she said evenly. "But he had a dog. So did Ford. I like cats better."

"So it had to be someone who knew the newspapers were valuable," Decker mused. "Someone who knew you kept so many, and someone who knew to come here late at night when you and your housekeeper were sleeping. Probably took as many as he could haul away in his vehicle in one trip."

Nada pursed her lips. "A lot of folks in town know I have these newspapers. The local paper did an article about me and my collection early last year."

"What about Ceil?" Rupert was still sneering at Cat.

"My housekeeper? Goodness, no! She's a Godsend. Wouldn't think of taking anything from me. Besides, she's not one to read the paper. Gets her news from the radio."

"Not one to steal...that's what you said about the gardener before your vases disappeared."

Nada ran her finger along the Reagan and Ford story. "By Jerome R. Watson and Patrick Oster, *Sun-Times* Correspondents," she whispered. "Dateline Detroit. The *Detroit Free Press* wouldn't've run this story."

"Want me to put those back for you?" Rupert volunteered.

Nada shook her head. "I think I'll read these today. And I'll put them back later. You'd only get them out of order."

"Ma'am?" One of the other officers stepped close, the one who told her she needed better locks. "I was just wonderin' why you keep all these newspapers."

She chuckled softly. "These newspapers are my life. You see, I have..." She frowned. "Until this theft I had at least one issue for every day I've lived. They mark the years for me. I so love the news."

"Three hundred and sixty-five times..." one of the policemen whispered.

"Times ninety-five," Rupert softly added. "Nearly thirty-five thousand papers. Most of them are in here."

"That's a lot of newspapers," Decker said. "Why the fascination?"

"Her father was a newsman. And she used to write for a paper in San Antonio," Rupert explained, "Before she married her second husband and moved to Wisconsin."

"So long ago," she said, her rheumy-blue eyes instantly bright. "I had just turned twenty when I got the job—on my own merits. My father was working in Santa Fe. That was sixty-five years ago."

"Seventy-five," Rupert corrected.

"I covered the social engagements, the only woman reporter on the staff. Church teas, marriage announcements, frilly things. The editor called me Nothing Newsworthy."

"What?" This from another policeman. All four were gathered around now, intently listening. Rupert had backed away to stand at a narrow window between the shelves. The snow was falling harder, and he scowled to see it collecting on his car.

"Nada," she told the policemen. "My name in Spanish means 'nothing.' And since I covered all the frilly bits, the things the other reporters laughed about and didn't consider news, the editor called me Nothing Newsworthy." She laughed again. "But sometimes I got the good stories. A church fire when I went there to cover a social. Turned out to be arson. The murder of a prominent young woman who I'd gone to visit to write about her wedding plans. I discovered the body. My first front-page story. The deacon who embezzled from the parsonage. That was news. I was Something Newsworthy then—at least every once in a while. And it was warmer in San Antonio."

She put all the papers on the floor and held her palms out toward the fire to warm them. "I suppose this theft will make tomorrow's *Journal-Sentinel*? If they consider it newsworthy."

"The reporters have access to our reports." Sergeant Decker motioned to his men. "And I am sure they'll consider this newsworthy. You'll probably get called by a reporter or two. We'll be checking with antique shops and pawn stores in the area, see if anyone is trying to sell your papers. We'll look at eBay. Those are the best option right now. Unless the fingerprints we took turn up anything."

"I hope you do find the papers."

"If anything does turn up, I'll call." Decker stopped in the doorway. "And see about better locks, ma'am. Please. Maybe an electronic security system."

She nodded and smiled, intending to take care of the former a little later today.

Boot followed the men to the front door, then returned to join the orange pair on the hearth.

"Gran..."

She pushed herself to her feet, leaning hard on the cane as she shuffled toward Rupert at the window. Boot abandoned the heat to follow and find a spot on the sil.

"I'm not worried about my inheritance, Gran."

"I know."

"I'm worried about you. All alone here."

"I'm fine. I just want the Sergeant to find my missing newspapers. I particularly want the one with the special on President Wilson."

"They'll do their best."

"And I'll get better locks. I promise."

"I'd feel better if you didn't stay here."

She made a tsk-tsking noise. "I want nothing to do with that nursing home, Rupert. You can keep your fancy brochures. Nursing homes are places to die. I'm old, and I'll die soon enough anyway. But I'll die here."

"You'd be plenty warm at Fox Manor, Gran. Three meals a day. There would be lots of people and..."

"... And no place to keep all of my newspapers." She placed her free hand on his back. "And they wouldn't let me keep my precious cats, either."

"Your cats." He made a huffing sound and fumbled for his gloves.

"They mean even more to me than the papers."

"I'll stop in to see you tomorrow. After work."

"Thank you, Rupert."

"And I'll tell Ceil to bring in more firewood on my way out."

"Thank you, Rupert."

She stayed at the window, watching her great-grandson make his way to his car and clear off the snow. She watched him head down her twisting driveway and out of sight. Then she returned to her chair and picked up the copy of the *Chicago Sun-Times* again, almost reverently turning it over to stare at the back page: RANGERS HAVE FEAST ON SOX PITCHING.

She drew her shawl tight about her and shivered as the fire started to die, read the sports article twice, and drifted off to sleep. Cat was curled between her feet.

Boot was still at the window. Ceil hadn't yet gone out for firewood. The cat knew the housekeeper's ever-slowing routine. She wouldn't be going out until almost dinnertime. An hour away. He meowed softly and looked to the Angora, a silent signal passing between them. Boot meowed again and got the attention of the orange pair, which rose practically in unison, stretched, and padded to the north wall of shelves—to the 1950s *New York Daily News* section. Together, the four tugged free paper after paper, careful not to take them all from the same stack, where their absence would be easily noted by the old woman. Then they pulled them to the hearth, under Cat's approving gaze, and nudged them into the fire. Another week's worth followed, along with the Lillian Braun book—just enough to keep Nada warm until Ceil brought in more wood.

About the Author

Jean Rabe, of Kenosha, WI, is a full-time writer who concentrates on fantasy and science-fiction, and who occasionally dabbles in military fiction and mysteries. In addition to Walkabout Publishing, Jean has been published by Tor Books, Daw Books, Harper Collins, Wizards of the Coast, and TSR, Inc. She has two-dozen novels and four-dozen short stories to her credit.

This and That and Tales about Cats is her first title from Walkabout Publishing, and gave her an opportunity to gather some of her favorite short stories into one book. In addition, she co-edited the company's Blue Kingdoms anthologies.

Jean is a native of Ottawa, IL, and spent several years in Quincy, IL, and Evansville, IN, where she worked as a newspaper reporter and news bureau chief, covering education, health, courts, plane crashes, and crime.

She has edited several anthologies for DAW Books, including *Pandora's Closet* and *Time Twisters*, both 2007 releases. And she worked as an editor for gaming magazines for several years for TSR, Inc. of Wisconsin, and the FASA Corporation of Illinois.

When not writing or editing, Jean visits museums (military and aviation museums are her favorites), attempts to garden, tugs fiercely on old socks with her two dogs, and tries to put a dent in her growing to-be-read stack of books. She loves country music and board, war, and role-playing games.

Jean maintains a web site: www.jeanrabe.com, and she hosts writing workshops at conventions.

www.ingramcontent.com/pod-product-compliance
Lightning Source LLC
LaVergne TN
LVHW012330100826
845148LV00017B/1697

* 9 7 8 0 9 8 0 2 0 8 6 7 2 *